There is a guillotine on the steps
of the U.S. Capitol building.
Three hundred members of Congress
and the Supreme Court
are locked in the basement.
It's a city divided.
It's a new American Civil War.
Twelve elite thinkers have been chosen
to fix things. They're called Reasoners.
Except one of them, Chase Selby,
realizes that reason isn't going to work.
He will have to destroy the country to save it.
The question is, can Chase live long enough
to do it?

A FEAST
OF
WOLVES

A FEAST
OF
WOLVES

A novel by

Wilson Coneybeare

INDENT
PUBLISHING

IndentPublishing.com

A FEAST OF WOLVES

First published in 2022

INDENT PUBLISHING
IndentPublishing.com
contact@indentpublishing.com

This edition December 2022

Cover design by Meredith Fowler

ISBN: 978-1-7780837-8-5

For Lisa, who fights all the time

Author's Note

I don't go in for authors' forewords. Get to the story. But in this case, a word or two of explanation might be necessary, because how this novel came into being was crazy enough, but the events that took place after it was written were even crazier.

About four years ago, in 2018, I wrote and directed a movie where more than half the action takes place in one room and the other half takes place with cops doing a lot of talking. I kept thinking, this has been great but boy, do I want to do something big. Adventurous! On a massive scale! Set in America and about America.

Things being the way they were, I came up with what I thought was a big enough idea: a civil war in America. Not the one with the cannons and the cavalry, but a modern one with iPads, TikTok, and lots of tech.

But I had never written a book before and I wasn't familiar with the freedom a novel gives you. Pretty soon, I discovered you can go anywhere and do anything. So I did.

I imagined and wrote about half the country warring against the other half, an armed insurrection, the overthrow of the U.S. Capitol, a guillotine on the steps of the building itself, and members of the government (including the Supreme Court) tossed into makeshift prisons – all backdrop for a hero who has to unravel it all. And what kicked it off? How about a nationwide virus that led to race riots, which led to anarchy in the streets – not just extremists, but pissed-off senior citizens, kindergarten teachers, truck drivers, nuns, and yes, people dressed in animal furs (I'm not kidding).

I have to admit, even to me it all seemed totally unbelievable and ridiculous, but I kept going and finished the book in 2020. I started to get a creepy feeling once it was done, however, because soon enough some of the things I had written about didn't seem so outlandish.

The idea was to roll it out online and gauge initial interest, so I began chopping the book up into "postable" sections. But then a thing called COVID stopped the world in its tracks.

We didn't preview the book online until October of 2020, and it caught a small but dedicated following. But soon enough, what became more significant was a weird serendipity as the real world began to unravel strangely like the events in the book. The riots of January 6, however, shook me most of all. The images on the news weren't of a guillotine on the steps of the U.S. Capitol, but it was a gallows and that was close enough.

I didn't want to seem to be taking advantage of something so terrifying, so we pulled down most of the book. After a while, though, I decided that fiction has a crucial role to play in understanding the craziness around us. So maybe people should decide for themselves. I also discovered something I hadn't really anticipated: The people who control big publishing and big agenting have their view of what people ought to be reading and I have mine.

Fortunately, the good folks at Indent Publishing came to champion the work and the result of their faith is what you're holding in your hands or looking at on your phone or tablet right now. This is the book that I completed in 2020 – in print for the first time. My crazy big adventure story that somehow wound up reflecting, by sheer accident, a lot of the things that have rocked this country for the past few years.

So here we go. Like I said, I don't like prefaces. Get to the story. So let's get to the story. Fortunately, fiction is still stranger than truth.

We hope.

Wilson Coneybeare
October 2022

Book 1:

A Guillotine in Washington

"But what is more divine, I will not say in man only,
but in all heaven and earth, than reason?"
– Cicero

"The extreme suppression of your rights deserves the
most extreme reaction you can dream up.
And it is never wrong."
– *Words of the Wolf*, pg. 22 (Free Kindle Edition)

1. *Pointy Shoes*

1

To everyone's surprise, and flying in the face of the Reasoner Compromise, they resumed culling on Friday night, although the leadership made it clear they were restricting themselves to junior civil servants and Capitol staff. There were a lot of pissed-off people when word got around about that, but even the most diehard Changer had to admit that in the first culling they'd kind of lost their minds and wasted far too many Senators and Congressmen in the rush of enthusiasm, and at least half of them outside prime time, when the eyeballs – particularly on the West Coast – were low. So what was the point of that?

They still made a good show of it, though. They randomly chose and dragged a young man from the staffer pen in the basement of the U.S. Capitol building. He was in his late twenties at most, a classic junior power broker in skinny suit and pointed shoes. He cried and screamed and yelled as they hauled him up the steps. Webs of gob latticed across his mouth and nose as he kicked back at them with those pointy dress shoes. "No!" he shouted. "No!" Three huge men – one in a Philly Eagles jersey, another in a Washington Capitals jersey, another shirtless but covered in tattoos – carried him feet first to the guillotine.

The crowd was really into this until they learned from CNN and Fox (almost everyone on the lower steps watched their own actions live on smartphones) that this guy wasn't actually a power broker at all. He was just a junior-level data-entry clerk in the government. Once that got out, most everyone lost interest and began talking amongst themselves. They cut his head off anyway, so as not to lose face.

Beavenstock, the Changer's leader, felt the crowd's disappointment. He had an instinct for those things. So he made a snap decision and assured everyone over the loudspeakers that there were still plenty of big fish to fry. They would most definitely be decapitating a Senator tonight if the weather held. That perked everyone up. Beavenstock chose Tobias Brubaker (R.-Iowa), about whom neither he, nor anyone in the crowd, knew anything. Fortunately, the weather not only held, but it cleared up quite nicely. So they decapitated Senator Brubaker and no one was disappointed. There were a lot of barbecues out on the Mall that night. You never leave the audience wanting less.

2. *Chase*

1

By August, Washington's train station had become something it hadn't been for sixty-plus years: important.

The airports had been shut down since April. At first this was because the Secret Service had determined that aircraft landing indiscriminately posed a very real threat to the White House specifically (back when they had something to protect), and then because the FAA had determined that *all* aircraft around D.C. were a threat to the region generally. This was after the first wave of protesters in Washington had somehow laid their hands on a shoulder-to-air missile. By sheer dumb luck, these jokers had managed to take out one of the engines on a United 737 right over Ronald Reagan National Airport. So that was the end of that.

Trains were better suited to the hordes that kept streaming into the city anyway. Every day there were more and more of them, everyone hoping there would be a second culling and that they hadn't missed the excitement. The country watched them on TV, and in time divided them into groups. First there were the diehard Changers, who unofficially wore a uniform of sports jerseys (Patriots/49ers/Colts/Seahawks). These folks could be mistaken for rabid football fans on their way to the Big Game, if you ignored the firearms and the wolf hats. Then there were the bikers, whom most people referred to as Harleys, after Harley-Davidson. In tense opposition to these were the people in tactical armor, weekend warriors tricked out from head to toe in combat or riot gear. Then there were the regular folks, moms and dads and kids who looked like they'd come to Washington for a weekend cookout. Almost all of these – and most of the Jerseys – had wolf gear: plastic snouts for the kids, cheap faux fur caps hawkers sold on the street for moms and dads, or more legit ones sold at sporting goods stores or Target or Walmart. Some hats even had the plastic snout on them, complete with bared teeth, but those you could only get online from Amazon.

2

That August afternoon, Chase Selby was on one of the few trains entering Union Station that didn't have crazed wolf-hat-wearing, gun-toting revolutionaries clinging to its side or squatting on its roof. Chase's was a special, which in this case meant an armored train six cars long with the middle fourth car and the caboose loaded with reserve military personnel.

Chase stood alone in the passenger car, which had been emptied expressly for his security. As he looked out at Washington passing slowly by the picture window, he knew he had less to fear than almost any other person in the city at that moment. Chase was a Reasoner, after all, and both sides had agreed – in principle, anyway – that only Reasoners could pull everyone out of the shit mess the United States had somehow made for itself. This agreement between the two warring sides – the Changers and the Government of Record (GOR) – was called the Reasoner Compromise, and while the language was iffy in a lot of places, in one area it was explicit: Reasoners were given special status. To be protected by both sides. At all costs.

Chase was looking south as the train inched its way into town. He saw smoke rising from somewhere in the near distance. Was that as close as the Mall? Chase didn't know Washington that well, but it seemed to him the reflecting pool and the long stretch of green grass called the Washington Mall was somewhere over there. He had been to the city only twice before, but obviously under entirely different circumstances.

There were angry – no, furious – people waiting on the banks of the rail line as the train slowed in its approach to the station. Just as many women as men, Chase noted with surprise. They shouted and hurled rocks and food at the train. Idiotically, some official had put a government emblem on the side of the train, so maybe that had set them off. Some joker wearing a hunter's red plaid jacket fired a potato cannon right at the window. Chase had been told to expect this kind of thing. He had also been told the train's windows were reinforced and bulletproof.

Still, though.

He stepped back.

Captain Holden, the able young state guard commander assigned to his security detail, returned to the car through the connecting door. Chase noted his costume change. Holden had been wearing a perfectly cut single-breasted business suit and open collar when he and the security team had escorted Chase onto the train at Princeton. Now the captain was in full combat fatigues, complete with sidearm – no, two sidearms – and a lethal-looking bowie knife. Apparently, he had just made the change. He was adjusting the cap to his liking, as if preparing for battle, and pulling on a pair of expensive-looking calfskin gloves. Chase had read in the dossier that Holden came from an exceedingly wealthy family, so maybe he had a dog in this fight beyond his patriotism.

"We're going to be at a full stop in four minutes, sir," the commander said. "I want to warn you of what to expect. Fucking savages!" This last was in response to a row of fat middle-aged men in Washington Capitals jerseys, who had just hurled a flaming seven-foot log (a telephone pole?) at the window of the train. Their exertion was so great, and the men so out of shape, that the three of them promptly fell over.

Holden apologized for the outburst. "My apologies, sir."

"I'm nobody you need to apologize to," Chase said.

"When we arrive, you'll need to wait approximately five minutes while we make sure the train is secure. You'll stand by the disembarkation door. Then Commander Guerra will escort you off the train. We've set up a security corridor and you'll be escorted to an armored vehicle that will take you directly to your accommodations. We've arranged for a motorcycle security escort."

"No," said Chase. "I want to go by the Capitol first."

"Sir?"

"To see it."

"Absolutely not."

"How am I going to be able to fulfill my duties if I don't even see it?"

"You can see as much as you want on CNN. Or Twitter or Instagram or Tik Tok."

"Things like that are different in person."

"Things like what, sir? I don't know that we've ever had anything *like* this, have we?"

He had a point, but Chase wouldn't be swayed. "All the same."

"You are aware they started again last night?"

Of course he was. Everyone was aware. Chase had, in fact, spent a good part of the journey from Princeton following last night's adventures on his smartphone. Reception, of course, had been terrific, and data unlimited, because the Changers were nothing if not technically capable, and the early takeover of the telecom companies had been one of their first shrewd moves, burning down Verizon's headquarters and murdering not just its CEO but its entire – and perhaps unnecessary – board of directors. As a result, Chase had been able to witness replays of last night's madness in full HD, including the final seconds of the life of Senator Tobias Brubaker in all their gory detail.

"That's why I need to see it," Chase said.

"They're savages, sir. Anything could happen."

"So let's get a look at the savages."

They were about the same age, around thirty, and Holden had the military stature, but Chase won the stare-down. He knew he would. His whole life people had said he was one of those who just seemed to know the right way to go. He wondered if that was the mark of a Reasoner. He hoped so, because truth be told, Chase had no idea what a Reasoner was, or what was expected of him. Now that he was in the city – or almost in the city – and was seeing the state of things, he wondered how he, or anyone, was supposed to be able to fix such a colossal shitshow.

3. *Loosing the Fateful Lightning*

1

Some said the government shutdown, which took up most of the early part of the year – a mind-numbingly stupid stare-down between the President and Congress that made everyone's life miserable and achieved nothing – had started it all.

And there was truth in that. After all, the shutdown led to the viral epidemic that spread like wildfire across the East Coast, up from Georgia all the way to New York. It was called VIRA and *that* was caused because the governor of Georgia refused to deem water and safety inspectors as crucial services during the shutdown. Nor did he have any interest in interfering with the business practices of Dynastic Chemicals Inc., a company that saw the shutdown as the perfect opportunity to flood the Middle Savannah River with more than 11,670,000 pounds of toxic chemicals. After all, the CEO of Dynastic Chemicals was a golfing buddy of the President's, and the President had shares in Dynastic, so where was the risk?

By the time it wound down, the VIRA epidemic killed more than 146,000 Americans, and created God knows how much economic turmoil and civil unrest.

Nowhere was this truer than in Virginia, where martial law had been declared. The cops in some of the smaller towns took this to mean you could shoot a lot of Black people after dark, which they decided to do with even greater frequency than usual.

Which is where the first guillotine came in.

2

It appeared on March 17, in front of the Lynchburg, Virginia sheriff's building. A lot of people thought it was a joke.

The civil rights group Black Force had come to Lynchburg in response to the curfew crackdown which led to the killing of a group of Black teenagers the week before. For his part, the sheriff said the police had no choice but to shoot the kids, because every time one of his officers – "good, God-fearing family men," he said, forgetting the women in the force, something for which he later issued a written apology – approached a Black teenager to ask him what he might be doing out after dark, the cop became so frightened for his life that he had to kill the Black kid sooner than he had planned to.

The VIRA epidemic had created chaos, but no one could have guessed that it was only prelude compared to Lynchburg. From here on in, things were about to get really hairy.

By the end of that first week of March, Black Force had wound up occupying the actual sheriff's office and making good on their threat to shoot any cop who tried to retake any part of the building. For their part, the cops were determined to do exactly that – retake their building and, specifically, the secret armory in the sub-basement. This contained an astonishing arsenal of semi-automatic weapons, which would be crucial if the cops wanted to keep the peace. To make all that happen, and to keep Black Force occupied and from discovering the arsenal for themselves, the cops kept up a barrage of gunfire from the weapons they already carried, which was satisfying for now but nowhere near as satisfying as using the stuff in the armory.

So it went, back and forth.

On the fourth day of this standoff, during a lull, the Black guys watched in amazement as some of the cops bravely scampered out into the open. Right there on the lawn, they quickly erected a sort of prefabricated gallows, complete with noose. This was an obvious reference to lynching and the Jim Crow South, and MSNBC and CNN made their outrage known. Shootings were one thing, but this kind of intolerant racial slur was outrageous.

Two days later, the cops awoke to discover the gallows gone and replaced by a guillotine – Black Force demonstrating that they too had a pretty bleak sense of humor.

It wasn't a real guillotine, of course. That kind of thing is hard to come by, even in Lynchburg, Virginia. Anderson Cooper would later report that it was actually lifted from a nearby prop house that usually rented it out to amateur theatrical companies putting on community theatre productions of *Les Miz*, always a crowd pleaser, particularly in Savannah or Asheville or Knoxville.

What the Black Force leaders didn't know and couldn't have imagined as they were engaging in a literal gunfight with the law enforcement officials of Lynchburg, Virginia was that they were giving inspiration to a group of irate senior citizens who had just seen their retirement savings disappear due to the latest investment house crash. The announcement of this disaster took place literally two days after postings of the annual compensation paid to the top five bank CEOs (average weekly pay packet: $532,000) were plastered all over the internet.

3

No one would ever know how exactly things went from a group of senior citizens in fleece and Tilley hats chanting "This is what democracy feels like" to moms and dads literally lighting the Goldman Sachs building at 200 West Street in Manhattan on fire, but things got out of hand in the Big Apple with lightning speed. Soon protesters were smashing most of the windows on the first, second, third, and half the fourth floors of the Citigroup building at 399 Park. On day three of the Streeter movement – which became the genesis for the nationwide protests over income inequality – a guillotine appeared right where the Merrill Lynch bronze bull stood, or used to stand. Here as well, no one knew where it came from, but no one missed the implied solidarity between senior white Americans and their Black brothers and sisters shooting it out with the cops in the town that had made Jerry Falwell a symbol of clean American living.

4

Violence inspires violence. The riots in Bentonville, Arkansas may or may not have been juiced by what went down in Lynchburg or New York, but for sure things wouldn't have gone so crazy had one of the Walton family not made the poor decision to step outside the retail giant's corporate office. He wanted to talk to the folks demanding living wages. At that very moment, the Walton scion explained, Walmart had in fact instituted a base wage of $17, which was considerably higher than almost all state minimum wages. This sounded good to some in the crowd, but not to a forty-five-year-old factory worker named Wes Montana, who didn't even work for Walmart but had watched his wife succumb to breast cancer the year before. Wes lost not just the love of his life but also his home, the sale of which was necessary to cover what the family's inadequate medical insurance (set up by Walmart) would not. So, being in the right place at the right time, Wes Montana smashed in the Walton scion's head with a brick, an image which was caught on an iPhone and went viral. A day later, a guillotine appeared in Bentonville, Arkansas.

5

The people of Lexington, Kentucky weren't shy. They made it clear they were very much inspired – some would say divinely inspired – by the events in Arkansas. Three days after Wes Montana clocked the Walmart scion, two nuns who worked as nurses at St. Nicholas's Hospital set about burning down the Humana building as well as the state Blue Cross headquarters. Both acts were performed in the name of the Lord and memorialized by the nuns themselves, who sent their videos into the cyber world by virtue of their Samsung Galaxies. Overnight, the two sisters discovered they had a lot of converts to their cause, and suddenly there was a run on tiki torches, which turned out to be very handy when it came to setting ablaze the offices of health insurance companies, or in fact any business related to the iniquities of private health insurance across the country.

Protests from the state's elected representatives – that Kentucky did not have the worst health care in the country (in fact, Arkansas did; Kentucky was only forty-third of fifty) – didn't cut much ice. It seemed kind of splitting hairs too. People clearly wanted change, and they were no longer interested in being polite or good citizens.

Perhaps that's why, sometime after Kentucky and right before West Virginia, when pissed-off miners led by a righteous powerhouse named Jeff Beavenstock literally blew up the state Capitol, one word was discovered the next morning, spray-painted into the smoking wreckage. "Changers."

6

Changers.

It meant all of them: Lynchburg, Bentonville, Lexington, Wall Street, anywhere the people were fed up and demanded change. "Changer" was the word from late March through April and into May.

Suddenly guillotines were popping up everywhere.

A big blade appeared in front of the state house in Texas after the governor decreed protesters would be thrown in jail for sedition; another popped up when the Department of Homeland Security declared that the United Federation of Public School Teachers protesting against pay discrimination were a threat to national security; a third appeared in Davenport, Iowa after the city announced they were raising taxes but had no plans to fix the water supply.

This was the crisis the news media called the "middle-American protest" or "the crisis in the small towns" and then, eventually, "the Uprising."

Then, two days after Davenport, on May 1, the public employees who make up most of the population of Washington, D.C. awoke to find an eighteen-foot-tall guillotine bolted to the mezzanine steps of the west front of the United States Capitol building, the side which looked all the way across the grassy Mall and the reflecting pool to the Lincoln Memorial.

This was clearly *not* a prop. With its counterweight released, it set the 88-pound blade rocketing downwards at a drop speed of almost 21 feet per second for a total drop time of $1/70^{th}$ of a second, delivering a wallop of 5,100 pounds of pressure per square inch. It could cut a human arm off at the shoulder in less than 0.005 seconds, and a head absolutely no problem.

This clearly, and finally, was the real thing.

7

CNN reported that as of 3 a.m. that Wednesday, the 66 as well as the 495, 395, and I-95 – and every other road leading into Washington – was jammed bumper to bumper. Soon, the Virginia and Maryland state police shut down highway access to the capital. Commercial bus service was also cancelled. Reagan National Airport had been shut down due to the anti-aircraft debacle. Dulles and BWI followed two days later.

If this was the establishment's best attempt to keep Changers from flooding the city, it was too little and too late.

The Changer cause had spread by social media. Soon, therefore, everyone who used Twitter or Facebook or Snapchat or Instagram or even a phone knew that the best way to get into the nation's capital was by rail, a form of transportation the authorities – most of whom flew on private jets – had completely forgotten about. Suddenly, railroads were back in full use for the first time since

1967, the year the Commerce and Trade Act, written by GM, Ford, and Chrysler, had done everything they could to destroy the use of passenger rail travel.

Ironically, many of the people who had renewed that bill on its 50th anniversary were herded into the basement of the Capitol building on May 22nd (a date later abbreviated to 5/22). Here they would live, the once High and Mighty, ears pressed to the walls or ceilings through which they were able to hear the crowd outside the nation's capital, yelling as loudly as any mob at the Superbowl or in a Roman Coliseum. But it wasn't the cheering crowd the terrified public servants wanted to hear. They wanted to hear whose name was going to be called next.

4. *Chase and the Guillotine*

1

The train finally stopped in the station. As instructed, Chase waited in the doorway between rail cars for the better part of four minutes.

The window which normally made up the top half of the door had been reinforced with a steel plate, so Chase could only hear, not see, the chaos on the other side. What he heard were crazy people shouting at one another, police whistles, and a loudspeaker mindlessly repeating the same instructions over and over: "Step away and vacate the platform area. This is a red zone. Repeat, step away and vacate the platform area. This is a red zone." A voice broadcast through a bullhorn delivered exactly the same message, except in this case it was pretty much screaming.

Two separate messages, for a very good reason. Washington was now a city divided, like old Berlin. Two forces – what remained of the U.S. government and the Changers – controlled it. And nowhere was this division and its resulting chaos on better display than within Washington's Union Station.

The door was suddenly ripped open. Commander Guerra – or someone Chase sure hoped was Commander Guerra – reached in and grabbed Chase's upper left arm. Without ceremony, Chase was yanked down the two steps and practically carried through a corridor of armed soldiers in full riot gear. They lifted their shields at odd moments and thrust them out. Chase was confused by this at first, but then realized they were deftly deflecting garbage and cans of food – tuna cans in particular – thrown by the mob.

Once they got him through the rear of the station to its vaulted atrium, Chase was shoved out the front doors and hustled toward an SUV that stood by the curb at Columbus Circle, the rear door opened at the last possible second. He did a double-take. The person holding the door was an enormous, pot-belled senior citizen wearing a leather Hells Angels vest. He carried an AR-15 – the gun of choice these days – held upright against his left arm. Three hundred and thirty pounds of belly and beard and yet he nodded politely to Chase like a doorman at the Dorchester. He actually said, "Good to have you with us."

Chase started to respond to this politeness with a politeness of his own, but Holden shoved Chase into the back of the car and hopped in after. The door was slammed. Someone smacked the roof. The SUV pulled away.

Inside the car, Chase pulled himself up and looked out the windows. There were motorcycles in front and on either side of them.

"Hells Angels?" Chase asked, looking back through the rear window at the man who had held the door for him.

Holden nodded with embarrassment. "They've announced themselves neutral, so we decided to recruit some of them as a secondary force. We're facing a manpower shortage due to the … " He hesitated just a second. "Reallocation. It's just temporary."

Chase started to respond, but a tuna can hit the car. "Pick up the pace!" Holden told the driver. He explained to Chase, "We're harder to hit the faster we go."

The Capitol was only a few blocks away. The motorcycles up front did a pretty efficient job of clearing a path, spikes and taser prods sticking out either side of the bikes and the lead cyclist firing a pistol in the air to herald their approach, but it was still a pretty thick crowd to plow through.

The route took them down Delaware Avenue and along Northwest Drive to the west side of the Capitol and beyond that, the wide, grassy Mall.

"Why the tuna?" Chase asked.

"It was something she said." Holden said. "On MSNBC or somewhere. She said, 'If you only have a garden hose or a snow shovel or a can of tuna, use it.' Churchill, or almost. She's shrewd. I can tell you, a can of tuna hurts."

She. The whole country knew who 'she' was. The whole world, likely. She called herself Sister Sheena, the ying to Changer leader Beavenstock's yang, one half of a very unsteady and volatile political alliance. She wasn't exactly a kid, but her youth pissed off a lot of people. So did her stridency. And appeal.

"Like she's ever used a shovel or a hose," Holden said. "All that street stuff is bullshit. I heard she went to Yale."

"I heard Stanford. Doesn't she come from California?"

Holden shrugged. "Like all the other bullshit, they took her literally. But it's weird she chose tuna. Cat food is cheaper but because it's more tightly packed turns out nowhere near as clean a yaw. That's a hell of a thing for her to know, don't you think?"

They were coming around the bend from Northwest Drive. The crowd was getting thicker and edging closer to the car on either side.

Chase gazed out at the snarling, misshapen faces screaming in at them. "It's worse than I expected."

"I told you, they're savages." Holden now had his sidearm out and was holding it up, ready for who knew what. He took the safety off. "And of course, they're more psyched up because of last night."

They took the right and then the left turn. The first thing Chase saw as they came around the bend were people perched on top of the Grant Memorial and the Peace Monument. Some of them had binoculars. More than half of them wore wolf hats.

Then Chase saw it. The top of it, anyway.

2

What the country called the Great Guillotine rose eighteen feet from its base, but because it was placed on the second terrace of the Capitol steps, it seemed to tower that much higher. And the great blade was up at the moment, so it caught the light. It seemed to beckon you forward.

At the moment there was a guard around the guillotine, made up of Changers in football jerseys ('Jerseys') and the weekend warriors in full tactical gear ('Tacticals'). It was this formidable force, as well as a rope strung across the stop step, that kept the crowds back. The rabble were clearly expecting more excitement today, because they were chanting and singing and seemed almost high. There were a lot of smartphones poised at the ready.

"They're hoping the Reasoner Compromise is broken," Holden said. "Because Beavenstock did the staffer first, then finished off with a Senator. That really riles them up."

"What do you mean??"

"They love it when you do a Congressman of any sort, but especially a Senator. So it's become a big finish thing with him. The only problem is, you can't control them the next day. It's like a drug. Like I said, savages."

The crowd forced the small motorcade to move away from the Capitol steps and down alongside the Mall.

Chase had expected to be shocked by the guillotine – and he was – but to his surprise, it was nothing compared to the Mall. That left him speechless.

3

Everything was so well set up. That's what struck him first. It was like an Independence Day picnic. There were camp chairs and beach chairs, umbrellas and coolers of beer and cold cuts and potato salad, as well as snack bars and barbecues every few yards and, down the side of Independence Avenue, food trucks. Children were on their dad's shoulders and moms had brought sunscreen. When announcements weren't being made from the Capitol mezzanine, music was playing from speakers clipped to the top of wheeled basketball hoops that had been placed every seventy-five feet or so, all the way to the Lincoln Memorial. At the moment, the song was *96 Tears*, which Chase had always liked. Everyone was armed.

Violence, he discovered, erupted quickly and was dealt with instantly.

As they were edging up 3rd Street, a man jumped out in the middle of Madison Drive waving a hatchet. Someone – one of the Jerseys positioned along the sidewalk, Chase thought – shot him. The body was quickly moved to the side. A five-year-old boy, surprised by the loud noise, dropped his snow cone and started crying when he saw it melting on the pavement. His mother rushed in and evidently promised him a new one, because the kid perked right up.

"Holy shit," Chase said.

"Have they told any of you why the Changers resumed?" Holden asked Chase.

"I just got here. I haven't been briefed on anything yet."

"It certainly does seem counter to the Compromise," said Holden, fishing for information.

Chase shrugged. "I imagine a lot of people are looking for a lot of answers." Then, Chase gave it a shot from his side. "How would one know if they intend to go again tonight?"

Holden shook his head. "There's no way of knowing until they put it on Twitter. But if they do, it won't be until eight at the earliest." Holden saw Chase's inquiring look. "They're always careful to catch the West Coast."

They were going up 7th Street now. Chase was unsure about his geography, but this seemed wrong. "I thought we were staying at the Hyatt."

"There was a problem with that."

"Booked?"

"In a manner of speaking. You'll be staying in one of the old off-site State buildings. But your meetings are going to be held at Treasury."

So many last-minute changes. "We were supposed to be meeting in the government accounting building," Chase said.

"You were," said Holden. "But they burned it down this morning."

There was a pause.

"Probably no great loss."

5. *The Reasoners*

1

Chase's motorcade drove across the "border" between Changers Washington and the GOR Washington, which was roughly Pennsylvania Avenue. Right past the Hyatt hotel. Chase leaned forward, peering across Commander Holden's body to get a better look at the hotel where he wouldn't be staying.

Clearly the problem wasn't that the place was closed. On the contrary, the Hyatt was a veritable beehive of activity, with all sorts of folks happily streaming in and out through the double sliding glass doors and plenty of others crowding the sidewalk. The problem was that most of the clientele of the four-star hotel were Jerseys, Harleys, or badass Tactical guys wearing civilian riot gear. Everyone was armed, with a good quarter of them carrying semi-automatic or even automatic rifles. The sidewalk litter baskets outside the street entrance were filled to bursting with fast food garbage, and three heavyset teenagers were busy jumping up and down on an overturned USPS mailbox. In other words, the Commander had been correct – the Hyatt was not available, but it was very much occupied.

The off-site State Department building which had been chosen in its stead turned out to be only a few blocks away. In contrast to the handsome Hyatt, this was a dismal grey bunker, tall for Washington, with a surrounding iron fence reinforced by razor wire. Clearly, it had been chosen because it could be protected.

Armed state guards stood at full attention every ten feet outside and inside the barrier, and roadblocks of Normandy fencing had been erected at each mouth of the driveway. As his car pulled in,

Chase saw that the men guarding the entry were in full combat gear with stars and stripes on the left breast pocket. No Hells Angels mercenary support here – strictly U.S. issue, although they had to be reserves or state guards, as per the withdrawal on Capture Day.

"Do not exit the car until advised to do so," said Holden. "We need to secure the area first."

Chase, who had absolutely no intention of getting out of any car until he was advised to do so, eyed the state guard, the razor wire, and the Normandy fencing. "This isn't secure enough?"

Holden didn't respond. He was looking in all directions through all windows at the same time, as if waiting for an attack. To Chase's eye, this seemed far less likely on the Government side of town. Since they had driven up from Constitution Avenue, the crowds had thinned noticeably, and there had been no overture toward the vehicle or its escort SUVs. In fact, for the last half-block since passing the Hyatt, you could have convinced yourself that you were in normal Washington. More than half the stores and coffee shops were open.

Apparently satisfied that it was safe to do so, Holden popped open the door and vaulted from the car to address a fellow Commander standing just outside.

Chase stayed in the back seat as the military men did their thing, which seemed to be saluting one another, speaking in hushed monotones, and exchanging papers.

A sudden rifle shot. Chase spun around in his seat. The escort Harleys, so handy in getting them through the Capitol crowds, were parked on the other side of the fencing, waiting dutifully. This turned out to be the source of the 'rifle shot.' One of the armored Harley Fat Boys had backfired.

"Professor!"

Chase turned. Holden was holding the door open for him.

He was yanked out of the car and, not unlike the scurry through the train station, rushed into the State office building under more than his own power.

2

Everything changed the second they entered the marbled reception area. There were friendly faces in here, or at least one. A young man in a blazer and striped school tie stood in the center of the vast polished atrium, holding a clipboard. He greeted Chase enthusiastically. "Professor Selby!" He wore a security badge and introduced himself as either Tyler or Skyler, Chase wasn't sure which. Whoever he was, he clearly had some sort of authority, for he thanked Holden and summarily dismissed him, saying he would take it from here.

"We won't need you until the tea," Tyler said.

To Chase's surprise, Holden responded to this discharge by turning about-face and snapping off a smart salute directed at … Chase!

He had never been saluted before, so he just nodded to Holden and thanked him for his help. Holden turned on his heel and marched toward a double set of crash doors which led to a corridor on the north side of the building.

3

Chase was relieved to be away from the guns. Tyler seemed relieved as well, but for other reasons. "You're all here now," he said as they rode the elevator together. "That's a good thing."

Chase noticed that Tyler had to start the elevator by swiping a card as well as turning a key attached to his belt. As if this weren't enough, he also entered a six-digit access code. "I will be your PSLO – personal services liaison officer – during your time here," Tyler said. "Which means you can turn to me for anything related to your stay."

"How many personal services liaison officers are there?"

"Six. Twelve Reasoners, six PSLOs. Two Reasoners per floor, with Director Brueler on Four. Here we are. Top floor."

They got off on a floor that clearly at some point had been the exclusive domain of executive directors and high-level bureaucrats. As Chase followed Tyler to the right, they passed a half-dozen closed doors, wide, set apart, of polished walnut, now sealed with crisscrossed aluminum braces. Someone had forgotten to remove the nameplates, however. "DIRECTOR, INTERNATIONAL ACTION ASSESSMENT," and "CO-ORDINATOR, ASIAN INITIATIVES AND FEASIBILITIES."

Tyler nodded at an armed guard standing sentry at the far end of the corridor, then unlocked the second-to-last door. He used both the key and the card. "This entire building was spillover State," he explained to Chase. "It was evacuated on 5/22."

"But why here?"

"As a State building it had been a high-level security location, so that meant reinforced entry and exit, daily sweeps for surveillance, easy to protect, and – " Tyler gave him a wink, "it had enough executive offices with their own ensuite bathrooms."

Tyler held the door open. Chase entered. He was standing inside what could easily pass for a luxury suite in any five-star hotel.

Tyler said, "It was determined that it would be easier to bring in beds and headboards and retrofit offices than to figure out how to make the Intercontinental or the Hyatt externally safe."

"They did a magnificent job."

"We aim to please."

Chase went to the window. Even though they were only on the sixteenth floor, from this angle he could see just over enough rooftops to get a glimpse of the Mall and, beyond that, a piece of the Capitol building. Not surprising, given that the Washington Monument was the tallest structure in the city and there were rules about how high you could build in D.C.

"Don't worry," said Tyler. "The windows are one-way, and destruction proof." Chase noted the careful avoidance of the word 'bullet.'

Chase turned from the window and considered the artwork on

the walls. He studied a portrait of James K. Polk. "Is that original?"

Tyler nodded as he squatted down to check the mini-bar. "They figured that as long as they were moving the entire contents of the National Portrait Gallery, they may as well place some of it in a secure location. It's assumed you won't spill anything on it or sell it."

"When did they decide to make the change?" Chase asked.

Tyler craned his neck around to look at him. He hesitated just a fraction of a second, barely noticeable, before answering. "Last night. When the Changers broke the Compromise."

"That probably meant a lot of scrambling."

Tyler shook his head as he rose out of his squat. "In my opinion, the Hyatt would never have worked. We were ready with an alternate, of course. So we just released it. I hear there are Changers with AR-15s hanging around the lobby now, getting drunk and reloading. Maybe they'll accidentally shoot one another. Hope springs." Tyler disappeared into the bedroom and called back. "The linen is fresh and you have a change in the lower drawer of the dresser. You can always call down for extra. You will have daily maid service if you want. I made sure there are four pillows on the bed – I always like extra myself – and two more in the closet. I hope that's sufficient."

"It's more than enough. Thank you."

Tyler emerged from the bathroom. "Your Wi-Fi information is on the desk. You'll need it. Cellular service is non-existent here – part of the security protocols, I'm afraid – but the Wi-Fi is government protected. And you must only use *that* Wi-Fi. And obviously you wouldn't use cellular for any official business."

"No, of course not."

Chase, having just driven past the U.S. Capitol building with the eighteen-foot-tall guillotine out front, wasn't exactly sure what 'government-protected' meant, but he appreciated the spirit. A large part of him was truly sorry to be doing without Free-Fi, though, the lightning-fast cellular and Wi-Fi service that he and the rest of the country had come to enjoy free of charge, courtesy of the Changers' can-do tech.

Tyler gestured to an old-fashioned red telephone on the coffee table. "That's your government-issued communications lifeline."

Chase looked. "Also from the museum?"

"Our people say analog is almost impossible to crack."

"Can the Reasoners call one another?"

It was a question Tyler hadn't anticipated. "For now, you can only call your PSLO or their surrogate."

"What about individual security? Within the building?"

"There will be one armed military personnel per floor. It's unnecessary, though. You can rest assured this is the safest building in Washington."

Chase could have pointed out that the White House was supposed to be the safest building in Washington, but he decided to let that go. After all, as far as anyone knew, the White House was unoccupied at the moment.

"Director Brueler has called for a meeting with the GOR for later this afternoon," said Tyler. "That will be at three. That still gives you all plenty of time to refresh, and you can be on time for tea."

"You mentioned that to Commander Holden. A tea."

"On the fourth floor, in less than an hour. Boardroom One. It will allow you to meet all your fellow Reasoners for the first time."

"I see."

"Your daily schedule has been sent to you via secure text and is also printed and on the coffee table. It will be left under your door every night."

"Thank you."

"There are also research binders and background material on the desk by the window."

They stepped out into the hall and Tyler showed Chase how the lock on the outer door worked. Chase peered down the long corridor past the elevators and saw his neighbor moving in on the other side of the building; a tiny, older man in a nondescript beige raincoat. A young woman in a blazer identical to Tyler's was opening the door for him.

Chase could hear her giving the same speech Tyler had given him: "There are twelve Reasoners, two per floor, and six Personal Services Liaison Officers per ... "

"I didn't know he was so small," said Chase.

Tyler looked up. "Excuse me?"

Indeed, the old man at the end of the hall was thinner and smaller than Chase had ever imagined, but the odd droop of his head and the half-pitched smile were unmistakable.

"Hamer," Chase said.

Tyler followed Chase's gaze down the hall. "Is there anything else I can do for you right now?"

"He won the Nobel Prize before he was forty. Did you know that?"

"I'm always accessible through the red phone."

"Then he did it again. Economics *and* Physics. I don't know if anyone else has ever done that. No native-born American, certainly."

"Anything, at any hour, day or night."

Chase focused back in. "Yes, there is."

Tyler seemed crestfallen, like he'd lost a bet. "Of course."

"A pair of binoculars. High-powered. Military-grade."

"May I ask – "

"Thanks," said Chase.

Only the slightest flicker from Tyler, a look that said, 'Oh, so you're one of *those* assholes.' Aloud, Tyler said, "Of course. I'll get them for you right away." Then he added, because he couldn't resist, "We would of course make a record of something like that."

"Of course," Chase said.

Tyler made to go. "And remember: Always use the red phone."

"Why only the red phone?"

Tyler shrugged. "You know what they say. 'Good Times Bad, Bad Times Really Bad.'"

With that, Tyler left Chase alone.

6. *Wolf Words and Windows*

1

The quote was inaccurate. Tyler was using the T-shirt version of it. The actual sentence in the book was, "When times are good, you need good government; when times are bad, you need terror to make them *give* you good government."

For slogan purposes, however, sometime around April this had been shortened into "Good Times Good, Bad Times Really Bad." It was a threat, which came from a book that was basically a collection of threats.

It was later estimated that less than a hundred people had actually read or ordered the tract *The Words of the Wolf* (later, folks just shortened it to *Wolf Words*) when it had been published more than four years before, courtesy of one of those print-on-demand publishing houses. Its authorship was attributed to the pseudonym "The Wolf." After that inauspicious debut, it had disappeared without a trace, its true author or authors unknown, its purpose almost as inscrutable as many of its sayings and aphorisms, even if its point was clear: Citizens should "reinstate" the American Constitution by any means necessary, especially violence. The book went to great lengths to explain why that wasn't such a bad idea.

Then, after the government shutdown had lit the spark and the epidemic had fanned it into flame, quotes from *Wolf Words* were suddenly and mysteriously on the lips of every insurrectionist leader and tuned-in, pissed-off American. It became a sort of jingoistic framework upon which folks could hang what was being touted as a new, Second, American Revolution. And the more it was quoted, the more people read it, and the more it spread.

And why not? An outrageously pissed-off America wanted its own *Das Kapital*, written in plain simple American language that laid the case and the objective out plainly. They found it on Amazon for $12.99.

"When your leaders tell you the truth, that's freedom; when they keep lying to you, you're living in a dictatorship."

"Sometimes the leaders must die so the country can live."

"When the leaders of a country believe they're the good people and the people they govern are bad, it's time for the leaders to go."

And, to some, the most disturbing of all: *"If you want to create true and unquestionable Justice, first you have to create true and unspeakable terror."*

In a matter of weeks, against the backdrop of the Uprising in the small cities, these invocations were everywhere: Someone started a Wolf blog, a group of privileged kids at Duke started a Wolf website, and boldly, folks began to represent themselves as the Wolf on Twitter and on Instagram. The real key was the book itself, however, which now became a national bestseller and was sold by the skid-load not just through Amazon, but soon at Barnes & Noble, Target, and CVS. Soon, an ebook was offered up free, which meant everyone – *everyone* – had it on their phone, an AAA roadmap for a revolution and easier to understand than Ikea bookshelf instructions. Here, finally, were some goddamned answers.

It was perhaps even more appealing because there didn't seem to be an actual author. Some of the Uprising's original and most violent leaders, especially the Black Force guys in Lynchburg, began to suggest that maybe *they* were behind the volume of revolutionary wisdom – but that was a claim pretty quickly disproven. Then there was a long investigative piece in the *Washington Post* that pointed to a cadre of academics out of the University of Massachusetts, Amherst; supposedly they had written the piece as part of their thesis, and something of a joke at that. This claim was also disproven. Jeff Beavenstock was an impossible candidate and the four-year-old print-on-demand edition almost surely erased Sister Sheena due to her age. The only thing experts could agree on – and soon there actually *were* experts – was that inconsistency of spelling and grammar suggested more than one author at work and likely more than three. Five seemed to be the generally accepted number.

What the academics missed was that it didn't really matter.

What mattered was the effect it had on people, and the fact that it was an immediate and identifiable brand; you couldn't go wrong with a cartoon wolf snarling at you. That image was reprinted on everything from keychains to backpacks to gun holsters. The Wolf brought home the message to every pissed-off American out there. "The extreme suppression of your rights deserves the most extreme reaction you can dream up, and it is never wrong." In other words, 'Get as mad as you want and be as extreme as you want, it's okay because people really *did* fuck you over as badly as you think.'

The way Chase viewed it, the problem wasn't when the Changers quoted the Wolf, or even when maniacs in Chicago Blackhawks jerseys marched down the main streets of America chanting its simplistic aphorisms; the problem was when a Government keener like Tyler casually tossed off a quote without entirely realizing what he was doing. If you looked at it from that perspective, the Changers weren't an aberration of the nation's culture, they were becoming part of it.

2

He cleaned up in the bathroom, which was as modern as any found in a new Park Avenue condominium. While he was drying his face, there was a discreet knock at the front door. He padded out to peer through the peephole and discovered there was no peephole. Something they missed. He opened the door.

A Personal Services Liaison Officer in a blazer that matched Tyler's – in fact, this PSLO looked pretty much like a seventeen-year-old mini-me of Tyler – had Chase's luggage behind him and a small leather satchel under his arm. "Dr. Selby?"

Chase opened the door wide and held out a hand. "I'll take that. And please, put the bag in the bedroom."

As the young man wheeled the bag in, Chase opened the leather satchel. Inside was the finest pair of binoculars he had ever seen.

The young man came out and asked if there was anything else he could do. Chase said no and asked if he was allowed to tip him.

"No, sir. Besides, it's my honor." He gave Chase an odd, awkward little salute, a bow, and then left. Chase's second salute of the day.

He didn't know what to make of this new phenomenon, but he hoped it didn't recur. He didn't like what it suggested. The Reasoners, by definition, were meant only to be reasonable. While they had been given enormous, sweeping powers, they were not meant to be a replacement for the U.S. government nor any elected representatives, even if the elected representatives – those that were still alive, anyway – were teetering in their power, or had already had it taken by force.

He locked the door behind him and went to the window with the binoculars.

They were so high-tech. At first he had trouble even adjusting them. Once he figured out the basics, however, he was able to focus on the office tower across the street. But when he looked beyond that to clear sky and took the zoom out as far as it would go, he was rocked back on his heels by the sheer power of the lenses.

Once he made adjustments, he focused in on part of the Capitol building itself and the area around the guillotine. Not close, but close enough. His view was partly blocked by buildings, so all he could see was the top of the frame high above the heads of the crowd. Right now, the blade was up. He remembered Holden telling him that Beavenstock always waited for best coverage on the cable news nets, which was never before eight.

He could also tilt down and get a pretty good look at the crowds on the Mall. They were stretched all the way west to the Memorial. Through the lens, it was a silent show of almost genial confusion. There was an energy to these people, a pulse, an excitement. They were expecting *something*.

He moved to the other end of the window and stepped in so close that the lenses touched the glass.

Joy. That was it. These people had the joy of violence in them. You could see it in their faces, in their movements, the way they called to one another, in their too-loud, exaggerated gestures. Somehow it made a mockery of Chase even being there.

How could you erect a barrier against this kind of force? It seemed absurd. All the precautions and preparations in the world wouldn't protect Chase or any of the other Reasoners from harm if things went wrong. Fighting against this kind of exalted, willful anger and energy was whistling in the wind, or spitting in the eye of a hurricane.

Chase checked his watch. 1:30.

He laid down the binoculars and slipped off his shoes and began climbing on the furniture. A half-hour wasn't much time to disable all of the surveillance devices he was sure they'd planted, but he could get a good start on it.

The simple fact was, he could act the role they wanted him to play – yes, he could do that – but he couldn't allow himself to be watched or recorded. Because they had made a mistake about him. From the beginning.

7. Recruitment

1

At the time, Chase had just been transfixed by her hair. He couldn't take his eyes off it.

A wig. It surely had to be a wig. But maybe not. Perhaps it was just an incredibly bold dye job to match the cut, which was a jet-black flapper bob that ended abruptly at the jawline – saucy and piquant on a woman of, say, twenty; on a woman of eighty, however, which the Senator surely was, it was really something else. So was the Victory red lipstick. So were the rings which adorned each gnarled finger. Add the stylish Dior pantsuit and owlish Woody Allen eyewear and the whole package said, "You want to laugh at me, and I'm encouraging you to laugh, but you can't laugh, because I am the very embodiment of power."

Her hand reached across the table and rested on Chase's. It was downright flirtatious, as was the honey drawl that went with it. "Things have progressed with our little project, Chase," Senator Sofia Puccelli said in an almost Marilyn or Jackie breathy whisper. "So, you deserve to know where we are."

"We?" he asked.

Eighty or not, there was still sparkle in her eyes. "*You*, Chase, are about to become a very important person."

It was still four months before he would board an armored train to go to Washington, D.C. and long before he would be saluted by a U.S. Army Commander and a bellboy. So Chase could be forgiven for almost laughing when she said, "a very important person." He was, at that moment, nobody.

Well, maybe not entirely. A tenured professor at Princeton, yes, one of the youngest in its history, yes, but that was Princeton important, not *important* important. He was the author of two rather dry books – one on the genesis of the U.S. Constitution, another on the nature of American patriotism – but very few people had bought these books and even fewer had read them. Despite his dozen appearances on television and maybe a dozen podcast interviews, no one stopped him on the street. So, on this unseasonably warm early spring afternoon, he viewed himself as simply a young man with an exceptional academic CV, which in the Princeton environment meant he was entirely unexceptional.

Chase was fine with that, but the octogenarian holding his hand had spent forty years surrounded by people who more than anything else in life wanted to be *very* important, so she laid it on with a trowel. "Because of your importance," the Senator continued, "we feel it's time to brief you fully. Bring you up to speed. About how things have suddenly accelerated."

"Because of the crisis?"

That's what it was called then. Sometimes it was 'the crisis in the small cities,' but for the most part it was 'the crisis' or, a new phrase, 'the Uprising.' Whatever name you gave it, it was hard to grasp that while Chase and these two visitors from Washington were sitting on a porticoed patio overlooking the lawns of Princeton stirring cappuccinos, a gentle breeze riffling their hair, a good two dozen smaller American cities were in the middle of insane, violent revolution. Just that morning Chase had read about two nuns trying to burn down an Anthem Blue Cross building in Kentucky. Could that be right?

"Why do you assume our little project and the crises are linked?" asked the Senator.

"Aren't they?" Chase sipped his cappuccino. "Why else would you be here? Surely two such highly placed public servants could be doing better things while one half of the country is trying to figure out how to destroy the other half. Therefore, yes, I assume they're connected."

Senator Puccelli looked at him a good long while, as if trying to determine if he were man or mouse, then let out a delighted hoot of laughter and clapped her hands together. Her hoopy bracelets jangled. "You're wonderful!" She looked at the man with her. "Isn't he wonderful?" She leaned in on Chase, even closer. "All right, Chase, then *you* tell us! Show us how clever you are."

Chase shook his head. "I'm not so clever. And I haven't thought very much about your project since last summer, so I can't tell you anything."

That was only partly true. In fact, he hadn't given their thinktank – or whatever it was – *any* thought, not since his last interview at the Holiday Inn. Months before, when they'd first approached him, there had been no crisis, no burnings of banks, no shootouts with Virginia's finest, not even an epidemic named VIRA. There had only been the murmurings of discontent over a stimulus bill that might lead to a government shutdown.

Senator Puccelli turned to her companion, the big, rumpled man with the walrus mustache. *Literally* a walrus mustache. Another anachronistic hair choice.

The man gave Senator Puccelli a small nod.

She turned back to Chase. "Well, obviously there is a connection. Although I must be clear that our project started long before all this madness. Back in the dark ages, when a wolf was just a wild dog." She laughed at her own joke. "I can't even read *that* trash!" She nodded at the walrus man. "Dr. Barnhardt is one of the project's architects. I think he can explain it best."

Finally, Dr. Ross Barnhardt looked prepared to speak. Maybe. First, he adjusted his ass in the uncomfortable metal garden chair, then studied his knuckles, then he actually smoothed the insane mustache. These two, Chase wondered in vague amazement, are the face of power in D.C.?

Barnhardt's voice was like sandpaper. He sounded like he was in the final stages of throat cancer. "This actually started as a mere theoretical concept. The science is in how we make our choices. Your name wasn't just pulled from a hat."

"That's good to know," Chase said amiably enough. "But what's it about? What's its purpose?"

Dr. Barnhardt adjusted his ass again. Here was a man who would likely never be comfortable with the furniture he was given. "Well, when it started, it was simply a basement concept that didn't attract a lot of attention. Because no one was really sure of its application. It was all theoretical."

"I know I filled out a lot of forms," Chase said, prodding the man to focus. "And I know I had few options in the matter … "

That was putting it mildly. When they had first approached him, he rebelled against helping them in any way. Then the college's counsel made it clear that he didn't really have any choice in the matter, and that it was wiser to fill out all of their forms and background checks and sit for two interviews in the Holiday Inn ("consider it like being tested for the draft," he was told) than kick up a fuss. The alternative was that some of his research grants would be at risk. "All major universities have a close relationship with the Feds," the school counsel said. "And to pretend otherwise is to be naïve." So Chase went along with it, assuming he was being used as a test subject at best or at worst being head-hunted to work for one of the intelligence services or some equally absurd branch of the government for some low-level make-work thinktank. Which he would later turn down.

"So tell him," the Senator said to Barnhardt.

Dr. Barnhardt adjusted his ass again. "It's really your enterprise now, Sofia."

"Oh no," she said. "Not mine." The girlishness in her voice gained a bit of edge.

Dr. Barnhardt explained to Chase. "It was really Howard Pierpoint's. Before he died."

Finally Chase's curiosity was piqued. Pierpoint? Did he hear that right? Everyone knew who Pierpoint was: a historian and psychologist but also a vigorous anti-capitalist of the old school, and exponent of 1930s radicalism. Since Nixon, the man had been in a kind of perpetual war with the system.

"Pierpoint worked for the U.S. government?" Chase asked skeptically. "What department?"

Neither wanted to answer. Finally, Barnhardt said, "Defense."

Chase felt a cold finger tracing down his back. Defense? Wherever this was going, he didn't like it. If, in fact, any of it were true.

"And with the DNI," the older man added.

"That's the Director of National Intelligence," the Senator said helpfully.

"I thought this was some thinktank," Chase said, slowly. "Your people said it was a test of – what did they call it? 'Alternative methods of maintaining governmental integrity'?"

Barnhardt sat forward. He looked at the other café patrons before shifting to a quiet, intense voice – kind of like Dick Cheney whispering to the boys in the silo. "After the Middle East incursions – after *that* debacle," he said, "Howard had a notion that we might one day reach a point in this country where civilian leadership might be unable to distance itself from entrenched commercial interests. Do you understand what I mean? Unable to act exclusively in the chauvinist interests of the United States. He imagined the temporary collapse, or maybe more than temporary, of the traditional governmental structures. So Howard began to consider the notion of a panel of mandarins to be brought in during a potential time of crisis to help create the smoothest possible decision-making process."

Traditional governmental structures, smoothest possible decision-making? But the word that stuck out most with Chase was 'mandarins.'

Barnhardt shrugged. "A team of thinkers. For want of a word, we call them Reasoners. Working for but outside the traditional lanes of government. As Howard stressed, only in a time of crisis."

"Outside?" Chase liked the sound of this less and less. "To do what?"

Dr. Barnhardt counted off one calloused finger. "Primarily to evaluate and contemplate and advise. Also, to – "

"To stop the crazies from destroyin' the country!" said the Senator. "To force upon the President real solutions to real problems outside the political realm! And to work around Congressional entanglements."

"Force? Upon *which* President?"

"*Any* President."

"You do realize what this sounds like," Chase said.

Barnhardt shook his head. "The Senator misspoke. Not to replace existing Presidential power. Just in case something happens. How we could stabilize decision-making in a potential time of crisis. To create the most streamlined process possible."

"Except," Chase said, "the President already has something set up for that. Every President does. It's called a Cabinet. And the people have something too. It's called Congress."

Barnhardt leaned forward, continuing as if Chase had never spoken. "What fascinated Howard – what got him going – was figuring out who would comprise such a panel and how such an apolitical body could be assembled. What standards would be required. It was the psychological profiling that interested him, determining what kind of mind was best suited to – "

"No!" shouted the Senator. A few of the other heads on the patio turned. "No, no, no. You've told him enough." She gestured to Chase as one might gesture to a particularly gifted child standing beside a piano. "Have *him* tell us."

Barnhardt looked at her, considered what she had said, then looked to Chase. He sat back and waited.

Chase knew when he was being tested, and he didn't like it any more than he liked the sound of their project. Yet he also knew the answers to some of their problems. They were obvious. "Well ... " he said slowly, "if you're talking about a panel of super advisors and not administrators, you're talking something far more focused than the Cabinet and probably not answerable directly to the President.

So, no lawyers. Too many lawyers within the legislative body already, and obviously SCOTUS has its own constitutional mandate, and that can't be crossed. Age cross-section, sexual, economic, immigrant, native-born. Racial representation would matter but not as important probably as experiential background. But they would have to have seen something of the world. Adversity? Yes." As he was talking, Chase could now see how 1930s socialist Howard Pierpoint's interest was captured; this was social engineering and psychology and the re-creation of the American compact all rolled into one. And it tested the strengths and elasticity of the Constitution. Perfect for a man who had little respect for the nation state to begin with. Unfortunately, Chase, who *was* a patriot, had bad news for them. "Of course, versions of this have been done before."

Now it was their turn to look baffled.

He continued. "Many times. FDR's Brain Trust. LBJ's Wise Men. JFK's Ex-Comm … "

"No!" said the Senator. Again heads turned. She leaned in and whispered. "That was free advice and there were no balls in a vise. No consequences. And half of them were Cabinet officers. The purpose of our project was to imagine what kind of people we'd have to draw together for the *sake* of reason and to meet outside the constraints of executive overview."

Chase turned to Barnhardt. "What was the word you used earlier? Reasoners?"

Barnhardt nodded.

"So, a panel of elites who simply must be … reasonable?"

Now the Senator nodded.

"And you want me to what? Advise on your choices?"

Barnhardt and the Senator looked at one other, flummoxed. This they hadn't expected at all.

"You misunderstand, Chase," the Senator said finally. "You have been chosen to *be* one. A Reasoner. That's why we're here. This has been in the cards a long time. Long before we contacted you, even."

Chase stared at her. "Pardon me?"

"We drew up a dossier on you, observed, and only then did we approach."

"Observed?" Chase felt his jaw clench. "What kind of observations?"

"Not invasive. Just keeping tabs."

He was surprised at how angry he was. "Going back how far?"

"Well the project didn't start yesterday, did it? Three years ago, at least."

Chase was stunned. "Three years?"

The Senator grinned. "Even a patriot like you knows not to trust the government, Chase. Look, I wouldn't be upset. This is only a 'what if' project and a shaggy dog one at that. It's only in the past few weeks that a few sober minds have decided this program may have some real application after all, if things go … poorly. And they want to move it to the next level."

"Poorly like in the cities?"

"Yes. We may need something exactly like this before a bunch of fools rip this country apart."

He calculated. Three years. Long after his time in London. Just after his first book. After the Princeton Project got him the profile in *Slate*, then *The New Yorker*. After.

"How many people have you been looking at?" Chase asked.

"In the very first round?" asked the Senator. "Just over three hundred."

Chase stared at them. "You expect three hundred people to get together as some sort of American Politburo and come up with reasonable solutions to difficult problems the government can't solve themselves?"

The Senator laughed. "Not three hundred at the *end*. We winnow the candidates down. Like picking a judge."

He could see how that would work. Their first pass would be easy. Almost a game. Simply list the purportedly finest and most interesting minds in the nation across a broad range of disciplines and over a reasonable age range. There would be Nobel prizewinners, journalists, economists, writers, educators, and social activists. But soon enough, the obvious problems would present themselves; prospects would have to be free of ethical conflict, which might take as many as half of them off the list. They would all have to be actual American citizens, which would knock off a few more. They would also, most importantly, all need to be noted for their temperament and reason as well as their accomplishments. What good was a Reasoner who wasn't reasonable? This would strike the greatest number from the list. Alphas are seldom the most reasonable people, and the first criteria meant you needed alphas.

So, a chosen panel of pragmatists to help make reasonable decisions in a time of crisis when there was no one left in America to be reasonable. Working around the President. Around the Cabinet. Around Congress itself. And somehow, people who ran the ship of state thought this might be necessary one day soon.

"Are the people in your world really that worried about what's going on?" Chase asked.

Senator Puccelli spoke carefully for the first time. Chase felt she was choosing her words with rehearsed precision. "There are concerns, within certain levels of the legislative branch, about the President's viability to handle the Uprising. Especially if things escalate and go in the wrong direction."

"Viability? What does that mean?"

"He may not be able to stand by his own decisions much longer."

Chase didn't know what that meant, but he knew he didn't like it.

"That's why the project has been picked up again," said Barnhardt finally. "Some feel there's no more time to wait."

"To do what?" asked Chase. He felt more and more uneasy and he liked these people less and less. "You folks aren't seriously worried about these … " He had to search for the word. "Changers?"

"Yes," said the Senator.

Chase didn't know what to say. "I'm sorry," he said, "but I don't think I can go along with any of what you have in mind."

Her eyebrows went up. "Chase, this is your country calling you."

"I don't know who is calling me," Chase said, "but it doesn't sound like my country. What you're talking about is actually unconstitutional, which I'm sure you know. You're saying a government thinktank project that arose from somewhere deep inside the Defense Department is now being proposed as a reality in a moment of crisis that in fact doesn't really exist yet. So it sounds, if put into practice, and coming from a proto-military structure, more like a … coup." The word lingered. "A coup against the elected United States government. I mean, if it's coming out of the Defense Department, how is it anything but?"

They stared at Chase. This was not what they had expected from him. At all. Stalemate.

Chase stood up. "You've wasted your time focusing on me. I had no way of knowing that this is what you had in mind. I assure you I'll keep everything you told me in strictest confidence, but it's a bad idea for all sorts of reasons. The biggest one is obvious."

"Which is?" asked Barnhardt.

"This is a democracy. People are elected to solve problems and run things. That's how we've always done it." He looked at the Senator. "The United States government doesn't need people like me to make decisions for them behind closed doors. It needs the people who were elected *by* the people to do their job out in the open. That means you."

The Senator snapped. "And if the people who elected them no longer want them to do their job? Or they simply can't do their jobs because the system is so corrupt?"

"We're nowhere near that yet," said Chase.

"Young man," she said, "we're already *past* that."

He stared at her. He had no idea what to say. So he simply turned and walked away. Later, he would realize he hadn't paid for his cappuccino. It probably didn't matter. He wouldn't have been able to pay even if he had remembered. His hands were shaking.

8. *Choosing*

1

He had just turned off his light and now someone was knocking on the front door of his bungalow. He checked the time. It was just after one o'clock. The knock soon turned into kicking. When she called out, "It's me!" he recognized the honeyed voice instantly.

Chase turned his light back on and reached for his robe.

He padded across the living room, which is where he slept. Since he'd moved into the little wartime bungalow four years ago, he'd made his bedroom in the living room and outfitted the bedroom as his study, which afforded him the most isolation when he was working on something serious. It meant, however, that books spilled across both rooms, and as Chase was a stacker-upper and not a shelver, he had to step around small book towers just to open his own front door.

She was standing on the front porch, shivering in a too-light but most definitely designer raincoat. The temperature had dropped since the balmy afternoon on the patio. "We did not adequately represent who we are," she said. The sweet lilt was still in her voice, but there was something else in it now as well. That edge.

"I thought you did just fine," Chase said, truly sorry he'd answered the door. "I'm just not interested."

"Well, you're wrong about both those statements. Invite me in for a drink."

She pushed past him before he could answer. He closed the door after her. To his surprise she went right for the bed and removed the comforter and wrapped it around herself, then dropped into his comfy reading chair. She looked around. "Mother of the savior!" she said in amazement. Then: "Darling, do you have something to drink?"

He went into the kitchen to find whatever he had under the sink. "Mother of the savior what?"

"Your digs," she said. "Live up to all my expectations."

He returned with a bottle of Southern Comfort and she brightened considerably. "Now that's a good boy!" The only clean glasses he could find were wine glasses, but they would do. He filled two halfway up and handed her the smaller one. She took the larger one.

"What do you mean?" he asked. "That you didn't adequately represent who you are."

"I made a mistake in deciding to only give you half the picture. I have been remiss."

"No, I think you did just fine. I just don't want to be involved and I don't intend to change my mind."

"Well, I'm afraid you're going to have to."

"Why is that?"

"Due to the half of which we have not yet spoken. Of. Yet. That half." Chase wondered how many drinks she'd already had that evening.

"Meaning, exactly who you are?" he asked.

"Exactly."

"But I know who you are. You're a United States Senator in charge of a project that – "

"Ha!" she shouted. "That is your *first* misapprehension."

"You're not a U.S. Senator?"

The Senator sat forward, her 80-year-old knees gracefully drawn together. She delicately turned the wineglass of Southern Comfort in her hand. "It is Ross – Dr. Barnhardt – who is in charge of the project for the United States Defense Department, as I already told you. He represents them in this matter."

"So you are the one speaking for Congress."

"Again, wrong. Or partly wrong."

"So you represent some other interested party as well as Congress?"

"You see!" she said with great delight. "That is why I know you are so right for this project."

Chase was intrigued, despite himself. "So who do you represent, Senator?"

"Only in this case, mind," she said. "Only in this case."

"Which case?"

"The recruitment-of-you case." She sat forward and fixed him with a very steady gaze. "My boy, in this very unusual case, you are looking at a representative of the so-called Changers."

Chase was at a loss for words.

The Senator smiled. Weakly. "But before we go on, we must be clear: I am most obviously still a representative of the United States of America and my belief in it is whole, it is absolute, it is my rock, it is my redeemer. No, I am still a U.S. Senator but, in this matter – choosing the Reasoners and this one in particular – I am a Designated Hitter for the other side."

"I don't see how that's possible."

"Chase, it is clear to me from our earlier encounter that you and I share differing views on where this nightmare is going. These Uprisings."

"I don't think that it *is* a nightmare. Yet."

"And if it becomes one? One even you recognize? What do you think will happen then?"

He thought a moment to make sure he said what he believed. "Eventually, the military is going to have to clamp down and put an end to all of it."

"And if they can't?"

"That seems unlikely. For the most part, these people are just maniacs with tiki torches and Twitter accounts."

"Well, don't be so sure this country is as strong as we think we are, or as state-of-the-art as we think we are, or even as organized.

And tiki torches have power. For a long time now I have believed that our great skill isn't doing things so much as believing our own fairy tales."

"A U.S. Senator truly believes pockets of citizens who quote a non-existent wolf are going to – "

"Are going to be in Washington soon. Yes, Chase, I do. And God knows what they're going to do once they get there."

"Nothing."

"Because the military will stop them?" She snapped. "And how have they done so far? Haven't we already had a dress rehearsal for that kind of chaos? Not just in D.C. but on Wall Street and in Davenport and Lexington and in Wheeling? Have you paid attention to that Beavenstock man? He is *terrifying*. And brilliant."

Chase tried to remember which one was Beavenstock. There were a lot of people who claimed they were the one true leader of the Changers. He had an image of black coal smoke. "The miner?"

"Yes, he's the miner, if you accept that Lech Walesa was just an electrician. Take a closer look at what he's done. He's convinced a small army of his fellow workers to torch an entire city without blinking an eye, and with almost military precision. Those people did everything he said. And that business with the TVA … "

"I'm sure that if D.C. is even in a hint of danger – "

"Chase, have you ever heard of something called the *Posse Comitatus Act*?"

Chase nodded. "Of course. Power of the county."

The Senator brushed a loose strand of jet-black hair back behind her ear. "I *do* so like a very bright boy! Yes. And that's what it means. It was put into effect after the Civil War, and it forbids the use of the United States military to enforce domestic law. Even in the event of an insurrection. The Act can only be countermanded under explicit and direct orders from the President. That's not a big issue in itself, and we've obviously seen our Presidents issue that order any number of times – the Civil Rights movement, Detroit in '67, Rodney King

– " She pulled the blanket tighter around herself. "But in this case, with this President … "

Chase recalled her words that afternoon. "There's an issue with him, isn't there? Something no one is saying."

Senator Puccelli did an odd thing. She put her arm across to her shoulder and leaned her chin upon her elbow. It made her look like a little girl. "Let us be clear," she said. "He is a very, *very* weak man. His act was good in the beginning, or good enough, but I think we all know now it's just bluff and bluster. Did you know he has never actually fired anyone? He's never run any organization at all. And he's frightened of horses."

Chase raised an eyebrow.

She smiled. "That really struck me, too, the first time I heard it. It tells so much, doesn't it? Please don't get me wrong. I quite like him. He has a decent courtliness that I think he learned from old movies. He's charming. I have spent many enjoyable hours in his company. But he is so very, very weak."

Chase persisted. "But there are safeguards in the event of a national emergency, Senator, and constitutionally he has an obligation to … "

"To what?"

"He will have no choice but to rise to the occasion."

"Well, he hasn't so far, has he?"

She had a point. The government shutdown had been absurd, and the epidemic that followed it had been a complete botched response by the federal government. But it had been the first insurrections which had revealed President Drury's true problem: He was terrified of his base. As a result, so far local police, state police, and in some cases the National Guard were the only ones to respond to the violence that was spreading across the country. The President had refused to step in. He even refused to federalize the guard when the New York governor had pleaded for it, primarily because he had been elected on a promise that the federal government would stay out of all state affairs. President Drury knew his base would turn on him, and that was something his ego couldn't handle.

"Mark my words," the Senator said. "We are not what people think. And as a result, if things go very wrong, we may need the military for other protections. Besides, are you able to imagine American troops firing and killing American citizens on American streets, no matter how many pitchforks and tiki torches come out?"

"Yes," said Chase.

Now it was time for her to look surprised.

"1932," he said. "The Bonus Army. Hoover had MacArthur fire on veterans wanting their army bonuses. Right there on the Mall."

"*Hoover?* You're going with *Hoover?*"

"I'm just saying it's been done. So what did you do, Senator? You anticipate the very worst, so you opened a back channel to the bad guys?"

"Come closer."

He sat down on the ottoman in front of her.

She held out her glass. "I would like some more, please."

He refilled her wine glass.

"Chase, you're a big enough boy to know that there is no such thing as politics that is pure. Everything can be corrupted, and everything can be cracked."

"So you reached out to one of the leaders of the Uprising? Or they reached out to you? Who? The Black Force? The Wall Streeters?"

She seemed appalled. "*Don't insult me!* Those old codgers? No, no, by the time the Changers get to Washington they will have whittled down the number of so-called Changer leaders down to two. True leadership always emerges. It will be down to that young woman and the miner, as you call him."

"So it was the miner you reached out to?" Yes, it would be the man. Senator Puccelli knew about powerful men. "Isn't that borderline treasonous? Like entering into discussions with terrorists?"

"One man's terrorist is another's man's political rival. Lincoln sent emissaries to talk to Jeff Davis. No, it wasn't Mr. Beavenstock directly – that really would feel like treason – but suffice to say it was people who have his ear and will be very important if things go the way I imagine."

"But why?"

"Because I am a realist, Chase. And when I see what is happening around the country, and when I look at who is in charge in Congress and who is sitting in the White House, I know we need some seriously long-term planning. So a few of us – a couple of Senators, a couple of House members, some of them very senior – dragged that old commie Pierpoint's idiot idea of – what would you call it? An American politburo? I almost bust a gut! – out of mothballs and I shared it with my Changer contacts."

"And what conclusion did you come to?"

"An agreement, not a conclusion. A kind of compromise. That if things got to a certain point, if the wheels truly came off, then the Reasoners plan would go into effect. That was something both sides could agree to. A maybe. A possibility."

"In other words, you bought some insurance because you think our government might fall?"

"Oh no, honey!" she laughed. "Simply not be able to defend itself. You think that's an outlandish notion? You need to spend forty years in the Congress. Then you'd see what the right set of circumstances at exactly the wrong moment can do. Consider our perfect storm as we sit here tonight: a hopelessly weak and corrupt President and a Vice President who is even weaker, both of them the butt of every joke on every late-night television show. Dean and Jerry. None of the intelligence agencies trusts them and why should they? Those two fools have done nothing but degrade and set those agencies against one another for their own political and monetary gain for the past three years. The military thinks even *less* of them – *and* the Senate majority leader – than the intelligence agencies. So who knows who would really take orders from who if push came to shove? It's not hard to picture American troops deciding to lay back rather than fire on American citizens even if the President told them to do so."

Chase couldn't believe what he was hearing. "Is that what you think? The President doesn't order the troops out because he's terrified they might not follow his orders?"

"Let's table that for a second. What we're talking about is the long game. With Howard and Ross's Reasoners project, I stumbled across something that might buy us time if things get truly frisky and be radical enough that the other side just might buy it. You understand? *It might be the only thing the two sides can agree on.*"

Chase took this in. "So why did you say I have no choice?"

"Because you don't."

"Me specifically."

"You very specifically." She sat back. "I was forced to share with Changer friends a list of our three hundred top choices. From there, it was sort of like choosing sides for basketball. They crossed off a name, I crossed off a name. That's how it went. You wouldn't believe how limited their knowledge is of public affairs. It was really rather repulsive. But then ... " She hesitated. "Chase, sometimes a girl needs the boy to move even closer."

Chase had no idea what she meant, but the Senator was not a woman to be denied. He nudged the ottoman, which was on wheels, closer to her. She gestured him even closer. Then again closer. Finally they were touching knees. To his surprise she suddenly reached up and put her hands on the back of his head. He thought, my God, she's going to kiss me. And indeed, she drew his head right to hers until they were touching foreheads. He took in her fragrance, which was surprisingly subtle, and the red wine on her breath, which the Southern Comfort had not masked. But her fingers were like iron.

She didn't kiss him. Instead she whispered. It wasn't quite the Marilyn-Jackie voice she'd used that afternoon, but it was intimate, like they were siblings with flashlights under the covers. She said, "They gave *us* a name. That wasn't the deal, of course. We were supposed to be the ones supplying names and they got a certain number of cross-offs. But one day they just presented a name. At first we balked, but then we realized it was a name that was already on *our* list."

"And whose name was that?"

"Yours."

Chase looked into those dark green eyes, uncomprehending.

2

When he managed to speak, it came out as more of a laugh. "I don't believe you."

"Don't you?" She certainly wasn't laughing.

"What does it mean?"

"You tell me." No, not a hint of laughter.

"I don't know any of those people."

"Well they know you."

"I've written two books. I've been on TV. Podcasts. Maybe – "

She cut him off. "Chase, I need to be clear. You are the *only* person they requested. That suggests that for some reason, they mean something to you. And you mean something to them."

"I don't know anyone in the Changer movement or anyone associated with any of that insanity if that's what you're – "

"You're not answering the question."

He tried to pull his head back but her fingers kept their vise-like grip.

"I told you."

Finally she let him go. He sat up and rubbed the back of his head.

She held her glass out for a top-up. He obliged. "Of course," she said, rather conversationally, "such a turn of events raises a number of issues of concern. One is obvious: that you're some sort of agent for the Changers. Well, that's actually not against the law and in fact it might work to our benefit – "

"I just told you I don't know those people, and you don't for a second believe – "

She raised her voice, riding over him. "– but the more *frightening* thought is that there's something dangerously flawed in the

methodology we used in choosing our Reasoners. Our assessors –
and Dr. Barnhardt in particular – gave you top marks. You sailed
right through. Yet those psychopaths see something in you that
helps their cause. So does that mean we missed something? It would
seem so."

He bit down on his annoyance. "I would imagine you gave me a
second look after such a surprising endorsement."

"Surely *not*."

He was, again, surprised. "You kept your concerns to yourself?"

"No one knows about my back channel to begin with, so how
was I going to tell Barnhardt? This was something I had to solve
myself."

"And have you?"

"That's what I'm trying to do. Here. Now."

London, he thought. That's what you're missing.

"You know, I could make you tell me," she said.

"Pulling fingernails?"

"No, but the power of a Congressional subpoena has certain
charms."

"Really? Last I heard, nobody pays attention to those things
anymore."

"Chase, I need to know."

"Senator, I think you should go."

She considered him a moment, decided he was serious, and got
up. She balled up the duvet and started to hand it back to him, but
then became thoughtful. "Chase," she said, "I used to think nothing
frightens me. Now, however, I'm not ashamed to tell you I am
frightened."

"Of?"

"Us. We can't seem to do anything right anymore. Has no one
noticed that but me? We can't win a war, our cities are full of rage,
our bridges fall down, and our towns are dying of a drug epidemic
dumped on the public by Wall Street scum. We can't stand up to
what's coming, and you want to know why? Because we've turned

ourselves into a happy, arrogant, Third World nation with First World luxuries. But we're no longer equipped to build a rowboat, little less fight a second civil war. You know what that means? That means our people – the angry ones, the one who still have energy – are probably going to rip us to shreds."

Chase didn't know what to say. Finally he took the duvet from her and managed a feeble, "I just don't think that's going to happen, Senator."

"But it *could.*"

He led her to the door.

"Make me a promise," she said. "Say 'maybe.' Not 'no.' Call it a Politburo, call it whatever you want, but say 'maybe.'"

He opened the front door.

She sighed and drew her raincoat on. She took a card out of the coat pocket. "Use the back number when you change your mind."

"I won't be changing my mind, Senator."

"There's just one more thing I have to say. Because it's important." She leaned in and whispered one inch from his ear. The Marilyn-Jackie voice was back. "I know about the girl."

He was frozen in place.

She went on: "You lied in every single one of your interviews, didn't you? Oh, don't worry. I didn't tell. Frankly, I believe it spoke to your character."

Then she did give him a kiss. On the cheek. But it was still a woman-man kiss.

He watched her walk across the dark street, not toward her car but toward one of the greenways that wound through campus. She stumbled on one of her three-inch heels but righted herself instantly and continued to walk away with consummate dignity. She didn't look back.

It would not be the last time he saw her.

9. *The Fall*

1

Senator Sofia Puccelli had been right. Chase had been wrong. Events piled on top of one another.

On April 26, the President went to Camp David to "think through" the crisis. The man seemed terrified. And for good reason.

The Changers had indeed come to Washington. They marched down Constitution Avenue and set up camp on the Mall. On May 1, the eighteen-foot Great Guillotine was erected on the Capitol steps. It was protected by an army of Changers, mostly Jerseys and Tacticals, who were extremely well armed – so well armed, in fact, that when the Capitol police and the D.C. cops decided to remove both blade and Changers, they wound up in a two-day firefight that ended in a standoff. Apparently, in addition to having more weapons than anyone had anticipated, the Changers were also pretty good at tactics.

On the third day, around dawn, the D.C. cops and Capitol cops retreated. Americans tuning into CNN had to reckon with the fact that the Changers now had possession of the west front of the Capitol building.

Under orders from a rogue Lt. Colonel Nunes, the U.S. military stepped in, surrounded the Capitol and waited for orders. They were backed up soon enough by the D.C. militia. But no one was quite sure who was going to issue the orders that, in fact, never came.

That gave the Changers plenty of time to talk to cable news.

The Great Guillotine, the Changers told the country (specifically Jeff Beavenstock, speaking from the Capitol, and Sister Sheena, talking from a Sioux rights uprising in South Dakota), was merely a symbol of protest which they intended to leave on the Capitol steps until such time as the U.S. government gave in to their three-page list of demands. These demands gave the American people what they deserved from their government and reinstated the Constitution as they understood it. The Changers, in other words, weren't taking the United States government *away*, they were giving it back.

On May 2, the government announced that the President had been moved from Camp David to an undisclosed location. For some reason, this caused Lt. Colonel Nunes and his troops to stand down, saying he awaited orders from General Van DeVere, Chairman of the Joint Chiefs and Commander of the Armed Forces, who personally was awaiting Presidential orders.

Despite the sudden lack of real armed federal support, Congressional leaders said they refused to be cowed, and would stay on the job. The National Guard and D.C. police wound up having to escort them to and from work, making their way around the cordon of buses which protected the front face of the Capitol. A lot of people thought this was a real show of courage. It was, in a way. It would also prove to be fatal.

On May 14, Vice President Fox, under enormous pressure from the Cabinet, went to have a private meeting with the President.

That evening, the Vice President had another private meeting – this time with the congressional leaders of both parties. The Vice President, who had quit smoking thirty-two years earlier, asked for a cigarette and smoked half a pack.

The following day, it was announced that the 25th Amendment would be invoked and Vice President Fox would assume the Presidency almost immediately, which is pretty much what happens under the 25th Amendment: The Cabinet and the VP decide the President can no longer perform his or her duties and that's the ballgame.

A problem arose almost immediately. That very night, Sister Sheena tweeted the observation that while it's true that foxes eat chickens, wolves eat foxes.

No one missed the implicit threat to his personal safety, least of all a Vice President with the last name of Fox who was facing a national insurrection led by heavily armed citizens who followed the deranged writings of something called the Wolf.

Whether these threats had teeth or not, Fox must have figured they did. Something sure happened, because by morning it was announced that the Vice President had had second thoughts and while he would go along with the invocation of the 25th Amendment, he would need to resign immediately thereafter, citing "health concerns for himself and his family."

Constitutionally, the Speaker of the House was next in line but there was no announcement that she had been or would be sworn in, or the legal mechanisms by which that would take place (this unwarranted confusion was caused by the President's party in Congress, which was not the same party as the Speaker of the House. Unaware that both the President and Vice President *wanted* out, they stalled things in the Senate, not accepting either resignation and pressing that the President pro tempore of the Senate was next in line, this despite the Presidential Succession Act of 1947).

Into this void, with things getting hotter and the Changers cause growing, the leaders of the House ordered the military to step in and protect Washington, D.C., placing it under martial law. As far as the Senate was concerned, this was obviously a power grab. This left the Commander of U.S. Forces, General Rasimus Collier "Bud" Van DeVere, getting conflicting orders from just about everybody.

On May 16, military lawyers announced that until such time as a line of authority was properly clarified, the U.S. forces could not engage in any offensive action against its own citizens.

Unbelievably, the U.S. Congress turned to the *courts* to decide if the military had the right to step into the crisis without clear executive authorization. In short, this left General Rasimus Collier "Bud" Van DeVere with troops at the ready but no firing pin.

The Changers, standing on the Capitol steps they now controlled, said that if any action spelled out what was wrong with the country, this was it. The courts! Sister Sheena, who had yet to appear in Washington, spoke via Zoom to the crowds on the Mall (she had left South Dakota and was now in Appalachia) and whipped them into a frenzy. Anderson Cooper said it felt like a dam was about to burst.

On May 20, the Supreme Court of the United States made its ruling. "The Congress itself cannot act as Commander in Chief and order the United States military to take arms against its own citizens without the authority of the executive, and adopting such a role would be, in effect, a military coup." In response, General Van DeVere made it clear that he would stay at his post and maintain his command "defending the nation and its resources from all threats foreign and domestic" but he could not act against the court, or be drawn into a political battle.

With that, the Supreme Court announced it would adjourn itself on May 23.

They could not have chosen a worse date.

That's because, as a result of the court's decree, on the morning of May 21st, all federal military forces pulled out of Washington D.C. at 6 a.m. That made May 22nd (5/22) what would become known as "Capture Day." For reasons no one could later cite, more than three hundred members of the House, more than eighty-five Senators, and a full complement of Capitol staff went to work that morning, clearly wanting to be seen as brave and resolute in a crisis. There was, for sure, a lot on Twitter, Snapchat, and Instagram about work continuing and leaders attempting to find a solution because, after all, "we are Americans and we all believe in the American Dream," but it all spelled disaster.

The Changers struck at 2:42.

The timing was perfect. The visuals were electric.

America glued itself to images of Changers in the hundreds – no, thousands – spilling out onto the streets, seemingly from nowhere. Some were in sports jerseys, some in tactical gear, some in biker wear, cammo gear, T-shirts and jeans, but all of them were armed. And incredibly well organized. A mob, yes, one commentator remarked, but a mob trained by General Sherman. That would be Jeff Beavenstock, onetime miner.

The firefight with the police lasted only an hour. Police were pushed back north of Constitution Avenue. Soon, the Potomac and entire sections of D.C. – including the Capitol, the Mall, and a huge number of administration buildings – fell into Changer hands. The city was split in two.

But there was more.

At the end of the day, a stunned yet incredibly well-protected news media (the Changers had built them special scaffolding to the south of the Grant Memorial, and even made sure to supply padded folding chairs) announced to the nation that locked in the lowest levels of the U.S. Capitol were some two hundred and seventy-five members of the House, sixty-two Senators, and seven Supreme Court Justices (two had literally been out to lunch). Sharing the space with them were more than three hundred staffers, with an average age of thirty-four. No one knew what was going to happen next, but they sure knew something would.

They didn't have to wait long to find out. The First Cull, as it would be called, started on May 27. The entire world watched in disbelief.

Over the course of three days, the Changers decapitated five Supreme Court Justices, ten Senators, and fifty-five members of the House of Representatives. More than eighty staffers were killed. Lobbyists and lawyers were given special mention.

2

Chase Selby watched it all from his bungalow in Princeton. At first, he clicked between MSNBC and CNN and Fox, but soon realized that the camera feed was actually the same, which meant the Changers themselves were managing the filming of the beheadings and supplying the cable nets directly. Maybe that explained why the images were razor sharp and professionally rendered. Nothing was left to imagination and the Changers weren't letting the cable nets turn the cameras away at the gruesome bits.

Then, on the Sunday night, Chase saw something he had thought he might see but hoped he wouldn't.

He was tuned to MSNBC when he saw a woman of perhaps eighty, wearing a 1920s bobbed haircut and Woody Allen glasses, marched up the steps of the Capitol and told to kneel with her head under the blade of the guillotine. She tripped just once on one high heel, but then righted herself adroitly and strode toward the kneeling spot with complete dignity.

When the blade dropped and her head fell into the blue plastic recycle box in front of the device, Senator Puccelli suffered the final ignominy. The hair was revealed to be a wig.

Chase called the number the Senator had given him.

3

Less than a week later, a young, very fit man named Commander Holden knocked on the front door of Chase Selby's bungalow at Princeton.

10. *Meeting Reasoners*

1

Boardroom One, on the fourth floor, was large and broadloomed in cheap but serviceable airport lounge carpet. The row of lights which had once hung over an immense board table had been clipped up near the ceiling, with the board table pushed to one side of the room. It now offered a tempting buffet of croissants, cakes, fruit, vegetables, and tea and coffee. There were two caterers fussing about.

The room was guarded by two D.C. militiamen who respectfully stepped back as Chase approached. Presumably, they knew him by sight.

It was a grim group of tense people, most of whom clearly didn't know one another. There were maybe seven or eight of them milling awkwardly around the buffet table. Chase thought he recognized three or four faces from television or the internet or a book jacket, but he wasn't sure.

A man and woman stood apart, studying the others. The woman seemed brittle and angry, a dyed blonde in her mid-fifties who looked like she'd stepped out of the shower in the past hour. Maybe she had. The man was a smooth and handsome late sixties and reminded Chase of Mitt Romney.

Coffee in hand, Chase went over. He introduced himself.

"The Twelve Steps That Made Up the American Revolution," said the woman, offering her hand. It seemed a purposefully bad attempt at remembering the title of Chase's second book.

Chase shook. *"The Twelve Decisive Steps to the American Revolution."*

"I've heard of that," said the man. "Why twelve?"

"It's an easy number to remember."

"We are twelve."

"So is a jury," said Chase.

"And disciples."

The woman turned out to be Kirsten Pappason, President of Primateur University. Chase should have recognized her. She was well known for her book-a-year and TED Talks about the future of developing world government. Despite being a hardcore academic, she was very popular on social media. The man was Malcolm Agniew, known for his philanthropy and dispensing his family wealth to where it would do the most good. He had been a medical doctor, Chase vaguely recalled, which maybe explained why he focused on the creation of clean water resources. He had been director of UNESCO or UNICEF, Chase wasn't sure which.

Pappason was drinking a healthy glass of wine. Agniew had nothing.

"You're awfully young," Pappason said to Chase. She peered around him to consider the others at the buffet.

It was impossible to miss. The Reasoners were an equal mix of sexes and a polyglot of ethnic backgrounds. No politically correct stone had been left unturned.

"I'll wager you're the youngest Reasoner," she said.

Agniew tried to lighten things. "It's a cinch I'm the oldest."

"I don't think so," Chase said.

"Oh?"

"You haven't met my neighbor yet. I haven't either, but I saw him being checked into his room with his PSLO."

Pappason suddenly changed the subject. "Do you think we have enough personal security? Especially after last night? I don't!"

"How much personal security is necessary?" asked Chase.

"They broke the Compromise!" said Kirsten Pappason. "That poor Senator Brubaker. So where does our treaty stand now?"

"Not a treaty exactly," Agniew said. "The Compromise is just an agreement. And there was nothing in it about a true cessation of hostilities. They should have got that, but technically all they were given was an understanding that we, as a delegation, would be safe. That's all."

"But we can't move forward if they've started executing people again," she said. "They might be slaughtering more. Right now."

"They're not," said Chase.

She looked at him. "How do you know?"

"Because I just drove past the guillotine."

Heads turned and coffee cups paused in mid-sip. He not only had Pappason and Agniew's attention, but now everyone at the buffet table was focused on him as well.

"How in the world did you get *there*?" Kirsten Pappason asked, clearly horrified, jealous, and intrigued. "And why?"

"I requested it." Then, not wanting to get Commander Holden in any trouble, he amended himself. "Forcefully."

One of the men at the buffet table stepped forward. A plain, lean man with an Eastern European accent. Chase could almost, but not quite, come up with his name. Conescu? Conscue? "And?" he asked.

"And the blade is up."

A striking-looking woman in her early forties said, "What I think Dr. Calinescu means is, what does it all look like up close?"

Chase thought about his answer carefully. "Like a tailgate party," he said finally.

There were looks of confusion, but finally nervous chuckles. Before he could explain further, the twelfth Reasoner arrived, and all conversation ceased.

He was even smaller and thinner up close. And shabby, but it seemed a duplicitous shabby; the corduroy suit and the threadbare Oxford collar sold the image of a high school math teacher, but the energy in the green eyes and the slightly erratic, jingly manner let you know under no uncertain terms that there was a fireball of intelligence and energy in there.

Tay Hamer, émigré from Brezhnev's Soviet Union, American citizen, had won the Nobel Prize. Twice. He was considered one of the finest minds in the world, and his disciplines stretched, incongruously, between science and the humanities. He had pioneered work on micro-particles and laser light, expanding the world's understanding of radiation pressure, while in economics he was lauded for his theories on Economic Trade Activity and National Economies of Scale.

Seeing he was the focus of attention and the last to arrive, Hamer addressed the whole room. "I am so sorry! I couldn't understand how to operate the shower door." Then he spied the buffet. "Tarts!" He reached for a large plate and moved in on the pastries without a second's delay.

Kirsten Pappason went over and introduced herself immediately. "I don't know if you'll recall, but we met in Davos."

Hamer nodded. "I have been to Davos many times." He nudged the pastries with the end of a dessert fork, determining if they were fresh.

"We were just talking about security," she said. "Our safety. Do you think – "

"I think they've done an excellent job," said Hamer. "Don't you? I feel very safe."

That threw Pappason off her stride. "But obviously, after last night – "

"I don't imagine our hosts could have done anything about last night. Undoubtedly there are other forces that caused that. I believe those are empire tarts." He pointed to a tart with white icing and a maraschino cherry center. "I haven't seen these in years." He looked to Chase. "Could you?"

Chase did not understand at first, but then he did. The old man was asking for help. For whatever reason, his arm was not able to reach across the table. Later, Chase would realize that Hamer couldn't lift his arms beyond his shoulder sockets. Chase reached out to put a tart on the man's plate.

"We're neighbors," said Hamer.

"Yes," said Chase.

"You're the one who wrote the book about the Continental Congress," said Hamer. "I liked it."

"I'm flattered," said Chase.

Hamer turned to Pappason and said abruptly, "I would assume that someone has decided to ramp up the grotesqueries in order to gain a stronger hand in these very discussions."

Pappason clearly didn't know what the old man was talking about.

Hamer shrugged. "Her handiwork, I suspect. Not his."

Her.

"So the events of last night were not in spite of our arrival, but because of it," said Chase.

Hamer nodded. "Exactly."

Hamer carefully sliced a pecan tart in two and put one half on his plate. "They want to come to the table with a full deck of cards. We are that table. She's clever like that."

Hamer had now placed two more tarts on his plate and drawn himself a cup of tea. He looked around the room, and lit up when he saw the tall, thin European man, Dr. Calinescu. "Albert! I didn't know you would be here!"

As Hamer made his way to one of the smaller tables, he whispered to Chase. "Which one is Brueler?"

"I don't believe he's here yet."

Chase held a chair out and took the older man's plate. Hamer nodded appreciation and took the plate back once he was seated. "He was a labor negotiator. Don't you think that's very smart of someone? I do. Supposedly he forced the Ford company to retain its operations in America. I had a Ford LTD once. I loved that car, I swear to you, more than my children. And apparently he was very useful in the Middle East negotiations. I would have no idea how to even begin to do anything like that."

Agniew clearly wanted to be part of the conversation or at least in Hamer's orbit. He joined them at the table and sat down, unasked. "I met him. Years ago."

As Agniew began to explain where and when he had met the man who would be their operational director (Brazil, world conference), Chase studied Kirsten Pappason as she, too, quietly joined their table. Pappason's presence made Chase curious. He could name a half-dozen women who were better qualified and perhaps better suited temperamentally, so how had she been chosen to be a Reasoner? Chase began to wonder about the whole process.

Suddenly, Commander Holden was in the doorway, this time in dress blues. He had an announcement. In five minutes they would be escorted to cars and from there taken to a secure location for their first meeting.

Chase, sitting beside Hamer, said to the older man, "Why aren't we meeting in the same building in which we're staying? It seems a risk."

Hamer carefully sliced the icing off the top of a chocolate cupcake and discarded the cake part. "You must not forget that no matter what," he said, "this is still a government operation."

11. *Oaths and Prayers*

1

Tom Brueler turned out to be one of those men born to sit at the head of a board table and yet he was a mass of contradictions. Chosen as the Director of the Reasoners, he was not a Reasoner himself. A bald bull, he wore beautifully cut suits which probably cost thousands of dollars and yet you still had the impression of someone who shopped off the rack at the suit outlet by the highway. The fountain pen was Montblanc. The wristwatch was Piaget. The shoes were Testoni. But he still looked like the owner of a chain of very prosperous sheet metal yards. Maybe it was the mustache.

Brueler and the twelve Reasoners were seated around the massive – truly massive – board table in one of the equally massive marbled conference rooms within the Treasury building. Though currently abandoned for official purposes, the Treasury, it turned out, had avoided falling under the control of the Changers. Therefore, the Reasoners would be living in the State building but holding their discussions and meetings in the Treasury building. Chase wondered if it was just because of the marble.

Brueler nodded at the security guards and the PSLOs who were standing against the walls. They left the room.

When it was just the thirteen of them, Brueler removed a thick file folder of papers from his battered briefcase (Berluti) and opened a calfskin writing folder and went to a fresh sheet of paper. "I think we should begin by introducing ourselves."

Seated at Brueler's immediate left, Kirsten Pappason introduced herself with academic credentials first, but got to her bestselling books with no delay; Howard Agniew mentioned only his philanthropist organization. The tall man with the Eastern European accent was indeed Albert Calinescu, Romanian-born historian with a specialty in developing civilizations. Chase knew of him but hadn't read his work. It made sense that he and Hamer were old friends.

Pen-tapping Brian Gleeber, mid-forties, introduced himself as a statistician, even though everyone probably knew him better for his lectures and papers on political theory and dynamic waves of liberalism.

Dr. Hydy Horvat, the attractive woman in her forties, simply announced herself as a doctor with a background in anthropology.

General John G. Williamson, easily now in his seventies, introduced himself as a consultant to the Carter Center and an ex-associate director of the UN. He was a stocky fireplug of a man.

Alyssa Swoot, who couldn't be more than fifty, said she was one of the "most successful independent newspaper publishers" in the country.

Vin Jansert was known to everyone. Not just everyone at the table, but everyone in America. Even within this setting, he didn't disappoint; he loudly described himself as a "vigilante provocateur," named his publications and listed all the places he had been banned as solid examples of the left's assault on free speech. Chase could not imagine how in the world Vin Jansert had been chosen as a Reasoner.

Reverend Sarah Campbell meekly gave her name and denomination. She didn't mention any of her books.

That brought them to Ambassador James Macomb. *Here* was a man who knew how to wear a twenty-thousand-dollar watch and a ten-thousand-dollar suit, which is what in fact he appeared to be sporting, to say nothing of the polished snakeskin cowboy boots, which surely cost more than most mid-sized cars. Macomb, aka The Gentleman from Texas, was as smooth as his reputation, and referred only to the ambassadorship and his role in the U.S. Treasury when introducing himself. He didn't mention any White House affiliation, nor his more than fifty years in the dark corridors of power.

Seated beside Macomb, Chase introduced himself last, and as he heard himself speak – he mentioned both books and the Princeton association – he was surprised to realize that he had as much reason for being there as any of the others. He also realized that he had been right about Tay Hamer. If Vin Jansert was their cheap celebrity, Tay Hamer was the top of the intellectual food chain.

Brueler introduced himself quickly and directly. "I'm Tom Brueler. No title. I was asked to chair this group not because I have any particular insights or skills, but because my specialty is organization and management. I did work in the private sector. I have done work with the federal government. I have worked overseas. Let's be clear, however. I am your advocate. I am your advisor. I am your Clerk of Session. I am, thank God, *not* a Reasoner." There were polite chuckles. Brueler, however, didn't even crack a smile. Instead, he did a studied sweep of the faces around the table.

"Before we begin, I want to make sure we all understand what this particular playing field looks like. Every one of you was recruited after much research and deliberation. But I will offer an opinion – and it's only an opinion and one of the very few I'm going to give during these sessions. I think you're the right people and you're here for the right reasons to do the right job."

Kirsten Pappason leaned forward and got right into it. "I have a question."

"Yes?"

"Are we safe? Was it wise to bring us here if a second cull is about to begin?"

Brueler sat forward as if pleased to be engaged in battle.

"Let's address that head-on. We don't know if the events of last night signal the beginning of a second cull. For the Changer leadership, it makes no sense to reject the Compromise so early in the game. Up to now, they appear to recognize – as much as we recognize – the important role this body can play in knitting the peace back together. So I believe last night – the killing of the staffers and Senator Brubaker – was one thing only: red meat for the masses."

Whoever this Brueler is, Chase thought, he was more than just a hired labor negotiator. Chase glanced at the man on his right, the other master negotiator in the room, Ambassador Macomb. The smooth old fox was studying Brueler with interest. When he crossed his legs, however, Chase thought he spied Velcro garters just above the top of those expensive boots. No, not garters. Holsters? Was it possible the Ambassador, a Texas native, had come in here armed? Maybe that explained why he wasn't particularly vexed about the subject of personal security.

"But rest assured," Brueler said to Kirsten Pappason, "your safety is guaranteed."

"But if they were able to do that last night," the Reverend Sarah Campbell said, "does that mean no one negotiated a proper and complete ceasefire for our time here?"

Brueler turned his smooth calm on the Reverend. "Actually, Reverend, a ceasefire refers to conscripted soldiers with government-issued firearms. Mobs are more often a law unto themselves. I think we'll all agree that despite their capability and obvious handiness, we're dealing with a mob, not a military unit. But still, I believe you are safe."

"Why do you keep saying that?" asked Pappason, clearly looking for a fight.

"Because of this." Brueler reached in his calfskin folder and drew out a sheaf of maybe a dozen pages. He handed them over to Pappason, who quickly realized the other sheets were copies to be passed along. Everyone got one. "We received it early this morning," Brueler said.

Chase realized he was studying a copy of a letter – on Plaza Hotel stationery, no less – which had been written out in an elegant if spikey script that seemed to belong to another era, and might have but for the fact it was rendered in Sharpie.

"If I may do the honors," said Brueler. He cleared his throat. He read aloud in a clear, deep voice. "'For now, we are honoring the Compromise and the agreement we signed to protect the Reasoners because unlike the Government of Record of the United States, we are people of our word. However, to gain more advantageous understanding of the plight of the people of those said states and their needs which have been denied by the bullshit corporate oligarchs and privileged slave masters, and to make clear the purpose of our cause, there will be no reprieve for those cocksuckers who have lied to and abused the deserving, hard-working patriots of this land, who have been duped by the warlord masters who have wrested control of the nation and its freedoms and liberty."

At the bottom, in a jagged sawtooth signature, they all read: 'Sister Sheena.'

"Well now," said Vin Jansert. "She never *does* fail to excite, does she?"

The Romanian, Calinescu, was confused. "I'm not sure I understand. Is she telling us that the Changers guarantee our safety while at the same time reserving the right to go back to slaughtering any of the three hundred people still imprisoned in the Capitol?"

"That's how I take it," said Brueler.

"So did she order the resumption herself?" Vin asked.

Brueler shook his head. "Not directly. Beavenstock is the one who owns those Capitol steps and every single soul on the Mall. The Jerseys, the Tacticals, the Harleys. But Sheena and Beavenstock share a common goal, so when they have to – "

"They do each other's dirty work," Hamer said.

Vin Jansert waved the letter and said, "But no matter what, this letter is the only thing between us and a blade literally hanging over our heads!"

They all spoke at once.

General Williamson banged on the table. They all came to order.

The old man's voice sounded like an earthquake starting to rumble. He spoke so quietly you had to lean in to hear him. "The only response to your observation, Mr. Jansert, is yes. That's all we've got. But despite that, I for one am going to give this job everything I've got. For one very good reason." He fixed them all with a steady gaze, going from one Reasoner to the other. "The person who recruited me to this job is dead. Likely the person who recruited you is dead. So if only for them, we go on. Otherwise we give the nation over to the mob, go home, and wait our turn. I'm not doing that."

There was silence. Finally Tay Hamer said, "Very good, General."

Brueler leaned in. "I think the General raises a very important point. We must focus on *why* you're here. All of our institutions have failed. You've been chosen to be the last responsible people in America. You're supposed to use your reason to draw conclusions, formulate a plan, and get us out of this mess. It has been agreed that your conclusions will be accepted by both factions, within … reason."

Dr. Hydy Horvat raised her hand. Brueler nodded.

"Except if our conclusions fall on deaf ears," she noted, "we have no actual constitutional power."

"So this could all be a huge waste of time," said Vin Jansert.

Voice rose again. Then a single voice erupted, "Yes!"

All heads turned.

Chase hadn't even recognized his own voice. It had sounded so firm. He realized he liked the sound of it. "It *could* all be a waste of time." Chase pivoted his attention to Vin. "Actually, it likely *will* be. A panel of the last reasonable people in America? It's more likely they'll just ignore our recommendations and decide to walk us up to the blade." Chase studied the others. These were some of the most original thinkers in the country – academics, diplomats and scientists – but there was something else about them, something he couldn't quite put his finger on. Something that didn't work. "That said, the very nature of this country and its history, has been the taking of risks if they're worth the effort and despite the odds. That alone is worth it, don't you think?" He thought of Senator Puccelli's head in a blue recycle box. "Considering the stakes, and, as General Williamson said, in honor of the people who brought us here."

No one spoke. Then the Reverend raised her hand.

Mr. Brueler recognized her. "Yes, Pastor?"

"What is the agenda for the rest of today?"

"I've moved up our meeting with the government of record to within the hour. I felt that was crucial – to know exactly where they stood. I assumed no one would object."

"I was going to recommend something first."

Brueler looked just the slightest bit hesitant. "Yes?"

"That we ought to perform an exercise together. As a body."

There were uncomfortable glances around the room.

"What kind of exercise?"

"I would propose an oath and, for those who wish to participate, a prayer."

This was met by further silence.

"I'm sorry, Reverend," said Brueler. "I hadn't prepared anything of that sort."

"I have." The Reverend reached across the table and pushed toward Brueler a piece of paper from the pad she had been scribbling on. "It's not profound, of course, but I believe the act itself … "

When Brueler was done reading her sheet, he said, "May I?"

She nodded. Brueler pushed back his chair. Following his lead, all the Reasoners stood. Brueler read from the Reverend's sheet. After a few lines or two everyone followed along, repeating aloud.

"As a citizen of the United States of America and all that means and has meant, I affirm that I will do my utmost both physically and mentally to bring this nation and its peoples to peace and order where the liberties and safety of all can be preserved and maintained as they shall choose. I so affirm."

They all repeated, "I so affirm."

The General looked over at the small woman approvingly. "That was very fine, Reverend."

The Reverend looked at the rest of the table. "As for the prayer … "

There was an even more uncomfortable silence. It took awhile for Tay Hamer to realize people were looking at him. He nodded at the Reverend. "Well, I for one would very much welcome a prayer.

And that is coming, Reverend, from a former Soviet at that."

There were good-humored chuckles.

The Reverend lowered her head. "Let us pray." Heads were lowered. The Reverend reached out and took a hand of each of her neighbors: Calinescu and Vin Jansert. Jansert looked taken aback but, to Chase's surprise, he didn't withdraw his hand. Chase held onto Kirsten Pappason and the Ambassador. "Heavenly father, as we engage in this task, please give us the wisdom to think only of our fellow man and woman, of the children of this land. We know what has brought about this moment: avarice, arrogance, greed, and stupidity." Chase felt the circle tense just slightly, but the Reverend kept going with no hesitation. "May we be spared these sinful traits as we attempt to bring, with Your blessing, peace. In Your name we ask this, Amen."

There were murmurs of 'Amen.'

When they sat down, it was clear that a transformation had taken place. Strangers were now a unit. The Reasoners were a team.

The Reverend, of all people.

12. *Warren Potsburger*

1

The day that Bella walked out on him was the day Warren Potsburger decided to go to Washington to cut off someone's head. That wasn't *exactly* his motive, but he sure wanted to get back at somebody, anybody, for the sorry state in which he found himself.

The way Warren saw it, it didn't matter whose head it was. Warren wasn't big on the specifics of politicians – lying sacks of shit are all the same – but the way he saw it, if they lived and worked in Washington, they'd probably had a pretty strong hand in masterminding his current misery.

In truth, Warren made the decision to go to Washington even before Bella pulled out of the driveway in the brand-new GMC pickup (his), leaving the house (his, or his until the 30th when the bank stepped in), the goddamned dog in the back seat (his, or his until recently, when it had turned on him, *again* her doing), and off down the street and out of his life. *She* thought. That's what kept Warren from blowing his brains out: *she thought*.

Warren had been thinking that if he got himself to Washington, from there to the Capitol, and from there to the front steps where all the action was, then he would wind up on Fox or CNN. At the very worst on the net. Then Bella would see him. And Bella would start to see just what she was passing up.

Warren was too stupid to come up with the word 'revolutionary,' but he did summon up the word 'warrior,' because that's how he was starting to picture himself. A goddamned warrior, standing right up on the steps with the real shitkickers, holding up a guy's severed fucking head. Warren very much wanted that. He even went to Walmart and bought himself a bandana to wrap around his own head so he'd look that much more terrifying. He already had very good wrap-around sunglasses. A true badass.

The first problem that presented itself was that Warren was unsure where Washington was. Wherever it was, he knew he couldn't drive because, of course, the bitch had taken his GMC. He thought of borrowing a car but he couldn't come up with the name of a single person in Rozberry who would lend him a shotgun with which to blow his brains out, let alone a car with which to drive to Washington. His mind switched to the train. Before the cable died, there had been all sorts of news reports about people climbing inside or even on the outside of trains going to Washington, and the Beaver guy had said come one, come all, take the train, so why not?

Warren had never been on a train in his life, but he imagined that if they went slow enough, he could hop on one with relative ease. He'd seen Johnny Cash do that in a video, and it didn't look too hard. What he hadn't expected was just how many others had the same idea.

The train station was in nearby Stubbensville, Ohio but when the train pulled in you would have thought you were in fucking Pakistan. That's how many people were crammed together on top and hugging the sides of the thing. Warren thought of those movies where peasants were trying to get across the desert, except of course there were no peasants in America and Americans didn't know anything about managing themselves peaceably using this kind of travel. Everyone jostled everyone else and there were angry words and fistfights. Even when the train was moving through dangerously narrow tunnels, people just couldn't help beating the hell out of each other.

As it turned out, Warren would find himself involved in no fewer than four fistfights that first day. After the fourth, he concluded this wasn't really what he had in mind. He had been after some glory and badass head chopping; he hadn't counted on being surrounded by truly crazy people who simply weren't, by Warren's sights, civilized. They spat, pissed, and shat wherever they liked and, if you made the mistake of getting up, they took your seat. When you went to sleep, they took it upon themselves to go through your stuff. These people were animals.

When the train pulled into a station – any station – everyone scrambled like bugs off a burning log. They were after the train station restrooms, the vending machines, and any fast food kiosk that would serve them before the train pulled out again. Warren didn't take any chances with the restroom. He pissed by the side of the rail tracks and got back on the train before anyone could take his seat.

2

Like many another first-timer to Washington, Warren was not prepared for what greeted him. He tumbled off the train – was pushed, actually – well shy of Union Station because the track was blocked up ahead – and in the scramble down the embankment, he broke his arm. He survived because he did the tuck-and-roll, but before he could even stand up, someone took his suitcase. Three teenage boys then body-checked him and wrestled him to the ground for his money. Then two older men offered to help get Warren's money back for him. They didn't succeed, but they were able to rape Warren at knifepoint behind a dumpster two blocks away.

Washington has always been difficult for out-of-towners.

Warren lost his front teeth before ten o'clock. Finally he found his way, arm broken and unset, to Constitution Avenue and the Capitol building itself, home of freedom and democracy. It turned out he was lucky, because word was that they were going to see some "serious action" tonight, which Warren assumed meant head chopping. While Warren was getting this information, a kid who had eaten too many hot dogs and was hopped up on Red Bull threw up on Warren's feet.

Somehow, Warren felt, he was made for better things.

What he didn't know, in fact couldn't have imagined, was that he was being watched. He might have cried had he known. The notion that in this hell on earth, this melee of madness, someone had singled him out, cared about him in any way and actually viewed him as having some value and worth, would have caused him to cave in on himself.

In fact, Warren Potsburger had tremendous value, and soon everyone on the Mall would know it. Everyone in the melee. Everyone in America, actually, and most of the world. He just didn't know it yet.

13. *The GOR*

1

The Reasoners were about to commence their first meeting with the GOR, the government of record. Already it was like nothing any of them had anticipated.

There were more than thirty of them, first of all, and they entered the room as if the meeting were their call, in their offices, and on their terms. In no way did they look like the representatives of a defeated, or at least fatally compromised, federal government.

They were also impeccably dressed in business wear and outfitted with leather folders and laptop satchels and tablets. They shook hands and passed around creamy white government business cards, not just to Brueler and the Reasoners, but to each other. They distributed other printed materials, reports with titles like *Objectives in Managing Dissent* and *State Report Alerts*. Chase guessed that the young people who did the handing out were assistants, but he had to wonder where exactly the materials had been printed. As far as he knew, the Government Printing Office was currently being used as a morgue.

Due to numbers, the government people had to take one whole side of the immense table while the Reasoners took the other. There was a lot of shifting. A dozen of the younger government people automatically took chairs against the walls. They efficiently opened sleek laptops to take notes.

The chief representative for the government turned out to be Miles Mallickey. *Miles Mallickey*?? Representing the entire United States government? This took just about every Reasoner – even Brueler – by surprise.

Mallickey was not an impressive man. He was diminutive, with a 1970s side part, big hair to match, and a strangely froggy mouth. He wore a poorly tailored hunter green suit and a large digital watch. What he lacked in bearing, however, he made up for in a sort of "what makes Miles run" determination. Every American had, at some time or other, seen Miles Mallickey on television. A few even knew that back in the dark ages Miles had once actually won a seat in the House of Representatives. He never repeated the feat, but that one term had been enough for Miles. It put his toe in the door.

He stayed on in Washington in a number of Cabinet positions for the next twenty-odd years. All of this meant that Miles Mallickey knew not just every back lane of Washington, but how to manage both legislation and egos.

Brueler introduced everyone politely, but once they were seated, zeroed in immediately on the obvious question in the mind of every Reasoner there. "Mr. Mallickey, can you vouch for your standing here?"

Miles reached back to one of the aides sitting along the wall. The aide handed him a piece of paper, which Miles handed across to Brueler. "I am speaking with the full authority of the United States government," he said. "I am the highest government authority available at this moment for this purpose and have complete authority to bind the government in any manner as these talks may necessitate."

Brueler read the letter of authority. Surprised, he handed it to Agniew, who shared it with Tay Hamer and then Kirsten Pappason. It made its way down the table. "Mr. Mallickey, that document is three weeks old," Brueler said.

"The date isn't material!" The Mick, it seemed, was ready for a fight.

"Two people who signed it are now dead."

"It hasn't been rescinded, Mr. Brueler. Therefore my authority is as unassailable as your own." Mallickey opened his leather portfolio. "Look, we have a lot to cover, and my people and I have more to do today."

A raised eyebrow from Brueler. It was hard to imagine a meeting more important than briefing the folks who would decide the very future of the United States, but apparently Miles had places to be.

Miles clicked a pen in his hand. "What can you tell us?"

There was a long, still silence. Brueler looked to the Reasoners. The Reasoners looked to Brueler. The government people looked to the Reasoners.

"About what?" Brueler finally asked.

"Van DeVere," Mallickey said.

"What about him?"

He shrugged. "Well, on our side we've drafted a legal demand to the General to recant his position and to justify any refusal to defend both this city and to verify his protection of any and all other federal installations. We have also outlined a possible charge of dereliction of duty and how he risks being stripped of his command. This chaos has to stop, and order has to be restored. You need to make this position clear to Van DeVere. We need to take these people out as well as anyone else threatening the sovereign control of the United States government."

Agniew asked, "Take who out?"

"The Changers."

"All of them?"

"Of course."

Agniew was so stunned, he struggled with his response. "But … Congressman … by anyone's estimate there are millions of them across the country and at least a half a million in this city alone. So … that's your solution?"

Mallickey shook his head. "That's *your* solution. That's what you're going present to General Van DeVere."

An assistant reached forward and placed a can of Coke in front of Mallickey. He cracked it and swallowed half. Clearly, the Mick was done. He had shown his tough guy *bona fides*, and was waiting for a response.

Finally, General Williamson spoke in his low earthquake rumble.

"Congressman, you are aware, I assume, that the Supreme Court of the United States ruled – "

Mallickey waved that off. "A different time, General, and, if you missed the headlines, only two Supreme Court justices still have their heads on, so – "

"I think you'll find their rulings still stand," the General persisted. "And any military officer, and certainly someone of the character of General Van DeVere would never – "

"Yeah, yeah, honor, manhood, et cetera," said the Mick. "But I think you'll find the General was constrained in taking orders from a representative of the *Congress.* Our legal argument – and it has complete support from more than *three* Harvard and Yale scholars – is that with the invention of the Reasoner Compromise, we have a whole new power structure, none of which the court was able to take into account. So, there's nothing that prevents the Reasoners from telling DeVere to get back to work."

The silence that greeted this seemed to go on forever.

Finally, Ambassador Macomb crossed his legs elegantly (armed, definitely armed, Chase thought) and asked gently, in that buttery southern lilt, "If I may?" There were nods from the other Reasoners. His manner was so courtly, who could refuse him? The Iron Butterfly, they used to call him.

"Congressman Mallickey, there may be confusion here about exactly what our duties are and where our powers lie."

Mallickey shrugged. "I'm happy to clarify if people need me to clarify."

The Ambassador smiled and continued. "In fact, we are intended to be an impartial body, tasked with assessing and hopefully providing a direction that will bring the two parties together to reunite the nation as a whole. To be, *literally*, the last reasonable minds to put an eyeball to this most vexing of conflicts. You, however, are talking as if we are in the employ of yourself and the Government of Record, and that, I'm afraid, just isn't so. As well, it should be noted that the Reasoner Compromise explicitly prohibits us from any direct contact with the commanders of the United States military without expression permission – ”

“Sure, sure, sure,” Mallickey said. “That’s what we all *said*, but if we just hold it at that – I mean, if that’s all you do – then how the hell do you expect to get things back on track?”

“Well, for starters,” Vin Jansert jumped in, offering that trademark smirk, “I sure as hell thought we’d be helped by someone like, say, the President of the United States – or whoever is acting as President. I didn’t think our first meeting would be with a cut-rate leftover Congressman.”

Mallickey seemed shocked by the demand, if entirely unoffended by the attack on him personally. “The President is in isolation, and certainly doesn’t report to you!”

There were looks around the table. Ambassador Macomb tried again. “Perhaps it would be advisable to verify our understanding of where we *are* on executive authority. By that I mean, what *happened* to the President.”

“Which President?” Mallickey asked.

Before the Ambassador could answer, Vin Jansert interrupted again. “Start with Drury! After all, he was the last person actually elected to the damned office.”

Mallickey offered an angered shake of the head. “That’s been extensively covered in the news media. There’s no reason to go over that.”

“Let’s try anyway,” said Kirsten Pappason.

Mallickey studied the faces in the room. After a moment, he managed, with no small amount of discomfort, to say, in a weirdly flippant manner, “Regrettably, President Drury was not able to fulfill his constitutional duties.”

“What does that mean?” asked the Ambassador.

“It means exactly that.”

“I think you’re going to have to do better than that.”

“The *President*,” Mallickey said carefully, “is a patriot, and as such was extremely upset by the guillotine appearing on the Capitol steps and the flouting of civil law. As a result, he was moved to Camp David for his own safety."

"That's not what I heard!" Vin Jansert said. He looked at everyone around the table. "I heard he had a shit fit. Screaming and yelling and losing his mind. Everybody's heard that!"

(Senator Sofia Puccelli's words were clear in Chase's memory. "He is a weak man. A very, very weak man.")

Mallickey gave Jansert a very cold and very troubled look. "Let's agree that when the Vice President went up to Camp David to see him, he determined that the President would no longer be continuing in his constitutional role. That was to be passed on to the Vice President, as per the 25th Amendment."

"But then they threatened to kill the Vice President," Vin said. "And his whole family."

Mallickey nodded slowly. "For personal reasons, while the Vice President agreed to invoke the 25th Amendment, he elected not to assume the office."

"Can he do that?" asked Hydy Horvat from the far end of the table. "Just refuse? He was sworn to take over the Presidency if the President was unable to."

"The Vice President chose not to take those responsibilities upon himself," Mallickey persisted.

"And from there?" asked Brian Gleeber. It was the first time he had spoken.

Mallickey stayed true to the home team. "As you all know, it was decided that the mantle of the Presidency would best rest with the Speaker of the House. The Senate's objection to that is obviously a matter of long public record."

"When was she sworn in?"

But clearly Mallickey didn't want to answer that question. "Look, folks! Everyone *knows* this. We're wasting time!"

"Humor us," said Agniew.

Mallickey sighed. "Immediately after 5/22. And just as you all also know, she was immediately moved to an undisclosed location for her own safety. But I assure you she is issuing directives through surrogates and has always been in complete control of the government."

"Yet here you are," said Vin. "Making deals for the government. And not her. And here we are. Asked to step in. To solve the government's problems."

"And when was the last time she – Ms. Joles – made contact with General Van DeVere?" Pappason asked.

Mallickey seemed baffled by the question. "I thought I explained. We haven't talked to those people for *weeks*. That's why we're tasking you."

There was silence.

"Well, I now understand one thing." They all turned. It was General Williamson.

"What's that, General?" asked Mallickey.

The man straightened himself in his chair. "The problem you're having with General Van DeVere."

"It's not my problem," said Mallickey. "It's the nation's problem. He's hiding behind the court's decree when he should be fighting for his country!"

"I'm afraid it's the same problem that kicked off some of these confusions," said the General. "He's clearly waiting for the appropriate authority to instruct him."

"He responds to the commands of his Commander in Chief and the United States government."

"And who is *that*, Mr. Mallickey?"

A very awkward silence from the Mick.

The General went on. "Look, I've met General Van DeVere once or twice. He is a hell of a human being – solid father to those two kids, been married to Hannah since his first posting – as well as a hell of a soldier. And he's extremely well educated. His thesis was on Madison's responses during the War of 1812, did you know that? The Monroe Doctrine is his thing. My guess is that whatever he's doing, or not doing, he is doing or not doing because he is waiting for appropriate civilian authority. In the absence of the President, or a Vice President who has succeeded the President with proper constitutional authority, he is at a loss in terms of following the direct chain of command."

Mallickey stabbed the table. "The Speaker of the House, Emmeline Joles, assumed the Presidency! The order of succession is intact."

"But how do we know that she got there according to the rules?"

Mallickey was at a loss for words. He looked ready to explode.

The Ambassador read Mallickey's confusion and tried to step in. "I'm afraid the General has something here, Congressman. And thus we are reminded of the importance of ceremony." The Ambassador offered a small, indulgent smile. "If none of us knows precisely why the President was relieved, and none of us were there when the Vice President decided to absent himself, how do we know that the Speaker of the House has the appropriate authority to have assumed the Presidency at all? And without a lot of pomp and circumstance and seeing all the folks in charge nodding their approval at the new President's ascension, is she in fact the highest civilian authority from whom the General should take his orders? We have these ceremonies for more than show, you know. Without them … " He offered up a boyish, aw shucks grin. "Well, it just sort of gets away from you, doesn't it?"

Mallickey snatched back the paper he had given Brueler and pretty much waved it at the table. "This! This is the only authority that General Van DeVere needs!"

"But that's *your* authority, Mr. Mallickey," drawled the Ambassador. "It does not guarantee who is Commander in Chief."

For a moment it looked like Mr. Mallickey just might tear the paper in two. Or himself.

Finally Chase spoke. "Has something happened, Congressman, that you need to tell us? Something that the people at this table do not know but should?"

Mallickey looked baffled. "I don't know what you mean."

Chase went on. "Because you seem a man worried about something far greater than General Van DeVere's poor understanding of the chain of succession or his intransigence in the face of a court order. And earlier, I noted, you said in your legal position that the General was not just to defend the city but also to – how did you put it? Verify his protection of any and all other federal installations? What does that mean, Congressman? Are we missing something?"

Mallickey stared at Chase with undisguised fury. Was silent. For too long. Finally, he looked down the table at the Reasoners and seemed to relent. "Well, it's very hard to explain," he started.

14. *The French in Vietnam*

1

Mallickey had all their attention now. He took his time gathering his thoughts. "The most important thing to recognize about these people, these Changers," he said, "is how much they lie."

Vin Jansert said, "*That's* the most important thing to recognize about them, Mick? Not the head chopping?"

There were stifled grins, but Mallickey was not a man to recognize irony. He just went on. "A case in point is Russell, Kansas. Sooner or later, you people are probably going to hear about Russell. I just want to make sure you all understand that everything the Changers say about that incident is a lie. It's simply one of the many stories they've cooked up to excite those headcases on the Mall."

There were confused looks from all of the Reasoners. Finally, Brueler leaned forward. "Perhaps you should tell us what that story is, Congressman. I don't believe any of us know about or have ever been to Russell, Kansas."

Mallickey tapped his pen against the table, as if deciding to tell or not. "As I'm sure everyone here knows, there are many LF – Launch Facilities – for nuclear surface-to-air missiles across the continental United States, particularly in the Midwest. Silos, if you will. There are two such silos within the military installation outside Russell, Kansas. Top secret, of course, and heavily guarded. The Changers however, have concocted a lie and are trying to convince all their toothless deplorable hicks that recently a contingent of Changer psychopaths in pickups and SUVs made their way to said site, heavily armed, and got through the perimeter by murdering two military personnel at the front gate and, once inside the compound, hauled out the personnel manning the actual WMDs and now have unfettered access to the nuclear weapons facility."

There were looks of stunned amazement around the table. Finally, someone spoke. Kirsten Pappason. "Is there any truth to it?"

Mallickey burst out laughing. "No, no, no. As I said, the story is apocryphal. We're sure of this because we have it on good authority nobody hauled anyone out of anything. The point is not the incident itself, but how this lie has spread and is maybe being used."

Chase turned to Mallickey. "When was this supposed to have happened?"

Mallickey consulted some notes in front of him with unusual caution. Finally he said, "The best we can ascertain, somewhere near or maybe around August 6th, possibly."

The Reasoner side of the table erupted. "Ten days ago?!?" Vin Jansert pretty much yelped. "This happened ten days ago??"

"This apocryphal *story* says it happened ten days ago," Mallickey clarified. He tried to keep the tough guy act going, but he looked nervous.

"But how do you know the story is apocryphal?" Jansert asked.

"Excuse me?"

Chase picked up Jansert's thought. "You keep saying it's definitely a lie. What part is definitely a lie?"

Mallickey turned to Chase. "We have received unverified intel that suggests a couple of yahoo Changers did approach the facility and attempt to overtake it, but more reliable intel makes it clear the whole story is inaccurate."

"Meaning they did or didn't approach the silo?"

"Well, whether they did or didn't, I assure you, no one hauled anyone away. I repeat: No one hauled anyone away."

Chase thought about that awhile. Finally, he asked, "When you say, 'no one hauled anyone away' is that because the Changers did not *succeed* in hauling anyone away who was guarding the silo or because there was no one to haul away?"

There was dead silence in the room. Mallickey didn't like where this was going. "What are you asking, Mr. Selby?"

"Professor," Chase said, making a correction he almost never made. Truth was, he just didn't like Mallickey. "I'm asking if that's why you're confident the story is apocryphal. Is it because they were never there or because your intel says there wasn't anyone guarding the silo in the first place?"

Finally, when Mallickey spoke, it was awkward and stilted. "We have had reports that it may not have been adequately protected. Yes."

There was an audible gasp from some of the Reasoners. The government people along the wall looked down at the floor.

"Meaning?"

"Meaning that we have some reports – unverified – that a number of people simply abandoned their posts at some point prior to the 6th."

"How much prior? And why?"

"Well," said Mallickey, "our understanding is that it's possible there may have been discontent within the ranks for some time."

"Discontent? What kind of discontent?"

Mallickey hesitated. "Of a payroll nature."

Brian Gleeber, the statistician Reasoner, spoke up. "But the government shutdown was in February."

"Well obviously it wasn't since the shutdown," said Mallickey. "There was a slight hiccup getting paychecks going again after the government shutdown."

"So when was the last time the people manning the silo would have been paid, Congressman?" Gleeber asked.

Mallickey looked at the ceiling and made a show of doing a lot of calculations. "Well, figure they're paid biweekly and their last payroll run was before the shutdown, then the hiccup, as I say, then the Treasury startup after 5/22, but certainly they were paid before then. I'm almost sure."

Gleeber persisted. "But you said this incident was supposed to have happened less than two weeks ago."

Mallickey looked caught. "Well, that's when the Changers were supposed to have appeared on the scene, yes. As for when the primary personnel may have abandoned the facility, if they in fact did – "

Vin Jansert said what was on everyone's mind. *"We had a missile silo completely unprotected since mid-May??"*

Mallickey practically leapt out of his chair. "We don't know that! We don't know that at all!"

"But it could be," said Chase.

"A lot of things *could* be, Professor!" said Mallickey. "And obviously the facility isn't unguarded now."

"Who *is* guarding it?"

"Our understanding is the United States military has reasserted control."

"Which is in practice under the command of General Van DeVere."

"Yes."

"Who you admit has no contact with Emmeline Joles, Commander in Chief for the GOR. Or you."

Like a rat surprised to hear the trap click into place above his head, Miles Mallickey just stared at Chase. "It's protected," he said. "Of course it's protected."

"By someone. But how do you know who?" Pappason asked. "Why do you assume it's the U.S. military?"

There was a long silence before Mallickey said, "Well, that's what we've *heard.*"

Chase realized he had written a phrase down on the notepad in front of him. It referred to another place and another time, but it also told of a nation being led by people who just couldn't figure out what time of day it was.

"The French in Vietnam," it said.

15. *A Face in the Crowd*

1

The plan was that the Reasoners would eat dinner together in the boardroom on the fourth floor of the State building. Time had been allotted, however, for unpacking or taking a nap first.

Instead, Chase returned to his room, locked the door, picked up the binoculars, and focused his attention on the window.

He had figured out how to manipulate the extremely sensitive zoom so that he could see as much or as little of a scene as he wanted. This lent a cinematic quality to what he was watching, a sense that things seen through the lens were staged and unreal.

Which might explain why, with the day winding down, the people on the Mall didn't look any different from a crowd after a championship football game, a free open-air concert, or an afternoon of drinking or goofing around in the sun. They wore T-shirts and tank tops and shorts and jeans and Nikes, hats and sunglasses and sunscreen and backpacks. They carried water bottles or drank soda. And they ate. A lot. This was managed pretty easily, thanks to the hundreds of food carts and trucks spilling all the way up through the Mall and along Constitution and Independence Avenues – hot dogs, pretzels, hamburgers, shawarma, corndogs, and every manner of frozen treat. Spills of popcorn and kettle corn spread beyond the Mall into the streets, making what had once been road look like a cheap shag rug. Dogs had a field day.

But there was something else thrumming underneath all this Americana. Something perhaps as much a part of the national spirit as the corndogs.

It was the sense of menace. Of unpredictability. Chase could feel it even through the bulletproof glass and from the distance and the height. It felt warm to the touch and was almost alive, like when you put your hand on the hood of a car cooling down after driving a few hundred miles. It was the sense of a perpetually roiling snake pit.

There was the Great Guillotine at the end of the street, of course. That certainly lent a creepy tone, but there were other things just as unsettling. The costumes, for one. Not the folks in the jerseys or the wolf hats or the ones in tactical gear. Those seemed almost mundane after a while. No, there were more sinister costumes that startled you because of their incongruity. Chase saw three kids in wolf baseball hats eating ice cream cones, yet passing unexpectedly behind them was a robed executioner, complete with black mask and sword. There were a lot of Grim Reapers as well, almost always accompanied by a scythe. Guy Fawkes outfits were expected – they seemed to go everywhere – but why were the animal costumes so unsettling?

Perhaps because they weren't just *any* animals. The focus seemed to be entirely on killers. Wolves, obviously, but also tigers and panthers and leopards. In one case, Chase had to zoom in and tighten the focus just to make sure he was seeing what he thought he was seeing, but yes, one of the panthers walking past 14th Street had painted the ends of its canines blood red.

Who were the people who donned these outfits? What made some of them choose to walk on all fours? When the Uprising had first started and Chase had followed events from Princeton, he imagined he knew who the Changers were: the great unwashed, the downtrodden, the kicked-around, the deplorables, the hicks … and yet, still his countrymen. Looking out at men dressed as mountain lions circling children, he wasn't so sure of that. Not anymore. Too many of these people were removed from any reality he knew or valued.

When you looked at them from this distance, it was hard to believe that these people had real jobs. Or families. Or skills or responsibilities. That they wept at births or cried at funerals. But most of them had to have all of these things. The odds alone …

In only a few cases did Chase see the eyes of true madness. The rest were just dragging around the look of the angry and desperate – people who had simply come to be *part* of history, not necessarily to make it. What Chase couldn't bridge in his mind, though, was the willingness of these folks to accept their role as extras in a horror movie of such unspeakable brutality.

But maybe they didn't all accept what was happening. Not with equal relish, anyway. If you watched from the window long enough, you began to suspect that some of them – the ones down at the Lincoln end of the Mall near the monuments, most likely, or the ones throwing Frisbees – might not actually see themselves as part of what took place up on the Capitol steps. Perhaps these folks figured they were just window dressing. Sure, they were there, but they weren't *really* like the yellers and the screamers, the crazy ones who felt no compunction about doing the grisliest shit imaginable in the name of freedom. Guilt and complicity ended somewhere around the middle of the Mall, like a wall between the body-checking hockey player and the popcorn-eating crowd.

Chase trained his binoculars on the distant left and the Capitol steps. This was a slightly obstructed view, but still, he could see arms raised above the crowd and what appeared to be people literally thrown into the air. At first he thought this was part of some new sacrificial rite they'd dreamt up, but after zooming in he decided it was just the more zealous of the celebrants crowd-surfing and mosh-pit diving in fevered jubilation, probably hoping to encourage more culling tonight. And somewhere they had started burning something. Thick, black smoke was wafting through the air. Vehicles on fire?

These people up at the Capitol end, Chase suspected, were the seriously hardcore. These were the folks who lit the torches and screamed with joy when the guillotine blade came down. They sang the sports stadium anthems such as "hey, hey, goodbye" and Queen's *We Will Rock You*. These were the henchmen of this great uprising, as necessary as storm troopers on *Kristallnacht* or the Hells Angels at Altamont. Beavenstock's people.

Then Chase saw her.

He felt his heart skip a beat.

Not up on the Capitol steps, but farther down, past the Grant Memorial. It was only for a split second – just a face in the crowd – but what was so arresting, what literally rocked him back on his feet, was that while everyone else streamed past his lenses unaware he was spying on them, she appeared to be looking right up at him.

She was the most beautiful woman he had ever seen, even if she was wearing the silly floppy garden hat he had made such fun of.

Then she was gone, blocked by someone in a Patriots jersey.

Chase frantically readjusted the binoculars and widened out the zoom. He stepped up on the vent grid at the bottom of the window so he could get closer. He pushed himself against the bulletproof glass.

The hat. Find the hat. It should be the easiest thing to spot.

He tightened the focus and scanned first right to left, then left to right. Nothing. He tried again. Nothing. He had lost her, if in fact he had ever seen her. Which, of course, he couldn't have. That was the thing. She could only be a figment of his imagination.

He finally put the binoculars down. He had never felt sadder in his life. So, the window wasn't just an object of fascination. It played with you. The window was pornography.

He made himself promise he wouldn't look again.

16. *Naked Breasts*

1

"This isn't right," said the woman in the leather and denim dress with the criss-cross top that *almost* revealed her breasts. "Lookit all this bullshit. It's all wrong."

Warren Potsburger agreed, but mostly he was focused on the woman's breasts. They were a good size, and even if they were sagging a bit, they were still breasts. The full sides of them were exposed by the way the woman (Tempest? Tempo? She had said it was a name like that) had folded, or not folded, one side of her top over the other side. Warren's entire goal in life at that moment was getting to see a brown nipple. Happily, this seemed likely, considering the way Tempest (Tempo?) leaned in and out as she waved the 9mm handgun around when she gestured. Or when she tossed each finished cigarette in the general direction of the Washington Monument.

The sun had gone down an hour ago, but it was still unbearably humid. They were sitting on the side steps of some art gallery, just the two of them, watching everyone else rushing past. No one, apparently, wanted to miss the fun. On the south lawn of the African-American Museum, they'd stacked up three UPS trucks and lit them on fire, sending tendrils of black smoke winding around the Washington Monument, which was only a few hundred feet away.

"I didn't think it was going to be like this," Warren said.

"I didn't think it was gonna be like this either," Tempest the philosopher agreed, leaning forward just enough to give Warren the startings of the beginnings of a possible glimpse of nipple.

It wasn't that Warren was particularly starved for sex, although Bella hadn't been with that particular program for months (and the way he was seeing things now, her turning borderline frigid was one of the culprits for him winding up here). And it wasn't like you couldn't see people practically fucking in the open here on the Mall, especially after dark – at least until a brigade of men in white T-Shirts that read 'White Men for White Families' came by and baseball-batted anyone caught with their privates out. The issue was that a nipple meant softness and humanity, and even if Warren couldn't quite put that into words or even thought, he had an instinctive sense that he needed to touch some humanity – or, at least, this very unkempt and unbathed stranger's breast – before his brain cracked open and spilled all over the pavement, which was already sticky with Dicky D's and snow cones and what looked like urine and human blood.

They had set and wrapped his arm at one of the many Red Cross tents that dotted the Mall all the way from the Capitol to the Lincoln Memorial. Warren had almost cried when he discovered these tents, and was so grateful when the nurse took care of him that he *did* cry, and spent the rest of the afternoon wondering if he should get the nurse flowers.

As it turned out, finding flowers was something he could imagine more than do. Warren still wasn't made for walking, as his asshole still ached like it was on fire, the result of the welcome he'd received from those freaks at the train station. The Red Cross people in the tent had asked him a lot of questions and he had volunteered much, but he had not had the nerve to tell the nurse about that particular injury, or the fact that his jaw still hurt from where his teeth had been knocked out.

Truth be told, his stomach wasn't so chipper, either. He suspected that this might actually be his own fault – the result of a corndog he had eaten, or eaten at least until he had spied the maggots on the other side. Whether his belly ached from the dog itself or the maggots or the resultant retching was anyone's guess.

"Burn, baby, burn!" they were yelling over at the Post Office truck bonfire. This was matched by a chant of, "One, Two, Three, Four, we don't want your fucking government!" This had sounded wrong to Warren the first two thousand times he'd heard it at similar impromptu protests throughout the day, but now it seemed as natural as *The Star-Spangled Banner.*

"I wanted to make a statement," Warren told Tempo.

She turned to him, clearly pleased to have found a kindred spirit. "I did too! I thought I'd be heard! You know? But we're not being heard. We're nobodies here."

"I am, anyway," Warren agreed. "I don't matter shit." And in that second he knew he didn't. Anywhere.

"'Cause our voices aren't being heard. Those fuckers."

"Sure as shit, those fuckers," Warren said.

"Neither of us do," she agreed. "You feel that deep down, don't you?"

They both thought about that a good long time.

Finally, confused, Warren asked her, "Which fuckers are we talking about?" Suddenly he missed Bella so much he thought he'd break in two. Maybe he didn't care that she'd taken his dog. Or his truck.

"The way I see it," said Temple, "they're all fuckers. Fuck them all."

"Yeah, I agree with that," said Warren, "fuck them all." He looked at the chaos that surrounded them. "But how do you get people to notice you here?" he asked. "Because if you ask me, here, no one's noticing anyone."

"*These* hobos?" asked Tempest, lighting a new cigarette off the old and throwing the old one onto the ground, an action that almost but not quite revealed a wonderful, if dirty, nipple. "They're all low-class scum. That's the problem."

Warren looked at the group gathered around the burning postal trucks. "USA, USA, USA!" they chanted. Three women in the distance, on a nod from one another, lifted their tops, revealing *six* nipples. Shit, thought Warren. His life really was a matter of always being in the wrong place at the wrong time.

"You probably don't want these hobos to hear you," said Tempo or Tempest. Temple? "What's the point of that?"

"Ye-eah," said Warren slowly, not sure what she was talking about.

"You gotta do something so the *world* hears you. Not just them."

"Yeah," Warren agreed.

"When the world hears you, you're no longer just part of this shit. Then it starts to *mean* something."

Warren pictured himself doing something big enough to mean something. At least big enough that they would put his picture on CNN. That had been the plan when he'd left home, after all. If he wound up on Fox or CNN – for sure if that happened – then Bella would come back to him.

"How do you do something so the world will notice you?" he asked.

"You make a noise, Warren," Tempest said.

Warren wondered when he had told her his name. *Had* he? They had only met twenty minutes ago. She just started to chat on the steps. "You know how to make a noise, don't you?" asked Tempo or Tempest or Temple.

Warren grinned as if to show confidence, as if to say, "Are you fucking kidding me? Of course I know how to make a noise!" But he wasn't fooling anyone. And with all those teeth gone he probably looked like Jed Clampett's stupider nephew. And his ass ached. Suddenly, the more he thought about it, the more he wasn't sure why he had looked down on high school so much.

"You make a noise with a noisemaker, Warren."

"I don't have any noisemaker," said Warren.

"Sure you do." And with that she slapped the gun into Warren's hand.

He stared at it. It was the first good thing he had felt in days. It was the first time he had felt any sort of power since he got on the train.

"Look at me, Warren."

He looked at this dirty woman. She held his gaze like she owned it. "Warren, I'm gonna tell you *exactly* how to make a noise. And exactly when. And it's gonna be soon. But you gotta promise me you're serious about wanting to not become one of those fucking hobos. And in exchange … "

She grabbed his other hand, his left hand, and shoved it inside her dress, slapping it right onto her very warm and slightly sticky breast. "I'm gonna let you feel that first. Then I'm gonna suck you. And day after tomorrow I'm gonna do the same thing and the day after and the day after that but then only after you do what I want you to do."

Warren thought. Fast. He knew he was being set up. But how much is a setup a setup if you're actually getting something out of the deal? His brain tabulated and he came up with what he felt was a pretty good counteroffer. It showed he hadn't fallen off the turnip truck yesterday. "And a guarantee I get on CNN," he said. He pictured Bella and her mother sitting on the old sofa watching from the front room of the old lady's house on Cabbel Street.

"And you get on CNN, *guaranteed*," said Tempo or Tempest or Temple or Temptation.

One of them was her name.

17. *Dining*

1

For dinner, the boardroom had undergone another transformation. The afternoon tea setup was gone, replaced by three circular tables draped with white cloths. The lights had been brought down low, and candelabra placed at the center of each table. It felt like a Victorian restaurant, complete with waiters taking orders from a fixed menu. Chase was amazed. Who had set this up? Who had decided this was appropriate to the moment?

Seating had been pre-arranged, but when Chase entered the room, only three Reasoners – Brian Gleeber, Hydy Horvat, and Calinescu – were actually sitting at a table. The other Reasoners were gathered by the window. At first Chase thought they might be trying to get a look at the burning postal trucks out on the Mall – Chase himself had been studying them only moments before from his own window – but it turned out the group were just trying to stay out of earshot of the waiters, who were setting up glasses and pouring water.

Tempers were high. The subject, no surprise, was Mallickey's nuclear bombshell.

Kirsten Pappason looked genuinely terrified. She was berating Brueler. "We were all *told* that the armed forces were under control. Sidelined, all right, but at least the military structure and its other responsibilities were holding. Things were *safe*."

Agniew looked almost as frightened as Pappason. He asked Brueler, "Did anyone ever talk to you about a potential nuclear threat?"

Brueler gave Agniew a hard look. "Mr. Agniew, I'm an administrator – "

"How is such a threat, such a *potential* threat, not front page news?" This was Pappason.

Vin Jansert joined the group, a glass of water in hand. "You mean, how could a maybe abandoned silo in Russell, Kansas not make the front page when no one's even sure who the *President* is?"

Brueler said, "Obviously, I would have informed you all had I even an inkling anyone was concerned about – "

"Oh, those government people are concerned, all right," said General Williamson. "We all saw that. I honestly don't think they have control of anything."

"So your advice in this situation is?" Brueler asked the general.

"First thing always with government, find out if the story's even true."

"And who would likely tell us that?"

"Talk to DOE. Energy. If they still exist."

Brueler looked to Ambassador Macomb.

The Ambassador nodded. "The General's right. Department of Energy, but do Defense at the same time. Play them off each other."

Brueler grimaced and sipped his drink. Not water. Scotch. "Unfortunately, there's no Cabinet-level administration left at either."

"At *either?*" The General was shocked.

Brueler nodded.

There was silence as everyone tried to wrestle with the possible ramifications of that.

But Brueler, of course, was a man who had been manufactured to find solutions to everything. He consulted his phone and tapped in a few requests. "I do know someone who is – or was – Acting Deputy Director of DOE. He might be able to help. Salaman McHumphries. Anyone know him?"

There were blank looks all around. Clearly, neither General Williamson nor Ambassador Macomb were used to dealing with such low-levels as McHumphries.

"Let me see what I can do," said Brueler.

A distant voice said, "Or you could ask the Wolf! That might be quicker."

It was Tay Hamer, who had seated himself quietly at table two. The Reasoners at the window looked back at him. He shrugged. "Of course, I don't really mean the Wolf as in the *Wolf*, I mean that as we have an official line of communication open to the Changers ... We are meant to sit and talk with them soon enough, are we not? As we have with the GOR? So why not move things up? Suggest we wish to talk to them immediately. Tell them we have heard some troubling news about nuclear weapons, and we want to know if they could send someone over to talk on the matter."

All eyes went to Ambassador Macomb, the master diplomat. He shook his head slowly.

Hamer's eyebrows rose. "No?"

"Much less than that," Macomb said. "More oblique. Just say there's a serious subject we need to discuss as soon as they can send their representative to us. Make it sound serious, but for all they know it could be about scheduling matters. But insist. I believe these people understand insistence."

Brueler slipped his phone in his pocket. "Give me an hour." He strode out of the room.

"And what do we do in the meantime?" asked the Reverend.

"Well, I don't know about you, Reverend," said the Ambassador, "but I believe we should dine."

2

Chase's table was composed of the Ambassador, Reverend Campbell, Jansert, and an empty chair for Brueler. He had hoped to be seated at Tay Hamer's table, but the Noble Laureate was at the next table with Calinescu, Gleeber, and Horvat. Chase hoped the seating arrangement wasn't fixed for the duration of their tenure.

A waiter poured wine. Chase was surprised to see Vin Jansert discreetly hold his hand over his glass.

"What I don't understand," the Reverend was saying as she shook out her napkin and placed it on her lap, "is why this wasn't the first thing the government – or whoever they are – brought to our attention."

Vin Jansert snorted a laugh. "Because they're civil servants?"

The Reverend's expression tightened in displeasure. It had taken beheadings, but finally it was considered vaguely rude in America to mock public servants.

"I believe we must approach all sides with fairness and consideration," the Ambassador mused. "My assessment is that, rather than demonizing the people we saw today, we should take them for what they are: in shock. I would suspect their crime throughout the entire Uprising has been a misinterpretation of events, rather than willful or treasonous stupidity."

A waiter with a basket of bread came to Chase's side. Chase chose a roll with the aid of silver tongs. Again, he wondered who felt they needed silver tongs for their bread at this particular place and time. "What misinterpretation is that, Ambassador?" Chase asked. "Not six blocks from this building, systematic murder is taking place. The mob is in control. Who can misinterpret that?"

The Ambassador tasted the wine the waiter poured. He was the type of man who knew wine. "Quite a few people, I think. Maybe the majority. May I ask how you arrived in Washington, Professor?"

"Please. Chase."

The Ambassador smiled warmly. "Chase. If you came direct from Princeton, Chase, I'm assuming you took the train. As did I. My journey began in Houston."

"Yes," said Chase. "I came by train."

"And what did you see?"

"Chaos."

"You came through Trenton, Philadelphia, Baltimore?"

"Yes."

"And that's where you saw this chaos?"

Chase pictured in his mind's eye what he had seen. "Well, there were fires, although I couldn't see exactly what was on fire. In Philadelphia, the station was complete chaos, and of course you've probably all heard about the pillory on the steps of the Art Museum."

"Beside the Rocky statue!" said Vin.

Chase nodded. "I heard about that from Commander Holden, but I didn't see it." He turned back to the Ambassador. "The crowd in Baltimore was just a smaller version of Union Station here, minus the cans of tuna. And you could see smoke in the distance. According to CNN, that was the old town going up."

Ambassador Macomb smiled. "Perhaps not a barbaric turn of events. And in between? Wilmington or Elkton? How about West Chester, Pennsylvania? West Chester is a lovely village with fine historical significance. Washington marched through there on his way to his confrontation with General Howe, you know."

"I didn't." Chase tried to picture the nondescript town as he had viewed it from the train. "In fact, most of the smaller towns looked … deserted."

"Well it's hot, and summer, and it was Saturday," said the Ambassador. "In the age of universal air-conditioning, small towns are apt to be deserted in summer on a Saturday."

There was a pause as soups and salads were placed in front of them. The Ambassador had ordered soup and now made quite a show of adding salt and pepper and testing it while everyone waited for him to go on. "What I am getting at," he said finally, "what *we* will have to reckon with in our considerations, what is keeping Mr. Mallickey and his people and many more safe in their delusion, is that – to much of the country – all that is happening in this city and others is a … well, a television show."

The Reverend's salad fork stopped in mid-air. "Excuse me?"

The Ambassador nodded. "Of course, people are still going to the supermarket – even though there are fewer things on the shelves – and they're still going to the car wash and where I come from they still have Little League games on Saturday and afterwards the teams go to McDonald's. My son's old high school friend, Jess Strathmore, is one of the coaches for our side, and she says they're even going to go ahead with the championships this season." The Ambassador looked at all of them. "My point is, for a large proportion of the population, this is something happening 'elsewhere,' and because it is happening 'elsewhere' and hasn't touched them, they are not entirely unhappy with what is happening … 'elsewhere.'"

"You can't mean they *like* what they're seeing on CNN?" asked the Reverend.

The southern gentleman shrugged. "Most of us like a little chaos every now and then, as long as it doesn't affect us too directly. Don't get me wrong. I'm sure these are very patriotic people. It's just that, for most of them, it has been a long while since they saw the value of the federal government specifically."

"More than that!" said Vin, his mouth full of bread. "They hate it!"

"Let's say they have been *trained* to hate it," the Ambassador hedged. "In general, they are not disposed to favor our institutions. At all."

The Reverend seemed very uncomfortable with this line of thinking. "But surely beheadings – "

"Beheadings are abhorrent to everyone," agreed the Ambassador. "So again, thank God it's all happening, well … 'elsewhere.'"

The Ambassador had their complete attention and he knew it. He leaned forward. In the light from the table candle he looked like a Roman emperor, if you ignored the Ermenegildo Zegna suit and the loaded cowboy boots. "The genius of these Changers is what they have been careful *not* to do. It suggests a fine mind operating somewhere. For instance, here we have a nationwide riot with very little looting. That's unheard of. Local police departments are still being heeded and what they can't do, why, we now have others – including Hells Angels – ready to step in! So, we have complete bedlam in certain areas, and a sense of law and order where there needs to be law and order, which is most of the country. Fire departments still operate. On the federal level, elements of the government are still working. The Treasury, for one. They even put the Payroll Service back in order, more or less."

"And the FDA," Vin Jansert said.

The Ambassador smiled. "Yes. And Unemployment Insurance transfers to the states. They're unusual choices, aren't they? But cunning. So these madmen, these Changers, have taken over half of the government and brought things to a standstill but not interfered in certain crucial areas. Folks are getting their checks and their relief no matter what. And someone is inspecting meat and drugs. It's certainly an improvement over what happened during the government shutdown, isn't it?"

"That's the point!" Vin almost shouted.

The Ambassador nodded. "Almost certainly. During the shutdown and then VIRA, the government was still very much the law of the land but the Treasury was closed and the regular folks got nothing. Congress assured us that they were working day and night to open the government again, but of course, *they* got paid. Now, since the crazy people have taken control of so much, the Treasury is just humming along fine, regular folks are getting paid, and it's the Congress that's shut down and out of pocket." The Ambassador shook his head with something almost like admiration. "My point is that we must remove from our minds the original impression of these Changers as mobs with torches and pitchforks, with nothing more on their minds than 'burn, baby, burn.' I suspect that earlier than most of us recognized, a kind of shrewd cunning was ruling their day, and one of the key components was that smaller communities were to be unaffected. In many ways, they're protected for the first time in quite a while. Folks have not been asked to do without. And perhaps most importantly, there have been no media blackouts."

Chase was thinking. "And who do you figure is the fine mind behind this?"

The Ambassador chewed on this. "It's *possible* it's the young woman. I confess I have not studied her enough to understand what she's capable of. Has anyone? But somebody with a broad and, dare I say, cynical view of our culture has made sure that internet, wireless, and cable communication have all been protected. CNN is still on. Fox, MSNBC, even Bloomberg. The same as always."

"No, no, no, no, no," Vin Jansert protested with a laugh. "It's better! They're all *free* now. The bills just stopped coming! They socialized communication!"

The Ambassador reached for the wine, waving off a waiter and doing the honors himself. "My original point is we might be kinder to Mr. Mallickey and the remains of our working government, because they're struggling with something far beyond their comprehension. Their world has caved in, and the only thing they know to fight with are laptops, file folders, and business cards."

"And they're supposed to be our best and our brightest," said Vin Jansert.

"Apparently," said the Ambassador.

"No," said Chase. "They aren't."

They all looked to him.

"Who are they then?" asked the Reverend.

Chase shrugged. "The ones who *weren't* in the Capitol Building on May 22nd."

Main dishes started to appear. Brueler returned. He looked pale. He stood with his hands gripped around the back of his chair. "I have just spoken to one of my contacts in the Changers," he said.

The Ambassador raised an eyebrow.

Brueler nodded and spoke up, so everyone at every table could hear him. "I have just spoken to the Changers," he repeated. All talk and clink of cutlery stopped. He had their complete attention. "I let them know we needed to speak on a very serious subject. I didn't tell them what it was, however. To my surprise, they got back to me. Instantly."

"And?" asked Agniew.

"They said they are sending someone over to talk with us first thing in the morning. But they didn't use the word 'talk.' They said 'brief.'"

"Is there a problem with that?" asked Calinescu.

"In light of who they're sending, there might be."

"And who are they sending?"

"Sister Sheena."

There were confused and fascinated looks all around. "She's *here*? In *Washington*?"

Brueler nodded. "I was informed that she has an agenda she wants to address with us. I'm told it's related to fairly recent events. I have been told we will agree with this agenda the minute we hear what she has to say."

"And what is her agenda?"

"Surrender."

No one said a word.

18. *Sister Sheena and the Mattress*

1

Chase finally had a reason to turn to the binders Tyler had mentioned. The ones on the desk by the window.

As he thumbed through, it was obvious someone had assembled them with care and precision as well as insight and access to privileged information – to say nothing of an eye for what might be germane to discussions of democratic union.

And none of it was worth anything. It simply wasn't what Chase needed.

He snapped the binder shut and considered his laptop. Then the smart TV they had installed against the wall opposite the sofa.

Perhaps the thing was to *observe* her. He had seen her hundreds of times – everyone in the country had seen her hundreds, maybe thousands of times – but had he really focused on her as someone he needed to crawl inside?

YouTube likely wouldn't disappoint. Social media, after all, was her whole thing. *Their* whole thing. In less than half a year the Changers had used technology to make themselves part of the nation's living room, bus ride, morning wakeup, airport delay, and treadmill. By being readily at hand, they had managed to make the utterly intolerable reasonable, and the utterly unreasonable tolerable.

Chase used his VPN to bypass the government Wi-Fi they'd provided – which Tyler had instructed him to use exclusively – and prepared to log on to the unbelievably fast and efficient national Free-Fi the Changers supplied, which everyone suspected was unmonitored. Pretty sure. Probably.

Rash decisions could have incalculable consequences.

Fuck it. Chase needed to know.

He connected.

2

The leaders of the Uprising weren't technically fugitives anymore, especially as what remained of the U.S. government had agreed – despite shrill protests to the contrary – to enter into negotiations with them. This acceptance had come, more or less grudgingly, once the Reasoners program had been shoe-horned in as a possible path to reconciliation.

The Changers *had* been fugitives, of course. That spring, everyone associated with the violent overthrow of established order had been deemed America's Most Wanted at some time or other, even the oldsters in the Tilley hats on Wall Street. The federal government put out big talk of bringing folks in 'dead or alive' and issuing warrants for the arrest of and ceaseless searching for 'ringleaders.' But nothing happened.

Ironically, though, once they erected the blade of the Great Guillotine on the steps of the Capitol, things changed. Somehow with the madness of that first unimaginable shock of violence and the three-day weekend of blood – the first cull – the Changers had morphed from a renegade protest group into a sort of revolutionary force with a viable message.

Twenty-four-hour coverage helped. And endless repetition made the faces of the Uprising more familiar. Another thing that helped was that as time passed (and Senator Sofia Puccelli had prophesied this) the number of leaders in the Changer movement was whittled down.

Jeff Beavenstock had been a labor leader in coal country, and before that had served two tours of duty in Afghanistan. He had an odd, bad-boy, country singer charm. It helped that he looked like what he was: a no-holds-barred tough guy from West Virginia with wrap-around sunglasses, goatee, and sandpaper voice.

The other leader, of course, was about as far from that as you could get.

She literally stepped out of nowhere and took center stage in a single afternoon. The fact that she and Beavenstock wound up being the winning ticket was almost inconceivable when things started. However, once the country got a look at her, it seemed inevitable.

3

It was the end of March. A significant number of pissed-off L.A. County workers had gathered around the workman's compensation firm Tri-Star, in Long Beach, California. Tri-Star was notorious for its treatment of city workers injured on the job, seeing to it that they were denied their workman's comp benefits for as long as possible. It was a practice that most workers felt was beyond their ability to fight – after all, the city of Los Angeles itself had hired the firm – but after watching the killings in Bentonville, Arkansas, some of the more game Tri-Star screwees had a change of heart. Maybe they had more options than they imagined. And, having seen Citibank burn to the ground that weekend, people were feeling inspired to do more than write angry letters.

The sudden arrival of a phalanx of Long Beach and L.A. County cops, however, all standing at attention in full military riot gear, gave everyone surrounding the building pause. It was obvious the L.A. County cops were ready to shoot in order to protect the firm.

One or two ex-labor leaders, now newly minted Changers, were doing everything they could to encourage the crowd forward. There was a lot of shouting and calls of "now is the time," but the crowd barely moved a few feet.

Then she stepped into the camera shot. That's all. There was a void and she just filled in. And now, there she was, on national – international – TV, streaming live.

She certainly cast a striking pose. You couldn't not look at her. Everything about her said *feline*. The slight yet gracefully curvaceous physique, the drawn-back jet-black hair held in place by the black headband, the piercing green eyes, the rich and full mouth, the rigid posture, and the utterly humorless expression. She didn't look angry. She looked ready to strike.

"Listen to me!" she shouted. "Listen to me!"

Eventually some of them shut up enough to listen.

"If you just stand there, you know what you're doing?!"

No one answered. And, in fact, she didn't give them time to answer.

"You're letting men in suits who don't know your name and don't care the names of your children – or whether your children live or die – come in and rob your house every single night of your life!" That's how she *started*. "Night after night. You know what a good daddy or mommy does with a man who robs their house *one* night? They call the police. You know what a good daddy or mommy does if the robber shows up the *next* night? They shoot him. You want to know *why* they shoot him?"

The crowd was so stunned by her appearance that they hadn't picked up on the fact that they were supposed to answer. But she let them know. Real fast.

She shouted at them again. "YOU WANT TO KNOW WHY THEY SHOOT HIM??"

They shouted back. "Why??"

"Because the police clearly let *that* motherfucker go!" she shouted. "Which means that Daddy or Mommy are the *only* thing standing between their family and madness! So they *shoot* that motherfucker because they want a safe neighborhood, and they want a safe neighborhood because they are decent people!"

The crowd really liked that. They all moved closer.

"Today you are going to go into this building behind us and you are going to rip these people apart and throw their symbols into the street not because they owe you money – which they do! – but because you have *self-respect*! When you rip them apart, you are saying, 'I am a decent person and your indecency to me is going to end now! Not tomorrow when the police show up and do nothing, not next week when the courts decide to slap them on the wrist and go golfing with them, and not in the next century when the world has moved on to a different kind of criminal intent and has all but forgotten my very existence. Today, motherfucker!' You hear me? In the next few minutes those lying sacks of shit in that building behind me are going to be cowering behind those big photocopiers, but you are going to throw their corporate symbols into the street and reveal them for the sniveling, trembling animals they are!"

There were elements of the Uprising that were funny – hell, the first appearance of the guillotines was funny, in a way – but there was absolutely *nothing* funny about the arresting catwoman in the black combat pants and T-shirt that said "SURVIVE." She meant every word she said, and, as it turned out, the crowd did everything she said.

And if the media and the cops didn't quite understand what Sister Sheena meant by "their symbols," the crowd picked up on it right away. Photocopiers, laptops, telephones, filing cabinets, and desks. They threw all of them – as well as a number of executives at Tri-Star – out the window that day. It turned out she had a thing about desks and photocopiers.

"The modern whips of oppression," she told CNN that night, when she did an interview outside the now-windowless Tri-Star building, handling herself as adroitly as a twenty-year member of Congress. "Ask any person of color, any sister, any sufferer, if they haven't felt the whip of the desk on their back; the whip of the photocopier; the whip of the computer screen turned away from them. Ask them but don't you dare turn your back on them ever again."

A star is born and the world usually knows it. Instantly.

Such was the case with Sister Sheena.

4

An audience of Americans addicted to twenty-four-hour news and social media ate her up, either in revulsion or secret admiration. She offered something the battering ram Jeff Beavenstock couldn't: literacy, argument, and glamour. And if it turned out that much of what she said wasn't exactly off the top of her own head – she herself made a point of telling everyone who would listen about a slim volume called *The Words of the Wolf*, and by April a lot of people took her advice and were reading those words – it only added to the feeling that this was a real movement with a real ideology behind it, and not just a bunch of yahoos with pitchforks.

Part of her charm, of course, was youth. Not just her startling appearance, or the never-changing yet immaculate wardrobe of cammo pants and black SURVIVE T-shirt, but her willingness to engage with, debate, or intellectually outdraw people two or even three times her age. And she knew how to mix it up. If she sometimes went on too long quoting Robespierre, she was also smart enough to sneak in a few Malcolm X quotes, or Jay-Z. She knew how the media worked and she enjoyed it just as she enjoyed another exploitative tool she wasn't squeamish about at all: violence.

Educated people, particularly young people, suddenly had someone who seemed to reflect them, even if they didn't know exactly where she came from. Sister Sheena would not discuss her past, but the odd hint or two suggested she was also college educated, with likely a master's degree or more. Posters went up in dorms all across the country.

As for her uneasy alliance with Beavenstock, at first she seemed to dismiss him. After all, he represented everything she despised, possibly including being male. Soon, however, she tempered her rhetoric. She referred to him as the rifle. "And sooner or later," she said, "every self-respecting person is going to need a rifle."

When she saw how well that played, she pushed it even further.

"The Wolf reminds us," she said with quiet intensity, her jaw, as usual, rigid in anger, "there is no revolution without bloodshed. Not as long as we are human beings. Diplomacy can be bloodless, but not revolution."

Chase had heard this Sheena quote before, but sitting in his room in the revamped State building, surfing through clips on YouTube, he was amazed to discover that it came not from a Changer rally but from, of all places, *Good Morning America!*

Yep. There was George Stephanopoulos sitting opposite Sister Sheena, clipboard on his lap, asking the probing questions.

"Do you believe that this is where we are? In a revolution?" asked George.

Chase paused the clip. He checked the date. May 16?? Less than a week before they erected the Great Guillotine. Chase found it awfully late for George to be asking if there were a revolution roaring across the land. By that time, President Drury was on the lam and more than twenty smaller cities were on fire. New York was already in the full throes of street riots.

Sister Sheena was smooth, though. She didn't laugh in George's face or suggest that maybe he might want to look out a window. Instead she said, "A revolution only becomes a revolution when the people decide. It's not for me to say." Then, making clear what she expected of people, she said it: "There is no revolution without bloodshed. Diplomacy can be bloodless, but not revolution."

It may have been hackneyed propaganda, but it was great TV and she knew it. Everyone else knew it too. On CNN, Anderson Cooper lifted her up even higher – to full leader status – with his two-part prime-time interview, and Rachel Maddow was almost giddy in Sheena's company. These establishment journalists clearly felt burnished by her daring, just as movie stars used to like hanging out with Black Panthers.

Chase put Sheena on pause. He studied those hooded eyes staring down a foolishly grinning George Stephanopoulos. Sheena looked like she was one second away from pouncing. You wondered how long it would take before all of George was eaten.

5

5/22 was when the top blew off.

By late May, perhaps in an effort to deal with the madness of what had just happened, a new phrase entered the national lexicon. "This civil war." It was her phrase, of course, and she had snuck it in before Beavenstock had gone on his killing spree. "*This civil war is a righteous war*," Sister Sheena would say, and draw comparisons between that other conflagration that had ripped the country apart. The comparison had two benefits. On one hand, it reminded Americans that civil war was something the country had been through before, so no biggie. Two, it painted Sister Sheena as Grant to Beavenstock's Sherman. Simplicity is always appealing.

By then they had clearly decided to work together and support one another, even if Sheena never went near those Capitol steps. In fact, no one knew of an instance when she and Beavenstock were physically in the same room. Somehow that made the Grant-Sherman comparison even more apt. Violence bonded them.

Just like Sherman, Jeff Beavenstock inspired rock-solid devotion from an army of remarkably can-do folks. Back in West Virginia, when he had announced mass "trials" for local politicians, his self-described deplorables in their uniforms of football jerseys showed up en masse with their Black & Decker Workmate 425s. In no time, they were measuring, cutting, routing, and hammering together scaffolding and gallows. When Beavenstock wanted the Tennessee Valley Authority's power grid rerouted in order to bring light to the folks of northern Georgia – who had literally been left in the dark by their own utility company after the Middle Savannah River debacle – it was done in a matter of hours. So if you looked at it that way, it should have taken no one by surprise that, when he told his followers to literally storm the Capitol and sequester every inhabitant in the basement, Beavenstock's will was done.

Who knew how much they planned together? Or even if they did. No one. By the end of May, she would defend Beavenstock's deeds as "necessary" and Beavenstock would commend Sister Sheena as "our Thomas Jefferson." It was a union which one Washington columnist (now dead) described as the ultimate unholy alliance: Frankenstein's monster and Dracula's daughter.

6

Finally he found what he was looking for. It was a simple listing on the right side of the YouTube menu. A news clip from WNBC that simply said "Wells Fargo."

The preview showed a frozen closeup of Sister Sheena on the steps of a Wells Fargo branch in downtown Cleveland, addressing a crowd of locals.

Chase clicked "play."

Sister Sheena came to life, black smoke and flame billowing behind her.

"You are not after violence!" she told the crowd.

A few voices in the crowd begged to differ. They were very *much* after violence, and the sooner the better.

"Violence is not your objective!" she repeated. "No more than your objective in buying a hammer is to own a hammer! You buy a motherfucking hammer in order to nail two pieces of wood together. The hammer is just the *tool*."

Okay, now they got it. There was an eruption of applause and whistles. They liked this. This made total sense.

"What else are you going to buy when the front door of your house has split in two? You have to nail that door back together! You have to protect your family!" There were some cheers. The crowd always liked when Sister Sheena talked about the mythical family that needed protecting. That had become a trope with her and it worked. She turned on the cheering folks and fixed them with a steely stare. "So what are you going to do when the animals who should be listening to you have lost the ability to listen and instead threaten your family?"

The crowd got quiet. "Let's be clear: Not only do these animals think you're suckers, you *have* been suckers! Suckers for the billionaires who have taken your money and suckers for the billionaires who say they're going to give it *back*!"

Whoever had been operating the camera had been smart to stay on the closeup. As Sheena turned her head to make sure she was addressing the whole crowd, the flames devouring the Wells Fargo branch framed her perfectly. The part of the sign that showed the familiar horse and wagon was smoldering black as the plastic melted.

"That's all they do! They lie to suckers! They tell you they're gonna make sure you get your money back, or get more jobs, or get a wall to stop a bunch of brown people just as lied to as you." Sister Sheena turned to the folks on the side. "You know who believes that? *Fools* believe that, that's who! What good are more jobs if not one of them pays enough to live on? And how is a wall two thousand miles away gonna help anyone buy bread in Okla-fucking-homa? Or a good used car? Or a mattress?"

Chase stopped the clip.

Mattress? The word came out of nowhere. Why mattress? Chase didn't understand, but the crowd nodded at that word like they knew. It meant something. It meant something big.

Then Chase realized what it meant. It meant that unlike any other political leader of any stripe, Sister Sheena knew how much a mattress cost.

"You need real things and instead they give you plastic crap," she said. "Because they know you *believe* in plastic crap." She glanced over her shoulder at the melting Wells Fargo sign. "How about *that* insult? You look at it and think covered wagons, pioneers, America, home cooking! Don't you? I do! But look at it smoking. It's just plastic crap."

Sister Sheena turned back to the crowd and raised a fist over them. "I do not *want* you to set fires!" she shouted. "But you tell me what else you can do when they just won't listen to you? What else do you do? Well, I'll tell you!"

The crowd wasn't cheering now, they were full-throated roaring to get going. They wanted to be let off the chain. They also wanted to know the answer to Sister Sheena's question. Chase, watching, also sat forward. He too wanted the answer.

"You go out and get a motherfucking *hammer*!"

They stormed the Wells Fargo building.

They didn't just jostle the person operating the camera, they manhandled them. Then, as the camera itself struggled to settle on something, it found someone in the middle of the crowd who was not shouting, who was not raising a fist, who was not screaming for retribution.

She was, in fact, entirely at peace and looking right at the lens, almost as if she was looking directly at Chase himself, sitting in his faux hotel room two months in the future. The most beautiful woman he had ever seen. In that silly too-big gardening hat.

Chase stared at his TV and could not make sense of what he was seeing.

Rin.

Again.

Book 2:

Us Vs. Them

"If you want to create justice, first you must create terror."
– *Wolf Words*, pg. 6 (Barnes & Noble pocket edition)

19. *Rin*

1.

She unmanned him. That's how he always thought of it. Like an old 19th-century English novel where the staid and upright earl confronts the willful peasant wench. "Unmanned him."

Chase had already been in London two weeks. He'd come for a series of interviews about where he was going to do his doctoral work and was only starting to get the lay of the land (Edinburgh romantic but impractical, Cambridge an obvious step but unappealing). So far, he had enjoyed teas in quiet clubs and mainstays like Claridge's or the Langham, as well as private meeting rooms paneled with the decking of transatlantic steamers. That Saturday afternoon he was going to meet a Dr. Budden, PhD, King's College, who had suggested they have lunch and go over Chase's options. He would never keep the appointment.

He didn't know it, but his life destiny was wrenched off course the second he emerged from the entry turnstile onto the westbound platform at West Ham's outdoor station. He saw a young woman, around his own age, with luxuriant purple hair, kicking the living shit out of a subway car at the far end.

"Sonofabitch!" she shouted.

Clearly, an American.

She was tugging at something unseen, on which the doors of the train had closed prematurely. A suitcase, Chase realized.

The closed doors may have created a barrier between the girl and the bag, but they did not disengage one from the other. The girl held onto the long handle of the case with both hands while kicking at the doors with her black combat boots. These were a marked and appealing contrast to her short, soft, summer dress and man's jean jacket.

The hair, though. That's what Chase saw. There was so much of it. Long and ringleted. Like a heroine in an opera. Except it was purple.

For no reason he could later explain, he started to walk toward her. As he did, his eyes took in the whole scene: the girl, the bag handle, the train, the almost-deserted station platform, the red push button on the wall, and the frustrated driver in the left-hand side of the first car, only now starting to realize there was something wrong in one of the cars behind him. The driver checked his in-car monitors, trying to see what that problem was.

Chase offered up a "halt!" hand to the driver, then strode past him toward the end of the platform and the girl.

"Sonofabitch!" she kept saying.

Inside the subway car, passengers were also starting to react. Two teenaged boys tried to pry open the doors for the girl while clearly enjoying the opportunity of being able to destroy transit property.

"Fuck sakes!" she said, wrenching the bag to one side.

"Push the red button," Chase said.

She didn't hear him or see him. She kept struggling.

For reasons utterly unfathomable, the driver up front decided that whatever had gone wrong at the rear of the train was probably cleared by now, despite no supporting evidence. Suddenly the loudspeaker intoned its robotic "Stand clear of the doors, please, the doors are now closing," although clearly the doors had *already* closed.

The train began to slowly inch out of the station.

"Hey!" The girl's tone shifted from belligerence to panic, and the boys on the other side of the closed door began to laugh. No skin off their noses. The purple-haired girl began to run along with the train, still refusing to let go of the thin bag handle. She was heading right into one of the iron beams which supported the rain cover.

Chase moved quickly. His hand didn't hit so much as smash the red STOP button on the station wall.

The train jolted to a screeching stop.

The girl was yanked to the ground by the sudden stop, landing less than two feet from the iron beam which almost surely would have killed her. She did not, however, let go of the bag. Later, Chase would think that was it. Her character. Right there.

Soon enough, things pretty much righted themselves. The bag was back in the girl's full possession, the teenagers were back in their seats, and the annoyed driver was able to go on his way with his passengers, although the man seemed more interested in bitching about the paperwork he would have to fill out.

"Every time some damned fool pushes that red button!" he shouted in Chase's face. "Which is only for legitimate incidents!"

"This *was* a legitimate incident," Chase said.

The driver clearly thought otherwise. He continued to shout and point. So did the girl.

Chase didn't care. He was busy studying the right side of the girl's head, which turned out to be in complete contrast to the left side. Here, things were shaved down to purple stubble, a ying-and-yang contrast with the luxuriant ringlets on the left. Somehow, he thought, it made her even more beautiful, if such a thing were possible.

But then, she would always be that way to him. In public, or in private, she would always be the most beautiful woman he had ever seen. She would always take his breath away, particularly in bed, before and after sex, and especially at night with the curtains open.

Of course, this was not Chase as he had been for the first twenty-four years of life. Chase was a realist, not a romantic. Rationally, he also knew that most men believed the woman they were bedding was the most beautiful woman on earth – something women were utterly unaware of. But in this case, he believed he was right. She *was* the most beautiful. And, of course, not just because of her physical appearance, but her humor and her wit and her dark, canny spirit.

She unmanned him.

2

After the rescue of what turned out to be a fairly ratty suitcase, there was the coffee shop introduction at a little place across the street from the station. First, however, she felt it necessary to shout, "General Cornwallis did the right thing!" at the departing train, which made him laugh. She gave Chase a lopsided grin, then looked down at the bag. "Is everyone all right in there?" Chase laughed again.

In the coffee shop, he found out her name was Rin (for Katherine, a speech impediment issue for a little brother with the astonishing name of Adolphe), and she was in the U.K. trying to get a job with Granada TV news as a junior producer. She had literally been on her way to a sublet she had landed in Earl's Court.

"Why not BBC?" he asked.

She laughed a laugh he would come to know well. A sort of mad snort. "Are you kidding me? You think the Beeb is going to hire someone like me?"

"And Granada has significantly lower standards?"

"Let's fucking hope so."

Her use of profanity was terrific. Her daring, however, was even more amazing.

The plan to break into broadcasting in London was a perfect example. He finally wheedled it out of her that she had only had one previous professional job in broadcasting, and that was for a Midwestern cable operation in the States which specialized in collegiate sports. "Just enough experience for me to plausibly lie to a foreigner."

For Chase, who had completed every step of every procedure he had ever undertaken and who had never put together an Ikea product without carefully following all the instructions, her approach to this – to everything – didn't just seem reckless, it seemed to be daring the world. He asked, "Why don't you just go get enough experience so that Granada has no choice but to hire you? No plausible lying required."

She laughed. "I don't have that kind of time!"

"Why? Where are you going?"

"BBC, hopefully."

He laughed.

She laughed that she had made him laugh. "Well, shit, I have to dump those half-wits at Granada, don't I?"

At that moment he wanted nothing more than to stay all afternoon with her in the coffee shop. Forever, if he could. To stay with her, in fact, anywhere.

Later he found out the switch to broadcasting had been pretty recent. As she explained it, eighteen months ago she had dropped Sociology for Media Arts, and twenty-two months before that, Sociology had supplanted Political Science in the Digital Age. Previous to that, she had been working as a saucier at an off-campus restaurant of great pretension ("I read up on all that saucier shit in one day online," she said) and prior to that she had been selling "Black art" out of the trunk of a friend's car.

"You mean like Henry Tanner or Jacob Lawrence?" Chase asked.

"Who they?"

"Well, what is Black art, by your definition?"

"Sad, pathetic images of what it's like to be Black in America."

"That's all?"

She took a bite out of the second of the two very large macadamia nut cookies she had ordered. The second one was supposed to be his. She spoke with her mouth full. "It doesn't *matter* who painted it. It just matters that it's pathetically sad or makes you enraged."

"Why enraged?"

"Why *not* enraged?" she asked. "Imagine being Black but your whole life you're surrounded by artwork showing whites only. Like being the greatest actor in the world but because you're Black you can't play Hamlet or Willy Loman. Fuck that. *I'd* be enraged. In fact, I'd burn the place down."

3

Three days later he told Rin Darcy that he loved her. He had spent those days escorting her to a variety of job interviews across the London area – not just Granada and ITV and Sky but, because he'd persisted, BBC. She didn't land a position at any of them, but by then neither of them cared. By then they were only focused on one another.

That was Thursday, when the afternoon suddenly erupted in rain. They ran under Marble Arch for cover.

They were soaking wet when he turned to her and said, "Look, I have to tell you. I think I've got an unusual problem. Very, very unusual. What I mean is, I think I love you."

She laughed in his face. "Oh, Chase, you're so ridiculous!"

"What do you mean?"

"Of course you love me!" She reached her arms up around his neck, pushing her head against his. "You're so clever, but otherwise awfully slow. I've loved *you* since the button."

"Button?"

"The stop button. Who but you would know such a thing existed?" She told him he didn't even need to say he loved her as they were already, clearly, embarked on the first stages of a monumentally historic and passionate romance.

He laughed. "You can't *say* something like that! You have to let it happen."

"Says who?"

"The world."

"The world is full of boobs and religious crazies and people selling hedge funds," she said. "Fuck the world. This is about our romance. Tell the world to get its own romance."

"Our romance" always sounded to him like she assumed it wouldn't last, that there was a built-in timeclock, that love was always fleeting. But it also sounded monumentally historic and passionate. When he told her that she laughed again. "You're absurd."

If he was, it was for the first time in his life.

He canceled his return ticket home to the States, ignored the meetings about his doctoral work, and instead focused his attentions on the girl who fancied herself an ITV news producer yet had never really produced anything; the art dealer who didn't really understand the history of art; the student with four unfinished majors spread over five years of schooling. In so doing he discovered something truly surprising and wonderful. She could write.

She could write like a sonofabitch.

4

By then, he had basically taken up residence in her sublet flat on the top floor of what had once been one of the grand old terrace homes in Earl's Court, long since chopped into 14 apartments. She had landed the smallest one, accessed by the back stairs. The place perfectly reflected her complete lack of interest in practicality and function.

She was out that afternoon, pursuing her latest goal – a job as an interpreter at the Canadian embassy, despite the fact that she was not a Canadian and spoke only one language. She was convinced, however, that she could bluster her way through on high school French and a bit of travel German.

While searching for a wrench to tighten the forever-falling shower curtain rod, he came upon her writings in the bottom drawer of what was laughingly called the kitchen.

He *assumed* they were her writings, anyway. The cramped scratch was certainly hers – more a teenage boy's calligraphy than an educated young woman's – even though the subject seemed utterly alien to everything he knew about her.

"My father spent most of his life in prison," it began. "I was even conceived in a trailer placed in the prison yard for connubial visits. So, from the beginning, everything about our life was about someone being trapped behind bars."

It went on from there, loose cheap copy page after loose cheap copy page covered with spikey reminiscences about a girl who grew up in a trailer park in Shenandoah Pass, Vermont, and the miserable, religion-soaked existence that passed for a childhood for herself and her four brothers.

It was heartbreaking and riveting.

It was also, he knew, complete bullshit. Katherine Darcy, he knew, was one of two children from wealthy people in Illinois.

After four pages, he caught himself. What had he been doing? He quickly slapped the manuscript back together and returned it to the drawer, ashamed. He had violated her privacy. Broken trust.

And yet, now there were questions where he didn't want there to be questions.

Which was fiction? Which was truth?

Because no one's that good, he thought.

5

She must have somehow discovered what he had done because only four nights later, following a particularly manic sex feast – the first time she bit him – as they sat sweating and naked in the attic window, looking out to a sweltering London August night, she had an idea. Out of nowhere.

"We should do a backgrounder," she said. "Right now. About who we really are."

"What's a backgrounder?" He was trying to stanch the bite mark on his arm with paper towel.

"You know. My life up to now. Your life up to now. With plenty of pathos thrown in for good measure."

"You know about me," he said.

"I know nothing about you," she said.

"The basics, at least."

"Not deep stuff."

"Do you ever think that people our age talk too much?"

"You know, Manhattan, you really *are* a fool."

She had taken to calling him "Manhattan" after the bank, mocking his name, which she said didn't suit him in any case. ("I know no one less likely to 'chase' anything than you," she said. "I chased you," he said. "First time in your life," she said. He said, "If it's the only time I ever do it, it was the right time.")

Sitting in the window, Rin shook her head. "It's not talking too much if you give me all the juicy stuff and I respond with appropriate and overwhelmed sympathy. That's how it works. We do it like in the movies. You tell me how – let's say – your mother died when you were ten and it scarred you for life. I tell you how my father assaulted me. I'm talking good, big, thick steaks of heartbreaking truth. Really slap it down."

He laughed, but he was also thinking about the pages in the kitchen drawer. "How did you get to be so cynical?"

"I told you, my father abused me. Let me turn it around on you. How did you get to be such a hidebound prig? That's when you answer about Mom dying when you were ten. Then we stare at each other meaningfully, I hug and comfort you, and our relationship moves on to the next level. Music swells."

"So you're not serious," he said.

"I'm totally serious. You first."

"Okay," he said, distracted. The blood didn't appear to be clotting. "So, my mother died when I was ten."

"You can't use *my* examples! I mean the truth." She took over the paper toweling of his wound.

He watched her hand. She was gentle. "But my mother *did* die when I was ten," he said. "Nine, actually. And I was keeping to your script. You know, so the music can swell. So, did you father really abuse you?"

She laughed. "Of course not. My father never touched a hair on me in my life. He's a God. He fixes washers and dryers for a living."

Chase was surprised by this new version of her father. "Your father was a repairman? I thought you came from money."

"Money was Mom. You're dodging me, Manhattan. We're supposed to be talking about you."

"I'd rather hear about your mom."

She sighed. "Biggest bitch ever drew the breath of life. Not that I don't respect what she accomplished. Come on, boy – "

"What did she accomplish?" Chase asked.

"She became a millionaire at sixty. Manhattan Chase – "

But he persisted. "How? And did your dad stay a repairman? And what about your brother?"

"No. She left Dad for a guy with a house with a six-car garage and a hydraulic elevator. Steve Darcy, who adopted both me and my brother. Chase! It's supposed to be your turn!"

He reached for the bottle of wine on the table and filled the glass they had been sharing earlier.

"Luther," he said finally, giving her the glass.

"Who's that?"

"That's Dad," he said. "Luther."

She laughed. "You call your dad by his first name?"

He shrugged. "Since I was twelve. He told me he had decided that I was his equal, not his property, and the concept of fathers was an artificial construct anyway, so I should call him Luther."

"You're kidding."

"Word of God. Luther never told me what exactly my mother died of but I think it was some kind of awful pneumonia. They didn't believe in traditional medicine. It's a fraud perpetrated by Big Pharma. Did you know that?"

"So … your dad's some kind of hillbilly?"

Chase laughed. "Luther was *Doctor* Luther Selby, Professor of Sociology *and* Anthropology at the University of Missouri."

"Holy shit! And he's still in Missouri?"

Chase shook his head. "Dead. He didn't want traditional medicine for himself either. Cancer. I always thought he figured his superior intellect would beat it. My sister thought so, too."

"So you have a sister."

Another shake of his head. "She killed herself."

Rin looked at him a good long time. Finally, she got it. She reached for the wine bottle as if to pour it on him. "You fucker! You total fucker!! You had me going!" Realizing she couldn't throw the wine, she threw a pillow instead, then a paperback. "But you're good! But so awful! It's great! See? Secretly, deep, deep down, you're a sadist, twisting the knife in until I feel worse and worse. Oh Christ, we're all so awful."

Then she stopped. And stared at the wine bottle. She stared at it a good long time.

"Fuck," she said finally.

Chase gently returned the paperback to the table. "We're talking about the kind of guy told his children there was no Santa. My sister was eight, I was five. Because he didn't want us to believe in irrational things. He told me to go to prostitutes when I was fifteen to deal with my 'normal biological urges' because there was no logic in getting involved with real girls. He reasoned that the time they expect me to spend just trying to bed them would be lethal to my becoming a true scholar. He refused to recite the Pledge of Allegiance. I won't even talk about our arguments over 9/11."

"Jesus, Chase! Where did you *come* from?"

"What do you mean?"

"You are the most amazing person I've ever met."

Chase just looked at her. Intently. "Let's go again."

They did.

He never did speak to her about the writings in the drawer, and they never said anything more about how they grew up. Because things had already started to twist around by then, although they didn't know it. The biting was only the beginning. There was more that night. And more after that.

6

She asked him to slap her.

At first, he thought she was joking.

It was two weeks later. The heatwave was worse, and the city was deserted. They were in bed. They had already made love twice that night. "I want to know what it feels like," she said. "So unleash the beast within."

He laughed. "Do I have a beast within?"

"Everyone has a beast within. But *especially* you." She yanked his arm, placing his palm roughly against her left cheek. "Right here," she said. He realized she was serious.

He had no idea what to say. He had never had anyone make that request before. He had never been with a woman who would even consider such a thing.

"I've never done anything like that before," he said. He was going to add "and I never would" but then he realized – if she were serious – that he would be casting a judgment on her. Rejecting her candor. Was that the correct response? He weighed that. No, he decided, it wasn't. No more than laughing at the sound a lover makes in the throes of lovemaking or pushing them away for trying to kiss you. There were rules about those things. So, he amended what he said. "I haven't explored that."

She looked at him. Her lashes were so long. She blinked twice, then her face twisted into a mocking leer, almost masculine, and she shoved him. Hard. With both hands.

"You're scared, Manhattan Chase!" she said. "You're a coward!"

Then he knew she was serious. She wanted him to strike her. He didn't. Not then. Not the next time. Not the next time, nor the time after that. She asked two more times.

And then he did.

7

He was on top of her. She had her fingers dug into his shoulders. Too hard. "Come on, come on, come on!" she said. He tried to pull her fingers off him, but she wouldn't let him.

Then she said, "Do it! Do it now!"

She dug her fingers deeper into flesh until the skin broke.

It instantly yanked him out of the moment, but she drew him back, closer, and dug her fingers in again, deeper.

He was ready to stop, and she saw he was ready to stop. So she struck him hard across the face. She gasped at the change in his expression, then she slapped him again.

He slapped her across the face.

Punches, he knew from the schoolyard, almost never connect the way they're supposed to. Slaps are no different. But this one hit perfectly, the contours of his hand against her cheek, the bones against the fleshy part of his palm. He had used far more force than he had ever intended. Had he intended to use any force at all?

The look of shock on her face froze time. Her eyes were wide and she gasped. She was staring at him with wonder and amazement. Then it was replaced by something else. "Oh!" she said. Then determination to win the steeplechase. She gripped his body and forced him against her.

"Come on!" she said. Her eyes were alight as he had never seen before. "Come on, do that again."

He did. She cried out in pleasure.

8

"It's wrong," he said.

"Says who?"

"Says any metric of civilized behavior."

This was later. A fight. A real fight, the ones that were becoming more frequent. Sometimes he wondered why the neighbors didn't complain.

It was late afternoon, almost Christmas. A hellacious snowstorm was beating at the single-pane windows and if they hadn't been fighting they'd have been freezing.

"You just don't like what it says about *you*!" she said.

"That's ridiculous."

"It's true!" She laughed.

"Trite."

She went over and straddled him. "Nice boys don't hurt girls for that," she said. "Nice boys are reasoned; nice boys are sensitive; nice boys give back. So maybe nice boys don't expand their horizons."

He could tell she was excited by what she was saying.

"I'm nobody's victim," she said. "So you don't have to worry on that score."

That night he went too far. They hadn't even started out with intentions of having sex – or, at least, not that kind of sex. But one thing led to another and he just wanted her – in any way he could have her. He wanted to own her and consume her.

She looked up at him with hooded eyes afterwards. "You see? You're not who you think you are."

She accidentally left open an email on her laptop the next day. He read it. It appeared to be from her father. He had deposited money into her account, and some for her brother. This would be the brother Adolphe, but in the letter his name appears to be Robby. The signature line said he was an investment advisor at Dreyer's Financial.

Dreyer? Pronounced "Dry-er." As in washer and. Like what you might need a repairman for.

9

He read up on it, because that's what Chase knew to do. He wanted to reason out sexual psychosis. Yet nothing he read described them – or him. Eventually he snapped the books shut and clicked the computer screen off.

There were times now, he imagined, that she looked at him with fear. Not when they were having sex, not when they were naked or intimate, but when they were doing the most mundane things. When she was making a salad. When she was taking apart her phone to fix the screen. Once in a supermarket.

Was he who he had always imagined himself to be?

For the first time, he began to doubt.

10

Later, and many times over, he would think about how we always know. Somehow we always do. Even though it's the farthest thing from our mind.

It was a beautiful late spring Sunday morning and sun bathed the little Earl's Court flat. They made love "the nice way" as they called it – and still, more often than not, they did make love "the nice way" – amongst the tangled floral bedsheets they'd bought on sale at Tesco. "Oh my God, how can this be so good?" she kept saying as she rode on top of him. The sun streaming in the bedroom window haloed her hair, now almost fully grown out to a chestnut brown mane with purple tips, as yet unbrushed for the day. Her bare shoulders were warm to the touch, the small of her back moist with beads of perspiration. "My God, how can this be so good?"

While she showered, he threw on his old khakis, the ones with the paint stain, and his University of Virginia T-shirt. He shouted to her that he would get them something nice.

He went down to the corner store for coffee beans and some of those pastries the store sold from underneath the plastic dome on the countertop. He lingered a moment to watch the flatscreen TV above the cashier's head – reports of the U.S. President's latest atrocities and the battle within the British Parliament over terminating unemployment payments to union workers. He decided to buy a newspaper but took an unusually long time choosing which one.

When he got back, the bathroom was still steaming and the whole flat smelled of soap and shampoo and conditioner. But all of her clothes and things were gone. There was a note scrawled on the back of the receipt from last night's kebab order. "I love you so much." He sat on the edge of the sofa and let the plastic bag of coffee beans and pastry fall to the floor.

He would eat the pastries four days later, when they were stale. He realized he hadn't eaten anything since the night they made love, Saturday, when they had ordered the kebab.

He had known. Somehow. When he had touched the small of her back, he had had a glimmer of foreboding that he would never touch her there again. He knew she was going to leave him and this would be the last time. Their monumentally historic and passionate romance.

Somehow, he thought, we always know.

20. *Dangerous Weapons*

1

The marbled meeting room was silent in anticipation. The twelve Reasoners and Brueler were waiting.

Water and morning coffee had been laid out on four trays spaced down the length of the table, so for a while there had been the cracking of bottles being opened and the clink of coffee spoons. Then nothing but the distant thrum of traffic and loud voices outside and the whirr of helicopters somewhere overhead, the natural morning sounds of a city under siege. Reasoners checked the time on watches and there were discreet glimpses at cellphones.

Sister Sheena was twenty minutes late and counting.

At twenty-two minutes, Brueler made his second call. "Any news?" Before the party on the other end could answer, however, the double doors in the center of the room smashed open.

Commander Holden, back in full fatigues, stood in the doorway. "The visiting delegation, Director Brueler," he announced, and stepped aside.

Three massive men wearing Chicago Bears jerseys strode in, looking pretty much like bears themselves. Easily well over three hundred pounds apiece, they were mustached and goateed blocks of beef in wrap-around sunglasses and matching neckerchiefs. Two of them wore wallet chains locked to their belts.

These were followed by another three Jerseys, in this case a mix of Steelers and Buffalo Bills. These heavyweights were focused entirely on the ceiling, looking for God knows what. Maybe they were just awed by all the marble.

In the middle of this phalanx strode a tiny figure easy to miss if you weren't looking for her. Nia Kasha Blundt, as the FBI had identified her in the early days, aka Sister Sheena. Her security detail positively dwarfed her.

Chase would have bet the farm that she would appear in her usual cammo pants and SURVIVE T-shirt, but she took them all by surprise – which, he guessed, was the point. She had decided to forgo her revolutionary's uniform for couture black form-fitting slacks and a white silk blouse. The man's steel Rolex watch shone. She wore designer boots with a stiletto heel and carried a patent leather briefcase. Her over-sized sunglasses gleamed.

Half the men at the board table stood, including Brueler, who put out his hand. "Sheena," he said, as if it were a title and not a name – like "Prime Minister" or "Archbishop."

She ignored him, pulled out the chair clearly meant for her, and sat down. "Let's get into this." She slid the briefcase down to her feet, but not before Chase caught a glimpse of the word written in gold across its clasp. "EAT."

Brueler started to introduce everyone at the table. She cut him off. "I know who everyone is."

Brueler offered her a juice or water.

She shook her head. "A vanilla bean latte laced with almond milk and cinnamon."

There was an awkward silence. With no one else to turn to, Brueler offered an apologetic glance at Commander Holden. Holden nodded, as if the Starbucks order were part of a West Point education. He strode out of the room, presumably to rummage up a vanilla bean latte laced with almond milk and cinnamon.

Brueler gestured to the musclemen who had escorted Sheena in. "As you know, there's no need for personal security in this building."

"Yeah," she said. "But in light of the circumstances, they go where I go."

Kirsten Pappason leaned forward, clearly ready to take the first shot. "May I ask what those circumstances are?"

Sheena turned those giant sunglasses (like a wasp, Chase thought) toward the end of the table and Pappason. "Things have changed since we originally agreed to empower this body and entertain the concept of reconciliation with you."

"They certainly have," said Pappason. "You people started killing again the other night."

Sister Sheena shrugged. "The results of that change are fluid and random. Chaos is the child of dissent. Everyone here knows what I'm talking about."

Except, absolutely no one at the table had any idea what the hell she was talking about. Ambassador Macomb, reading all the other blank faces, took the initiative. "Perhaps you could offer us insight as to how you believe circumstances have altered."

Sister Sheena now pivoted her focus with almost machine-like precision onto Macomb. "There are several issues. For starters, we came into information that seems to indicate that you people are already operating in bad faith."

"That's pretty quick work," said Vin Jansert. "We only just got here."

Another machine-like head pivot as Sister Sheena turned on Vin. "We have information that one or more Reasoners are involved in a plot against the physical safety of the Changer leaders. Specifically, Jeff and me."

Jeff. In everything Chase had reviewed about Sheena, she had only ever referred to her once-enemy/then-competitor/now-ally as "Beavenstock" or "our friend from Wheeling." Now it was "Jeff." The Changers, Chase thought, were tightening up their act.

Ambassador Macomb spoke. "You're saying there's some sort of traitor to the agreement amongst us who is not working in the best interests of all concerned. That's quite an accusation."

Sheena didn't flinch one millimeter. "Accusations are for something that can't be proven. This can be proven."

"So who is the bad guy?" asked Agniew.

Sheena waved him off. "I don't have to play by your rules. To get into the battle of proof and refutation is to accept old standards. The whole point of the revolution is that we're not going to put up with that shit anymore."

It's word salad, Chase thought. Nothing more. But she was certainly good at it.

Agniew persisted. "So is this why you decided to resume your killing on the Capitol steps on Friday?"

Sister Sheena leaned in, happy to be engaged in battle. "Brother, hear me. I'm not responsible for the killing or death of anyone. Ever. But I can advise you that as long as your hollow dead man's system continues to try to destroy us and the will of the people, other true patriots and self-respecting Americans will take whatever steps are necessary to remind you of the power of the people."

Chase studied his fellow Reasoners. No one seemed to know where the meeting they thought they were going to have had gone, but this sure as hell wasn't it.

Sheena reached down for her case and removed a sheet of paper. "After much consideration, we've decided to continue to honor our agreement with you Reasoners despite your two-faced treachery. But you are going to have to make certain concessions." She handed the paper over to Brueler.

He studied it in confusion. "I don't understand."

"These are our terms."

"To do what?"

"To guarantee your safety."

Brueler read out loud. "The Chairman of Chase Manhattan Bank, the CEO of Boeing, the Director of Anthem Blue Cross, the two chief directors of Facebook, Bloomberg, and Google?" He looked at the others, baffled.

"It's not a long list," said Sister Sheena. "Fair's fair."

"What do you want from these people?"

"We want you to surrender them to us as a bond."

"What kind of bond?"

"A security bond."

A stunned silence around the table. If jaws could truly drop, they would have.

Then, finally, laughter from the far end. It was Vin Jansert. Hydy Horvat gave him a dark look. He just laughed harder. Finally Ambassador Macomb leaned forward and asked Sheena, over the laughter, "Are you asking us – for want of a better word – to *deliver* these people to your custody?"

"No," said Sister Sheena. "We are telling you."

Vin's laughter slowly died. The Ambassador sat back. "And you would guarantee that they would not be harmed as long as certain conditions, whatever those are, would be met?" he asked.

"No, we couldn't guarantee that," said Sister Sheena.

More silence.

Sister Sheena tapped a perfectly manicured nail at the list, which was sitting on the table in front of Brueler like an unexploded bomb. "Your behavior has a price, and this is it. Just like the 24.99% interest on Visa cards you forced every working person in this country to pay. 'There's nothing we can do about it.' Isn't that what the bank told working people whenever they tried to get that 24.99% interest rate lowered? There's nothing we can do? Which leads me to this."

She reached down to the briefcase again and this time came up with a stapled sheaf of twenty or so pages of copy paper with single-spaced typing on each sheet. She handed it over to Brueler. "I've decided to bring you into the loop on this. Jeff and his miners are hesitant on my sharing this, but I think it's valuable for you to know the direction we're taking."

Chase noted the choice in the derisive term. "Miners." She was talking about Beavenstock's people, the smarter ones who helped make the decisions and actually ran things. Some people had lately taken to call them miners, to distinguish them from run-of-the-mill Changers.

Brueler read the title of the document. "*American Constitution Reform?*"

She nodded. "It will serve as the foundation document for the new American constitution."

Brueler flicked through a few pages and read with surprise. "'Dissolution of the Supreme Court'?"

"No more bought-and-paid-for justice courtesy of Harvard Yard," Sheena said. "In fact, no more Harvard Yard. We're going to plow that right under."

Brueler read on. "'The power of the judiciary shall rest in the executive.'"

"Excluding state courts."

"'Excluding state courts'," Brueler nodded, reading forward. "And you're proposing this – "

"Not proposing. Presenting."

"– as a new American constitution?"

She put her fingers together. Those nails gleamed. "We didn't claw down the system so we could put things back the way they were. That toilet paper in the Archives building is just a boot on every neck that isn't white, rich, and privileged. Well, those days are obsolete now."

"You can't just take away the American Constitution!" Pappason erupted.

"Actually, we don't have to," said Sheena. "We have it. It's in a building we control. It's on our side."

Brueler leaned forward. "What I mean is, you seem to be proposing – "

"Bullshit."

Everyone stopped. Chase hadn't realized he was going to say the word until he'd already said it. Now all eyes were on him, especially Sheena's. Her mouth seemed to harden into granite.

"Bullshit what?" she asked.

"Bullshit is what you're proposing," he said. "Forgive me, we haven't been properly introduced. I'm Professor Chase – "

"I know who you are."

Chase gestured to her papers. "This is smoke and mirrors. There's a traitor amongst us, therefore you've broken the Compromise you people signed, so in exchange give us some human hostages and oh, here's a new rewritten American Constitution. You, more than anyone, know for a fact that we would never round up the top CEOs of American industry and hand them over to you. So you can what? Execute them along with the three hundred members of Congress you already have locked up? You know no one would agree to that. So what's your real agenda?"

For the first time, Sheena smiled. But it was an utterly mirthless smile. A dark, crooked, mischievous smile. "So," she said, "this is the voice of the Reasoners being reasonable. Funny, to me it sounds like the voice of the same old power elites to me. Sorry to tell you, brother Chase, but the days of me bending over at your lash are over. I speak with the voice of millions now. I speak with – "

"Fear."

Sister Sheena stopped.

Chase never felt more sure of himself. He pushed on. "The question *is*, what are you frightened of?"

Sister Sheena reached for her bag and got up. "I think we're done here."

Brueler was so startled that he blurted, "Miss Blundt!" before he knew it was out of his mouth.

She turned on him like a whip. "That's my credit card name, Angry Man!"

"Your *what?*" asked Brueler.

"My bondage name. Do I look like I'm in bondage now?"

Chase said, "Sister Sheena is leaving, Director Brueler, because it never was her goal make today's meeting productive, or even about anything. I don't know why but I assume we'll soon find out."

She whipped off the sunglasses. Her eyes were on fire. "Oh, you got that right! I don't need these conversations to be productive! In fact, I don't need these conversations at all. Not anymore."

"So something significant *has* changed since you signed the Reasoner Compromise?" Ambassador Macomb asked.

"You can be sure of that, brother," she said, addressing Chase even though the Ambassador had asked the question.

"I wouldn't put faith in me being your brother," Chase said.

"And I wouldn't put faith in everything I watch online at midnight."

It was the first punch she landed, but only the two of them knew it. He hesitated just a second, then pushed back that much harder. "It would be helpful if you told us what you really came here to talk about."

She took a good long time studying Chase, making sure to remember every detail of his face. Then the sunglasses went back on. "The former *United* States of America had over four thousand nuclear weapons. Over two thousand of those are in the United States itself. For these talks to continue as you want them to continue, you have to be sure that of all four thousand most likely, and two thousand most *definitely,* not one – *not one* – has fallen into the hands of the people you fear most, meaning the maniacs currently jumping up and down on the steps of United States Capitol. I can tell you right now: You can't be sure."

With that, she left the room, all six of her security team moving in step with her.

Commander Holden arrived with the vanilla bean coffee three minutes later. He discovered a room of Reasoners just as silent as when the morning had begun. And most of them were staring at Chase.

21. *The Reverend*

1

He was back at the window with the binoculars. He was looking to see – the ghost? The hallucination? The fantasy? Her, obviously. But there was something else, more complicated, which he didn't want to admit to himself. It wasn't just her. He needed to see *them*.

They beckoned him. Part of it was their proximity. At the moment, these people were the objects of the world's fascination and fear, and yet tonight here they were, live, streaming past Chase's binoculars, only a half-mile away but close enough in the lens that he felt he could touch them: a big fat man in a head-to-toe motorcycle outfit that was several sizes too small for him waving a handgun and shouting to who?; an older couple helping one another along the sidewalk, he with a plastic scythe in his hand and she with what appeared to be a bloody bedsheet in hers; a screaming woman with very frizzy bright orange hair, tied up on her head with elastic ribbons; two teenagers kissing under streetlight, lovely but for the matching wolf hats.

The journalists who had embedded themselves with these people (in the early days, intrepid reporters loved the idea of chronicling the voices of American deplorables from within) all said the same thing: They seemed so normal. Normal, that is, until Beavenstock and his Jerseys plucked a biggie out of the pen – a recognizable House member, say, or a Senator – and walked them up to the big blade. Then it was as if an electric charge coursed through the crowd, shooting from the Capitol. At that moment a metamorphosis took place which turned every individual into a single mad beast. The journalists weren't the only ones to write about this; the Mall people wrote about the phenomenon too. Some pretty graphic tweets said it was better than sex.

Chase was moving to the left side of his window to see if he could get any sort of view beyond the National Gallery, when there was a knock on his door.

He paused. Waited to hear it again.

It would be Brueler. He had been watching Chase as the meeting broke up. If you could call it a meeting. More like a two-hour shout-fest which commenced almost the moment of Sister Sheena's exit, most of it directed at Chase's impertinence. Chase suspected the Director had some thoughts for him.

He returned the binoculars to the case, snapped it shut, and slid them into the desk drawer. He felt guilty and wasn't sure why. He checked the drawer a second time.

No peephole, so Chase just opened the door.

It wasn't Brueler. It was, in fact, the last person he expected.

2

"I need a drink!"

"Help yourself."

Chase watched as Reverend Sarah Campbell made straight for the mini-bar. "I tried to sleep. Normally, I'm an early sleeper, but sometimes you can just tell two seconds after you turn off the light that there's not a chance."

She knelt to peruse the options. He studied her. She was a pleasing-looking woman in her late fifties, with a soft but not quite chubby face, and a haircut and color most likely from a chain salon. The persona she wanted to project was Mom, and it worked for her. But just as clearly, she was much more than that. Witness how she had finessed some of the finest and most spoiled American minds into first an oath and then a prayer.

The Reverend chose not one but two minis of Johnny Walker

Red. "My mind has been spinning since that damned woman. But you, Chase – May I call you Chase?"

"Please."

"You were terrific, Chase. You saw right away what she was and you rattled the shit out of her." The Reverend poured her Johnny Walker into a water glass. "Oh, I swear in private, by the way."

"I noticed."

She plunked herself down on the short end of the sectional couch. Some of her drink spilled onto her dark stretchy pants. She just brushed it off with her hands. "It shocks some people. Occupational hazard."

"What is she?" Chase asked. "You said I saw right away what she was. I'm not sure that's true."

"Oh, you know."

"I'm not sure I do. And likely a minister is a far better judge of character than a history professor."

She shrugged. "Well, I guess I'm assessing her based on the wisdom I've gained on my faith journey or I could be assessing her based on the life I left behind."

"I don't understand."

"Well, I wasn't always of the cloth, you know."

"I didn't."

"You know what I used to be? Guess."

Chase, who hated when people said "guess," shrugged. "Educator?"

The Reverend shook her head. "A whore. Surprised?"

"Completely."

She laughed. It was almost a cackle. Somewhere back there, this woman had smoked a lot of cigarettes. "I don't mean a physical whore. That would be more honorable. No, I was the CEO of one of the most successful hedge funds on Wall Street. Last thing you'd expect, right? But it's true. And I knew things. I was savvy. Also lost. And my soul was dead. You look shocked, Professor."

"A little."

"It's not uncommon. Many, many members of the clergy found their calling after mid-life. And often after a first half-life of serious moral turpitude."

Chase eased into the chair by the table. "So what does the hedge fund savvy side of your character say about Sister Sheena?"

"That she was on a fishing trip."

"What kind of fishing trip?"

"The kind where you use the bait of bullshit. You were right about that. All that idiocy about a traitor within the Reasoners ranks. Then that hostage list. Then, best of all!" The Reverend almost hooted with laughter. "Her constitution! I tried to go over it when I got back to my room, but I can't make head nor tail of it. You're a constitutional expert, Chase. You tell me."

Chase too had reviewed Sheena's "new" American constitution upon returning to his room. It turned out to be nothing more than nineteen pages of fury; an angry list of complaints about a world run by elites and sexist and racist avaricious white imperialists determined to keep society divided between the "haves" and "have-nots," all in the name of freedom and free markets. Then the document abruptly changed course and set out rules for a restructured society. The plan was a labyrinth of panels and bureaus which would guarantee that America was managed according to an utterly fair and proscribed grid assuming equality of outcome for all genders, races, ages, and religions. All of that would be overseen by a self-appointed leader who ticked at least three of the six "equality" boxes and could, or would, serve for life if so desired, based on a succession of six-year terms.

The first problem Chase had with this Mad Hatter document was where it fit in with the people he watched through his binoculars every day. Was this what *they* wanted? Sure, throw the bums out, but were they all on for a full tear-down of the system itself? Did those people – most of whom talked about "taking the country back" and chanted "USA, USA, USA" as heads literally rolled – believe that the way to get there was a terrifyingly narrow dictatorship dedicated to panels determining equal outcomes for all? Because that's all Sister Sheena's new American constitution was about, once you got past fomenting violent overthrow. Chase was pretty sure this wasn't what the folks on the Mall wanted at all.

"No," he said finally. "It's an absurd document."

The Reverend slapped her knee with glee. "Okay then!" she said. "So, I'm not so crazy! Which brings us to the biggie. I think she came in with a list of demands that she knew was absurd because she wanted to see our reaction. And our reaction would tell her what she really wanted to know."

"Which is?"

"What exactly the story is in Russell, Kansas."

That gave Chase pause. Yes, he thought. Yes, indeed. His respect for the Reverend went up even further.

She gestured with her glass. "Her behavior only makes sense if the following is true: We don't know the real story of Russell, Kansas, *but nor do they.*"

Chase took this in.

The Reverend continued. "Obviously, if we showed the slightest intention of even discussing her absurd demands, she would know that we're a lot more scared of the Changers than we used to be, and what would cause that? WMDs would be a damn good cause, I'd think. But if we laughed in her face – which is pretty much what you did, Chase – then she'd know that we were pretty confident *they* weren't the ones with possession of any silo anywhere, Kansas or anyplace else."

Chase processed what she was saying. "But according to Miles Mallickey, *someone* has control of that facility."

"But who? That man looks scared shitless. He definitely couldn't say for a fact that it was U.S. military who repossessed the silo. I think he's just hoping."

They looked at one another. "So there's a third party here?" Chase asked. "Someone we don't know. And they're in control of whatever's in the ground in Russell, Kansas?"

The Reverend arched an eyebrow as if to say, "Well, shit, yeah." They sat in silence.

Suddenly the Reverend leapt off the couch. Angry, Agitated. "You know what, Chase? I didn't sign up for this. Did you? I signed up to be wise and nod my head. I sure didn't sign up to manage anything, and certainly not nuclear bloody weapons. I don't know anything about nuclear weapons!" She turned on him. "Do you?"

Chase was looking at all the pieces as if they were floating in front of him, like some kind of holographic jigsaw puzzle. Sherlock, he thought. Finally, he said, slowly, "What identifies a Changer?"

"What do you mean?"

"How can you tell a Changer is a Changer? Physically."

The Reverend shrugged. "The way they look. The jerseys, I guess. The pickup trucks. The tools. The way they behave."

"So, imagine that at some point a group of people took over a silo in Kansas who everyone *assumed* were Changers. Certainly Miles Mallickey and the GOR thought they were Changers. But if your theory is correct, Sister Sheena and Beavenstock *know* they aren't Changers. They just look like them. And that's what really scares them."

The Reverend took that in. "You think a different set of yokels got their hands on WMDs?"

"It's possible."

"How dangerous would that be?"

"I have absolutely no idea."

"What I mean," said the Reverend, "is how hard would it be for a regular person – I mean someone like me – to set off one of those things? What would I have to do?"

"I don't know," Chase said. "But we do know someone who might know."

She watched as he reached for the white internal telephone.

3

Tay Hamer, Nobel Laureate and expert in the principles of the variables of radioactive pressure, looked at them. "So *what* is the question?"

The Reverend, who had evidently refreshened her drink in the time it had taken Chase to go down the hall, rouse his Nobel Laureate neighbor and bring him back, answered before Chase could. "If people – regular people – got their hands on some sort of a nuclear weapon, what could they do?"

"Ahh," said Hamer. He was making a careful study of the snack section of Chase's mini-bar. He gingerly picked out a Snickers bar. "So clearly you don't believe much of what the young woman had to say."

Chase and the Reverend glanced at one another. "How do you figure that?"

Hamer shrugged. "Because the three of us are talking. If either of you truly believed in the phantom traitor Reasoner, you wouldn't take the risk."

He had a point.

Hamer put back the Snickers bar and plucked out a small package of chocolate-covered peanuts instead. "So, you assume her demands were simply a feint, an attempt to get information. Perhaps to see if we're more frightened of them than they are of us."

The Reverend sat forward on the sofa. "It's the only thing that makes sense." Chase was watching Hamer, who in his snooping had come upon the binoculars. He was carefully turning the leather case over in his hands. He glanced back at Chase. "Yours?"

"On loan."

"May I?"

"Of course."

Hamer removed the binoculars from their case and went to the window. As he unwound the strap, he said, "As to your question, a warhead itself is not the issue. Launching it is. These things are not just sitting around ready to be knocked off the edge of a cliff with a fuse poking out."

"Well, these Changers have proven themselves pretty handy so far," the Reverend said.

Hamer nodded. "Yes, but hooking up cable TV and building scaffolding is not the same as cracking launch codes and exercising the protocols to direct an inter-continental ballistic missile."

Watching Hamer struggle to focus the binoculars, Chase found himself bristling. Then he felt embarrassed. Was he jealous of Hamer looking out his window? At his crowd? That would be ridiculous.

Hamer glanced back from the window. "You think the Changers are as confused and unsure about the Kansas story as Mr. Mallickey."

Chase nodded. "I think the real question is, are the country's WMDs being adequately protected while we work through this nightmare? Until we know the answer to that question, how can there be any kind of negotiation on either side?"

"He's right," the Reverend said. "Everyone's hands are tied."

"You don't believe Mallickey's assurances that the U.S. military has control?" Hamer asked.

"I'd love to," said Chase. "But it's clear he doesn't know anything for sure, which is why he was so desperate that we reach out to Van DeVere. I believe they're terrified that in addition to cutting the heads off public officials there's — what's the phrase? — a broken arrow out there. And where's there's one, there may be more."

"The thought is provoking, isn't it?" asked Hamer.

"Which thought?"

"That someone other than the U.S. military are coming across abandoned silos and taking control of them." The older man smiled weakly. "Like children coming across their father's gun left out loaded on the kitchen table."

The Reverend erupted. "Frightening? It's terrifying! And you know why? Because so far these Changers have been the dog who caught every fire truck they've ever chased. Every time." The two men looked at her with almost identical quizzical expressions. She laughed. "Well, that's how they've always seemed to *me*! When they took over half of the federal government and half of Washington, my guess is no one was more surprised than them. And amazed at just how easy it was. They caught a *huge* fire truck, but they didn't know what to do with it. I think that's why they agreed to the Reasoner Compromise in the first place. They're at least smart enough to know – or this Beavenstock is – that they were going to need some sort of structure and they were going to need help, even if it meant their revolution wound up a 50-50 compromise at best."

"You can do a lot with 50-50 revolutions," Hamer said. "The Roman Empire was built on it." He carefully returned the binoculars to their case. "To answer your original question, however, it strikes me as foolish for us to assume that all Changers are cut from the same cloth."

"Meaning?" Chase asked.

Hamer shrugged. "I'm sure they have engineers. I'm sure they have scientists. Maybe even nuclear scientists. I can tell you from bitter experience, scientific knowledge does not always go hand in hand with sociological wisdom. There are brain surgeons who believe in witches, microbiologists who believe that Communism will win the day, and chemical engineers who believe Jesus will come down any day now in a magical helicopter." He offered a brief apologetic nod to the Reverend. "All due respect."

"I'm a spiritual rationalist," the Reverend said. "Not a believer in fairy tales."

"Your point being – " said Chase.

"Given enough time, and enough of a brain pool, anyone can set off a nuclear weapon."

"In other words … " the Reverend said.

"In other words," Hamer said, "with control of any weapon of mass destruction, the Changers or anyone else will have won complete control of the United States."

They were silent as they contemplated that prospect.

"There's only one person who can tell us what we have to know," Chase said.

"Who's that"

"The very man Miles Mallickey wanted us to call. And the very man we're expressly forbidden to contact."

"So what do we do?"

"We break the rules."

"Already?"

"Already," Chase said.

22. *The Van DeVere Plan*

1

For a man who usually presented himself as militarily tidy and immaculately turned out, Brueler seemed tousled and unkempt in wrinkled khakis and a plain T-shirt. His bare feet were jammed into leather slippers. His hair was disheveled. Most of all, his manner was peevish. Perhaps they had woken him up, even though it was still only 10:30 at night. Now, sitting in the armchair closest to the window, he looked at his three visitors and seemed to dare the Reverend. "Take me through this again."

She did.

Hamer, sunk deep in the other armchair beside Brueler, his fingers steepled across his chest, added nothing. He was staring at the ceiling, deep in thought. Studying the group from the swivel chair by the desk, Chase noticed that Hamer had unconsciously slipped his loafers off. He had holes in his socks.

When the Reverend finished her explanation, she seemed markedly more sober than she had in Chase's room.

Perhaps it was the setting. Brueler's suite gave off a tremendous sense of purpose. It was smaller than Chase's but it was crowded with all manner of books, maps, and charts. The room of a man who was studying for a test for which he refused to be unprepared.

"So we do need a face-to-face with Van DeVere," Chase said. "Obviously not the kind Congressman Mallickey wanted us to pursue, but we need to know both what Van DeVere can tell us about the safety of WMDs, as well as his intentions."

Brueler considered this a good long time. "Right," he said finally.

"Right." He ran both hands through his disheveled hair, looked like he was about to get up, but didn't. A big sigh. "First things first," he said. Very slowly. "You are aware that the Reasoner Compromise expressly forbids – "

"Yes!" Chase and the Reverend said at the same time.

"That doesn't deter you?"

"Of course it deters us," the Reverend said, "but the stakes are getting high here. We need a line of communication and we need it now."

As Brueler chewed on this, Chase got up and moved to study the view from Brueler's window. It faced north, and from here Washington looked strangely normal. "We were thinking," said Chase, "you might know someone."

"You mean someone who knows someone who can get to the General? Who knows how to keep their mouth shut?"

"Something like that," Chase said. He was looking out the window at a lineup that snaked out of the McDonalds at 13th street. Wolf-hatted jersey wearers waited patiently with what looked like Washington locals.

"Well, I'm sorry to disappoint you," Brueler said. "If you want to kick FEMA's ass, or make the Federation of State, County, and Municipal Employees stop messing around with the retirement fund, I'm your man. But elite military commanders aren't in my circle. And even if I did know someone who knew someone who knew someone, what would I tell them? You want a back channel to set up a meeting? What does that mean? A phone call? Video? Skype? Zoom?"

Chase wandered over to the table upon which Brueler had spread maps of the region. Maps of Old Virginia? "No," he said, slightly distracted, studying the spread. Was Brueler some sort of amateur historian? "That won't work. Not from this building, anyway. Probably from nowhere."

"Why not this building?"

"Because it isn't electronically secure."

"How do you know that?"

"Sister Sheena told me."

Baffled looks.

Chase explained. "Last night, I decided to do a YouTube study of her. I watched a lot of news clips."

"Using the government service?"

Chase shook his head. "By its very nature the internal encrypted service is compromised. It's government. So I used Free-Fi."

"So how did Sheena tell you – "

"Directly. In front of everyone. 'I wouldn't put all my faith in what I watch online,' she said. She knew what I'd been doing the night before and what I was looking at."

There was silence.

"Okay, so that takes out cellular, Skype, video, Zoom," Brueler said. "Which necessitates a face-to-face. That's almost impossible, to begin with. For instance, where? He certainly can't come here. The only people who could look after his safety are his own troops, and that puts U.S. military personnel right inside the capital. And that …" He didn't need to go on.

The room was silent.

Finally, Tay Hamer spoke. "So we go to him."

"But we don't even know where he is," said Brueler.

Chase realized he had been staring at the solution for the past five minutes. "No," he said. "But we could tell him where to *be*." They all turned. Chase pointed to the map in front of him.

The other three rose and joined him at the desk. Chase reached for a pencil and drew a circle around the area of Mount Vernon, and below it to the west, the area of Fort Belvoir. "A military installation not ten miles west of Mount Vernon, down the Potomac but on the wrong side for the Changers, meaning the right side for us. No Changers in the whole region and it has deniability. Nothing like running into an old friend on safe territory. Who's to say it was even planned?"

They all studied the map. Finally, Brueler scratched the back of his ear. "It's possible."

"It has the promise of simplicity," Hamer agreed.

"But still," Brueler said, "we have no information that the General is in Virginia, or even on the East Coast."

"He has the United States military at his disposal," the Reverend said. "Surely he can catch a ride with someone."

"And if he can and does?" Brueler asked. "Who is going to meet him? The whole panel?"

There were awkward looks.

Finally, Brueler spoke. "Look, I have been appointed to administrate *for* you. I don't vote. But if I *were* to have a vote, I would say that such an expedition is not for the whole group. It's too dangerous. Keep it small. Keep it tight. With one spokesman."

"Professor Selby," Hamer said.

Chase looked up in surprise. Before he could say anything, the Reverend seconded the motion. "Why me?"

"Please," Hamer said impatiently.

Brueler agreed. "Yes, I think that's the right choice."

Chase felt some unnamed mantle had just been placed on his shoulders. He wasn't sure if he liked it, but he didn't *not* like it. He turned to Brueler. "How do we find out the status of Belvoir? Pointing at a map is one thing. Practicality is another."

"I probably can get that," said Brueler. "The big issue is security. Secrecy and security is going to be crucial for everyone."

"Definitely security," a fifth voice said.

They all turned. Ambassador Macomb was standing in the open doorway, immaculate in blazer and tie even at this hour. Behind him was a very worried-looking PSLO Tyler, lurking in the hall.

Macomb glanced back at Tyler. "Thank you, Tyler." Tyler retreated and closed the door behind him. The Ambassador stepped into the room. "You can't blame him. He merely asked if I was here for the meeting, and I said yes. Who would answer differently?"

"How long have you been standing there?" the Reverend asked.

"Only long enough to discern the four of you making fine plans.

I appreciate the making of fine plans. I came down here with the notion of making some fine plans myself. With the help of Director Brueler."

"About?"

The Ambassador sat in one of the armchairs and gracefully crossed his legs. "I'm deeply troubled by this Kansas business and what exactly the last known state of our triad is. Looking around this room, it appears I'm not the only one."

Chase sat. "We've decided to reach out to General Van DeVere directly. And, obviously, covertly."

The Ambassador didn't blink, but he did check a button on his jacket for a non-existent missing thread. "That is a very dangerous step."

"Yes," said Chase.

"Well, for what it's worth, I think you've come to right conclusion. Go to the heart of the matter, as it were. And how are we to make first contact with the General?"

"We're working on that problem right now," said Chase.

"For the price of admission, may I make a suggestion?"

Chase looked at the others, then nodded. "Please."

"Why not ask our own General about *the* General?"

"General Williamson?" the Reverend asked. "He said he's barely met Van DeVere. A casual professional acquaintance at best."

"I suspect if you press you'll find the General is being humble," the Ambassador said.

"What makes you think that?"

"Diplomatic ears. The General said a number of things about Van DeVere in our meeting the other day which sounded to me like he knew him considerably better than he wanted to let on. He knew the topic of his thesis – Madison – and his personal fascination with the Monroe Doctrine, that his wife's name is Hannah, that he married her during his first posting, and about his two children. What kind of casual professional acquaintances could say that much about you?"

The group looked at one another.

"Is it possible," the Ambassador asked, "that I bought my way into your little club?"

23. *Texting*

1

"You're assuming a lot," said General Williamson.

"Maybe," said Chase. "But if not you, who?"

General Williamson didn't look comfortable. He looked, if anything, cornered.

The General, Chase, and Brueler were in the small, private office Brueler had commandeered for himself in the Treasury building. The three of them were engaged in what the General had presumed was going to be some sort of a bull session after a day spent in stultifying meetings – in this case focusing on what was left of the Health and Human Service Department (three weeks ago a bunch of Changers, some of whom actually used to be social workers and RNs, simply took over the department at gunpoint). It certainly *felt* like a bull session. Brueler had his feet up on the desk. Both he and the General had a beer. Chase was looking out the window.

As soon as they started talking about Van DeVere, of course, it became clear this was no bull session. Anything but. Now they were down to brass tacks.

"Ambassador Macomb," said Williamson. "Is there anyone that man doesn't know?"

"Yes," said Brueler. "Apparently he doesn't know Van DeVere."

Williamson stifled a belch. "Bullshit. Macomb knows everyone."

Chase turned from the window. "Except we're not talking cocktail party acquaintanceship. Or even having sat in on the same meetings. We're talking about someone he trusts. That's what we need."

"And I've told you, all I've ever had with the man *were* cocktail party acquaintanceships and a few shared meetings," said Williamson.

"Yet you know about his thesis, his fascination with the Monroe Doctrine, when he got married, how many kids he has, and even his wife's name."

"Me and everyone else with access to Wikipedia."

The three men just looked at one another.

Chase sat on the edge of the couch. "We want to set up a meeting. All we need now is a private number. One that won't be intercepted. And assurance that the man himself will respond."

"And then what?"

"We set up a meeting to talk. Off the record."

"Mallickey's kind of talk? He's not going to respond to being told he's a traitor and will be stripped of his command. I don't know exactly what's going on, but he's not a traitor."

He does know him, Chase thought.

"The exact opposite," Chase said, without skipping a beat. "We want information and, if he tells us what I think he's going to tell us, probably we'd suggest he keep doing what he's doing. We just need to know."

Williamson gave him a cock-eyed look. "What do we need to know so badly?"

"If there's anything to the idea that there are WMD facilities out there that are unmanned, or manned but by the wrong people. How can we talk with the Changers – certainly Sheena – if we don't know?"

Chase could see that struck Williamson as logical.

Brueler clearly saw it too, because he quickly added, "Despite what Mallickey thinks, the Reasoners are in no position to tell the General what to do. So there's not going to be any of Mallickey's bullshit threats or grandstanding. As Chase said, it's just information gathering and verification.

Neither Brueler nor Chase said anything more. They let the silence be as awkward as it needed to be.

Finally, Williamson said, "I might know somebody who knows somebody who knows somebody."

"That's all we can ask," said Chase.

"But this has to stay in this room. Not the rest of the Reasoners. I don't want anyone else to know."

"Know what?" Chase asked.

2

The first message came in three days later. There was just the vaguest hint of light peeking through the curtains when Chase's cellphone vibrated. He reached over to the bedside table and checked it. The light hurt his eyes. He had to blink twice to focus.

A text message. A number he didn't recognize.

B here. It was Brueler.

Chase typed: **Okay.**

He's given me a number. Apparently direct.

Chased typed. **W came through?**

A moment. Then, finally: **Yes.**

A longer moment and then a number appeared. **202-555-0193.**

Chase stared at the number a good long time. Finally he typed: **This is the man himself?**

The answer: **This is the man himself.**

There were no more texts.

3

A half-hour later Chase was sitting on his couch. The blinds were open, revealing a pearl-grey sky over a perfectly placid Washington made of granite and brick and concrete. Like all cities in the morning, it looked dirty and deserted.

Chase was still in his robe. A freshly brewed cup of coffee sat steaming on the table. He kept staring at the phone in his hand.

202-555-0193.

I don't know what I'm doing, one side of his brain said. The other side said, I know exactly what I'm doing.

Nothing in Chase's life so far pointed to him understanding, appreciating, or belonging to the world with which he was about to engage. And if he pressed the SEND button, there would be no turning back.

The message he had written out on his phone said simply: **My name is C. Do you know who I am?**

He stared at the words awhile.

Finally, he pushed SEND.

He reached for the coffee. He'd made it with the Impressa machine they'd placed on top of the mini-fridge. It was still steaming hot. He blew on it and took a sip. It was delicious. Stronger than he'd expected, and he liked strong coffee.

Then he did what he swore to himself he wouldn't do. He got up and went to the window with the binoculars. Again.

He put them around his neck and waited a good while. Then he raised them to his eyes and began to focus on the Mall.

It was so early. There was nothing much to see but zipped-up tents and folks bundled into sleeping bags and wisps of smoke from fires which had burned themselves out from God knows what tribal madness. What else did he expect?

Her, of course. That's what he wanted to see. Even if it *was* a hallucination or a delusion.

Ping.

He put down the binoculars and returned to the coffee table. He picked up his phone.

Yes. Do you want to talk?

Chase took only a second to form his reply.

Yes. I want to talk.

He pressed SEND right away.

Chase hadn't felt so contented and at peace in years.

24. *Warren Calling*

1

For Warren, the gun changed everything.

At first it had felt strange. He couldn't even find a way to carry it. He tried it in his front pants pocket, but it kept digging into his thigh and he was terrified about shooting his dick off. Then he tried it in his back pocket, but it felt like it was going to fall out any second, and anyone could easily yank it away from him. He tried tucking it into the waist of his pants, but again the fear of dick blasting gripped him. Finally he settled on it tucked in at the small of his back. That felt good. Right. And if it went off, he was pretty sure that a bullet in one's ass wasn't fatal.

To his surprise, he almost instantly felt a new sense of power. More surprising, he imagined others felt it too. Moving through the crowds, passersby seemed to look at him differently, either because of the way he held himself or because of the way he considered them.

No one just assumed they had a right to knock his teeth out, and certainly no one attempted to anally rape him. These were huge improvements. A hot dog vendor even gave him a free hot dog, saying, "Don't worry about it," and two enormous guys who normally might have punched his head in gave him manly nods, as if he were one of them. So, was he? Even with the gun tucked in his belt, Warren wasn't sure.

Then came the three teenage punks.

It was Warren's fourth night on the Mall. He was standing at the perimeter of a crowd watching one of the bands performing at the

Lincoln Memorial. Bands were a big part of the fabric of life here. In fact, even while he was being ass-fucked by the two freaks who had attacked him after the train ride, Warren had been aware of incredibly loud and incredibly bad music coming from just beyond the Vietnam memorial. This turned to be not a real band at all but a bunch of punk musicians whose chief lyric seemed to consist of "Cunt! Cunt!" Still, you could hear some pretty good live acts on the Mall and that helped fill the lull between eruptions of extreme violence. On the steps of the Memorial that night, it was a heavy metal quintet who perhaps had never met one another before, and while heavy metal wasn't really Warren's thing, what else was there to do?

That's when the kid asked him for a cigarette.

He was just behind Warren, standing in the shadows cast by the trees along the reflecting pool walkway. "Got a dart?"

Warren turned back and saw a sniveling rake of a kid in a pink muscle shirt that said, "EAT THE RICH." He couldn't have been seventeen.

Warren said he didn't. The kid seemed to accept that and let Warren return his attention to the band. After a few minutes, though, the kid spoke again. This time he wondered if Warren wanted to see something. There were three chicks over there screwing one another. Right behind the benches.

This didn't interest Warren as much as it normally might, but the last thing he wanted to do was look like a fag. So Warren followed the kid.

In seconds, two more guys were behind them. Much bigger guys, although probably not a lot older than the kid in the pink muscle shirt.

They gave him one quick shove at the shoulders, and Warren stumbled into the gloom and the shadow of the trees. Another shove and he was down on one knee. They laughed. The kid in the pink shirt held out his hand. "Come on, man, give it to us." The biggest one began to undo his own belt.

Warren didn't know if the big guy was planning to flog him or fuck him, but he had been down this road before, literally, and he had no intention of finding out either way.

He reached into his back pocket for the small roll of bills the woman he had taken to thinking of as "Tempo" had given him, and on the way his hand brushed the butt of the thing hidden beneath his shirt.

The gun. He had forgotten about the gun.

In a matter of seconds, everything changed.

Suddenly the pink-shirted kid was down on the ground and the two big guys were backing up, their hands raised in innocent protest. "Hey man, come on, come on, we were just joking." Yeah, right. For his part, the pink-shirted kid seemed ready to shit his pants, and why not? Warren was hunched over him, the muzzle of the gun pressed to the stupid asshole's forehead.

Warren wasn't sure what he said. It was probably just a bunch of shit he'd heard in the movies: "Don't move or I'll blow your fucking head right off" or "You're one dead motherfucker" or "You better charge your phone, kid, because you're gonna be talking to Jesus soon."

All he really knew for sure was that the heavy metal music was screaming in his brain and the kid was shaking like a purse dog during a thunderstorm.

I could do this, Warren realized, pushing the gun so tight against the kid's temple that the skin puckered. I could really do this.

And he could. In more ways than one. After all, terrible things happened here on the Mall all the time, especially at night. Bodies were found every morning. So who would care about this asswipe? Or his two friends, if things came to that.

So why not? It would certainly make up for the teeth and the arm and the cornholing.

Then Warren thought about Bella. Not Bella coming to him and saying, "Oh, Warren, you're a good man, I know you'll do the right thing and let these pecker-fucks go," because Bella most times *didn't* think Warren was a good man and most likely would have said, "That's right, Warren, do the crazy dumb fuck thing *again*," but Bella on the couch with him and the dog. The three of them, on a nothing night. Maybe sharing a bag of salt and vinegar chips and doing what he liked best, which was watching *Star Trek* – original series, of course – and arguing through the whole episode. About nothing. Always. And the dog farting.

Which made Warren think about Captain Kirk. What would Kirk do in this situation? Warren was unsure about a lot of things in this world, but Captain Kirk vengefully ending the life of a stupid seventeen-year-old kid because he tried to take his wallet was one thing he knew for sure: Kirk would *not*. Kirk might start off raving out of his mind with anger and clenching his fists and pumping that vein in his temple, but in no time he'd pull his shit together and grimace and shove the kid away and say, "No! No!" and do the right thing. The kid would live.

Which is pretty much what Warren did, except that he kicked the kid in the shoulder as well, which twisted Warren's ankle painfully.

Pink Shirt and his buddies scrambled off like their asses were on fire and Warren watched them go. He straightened himself up, slid the gun back into the small of his back, and limped away from the Memorial and into the night, wondering just what the hell had happened to him. Was he truly changing? Was he becoming one of those guys who could handle everything? That might be good, because things were starting to feel strange on the Mall – stranger than normal, if such a thing were possible. But Warren had a sense that it might also be bad.

2

It had something to do with the Friday night killings. He had missed those by a day but he could still feel their energy. And the weird, confused aftermath.

Torturing civil servants and cutting their heads off, Warren imagined, required a frenzy so extreme that it was probably almost as good as sex. So, if you suddenly stopped it, you were inviting a shitload of sheer frustration. A bloodlust cocktease, if you wanted to look at it that way, and if you didn't get some relief soon, who knew what shit would go down?

But what *kind* of shit? That was the question.

Warren pondered this as he was getting yet another blowjob from the woman he thought of as "Tempo." His third of the day. He and Tempo were tucked in the doorway of one of the museums which backed onto the Mall.

Truth be told, Warren was getting sick of blowjobs. He had never imagined such a thing were possible, but there it was. And he was certainly sick of this woman. Yet, for all his newfound confidence and his new sense of self after threatening to kill the three teenagers, he still didn't feel strong enough to push her away or refuse to submit to her ministrations. Perhaps because Warren thought she was, in some way, the key to his new strength, and to turn her away would be to condemn himself once again to a future of high buggery and minor theft for as long as he was on the Mall.

Besides, how could he "get rid" of her? She always found him.

No matter where he slept or chose to spend his time during the day – and often that was sleeping on the monuments or under the trees on the south side of the Mall – she was able to hunt him down. And always, without discussion, she would drag him to a private or semi-private place and suck him off. That was becoming boring enough, but after the blowjobs came the true tedium when she talked about destiny. Destiny and Warren's new role in this world.

"Warren, I think we've all had our future written out for us, don't you?" She was firing up a cigarette almost immediately after spitting him out. She also picked a stray piece of tobacco off the end of her tongue. "Which means not just that we're not in charge of ourselves, but that we're not to blame for our actions. You hear what I'm talking about?"

Warren nodded his head, but in fact he had no idea what the hell she was talking about. And he didn't care. During most of these one-sided discussions, he chiefly thought about food. Lately his focus was the Hardee's Double Western Bacon Cheeseburger, which was two patties of beef with cheese, onion rings and special sauce, topped with extra onions if you wanted and why the fuck not? There was no Hardee's anywhere on the Mall, however, and Tempo had made it very clear that he was not to go more than one street north of Constitution or he would be entering "government territory," which she convinced him meant almost summary execution. "They see one of us try and cross back over the line, they'll take you out. That's it. And Warren, your destiny is not to be taken out."

Warren had decided not to test this assertion and just take her at her word. Confident as he was now that he was going about armed, he wasn't interested in engaging in a firefight with trained D.C. militiamen on the other side of the line. So, while he realized that all sorts of people streamed back "across the line" from somewhere beyond Constitution Avenue – many of them with McDonald's or Burger King or Dunkin Donuts in hand – he refused to even attempt the same. A Hardee's Double Western Bacon Cheeseburger was worth a lot, but it wasn't worth getting shot.

If he was able to get it up again, Tempo would suck Warren off one more time before she left him, usually with another meandering speech about destiny. Then she would disappear into the crowd. Today, however, was the first day it occurred to Warren that if he simply couldn't get it up again, chances are he wouldn't have to listen to more mindless shit about just how powerless he was over his own fate because it had all been decided for him, and that he was going to play a major role when it came to fulfilling the Master Plan, which Tempo said would soon be revealed.

She talked about the Master Plan as if Warren were as obsessed with it as she was ("I know you feel you must know, I know it consumes you to not know, yet you gotta believe when I say all will be revealed") but the truth was Warren didn't give a shit about the Master Plan. As Warren stood in that doorway, he was thinking about the kid in the pink shirt and why it had been *Star Trek* that had stopped him from pulling the trigger. The more he thought about it, the more he began to suspect it hadn't been *Star Trek* at all. Maybe it had been the image of sitting with Bella *watching Star Trek*, bathed in a cloud of dog farts.

What, he wondered, had been the big deal? Why had Bella lost her shit with him? They had had a pretty good – no, correct that – *perfect* life with one another. Even the dog. He just hadn't told her. Now he realized that what he really needed to do with his life – what his real destiny was – was to explain to Bella that he forgave her for all the shit she had foisted on him. Without that information, Warren imagined Bella was sitting at home in the living room, head in hand, crying her ass off and smoking too much, with her bitch of a mother yelling at her to stop being such a baby and just forget Warren, who was a useless shit to begin with.

That thought drove Warren crazy. The old lady would win if Warren didn't chime in and defend himself. But getting in touch with Bella and cleaning everything up was easier said than done.

The problem was that Warren's cellphone had been stolen almost the minute he arrived in Washington, and among the many things sold on the Mall, one of them wasn't cellphones. Tempo, it turned out, was no help. The one time he had brought up to her that he needed a new cellphone, she had assured him that she could get him one no problem. She'd bring it the next time they "met." That had yet to happen, and they had met (it seemed to Warren) innumerable times since then.

So there was a lot going through Warren's mind as Tempo sucked him off in the doorway of the American History Museum. Warren thought about how to get his message to Bella.

Then, as often happens when there is no solution, a solution presented itself.

It was one of the charred trucks lying on its side on the far side of the museum yard. There had been three of them, torched the first night Warren met Tempo, all United States Postal Service trucks. Warren remembered thinking that of all the U.S. government services he had a grudge with, the posties weren't one of them.

Now, looking across at the charred remains, he realized for the first time that they were *not* all USPS trucks. Only two were.

The one closest to the roadway had blue and white letters on its side. Some of the writing had been burned away, but you could still make out "E-L-L."

Warren wasn't a genius but even he could draw the conclusion that the first letter had likely been B and therefore the truck read "BELL." What, he wondered, was a Bell truck doing down here?

That's when he made the connection. The Bell truck must have been down here servicing the museum. Which meant, of course, that the museum had phones. Of some kind.

3

Having never been in a museum, Warren had no way of knowing that in fact every museum in the world still has a rank of pay telephones at the front or near the restrooms, and the unfortunate Bell truck had been parked where it had been due to a routine service call on those very phones. The driver was long gone or dead, the truck had certainly seen better days, but the rank of phones was likely still there.

Another thing Warren had never considered was whether the museum itself was open.

To his amazement, however, when he went up the stairs the next morning, the front doors opened easily. Then, when he went through the second doors, he discovered something else entirely unanticipated.

The lobby of the museum was completely deserted but clean. No litter, no tents, no dead bodies. It was also stiflingly hot – someone had clearly turned off the air conditioning weeks ago, and massive chain gates had closed off all access to the exhibits – but the marble atrium was open to one and all, including Warren.

That's what he thought, anyway. Then the three men stepped out of the gloom and pointed the AK-47 semi-automatics at him. "What the fuck do *you* want?" one of them asked. Their Patriots jerseys identified them as high-level Changer security. Elite.

"A phone," Warren blurted out.

"A *what?*"

"A phone."

There was a look between the three men. Then an imperceptible nod.

"Okay," said the head guy, gesturing with a toss of his head. "Over there. By the bathrooms."

"You guys living in here or guarding?" Warren asked, edging toward the bathrooms and making sure to never turn his back on them.

"What the fuck do you think?" asked the head guy. Pretty testy, actually.

"I just didn't know anyone was actually guarding the museums," Warren said. "I mean, everything else seems kind of up for grabs, so I figured – "

"Fonzie's *jacket* is in here," said the head guy.

That made sense to Warren. He nodded obsequiously to the guards and then turned the corner, only to be confronted by a row of a dozen telephones. Who knew?

Even more amazing: When he picked up the first receiver, he heard a dial tone. He checked his pockets for coins.

"They're free," a voice said.

Warren turned. The head guy was right behind him. His gun was down, at least.

"What do you mean?" Warren asked.

"All pay phones are free now," the guy said. "The calls don't always last long as you want, and sometimes they just drop, but they're free."

"So I just – ?"

"Yeah."

There was a moment, then Warren turned and punched in the only number he had ever remembered in his life. Bella's.

To his amazement, she answered. With great suspicion in her voice. She was probably looking at the area code and figuring it was a collector. "Who is this?" she asked.

"Me," said Warren.

"Warren???" she shouted. "Are you fucking *shitting* me??!"

Even the guard heard that. Apparently its sheer authenticity satisfied him, so he went back and joined his buddies, giving Warren some clearly needed domestic privacy.

Warren leaned into the wall and held the phone close to his mouth. "I have to tell you where I am."

"Where you are? I can't believe you're fucking *alive*!" Then she shouted off to someone. Loud. "Mommm!! You won't believe who I'm talking to! You won't believe it! You won't believe who's *alive!*"

"Listen," said Warren, his mouth almost touching the wall, "I don't know how long I have to talk or if this is a private line or anything – "

"*Private* line? What the hell are you talking about?"

"I just want to tell you I'm in Washington and I'm okay and I'm coming home – "

"Washington??" Suddenly the 'I'm talking to Warren the asshole' tone in her voice switched to 'I am now *worried* about Warren the asshole.' "What are you talking about? Jesus Christ! Tell me you're joking. Have you seen the TV? Do you know what's going on out there?"

"Of course I know what's going on," he said. "I'm right fucking here!"

"They started cutting off heads again!"

"A few nights ago, yeah," said Warren.

"They're doing it now!"

"No, they're not," said Warren. "I know because I'm maybe four blocks away. But they will soon. I don't know that for sure, but it's just a feeling. Things are getting weirder here. Look, I just wanted to let you know I'm coming home soon."

"Soon? You need to come home *now*."

"No, I can't do that."

"What do you mean?"

"I mean, I'm coming home soon but I can't come home *now*. They say there's something I have to do first."

"What could you possibly have to do in Washington? Who is they??" she shouted. "You don't know anyone in Washington!"

In fact, he did, and as Warren thought about Tempo while he had real-live Bella on the phone, he suddenly felt horrible regret and what was almost guilt about the blowjobs. The fact that he had enjoyed none of them – well, a few of them – eased some of the guilt, but it was still pretty bad.

"I'm just telling you I'm okay and I'll be home soon as I can."

"Why aren't you coming home now?"

"I told you. I just have to do this thing first."

"What thing?"

"I can't tell you."

"You *better* tell me!"

"I can't tell you because I don't know."

"How can't you know?"

"Because I don't."

"Warren – "

"Look, it's just something I have to do and then I come home."

Then that thing Bella had, that weird thing in her, kicked into place. "Warren," she said, her tone going all serious and real. "You need to come home now."

"I will. Like I said."

"No," she said. "Now."

"Absolutely."

"I don't like any of this."

"It's all good. I bet you'll be proud of me."

Now she was really panicked. "What the fuck are you talking about, proud of you??? I don't want to be proud of you! Get your ass home! You're too fucking stupid to be out there, Warren! Way too stupid!"

That really annoyed him. "Stupid, Bella? I was smart enough to get here, wasn't I? And even if I don't know what it is, I at least have a destiny, don't I?"

"What the hell did you just say?"

"I have a destiny."

"Warren? *Now.*"

"I will."

He could hear her starting to say more but that's when the phone cut out.

Warren stared at the wall awhile, waiting to hear more. But the line was seriously cold and dead. The guard had told him the phones sometimes cut out, and Warren guessed that's what this was. He hung up the receiver and looked at it awhile.

He had absolutely no idea why he had told Bella that he had something he had to do. That hadn't been what he had planned to tell her. Something just came over him. Warren had never felt more confused in his life.

Finally, he walked away from the phone. It never occurred to him to just call her back.

25. *The Crackle in the Air*

1

Chase had lied to Rin about his sister's death out of habit, not conscious duplicity. He said what he always said when pushed on the subject, and thereby repeated a tale as tidily complete as "he won the war for the slaves" or "he chopped down the cherry tree."

In fact, Bea had not died of cancer. She had cancer, yes, but she actually killed herself by leaping off the Bertram bridge just off Connecticut Interstate I-95, leaving her car running at the bridge's shoulder, the door open, the radio on, and the windshield wipers still wiping. It was an improbable end to the person Chase most treasured on the planet. And like Rin, he still searched for her in crowds, and often he imagined he saw her. Always the long cornsilk hair first, so startling when they were children. But he didn't actually imagine he *had* seen her, as he now did with Rin.

The thing was, while his sister's decision to end it all seemed spontaneous and unplanned, for the three or four days beforehand Chase had felt an inexplicable energy and crackle in the air. Something was wrong, but who knew what? And even though he had lived more than four hundred miles from her at the time of her death, he had still felt that crackle as if she had been standing beside him.

In the three days between the time he first communicated with General Van DeVere (*my name is C – do you know who I am?*) and the break of dawn when four Reasoners set out to cross the Francis Scott Key bridge in secret, Chase felt the same crackle.

Brueler had taken on the physical arrangements of the meeting, which would take place at Fort Belvoir. He brought Commander

Holden into the loop on security, as Chase had advised. So things were happening in the background even as the Reasoners settled into what felt like a routine. Yet still, Chase felt that crackle.

It wasn't in the work itself, though. That was anything but electric. The Reasoners now spent most mornings listening to people from the GOR expound on existing authorities, and the afternoon trying to decipher what they'd just heard. On Monday, for instance, some of Miles Mallickey's people took them through a grim casualty report, detailing who in government was no longer around and what key operations were no longer functioning and which were compromised but stumbling along.

These briefings amazed Chase. Three things in particular struck him:

1: that so many government functions *were* compromised and yet things still seemed to function relatively well (for instance, the IRS was almost entirely gutted and yet people still paid their taxes).

2: just how many government operations had ceased to exist and no one *noticed* (roads, highway regulations, as well as EPA) and –

3: that while a tremendous number of public servants were slaughtered on the altar of freedom, a lot more had simply run off, either in fear of being slaughtered for doing their job or for fear that they wouldn't be paid for doing said job.

This last particularly fascinated Calinescu, the Romanian. "Can I understand this?" he asked one of Mallickey's presenters. "Most of the collapse of the federal government agencies has been due to the fear of what the Changers *might* do, rather than what the Changers have actually *done*?"

A slack-mouthed millennial public servant in ponytail and power suit nodded her head. "Well, sure. Yeah." She pronounced 'yeah' as 'ya-ah.'

2

On the third day, Brueler ended the session – at least the part with an agenda – early. He said he had something to tell them all. Brueler and Chase had planned the departure from routine only that morning.

The other Reasoners sat and learned for the first time of the attempts to reach out to General Van DeVere. There was noticeable surprise around the table when Brueler announced that these efforts had finally proven successful.

Chase focused his attention primarily on General Williamson as Brueler lied and said that he, Brueler, had been the instigator of the contact and that he had kept the negotiations secret until he knew the odds of success.

Williamson managed to look as surprised as everyone else. You would never know that he had been the actual back channel to Van DeVere. Perhaps acting skill was an important element to a successful career in the military.

There were both a lot of questions and a lot of umbrage at the secretive initiative, but Chase was relieved that no one argued the value of the endeavor itself. Everyone had been becoming more aware of the potential threat from WMDs. Nor did they argue when Brueler seemed to randomly suggest that the Reverend, Chase, Hamer and Ambassador Macomb form the diplomatic party which would head out to Fort Belvoir. Until Agniew decided he smelled a rat.

"I suspect this list isn't random," he said. "But what is the point in arguing it?"

The Reasoners were, in other words, utterly reasonable.

Or, perhaps, Chase thought much later, they too had felt the crackle in the air.

3

On the morning of the 21st, folks on the Mall roused themselves, crawled out of their tents, peed on the lawn or trudged to the portable toilets, lit their camp stoves, began to make coffee, played music, and laughed.

Underneath it all was the thrum that said, "Something is going to happen."

And, as it turned out, it certainly was.

26. *The Bridge*

1

Commander Holden was in charge of the security for the trip, so everything was set to go like clockwork. By the second, not the minute.

The whole plan was that no one was to know there was a plan at all. Reasoners suddenly and without warning upping and traveling to another state for the day would be big news, even for a public more interested in the Capitol steps than the group of smarties brought in to powerthink the crisis. Reasoners were supposed to stay put, not go roaming off on secret missions.

Hence 5:30 a.m. And hence the three cars, not fourteen. Three black unmarked SUVs, the security car in the front and two Reasoners cars following, although Brueler confided to Chase that there were other perimeter vehicles which neither Chase nor any of the Reasoners would see. "But they're there. In case."

Brueler would not be with them. At first Chase had balked at this, but Brueler made an argument for his staying behind that Warren Potsburger would have understood instantly. "It's the *Star Trek* factor," Brueler said. "When Kirk and Spock go to talk to the Klingons, they go with Scotty and Bones and Chekhov. Stick with your main characters."

Tay Hamer, of all people, laughed out loud at this. The Reverend was unsure. But Brueler was an ex-union negotiator, so he knew about power at the table. "I have no authority to negotiate. You four do. It would be a waste of a ticket to the game."

This they understood. And agreed to.

In short order, of course, this eventually proved to be a fatal error.

2

At that early hour, the entire traveling party was gathered, blurry-eyed and perhaps still shower-damp, in the underground garage in the basement of the State building. The cars were running. Holden gave his security speech – more about the route from M Street and across the bridge than actual security – and then the car doors were opened. Everyone piled in.

Somehow, Tay Hamer and Chase had drawn the lucky card. They got the Escalade, the most luxurious vehicle. Holden told him it had once belonged to the Secretary of Health and Human Services.

Chase was ducking into the back seat behind the driver when he noticed Brueler whispering to a young aide who had just emerged from the security elevator and handed Brueler a sheet of paper. Brueler studied it, folded it, slipped it in his pocket, and caught Chase's eye. He stepped forward.

Chase moved away from the car and bent his head so Brueler could whisper in his ear. Chase could smell Brueler's aftershave and mouthwash. "We have a very strange communication from Mallickey," Brueler said. "About El Paso."

"Texas?"

"Colorado."

Chase turned his head and looked directly at Brueler, who looked pale. Chase had never heard of El Paso, Colorado.

"I don't know if Mallickey's playing games with us or not," Brueler said, "but this may need to be part of your conversation with Van DeVere."

"What's Mallickey saying?"

"Information he can't verify but which worries him. It has to do with the Cheyenne Mountain Defense Complex in El Paso."

"What information?"

"That the Government of Record should no longer consider the facility secure."

Chase felt himself grow cold. The awkward wording said a lot. Brueler went on. "The Cheyenne Mountain Complex is one of the largest land-based nuclear facilities within the continental United States."

"Did Mallickey say anything more?" Chase asked. "Or where he got this info?"

Brueler shook his head. "No, but it's a far cry from Mallickey protesting that everything is under control. The point is, we're probably not just talking about Russell, Kansas anymore."

"Or someone is peddling a story to confuse us all."

Brueler shrugged. "That also could be true."

"Okay," Chase said to Brueler. He got back into the Escalade.

3

They hadn't even pulled out of the garage before Tay Hamer, an actual Communist at one point in his life, further betrayed his childlike love of luxury.

"It's so fancy!" he exulted once they were cocooned in the back.

Chase smiled as the older man began pushing buttons and opening compartments. "Nuts!" he shouted. He had discovered a tin of gold-foil-wrapped cashews in the middle armrest. Then, puzzled, "I smell coffee."

Chase smelled it too. They searched for the source.

Finally, Hamer slid back a thin panel inset into the barrier between driver and passengers and discovered a brushed-steel carafe. It was warm to the touch. There were matching cups.

"Delightful," Hamer said. He poured a cup for each of them.

The car took an abrupt turn, and Hamer spilled some. "Shit!" He reached for a napkin.

Chase looked out the window. Their mini-motorcade was moving west along M street. The street was spookily deserted at this hour, and of course it was Saturday. It reminded him of those post-apocalyptic zombie movies; you half-expected to see a rampaging zombie force swarm out from the mouth of an underground parking garage, pointing and chasing after the cars.

Two streets up, identical white Yukons passed 25th street at the same time the mini-motorcade did, directly parallel. These, Chase assumed, were the perimeter vehicles Brueler had mentioned. Chase calculated that if they were entering Georgetown now, it would only be a matter of minutes before they crossed the bridge into Virginia.

"So what is it Mr. Brueler said to you?" Hamer asked.

"When?"

Hamer handed Chase his coffee. "Just now. Do you take cream? Sugar? I think that's what these little containers are."

"Black."

"All the better," Hamer said. He, however, happily sweetened his own coffee with three packets of pure grain sugar. "Something concerning?"

"Perhaps."

"Perhaps you'd like to share?"

Chase hesitated just a second too long.

Hamer shrugged as he stirred his coffee. "Or maybe it's something you shouldn't. You're a wise young man. If your instinct is to keep something to yourself, likely that's what you need to do."

"I'm not sure I'm so wise," said Chase.

"Do you think you'd be here if you weren't prized for your wisdom?" Hamer asked.

"Well, many of us aren't what we appear to be."

One Hamer eyebrow rose in surprise. "You have doubts?"

Chase hesitated just a second. He decided that he trusted the older man. "Yes."

"You have convinced yourself you're not as wise as you should be for the task placed before you?" Hamer asked.

Chase considered that. "Flawed."

"Oh well, flawed," Hamer said dismissively. "What does flawed mean? Being flawed is the gateway to wisdom. No great man is without sin. It's the nature of understanding. I have done terrible things in my life. Awful things. If I didn't have those moments to reflect upon, where would I be now?"

"I don't mean things I've *done*," said Chase. "I assume we've all done bad things."

"You mean you have some great moral deficit?" Hamer was looking at him over the lip of his steaming coffee mug.

Chase wasn't sure how much he wanted to say. Hamer saw this. He slowly lowered his mug.

The motorcade was now passing 30th street.

"Let me tell you," Hamer said. "Sometimes when I am drinking – when I am drunk – I find myself thinking about all of the friends I betrayed when I was younger. In the name of the purity of my politics. I condemned human beings who mattered the world to me, all because I knew about the greater good. These are the deepest regrets a man can have. 3 a.m. regrets. When you weep. And come face to face with your supposed moral deficits."

"I wasn't thinking about politics," Chase said. "I was thinking about basic character."

Hamer shrugged. "Politics can become your character. It's so wrong, but there it is. If I could take it back, I would. But I can't. Later, of course, I learned that even character is nowhere near as important as temperament. Perhaps that's what worries you. Something about your temperament?"

It was the way Hamer looked at him when he said 'temperament.' Chase had always wanted to tell someone about Rin. Hamer would be the first ever. Except what was he going to do? Tell someone without having worked out how to frame it? What end result did he hope to achieve? It was totally un-Chase-like.

The car made the right turn onto 37th street, closing in on the Francis Scott Key bridge.

"There was a girl once," Chase said.

"Was? Past tense?"

"Yes. At least, I think so."

Hamer raised an eyebrow.

"Well, I believed she was in the past."

"Tell me."

Chase started to explain. "I lost myself. I betrayed who I was. I don't know how else to put it. But I didn't regret it because of how much I loved her. Her name was Katherine. But I called her – "

They were jostled from their seats and Hamer's coffee once again spilled. "Good Lord!" he shouted.

Clearly, something serious had happened up ahead in the motorcade.

Chase moved forward and slid open the blind between the driver and the rear of the car. The security officer in the passenger seat was reaching for the walkie-talkie slotted in the front console. The security officer glanced back at Chase. "Sorry about that, gentlemen! Everyone all right back there?"

"One of us is a mess!" Hamer said irritably, mopping up the coffee spilled over his lap.

"What's going on?" Chase asked the security officer.

"Not sure."

The driver had to bring the car to a complete stop about twenty feet behind the Reverend's car, which had stopped thirty feet behind the first security car, the one with Holden in it. From this vantage point, it was pretty clear why the Holden car had stopped.

The bridge ahead was jammed with very angry people. They were waving banners and signs and some were brandishing light weapons – hatchets and baseball bats. They had positioned themselves in the center of the Francis Scott Key bridge and were making it clear that no vehicles were going across anytime soon.

Chase looked out the back window of the Escalade. The road was still clear behind them.

The security officer in the front said, "Sir?" He was holding the walkie-talkie toward Chase.

Chase took the walkie and pressed the TALK button. "Selby."

It was Holden on the other end. "Obviously this isn't supposed to be happening," Holden said. "I'm not sure what's going on. If it gets any hairier, I'm going to turn us around."

Hamer yanked the walkie-talkie out of Chase's hand. He expertly pressed the Talk button and asked Holden, "Do you think they know who is in these cars?"

There was a long pause, then a click. Holden's voice came across tight and controlled. "I hope these folks are just demonstrating for the sake of demonstrating. But of course this is our territory, not theirs. My guess is some Changers decided to advance north and press their luck. Another bridge would do wonders for them. I'm not sure why we didn't know about this, but I don't believe they could know who's in these particular vehicles."

Chase took the walkie from Hamer and clicked Talk. "Except they do."

"How would you know that, Professor?"

"The signs, Commander."

Hamer followed Chase's line of sight. "Shit."

There were only two or three signs in the crowd, but their meaning was clear. One said, "There's No Reason to Reason" and another said, "You Can't Reason with the Unreasonable."

Chase clicked Talk. "Wouldn't you agree, Commander, that these people appear to know *exactly* who is in these cars?"

The crowd began moving toward the front car. They were chanting something Chase couldn't quite make out, but it sounded like "You Don't Tell Us, We Tell You." Then they began rocking the first car, which was Holden's.

You don't tell us, we tell you!

You don't tell us, we tell you!

There was a crackle on the walkie followed by Holden's voice, no longer quite so steady. "Okay, let's turn this around."

Up ahead, the Holden car began to nose its way to the left, trying to nudge through the crowd of bodies and make a U-turn. The middle SUV, the one with the Reverend and Macomb in it, also displayed its back-up lights. The Escalade driver shifted into reverse as well. The mini-motorcade was now in retreat.

Chase handed the walkie back to the security officer.

"Where are those perimeter cars?"

"Which perimeter cars?"

"They were tracking us. I saw one of them back at 30th street."

"Well, I guess they'll be behind us now."

Chase looked out the rear window. "Shit."

All heads turned.

A mere minute before, the road behind the Escalade had been clear. Now it was filling up with wolf-hatted Changers, more signs and more light weaponry. Where had they come from? And so quickly.

The mini-motorcade was now trapped on the Francis Scott Key bridge, an angry rabble in front of them and an equally angry rabble behind them. The crowds shouted in unison, "You don't tell us, we tell you!"

In seconds, they were rocking the Escalade and hammering at the windows.

27. Warren's Duty

1

Today was the day. Tempo had said that just before she gave Warren Potsburger what she warned him would be his last blowjob until he completed his mission. This was just before she presented him with an extra-special treat – that which Warren had begun to crave most, other than a ticket home to Bella. It was a Double Western Bacon Cheeseburger from Hardee's. Where she had scrounged up such a thing so early in the morning, Warren had no idea, but more and more he had begun to suspect that Tempo wasn't really governed by the physical rules the rest of the world had to suffer with. After all, she found him whenever she needed him, and she often knew things were going to happen before they happened.

Warren, chomping down on his burger, looked out over the crowd on the Mall as Tempo pumped away at him. By now, his entire goal was just to find out what was expected of him, do it, and get the hell out of Washington. No, not true. He didn't even care particularly what they wanted of him. He just wanted to get it done and go. In twelve hours, he told himself, either way, he'd be a free man.

It never occurred to Warren to just walk. To just finish off with Tempo, finish off the Double Western Bacon, give it the big belch, toss the wrapper, thank the ill-bathed woman for the half-assed sex, and be on his way. No duty, no obligation. The problem was that she had somehow convinced him that he owed his actions not just to her, but to all of them, and most of all, to Bella. How was Bella to respect him if Warren came back from Washington with nothing to show for his trip but a mouthful of missing teeth and aches and pains in his ass best not explained? If his rebellion turned out to be one big fat fart? Tempo had suggested that despite what she said, Bella might see it exactly like that. Warren wondered if perhaps he had told Tempo too much about Bella.

He came, such as it was, and was finishing the burger. She, of course, was talking. But as Warren gradually tuned in, he realized that this time she wasn't talking about all that vague shit about destiny and being called to action. She was being *very* specific.

"You're going to have to go against the crowd," she said. "Literally, you're gonna see them all going one way, and you're gonna go the other. You hear me? You don't go where they go, you go where you're needed. This is all about going where you're needed. You understand me, Warren?"

Warren nodded as he took his last bite of the Double Western. In fact, he had no idea what she was talking about. He had never known what she was talking about.

He did, however, sense that something was going on this morning that was unusual. There was a buzz running through the folks on the Mall. Everyone seemed to be moving to the west, past the Lincoln Memorial and toward the river.

Tempo could see him studying the shifting tide. "They're what you ignore," she said. "You hear me? You have other things to do."

Now there were school buses lined up on the north side of the memorial. People were lining up to board. What the hell was *this* about?

People leaving? Was that possible? Were things on the Mall ending?

"Warren!" she shouted.

He looked at her.

She slapped him across the face.

He almost choked on the last chunk of burger.

"Stay focused!" she said.

"I'm focused!" He leaned forward and coughed out a good chunk of bacon and cheese. It hit the pavement.

"What did I just tell you?"

"To go in the opposite direction of the crowd."

"Why?"

"Because I have a job to do."

"That's right."

"And then this is over."

"Yep. After this."

"So, I go in the opposite direction, but then what do I do?"

"You use the gun, Warren."

"I do?"

"Sure. How else are you going to get on CNN?"

With that, she began to tell him how it would be.

28. *Back on the Bridge*

1

The three black SUVs were trapped on the bridge, surrounded on all sides by a shouting, shoving, screaming mob of Changers who had managed to whip themselves up into a frenzy over who knew what. "You don't tell us, we tell you!" they chanted. What did that even *mean*?

There was a squawk from the walkie-talkie in the front seat of Chase and Hamer's car. Holden was being rocked in the first car. They'd been stopped in their tracks while trying to turn themselves around. "Okay, we've obviously got a situation here."

Chase and Tay Hamer looked at one another. It was perhaps one of the greater understatements of all time. Hamer popped another cashew in his mouth.

Holden continued: "We're going to try and push our way through. Everyone hold their fire."

Fire? Chase looked at the two men in the front seat. Both looked extremely pale. The security officer wasn't just holding onto his ceiling strap and his left armrest, he was clenching them. The driver was also white-knuckling it, his hands carefully edging one over the other as he tried to inch the car to the left, wading through the sea of bodies. Was Holden really imagining that these two had the stones to open fire on a mob like this?

They pressed faces, breasts, and asses against the windows of the car, as well as tongues (one painted red, white, and blue) and what, for a micro-second, Chase swore was female genitalia.

Hamer said calmly, "It seems to me our mission may be in jeopardy."

Chase looked at him and was about to respond, but he became transfixed by the window behind Hamer. Someone was smearing something brown on the glass. Feces?

Then Rin came back.

Not Rin, though. Intellectually, he knew that what he had seen in the crowd on the Mall that first time had almost certainly been an image of Rin brought about by a woman or any number of women who, seen through binoculars at a distance of more than six hundred feet, had merely resembled her. The coloring had been the thing, perhaps because she had also moved like Rin in that slightly suggestive way, like she was gliding along a narrow path in the woods while trying to avoid her bare shoulders being brushed by branches. Somehow, he had convinced himself she saw him and lowered her eyes and the brim of her hat so that he wouldn't see her – just as Rin had.

But here it was happening again. Looking out the car window, Chase imagined he saw her in the rear middle of the crowd, an island of calm in a sea of red, white, and blue lunacy, the lovely lightly freckled face (the freckles she hated) looking up from underneath the summer hat. This wasn't just unlikely, of course, it was impossible. Yet, he couldn't turn away. In case she were real.

But she would never have belonged amongst such people. For all her ferocity – and there was ferocity – Rin was a thinker and a games player, a schemer even, but never gross or one to storm the barricades. She didn't even like the subway, which was ironic considering how they had met. She believed in brain over brawn, and this crowd, of course, was nothing but brawn.

You are a Reasoner? he asked himself. A Reasoner looking for phantoms on empty roadways, or angels within crowds of devils, or a silk fairy within a clan of trolls? What kind of a Reasoner is that?

Something hit the car. Hard. It jolted Chase from his thoughts. Then another one. He saw the next missile as it hit the window behind his head. A tuna can. They were back to lobbing tuna cans.

School buses were now pulling up behind them, just beyond the entrance to the bridge. Who knew where they came from? A big roar of approval went up from the crowd.

Still, though, their cars continued to complete their turn and inch through the crowd. But the school buses were a barrier.

Now there was another sound filling the air and almost drowning out the shouting mob. Aircraft engines? Was that even possible?

"Where do you stand on faith?" Chase asked Hamer abruptly.

"Faith such as the power of the Almighty to get us out of this sticky situation?" Hamer asked.

"Yes."

"Well, I guess it would seem contradictory for a Reasoner to believe in something that is, by its very nature, unreasonable – "

"Yes, that's what I was thinking," said Chase.

"But I am not as tied to reason as you believe we should be."

Holden's voice was shouting from the walkie-talkie in the front seat of the car. "Push on through! Just push on through!"

The driver of the Escalade, however, hesitated.

"Such stringent views must struggle with the fact that one of us is a minister," Hamer said. "Do you doubt *her* ability to reason?"

Chase thought about that. It was a very good point. "No, I don't. But only because I *do* doubt that the Reverend adheres to the mystical and magical. She strikes me as a woman who believes in the doctrine and moral teachings of her faith, not the physical myth."

"However, if she were suddenly to – "

"– see Jesus in the sky," Chase offered.

"Yes," Hamer nodded. "If she were to say she saw Jesus in the sky, you would say she is unfit to be a Reasoner?"

"Of course," said Chase.

"That's where we are different. The sighting of Jesus might not be neuroses. It could, in fact, be the very healthy and creative manner in which the Reverend's subconscious intellect engages in problem solving." Hamer nervously considered the crowd which was really rocking the car now. "We should all be so lucky."

The loud engines roared somewhere back in the road beyond

the bridge, and then they were suddenly quiet. Chase realized what they were. Motorcycles.

The car rocking was getting worse. Chase and Hamer had to brace themselves against the seats.

"You were once an avowed Communist," Chase said, having to raise his voice to be heard. "Did such tolerance fit in with your beliefs?"

"Of course not!" said Hamer. "As I said, I had no tolerance! But we all evolve. That which I eschewed I now hold dear as life."

Chase was surprised. "So, *do* you believe in God?"

"Oh, I believe in many things that can't be rationally explained, and yet which explain many irrational things."

"Such as?"

"Good. Evil."

"But God?"

Tay Hamer looked at Chase with a quizzical expression. "Young man, I believe in – "

That was when the world came crashing in.

Literally.

2

By the time the school buses arrived, some of the more energetic of the mob – all young men – had decided they wanted a better perspective on things. So, carrying backpacks full of tuna cans, bottles, and even rocks, they began to climb the steel superstructure which rose like an exoskeleton above the body of the bridge.

This was a temporary thing placed there by the District of Columbia, which had begun construction on the bridge before the city had been divided. Since then, no one had been able to figure out who was responsible for bridge repairs, so it remained unmanaged and uncared for. But if you had the nerve to climb it, it gave you an excellent vantage point from which to draw out your tuna missile or whatever you had dragged up there with you.

Obviously, however, if you were going to be engaged in such mountaineering, you probably weren't going to notice the guy who had climbed higher up and farther out on one of the struts than anyone else. That left him hanging over the water of the Potomac. If anyone had noticed him, they might have picked up a few details:

One, the guy looked both exceedingly stupid and determined.

Two, he didn't have a backpack, tuna cans, or rocks.

Three, he *did* have a gun. And he was aiming it right at the back window of the Escalade.

3

"Young man, I believe in – "

It was a pretty tantalizing phrase, up there with "and the murderer is – " or "the sole beneficiary turns out to be – " And like those phrases this one was left unfinished, in this case because a substantial part of Tay Hamer's forehead disappeared, replaced by a gout of dark red blood, at the same time the back window of the car exploded in a cascade of popcorn glass.

One completely illogical thought passed through Chase's mind as Hamer slumped onto the jump seat, staring vacantly up at the roof of the car: "You know, I really didn't think that was going to happen."

Then, when he looked down and realized his hands were covered in red, another inane thought struck: "That's blood from a Nobel Laureate brain. No ordinary brain will do."

At first the crowd around the car screamed and leaped back, but in seconds they returned, a tangle of arms reaching into the car through the shattered window, clutching at Hamer's most assuredly dead and slumped-over body, and Chase's very much live one. Like some mad spider.

Without thinking, Chase began to climb toward the front of the car. This was pure animal reaction, Jackie Kennedy on the trunk stuff. When one of the crazed mob grabbed his ankle, Chase kicked it off with mad hysteria, as if he had been swimming and suddenly an underwater serpent had clutched at him. "Get going, you motherfucker!" he shouted at the driver.

But the driver was battling to get *out* of the car, even though it was clear he would be eaten alive even if he could get the door open, which didn't seem likely considering the crush. But the flight instinct is strong.

There was another big bang, and one of the side windows burst in with another shower of glass.

"What happened to *bullet proof*??" Chase's brain screamed.

Now hands were reaching in for him from the side window as well as the back. He was like the last survivor in a zombie movie. One stranger's hand grabbed his other ankle, another grabbed his shoulder. Chase tried to wrench away. But his real focus was on getting the driver to either move the damned car or get out of the way so Chase could take the wheel. Instead, the driver was battling arms that had managed to reach in when he had been so stupid as to open his door that small crack.

The security officer in the passenger seat didn't move at all. He was staring ahead and speaking directly to the windshield. "We need to get moving," he said. "We need to get moving."

With Hamer's blood greasing every inch of leather upholstery, Chase's journey to the front seat was a slippery challenge. Just getting around Hamer's body was hard enough. He was slumped over the jump seat, and Chase had to shove him into the rear passenger side of the car just so he could climb into the front.

Chase was only dimly aware of the next gunshots. Had he been able to focus he might have noticed that they sounded different from the first two. These were bigger, louder, more explosive. They also seemed to come from directly behind the Escalade, whereas the first shots seemed to have come from above.

Another shot, from right up close near the driver, scattered the crowd back from the car. Suddenly the holds on Chase's ankles and his right shoulder were released. The crazy zombie people were scrambling away like rats from a fire.

An enormous man in a leather Harley-Davidson vest tore open the driver's door. He squished the utterly useless and now screaming driver against the catatonic security officer in the passenger seat. Without even bothering to close the driver's door, the Harley Man simply wrenched the car into gear.

Unlike the actual driver, this guy was in no way concerned about the crowd in front of him. He simply drove into them. The first three protesters made a crunching noise on impact and then disappeared under the car as if sucked up by some human vacuum cleaner. There was a small 'clump, clump' under the wheels, but not much more than that. Now people were screaming as they hadn't been screaming before. This wasn't "you don't tell us we tell you" anymore, this was full-throated terror.

If they needed any more reason to get out of the way of the car, the Harley Man gave it to them when he pulled out the largest handgun Chase had ever seen. It looked like a silver cannon with a serrated top. It came from somewhere under the armpit of his Harley-Davidson jacket. With it, he blasted out the windshield and anyone beyond it.

Now the crowd was genuinely motivated. They ran screaming and yelling back across the bridge like Godzilla was on the move.

Chase was so stunned by this display of – what? The first phrase that shot through his brain was "brutal violence" but the second phrase – "sheer usefulness" – seemed much more accurate – that he gave up on his attempt to climb into the front seat. It seemed unnecessary.

As the crowd melted away and the car headed back toward M street, Chase saw more Harley bikers up ahead, almost all with shotguns or handguns pointed into the crowd. Chase no longer felt fear so much as relief.

He looked back over his shoulder to see if the other cars were following. They were. The middle SUV was right on the tail of the Escalade, and Holden's car, stuck in the rear, seemed to be jockeying for position first on the right, then on the left. Clearly it had plans to actually pass the SUV and take position directly behind the Escalade.

That's when Chase became aware of a different kind of shouting. There was something going on above him. He peered out the window and looked up.

A half-dozen or more of the crowd were scrambling up the steel superstructure over the bridge. They were after the man who had climbed up and farther out than anyone else. This poor bugger was, in turn, crawling like a spider across struts and cross beams trying to get away. He wouldn't make it, of course. His pursuers were too close. And they wanted him too much.

Only when he saw the man drop a pistol did Chase realize he was likely looking at Hamer's assassin, about to be devoured.

They never got to him, though.

Just as a hand reached out and caught a loop of the assassin's jeans, the man fell from the superstructure onto the bridge roadway.

The crowd were like wild dogs in Africa landing on a gazelle and just ripping the shit out of it, head and guts first. A frenzy. Then a jubilant cry rose up. One word. For a second, Chase thought he was imagining it. Then another voice picked it up, then another. It was clear now. Perhaps it even made sense. But still, it sent a chill through Chase.

"Oswald!" they shouted. "Oswald!"

29. *In the Death Car*

1

Chase assumed he was being kidnapped. Or worse.

The Escalade had jerked itself around the parked school buses and was now careening at top speed east along M street, back toward the city and almost surely toward the Capitol building. The Harley Man at the wheel drove with crazed confidence, weaving through the beginnings of morning traffic at breakneck speed and using the accelerator where anyone else would use a brake. Chase read the speedometer over his shoulder. They were blasting through Georgetown now at 75 mph.

In the passenger seat, the security man had not moved a muscle since the first shots had been fired, and the driver was literally quaking beside him. So much for Holden's A-team.

Chase glanced back through the shattered rear window and saw that the Holden car and the SUV were keeping pace with them. The Holden car had finally overtaken the SUV.

"Where are you taking me?" Chase shouted to his self-appointed driver.

The Harley Man said nothing.

Chase was tossed to the side as the Harley Man wrenched the wheel to the left, deking around a delivery van which has just started to poke itself out at 28th street. This was, after all, the Government side of the city, and a lot of business still went on as usual, or at least tried to, even on a Saturday. "Essential services" the GOR called them.

In the passenger seat, the security officer finally attempted to react to events. He fumbled for something under his jacket. The

Harley man reached out and put the cannon gun against the security officer's head. "Don't even think about it."

Reluctantly, the security officer gave up his sidearm, a .9mm Beretta. The Harley Man took it and slipped it into his own jacket. He punched the security man in the face, knocking him out. Or maybe the guy simply went back into shock.

The Escalade blasted through Georgetown. They were now crossing the Rock Creek bridge and coming into the city proper. At the intersection with 25th street, two cars were edging into the road as their light turned green. Before either car got ten feet, the Harley Man – without once taking his foot off the accelerator – stuck his arm out the window. He fired his weapon five times, four in the air and the fifth at the front wheel of the car edging furthest out. The wheel blew instantly. "Don't even think about it!" he shouted as the Escalade blazed through the intersection. Regular traffic coming toward them either hit their brakes or plowed into one another. Clearly, this "don't think about it" thing was this man's preferred M.O. in a crisis.

Chase pictured himself being dragged into the pens in the basement of the Capitol, home to more than three hundred high-level civil servants (according to last estimates, anyway). Or maybe he would be yanked straight from the car up onto the Capitol steps and made to kneel at the guillotine, no delay involved. He imagined what it might be like to place your neck on the blood-stained support block and stare into the blue recycle bin and know that this crappy plastic would be the last thing you'd see on earth.

Suddenly there were vehicles on both the Escalade's right and left flank. Identical white GMC Yukons with smoked black windows. Chase recognized them from earlier. These were the perimeter vehicles that were supposed to come to the rescue if any part of the trip to Virginia were to go awry. Well, here they were, late but at least making a showing.

The Harley Man clocked them right away. "Tell those fuckers to back off or I'll kill them both."

It took Chase a second to realize who he was talking to. "Me?"

The Harley Man reached over to the security officer. He wrenched something out of his hand. The guy suddenly roused himself, however, and decided to fight back. He crabbed with his hands like a three year-old.

Harley Man just punched the security officer in the mouth again. Then he grabbed what he had been after. The walkie-talkie. He threw it in the back seat.

Except the walkie-talkie didn't land in Chase's lap. It landed in Hamer's very dead lap. The Nobel Laureate didn't register the walkie, of course. His face was forever frozen in a look of surprise, pure shock that someone had shot out his magnificent brain. His expression would say "oh!" for all eternity, as if he were somehow aware that he would never eat a tart or Danish or salty tasty treat again.

"Tell them to back off!" the Harley Man repeated. "And tell the others to stay close behind!"

"Why would I do that?" Chase asked.

"Why wouldn't you?"

Chase reached for the walkie-talkie in Hamer's lap. When he did, Hamer suddenly sucked in a great big breath.

Chase leaped back. "Holy shit!"

The Harley Man glanced back. "What?"

"He breathed!"

The Harley Man performed a two-second assessment of Hamer's state. Eyes still staring straight ahead, open mouth, slumped body. "He looks dead to me."

"I'm telling you he – "

Suddenly one of the white Yukons nudged the Escalade to the side.

"Sonofabitch!" the Harley Man said as he nudged back. "Tell them."

Chase clutched the walkie-talkie and pressed the Talk button. He shouted into the mouthpiece. "This is Selby! The white trucks need to pull off and you need to follow close behind!"

There was a long pause and then a series of clicks. Then Commander Holden's voice, cool and calm: "Professor Selby?"

Chase clicked Talk. "Selby."

Another long pause.

Chase clicked Talk again as the Escalade slid through another intersection and around a cluster of vehicles turning right at 22nd street. "Did you read me? Pull the white trucks off and make sure you stay with us."

A pause, a click, and then, from Holden: "Can you give us any kind of report? Are you and Dr. Hamer all right?"

It took a second or two for Chase to take this question in. Had he heard right? Finally he answered. "Are you fucking kidding me?"

He wanted to add, *Hamer was shot an hour ago at the bridge, how the hell haven't you guys heard the news?* But of course Hamer hadn't been shot an hour ago. From the time of the Escalade's rear window being blown out to this moment – Chase holding a walkie-talkie sticky with Hamer's brain blood – it might have been three minutes at the most. Four max.

A click. Holden again: "Who is driving the vehicle?"

Chase clicked Talk. "I have no idea."

A moment, then Holden: "Can I talk to him?"

Chase held the walkie toward the Harley Man. "He wants to talk to you."

But the Harley Man was busy yanking the wheel to the right so he could get around a delivery van parked with blinkers out in the middle of M street. "Busy," he said.

There was another pause – all these pauses were taking far too long – and then Holden's voice, even calmer than usual. "Professor, are you listening to me?"

Chase clicked. "Listening." Unclicked.

"We're not going to let anyone take you down to the Capitol. You know that's against the Compromise agreement and we are going to hold them to it. Reasoners are strictly hands-off. I want to assure you of that."

Chase stared at the walkie. He wasn't sure he had heard right. Finally he clicked again and held it to his mouth. For the first time, his hands shook. "The agreement?" His mouth was dry. "Hamer took a direct head shot. What agreement do you think matters at this exact moment?"

"Fucking assholes!" the Harley Man shouted at the white Yukons, which still hadn't backed off. As they all crossed 21st, he waggled the wheel of the Escalade first to the right and then abruptly to the left. The first white Yukon went plowing into a sidewalk planter and went up on its nose. The car on the left merely crashed into cars coming toward it in the westbound lane, with a teeth-rattling crunching noise and squeal, as all three vehicles did a strange do-si-do that ending in a spray of glass and plastic.

After a good long while, there was a squawk from the walkie-talkie. "Professor?"

Chase clicked Talk. "Yes?"

"Get down."

Chase didn't understand. Then he looked back through the missing rear window of the Escalade and realized what they were thinking.

The Holden car was thirty feet behind the Escalade and cutting ground fast. Chase couldn't recognize the driver, but he could see that the man in the passenger seat was leaning out the car window with an automatic rifle in hand. He was going to shoot directly into the Escalade and presumably, take out the Harley Man. While driving.

This was their plan?

Chase turned and looked back at the Harley Man. Then back to the Holden car. The driver of Holden's car was gesturing that he get down. Chase could just make out Holden in the back seat of the car, walkie-talkie to his mouth, also gesturing for Chase to duck down.

A flash memory then: the way the Harley Man had ripped open the driver's door of the Escalade back at the bridge, the manner in which he had plowed through the crowd and fired his cannon of a handgun to clear the road.

Chase had only a second to decide.

He did it sooner than that. Instead of ducking down, he moved to his left, so that he was directly between the Harley Man and the shooter in Holden's car.

The walkie-talkie shrieked at him. "Get down, Professor!"

But Chase didn't get down. He turned front and spread his arms across the driver's seat, protecting the Harley Man.

"What are you doing?!" the walkie shouted.

Chase caught a glimpse of the Harley Man in the rearview mirror as he looked back for the briefest of seconds. There was a look of approval. Perhaps even gratitude. Then –

The steering wheel pulled sharply to the right, then to the left, and then to the right again. Chase went flying. They almost went up on two wheels as the Escalade came around a third corner, blasted down a narrow avenue surrounded by business towers, and then took another sharp right.

Chase didn't know Washington well enough, but he was pretty sure they were nowhere near the Capitol building or the Changers/GOR border on Constitution. Or, for that matter, the State building.

Then he saw where they were. Up ahead was a big blue "H."

They screeched to a halt under the canopy, parked at an angle only inches away from the glass walls and sliding doors of the area marked as EMERGENCY.

They had arrived at George Washington University Hospital.

30. *Emergency*

1

The Harley Man leapt from the driver's side and was reaching into the back seat to pull Hamer out when the other two cars bumped up behind the Escalade and screeched to a stop.

"FREEZE!" someone shouted.

So everyone froze: the Harley Man, who had his arms around Hamer's chest and had him three-quarters of the way out of the back seat; Chase, who was helping the Harley Man with Hamer's feet; the Emergency medical team who were already whisking a gurney out the back doors and hustling it toward the Escalade; the two plainclothes security officers who had leapt out of Holden's car and were now in firing stance with military-grade Glocks pointed right at the Harley Man; Commander Holden, who stood just behind the security guys, a 350 Colt balanced on the opened rear passenger door of the vehicle; and Ambassádor Macomb and the Reverend, who were just starting to pull themselves out of their own SUV, which was parked askew and to the left of Holden's car.

All participants stared at one another.

Finally the Harley Man spoke. "You want me to put him down or what?"

A tremor of confusion went through the men with guns. No one was sure what to do. Chase took the initiative and put his left foot out the back door of the Escalade, which pushed Hamer's body forward. The Harley Man stepped back to give Chase room to get out of the car, while fixing his own grip on Hamer's upper body.

"Okay then," he said.

"Move!" Chase shouted at the Emergency medical team as he and the Harley Man jockeyed Hamer's body out of the car.

The Emergency team had been crouched at the entrance. At Chase's shout, they snapped back into action and hurried the gurney over to the left side of the Escalade. With practiced skill, the two nurses, the orderly, and the doctor took Hamer from Chase and the Harley Man, slid him onto the gurney, and whisked him into Emergency. Other medicos joined them. In seconds, Hamer was gone.

The guns stayed trained on the Harley Man. "Put your weapon on the ground!" Commander Holden demanded.

The Harley Man looked at Chase.

Chase looked at Holden. "No," he said. "This man is with me."

No one knew what to do.

There was something ludicrous about the scene: three armed men pointing deadly weapons at one empty-handed man, and yet they were clearly the nervous ones. Perhaps it was the Harley Man's size. He was immense. Six-six maybe, lean but not too lean, a long grey ponytail, a Fu Manchu mustache, and a good array of tattoos visible beneath the uniform of denim and Harley-Davidson gear.

The Reverend stepped forward. "Perhaps, if I may suggest … "

"Reverend, stay back!" Holden shouted. His voice shook. He cleared his throat, perhaps to steady it. Then, carefully measuring each word, he said to the Harley Man. "Weapon on the ground! This is your last warning."

Slowly, very slowly, the Harley Man reached inside his jacket and under his left arm. He carefully withdrew his weapon from its holster. For the first time, Chase had a good look at it. He had never seen a Desert Eagle 50 before, and he couldn't have named it under any circumstance imaginable, but to his eye it really did look like a cannon. No wonder everyone had scattered when this monster had fired.

The Harley Man held it out to Holden.

The first security officer stepped forward, never once lowering his own weapon, and reached to take the Harley Man's gun.

Which is when Chase stepped in. He reached for the monster gun and took it for himself. "I don't think you understand," he said to Holden. "I *said* this man is with me."

Chase thrust the gun back into the Harley Man's jacket, where it slid neatly into the shoulder holster. He returned his attention to Holden.

Holden, horrified by what Chase had just done, said, "With all due respect, Professor, we don't know who this man is."

"With all due respect, Commander, I know *exactly* who this man is! He's the person who just saved me from *your* security team and brought Dr. Hamer to the hospital. How or why remains to be seen, but for now I know all I need to know about this man."

There was a stare-down between Chase and Holden. Chase was livid, hot coals, and Holden knew it. He lowered his weapon. His two men looked for instruction. Holden nodded. They lowered their weapons as well.

"We need to put our focus where it belongs," Chase said. "The first issue is Dr. Hamer. The second is why exactly whatever the fuck just happened, *happened.*"

Chase turned and entered the hospital. The Harley Man walked no more than three paces behind him. Chase felt immensely better for that.

2

The Reverend hugged him. The Ambassador shook his hand, then an awkward, hesitant shoulder-to-shoulder man hug. "What can you tell us about Hamer?" he asked.

"It's a head wound, and bad," said Chase. "I thought he was dead."

"What happened back there?" the Reverend asked. "How did Changers know what we were doing? Where we were going?"

"If those *were* Changers," Chase said.

The Reverend was surprised. "Is there any doubt about that?"

"Just a feeling," Chase said.

The TV mounted in the far corner of the Emergency waiting room interrupted them. CNN was on and Jamie Baldwin was cutting in with a "Breaking News" report. "– a special report out of Washington: Word is coming out that more violence has erupted in the nation's beleaguered capital, this time at the hands of the newly seated Reasoners. The details are sketchy at the moment, but apparently there was an altercation – "

"What did she say?" the Reverend almost shouted in indignation. "What the hell did she just say??"

The Ambassador stepped closer to the TV. "Well, well."

Chase saw movement over Ambassador Macomb's shoulder through the glass door of the Emergency entrance. More GOR security vehicles pulling up. Presumably Commander Holden's people. They leapt out of SUVs and a troop truck and began to surround the hospital. One of the security officers began moving civilians out of the waiting room and into another part of the hospital.

"– one of the many bridges that links Washington with the Commonwealth of Virginia. Bob?"

CNN switched to a live shot of a correspondent standing in front of the entrance to the Key bridge. Behind him were emergency vehicles. Police were putting up CRIME SCENE tape and barriers. It looked like any crime scene in any major city, with nary a Changer to be seen.

The Reverend turned and looked at Chase and the Ambassador. Her mouth was open in shock. "How is that possible? Where did they all go?"

Bob the correspondent began filling in the details. "Jamie, all we know now is that some sort of extremely violent altercation took place here less than a half hour ago and there are at least two fatalities, maybe more. That's the result of a demonstration involving the Reasoners, the very people who have been entrusted to bring calm and order to this most violent moment in our nation's capital."

"Bob, that just seems crazy," Jamie said.

Bob checked his notes on a cellphone in his hand. "Apparently an angry mob was responding to reports that the Reasoners were attempting to leave the District of Columbia itself – and let's remember, D.C. is the only area where Reasoner safety has been assured, at least according to the rules of the Reasoner Compromise – for what has been dubbed a secret tete-a-tete with Commanding General Van DeVere, who is understood to be secured at a military base within northern Virginia. Such a meeting, of course, would likely be completely against the rules of the Compromise."

"Hold it, Bob," said Jamie. "I want to make sure this is all the viewers clearly understand this … "

Bob went off his notes and addressed the camera directly. "Well, the Reasoners were breaking their own agreement here if it's true that their plan this morning was to attempt to engage with the General – "

"– who has been thus far incommunicado for most of this crisis," Jamie added, with a sidelong glance at the camera, bringing her viewers along.

"Yes!" said Bob. "Definitely out of contact and a source of much speculation since 5/22."

"But now we know he's in Virginia?" Jamie asked.

"Well apparently the *Reasoners* know he's in Virginia," Bob said, consulting his notes again. "And that's the problem: According to our sources, they were attempting to enter into negotiations with the General with an eye toward turning military force against the Changers here in D.C."

The Reverend's hands reflexively flew up in fury. "*What* did he say??"

"I believe," the Ambassador said, "that we now have a very serious problem."

CNN Bob continued. "The Changers would clearly see such actions as a double-cross, this despite their own resumption of violence last Friday night on the Capitol steps. Either way, it's perhaps a move that could put the whole Reasoner plan into jeopardy. It's believed that when Changers got wind of all this, the decision was made to form a blockade on the Key bridge and prevent the Reasoners from entering Virginia. Things got violent and there are reports of shots being exchanged, although exactly who was shooting at who we don't know yet."

"Clearly," said Jamie, "all of this is coming in fast and furious, and we have to be careful and make it clear that we have very few verified facts at our fingertips – "

The Reverend turned to Chase and the Ambassador. "How in the hell can they say that? How can they even put that out there? This is unbelievable!"

"Yes it is," Chase agreed. "Except for the fact that it's true. Which is the genius of it."

That stopped the Reverend. She gave him a quizzical look. "But it's not true."

"Yes," said Chase. "It is."

On CNN the picture cut abruptly to a shaky replay of the events on the bridge, courtesy of some bystander's smartphone. It was hard to make out what was actually going on, except that the person filming had been on the Washington side of the bridge, focusing on the bodies scrambling across the steel superstructure in pursuit of the assassin with the gun. There was something about the way it was shot; Chase didn't entirely buy it as authentic and impromptu – almost as if the cameraperson knew what was going to happen before it did.

"I'm not sure I entirely appreciate your point, either," the Ambassador said to Chase.

Chase returned his attention to them. "We *were* trying to leave D.C., and we *were* doing it secretly. The plan *was* to talk to General Van DeVere."

"But not to convince the military to turn on the Changers!" the Reverend protested. "We were on a fact-finding mission. We weren't trying to turn the military on anyone. That's Mallickey's idiotic idea!" She appealed to the Ambassador. "Why would they report that?"

"Chaos," Chase said, "sells."

As if taking its cue from Chase, CNN's Jamie Baldwin changed focus. "And now we're hearing about all sorts of demonstrations across the National Mall in Washington, as word spreads that perhaps – and again, these are early, unverified reports – but perhaps some of those injured at the Key bridge were bystanding Changers."

"Changers??" The Reverend was livid. "Dr. Hamer was shot in the head!"

CNN went to footage of the Mall. It was top-quality professional stuff, taken from the scaffolded perch which had been built for all the news outlets. Usually the camera was pointed at the steps and the guillotine, but now someone had reversed the angle. The camera – at least CNN's camera – was panning across the east end of the Mall, showing all manner of Changers waving signs, guns, and fists. In the distant background, there was an eruption of flame, as if someone had let off a July 4th firework. Smoke rose up in the air near the history museum. Jamie Baldwin let everyone know that what they were seeing now were folks on the Mall as they were hearing first reports of what had happened. Anger and fury were spreading.

"These are people who cut heads off!" the Reverend objected. "Senators! Congressman! God knows how many innocent staffers! They have slaughtered five members of the Supreme Court! How much blood has been shed? And this – THIS – " She barely got the words out. "Makes them look like the aggrieved party!"

"No, Reverend," said the Ambassador. "It is merely an excuse."

"For what?"

"I fear," said the Ambassador, "we are about to find out."

On the TV screen, Jamie Baldwin was telling the world that CNN was just getting word that Jeff Beavenstock would be making an appearance on the Capitol steps soon. Apparently he had a lot to say about the "crisis at hand." And a lot, people hoped, that he intended to do about it.

31. *Beavenstock Speaks*

1

Something, Warren suspected, had gone very wrong somewhere. In fact, seemed downright fucked up.

"Fucked up" was exactly what he felt from the second he began to hear the word "bridge." "Bridge" this and "bridge" that. And the exodus. It seemed like half the Mall's population had moved toward the west, trying to find out "what had happened on the bridge."

Warren badly wanted to go with them. But he had been told. It had been laid down to him. In no uncertain terms. "You do not belong there. You belong on the steps."

At first, that seemed lunatic – and the urge to join the crowd was beyond his ability to resist. But then, amazingly, by late morning the tide had turned, and now people from the mystery buses were coming *back* from wherever they had gone, back from the bridge, back from beyond the Lincoln, back toward safety. Suddenly instead of the ripple of giddy excitement which had overtaken the Mall just an hour before, there was anger. A sense that something terrible had been done. Everyone was following the news on their phones. There were shouts of "those bastards!," even if some didn't, in Warren's estimation, look entirely sure what those bastards were bastards for.

As the crowd trickled back to the Mall, Warren realized that he had done the right thing by staying put. His instructions had been validated. So, following that line of logic, if he just did what they wanted, if he did his job, he would be fulfilling his destiny.

Getting a wolf hat was the easiest thing to do. The hawkers still had their tented souvenir huts erected all along Constitution Avenue, and business was brisk. Losing wolf hats was just as common as having them stolen, and the same was true for jerseys. In the case of jerseys, however, the whims of fashion also entered into the picture. When folks noticed that the Changers up on the steps, Beavenstock's people, had started to wear Panther jerseys more than any other, there was a run on Panthers. When Panthers seemed to be getting too popular, the Jerseys on the steps switched to Wild Cat jerseys, and so Wild Cat jerseys started to sell.

But Warren's instructions were clear: a wolf "original" hat – without the plastic snout – and a 49ers jersey; classic get-up from the first days of the Wheeling uprising. It's what Beavenstock had originally worn. Always, Warren was told, stick with original recipe, never crispy.

"You hear?" the old hawker who sold Warren the wolf hat and jersey asked. "He's gonna talk."

"Who is?" Warren asked.

"Jeff."

Warren acted uninterested, and let the old man take his time counting out the change. Inside his chest, however, Warren's heart was beating like a goddamned jackhammer. They were right, he thought. About everything.

Don't get distracted. Stay near the steps. Get up there.

Warren put his 49ers jersey on right there in front of the old hawker and started to walk at a rapid pace along Constitution Avenue toward the Capitol steps. All around him, the mob was also making its way toward the Capitol. They just wanted answers, and that's what they figured the steps would give them. Warren slipped in with the tide and put the wolf hat on as he walked, found it was too tight, adjusted the band, put it back on. Perfect. Somewhere along the way, he balled up his old shirt and threw it in one of the overflowing litter baskets. He didn't think he'd ever need it again, and he'd turn out to be right.

His rapid pace soon became something of a jog, and by the time he crossed 3rd Street, coming up on the Grant Memorial, the crowds were thick and he had to push his way through them. Jeff Beavenstock speaking was a big deal at any time, but if Jeff was speaking now, in anger, how good were the odds for a culling? Pretty good, folks figured. And word wasn't that Jeff wasn't just angry; word was he was royally pissed.

Unlike the others, however, Warren had no intention of standing around arguing with his fellow Changers about what Jeff might say or what might have happened at the bridge.

Instead, he weaved through them with purpose, gently turning shoulders so he could squeeze closer to the front. He did this with his newfound authority, and people seemed to accept him for what he appeared to be: someone in charge. And, of course, he was dressed like someone in charge.

Which is exactly how he was greeted when he got to the bottom of the Capitol steps. There was a rope there – not much of a barrier, but a barrier nonetheless – which separated the mere spectators from the Jerseys who actually carried out the badass stuff. Even in Changer land, there was a hierarchy.

Warren, sure that the wind was with him, just decided to step over the rope.

Unfortunately, before his right foot was even raised three feet, a *truly* badass guy with massive – truly *massive* – red sideburns, wearing a bandana, wrap-around sunglasses and a Vikings jersey, was on him. Right away. Surprisingly, the guy didn't carry the usual AR-15 or even an AK-47 or a Glock, but instead brandished a classic Spalding baseball bat, which he held high up in a choke. An ominous amount of damage had been done to the business end of the bat, and for just a second Warren pondered what kind of man would choose the meat and gristle of using a baseball bat to a gun.

"Where the fuck do you think *you're* going?" the guy demanded.

Warren Potsburger, sounding like no Warren Potsburger who ever existed before, shot back. "Where the fuck do you *think* I'm going?"

The guy, who Warren decided was not just wearing a Viking

jersey but *looked* like a Viking, was taken back by the surety in Warren's tone. "Well, you're not coming in *here*."

"Well I'm not walking around the back again. Here, hold this for me." To Viking's surprise, Warren withdrew his gun, handed it to him, and stepped over the barrier. "Thanks." Warren took the gun back.

"And just who the fuck are you?" Viking asked.

"Potsburger! Warren Potsburger!" Warren realized it was the first time he had said his full name since he'd arrived in Washington. It sounded good. It sounded right. For the first time in his life. Like a fist hitting meat. Warren Potsburger. "Who are *you*?"

Viking held up the baseball bat, as if this were some form of I.D. "Lowell Grange."

Warren had a sudden old-Warren moment as he looked in this guy's eyes. *He loves that bat*, Warren thought. *He loves it like I love Bella. Or worse.* Something else was in there too. The Viking seemed to be looking for a kinship, as if asking, Do you want to use the bat *with* me?

Fortunately, new Warren reasserted himself. "Well, Lowell, I know where I'm supposed to be. Where are *you* supposed to be?"

"Are you fucking with me?" Viking Lowell asked. "I'm where I'm supposed to be."

"I'm not fucking with anyone, but I'm not sure you are."

"I'm sick of this shit!" Viking said, brandishing his bat. "All this shit with you guys in charge!"

Clearly, Viking had anger-management issues. Clearly, he'd also mistaken Warren for someone else. Someone who mattered. Which was good. What Warren had wanted.

"I'll put in a word for you," Warren said. "But all of you guys out here have to tighten up." Warren wasn't sure what he was talking about, but it sounded like a serious charge to his ears.

Clearly Viking took it as a serious charge, because he was further infuriated. "Who says??"

"*He* says."

Confident he had somehow won the nonsensical argument, Warren marched right past Viking Lowell Grange, who looked furious that somehow his services were found wanting and maybe he needed to get his ass in gear. Then he looked at the business end of the bat again and Warren felt a strange tremor.

Trouble, he thought. Some of these people are not like the others.

Things were very different on this side of the rope, Warren discovered. Here on the Capitol steps – what they called the terrace – it was clear that everyone was some kind of security personnel – had an actual *job* – and looked down on the folks beyond the rope. Literally and figuratively.

Warren was surprised to see they weren't all men, either. And they weren't all white. There were a fair number of women and a pretty radical mix of Blacks, Hispanics, Asians, and Natives in the group. The only common denominator seemed to be that if you looked like a completely deranged antisocial killer, you belonged up here beside the Great Guillotine. Guns helped sell the picture for the cameras and hence the country. The world. There was a lot of tactical gear, a lot of balaclavas, a lot of Stars and Stripes face masks, a lot of cross-draw pistol vests, ammo belts, and knife sheaths. Warren felt practically naked with his single handgun, but no one seemed to give him a second glance. Obviously, they figured that if he was up here, then he belonged up here, and if he didn't belong, they'd figure it out soon enough and either throw him back in the crowd or beat him to death.

There were Changers up here who *weren't* tricked out: The bikers, for instance, seemed to content themselves with one or two firearms, and it was hard to tell just how armed the Jerseys were. There were also guys who just looked like regular suburban dads in jeans and polo shirts, as long as you ignored the gun belts or Shuka knife holsters.

The protectors of the steps stood around in groups, never taking their eyes off the crowd that spread from the lowest flight of the Capitol. Interestingly, though, they kept with their own: the Tactical boys in a combat line, clearly talking only to one another, the suburban dads standing around in a semi-circle like dads at any AYSO soccer game; the bikers the most relaxed, telling jokes and perhaps offering an amused chuckle or two as they glanced over at the weekend warriors in their combat gear; and the Warrior Women, who stood at the back taking in the most expansive view of the scene, chatting idly while loading, reloading, and rechecking their weapons.

Only the Jerseys moved freely between these groups. Most of them, like Warren, were wearing wolf hats. There was a relaxed vibe to Jerseys. They were the elite, and everyone knew it. This made a lot of sense to Warren. The only people he had ever seen on TV dragging a Senator or Congressman or staffer to the guillotine had been someone in an NFL jersey, and even the Grim Reaper – the name the media had given to the person who pulled the rope that dropped the actual blade, usually while wearing an NHL goalie mask – had always been someone in a Colts, Vikings, or 49ers jersey. Warren was not one to recognize the subtlety in the ordering of social hierarchies, but he could at least looks at facts: The Jersey folks did the actual hardcore killing, and they had history with Jeff, so that made them who they were. Beginning and end of story. Everyone else was backup.

It wasn't until he turned around to follow one of the Warrior Women with his eyes – probably fifty, with spikey blonde hair, no more than five feet tall if that, yet she moved with the swagger and confidence of someone who had caused a *lot* of trouble to a lot of people in her life – that Warren realized he was less than six feet from the Great Guillotine itself. When he recognized that, and stopped to look at it, it took his breath away.

For one thing, it was much bigger than he had anticipated. And it was *old*.

The wood was more like brown rock than anything that had come from a tree. The ropes were thicker than they looked on TV, and appeared lacquered. The blade was down now and locked into its "safety" position within the stock, but still you could see the strange rust-colored curved neck rest made out of what appeared to be terrycloth. To make the victims feel more comfortable? At the moment, there was no blue recycle bucket placed on the other side of the base, but there was a whole stack of them – at least seven feet worth, each neatly fitting in the other – leaning against the back wall by the second flight of steps. Sandbags held the guillotine's base in place. Warren bet you couldn't move the thing without a truck and winch.

It was magnificent, and it made Warren feel truly good about what he had been sent to do.

Suddenly, there was activity from the landing one flight above them. A whole bunch of Jerseys were coming out of a center doorway and moving in a sort of flying wedge down the steps. All the security folks on the lower level snapped to attention. Weapons were cocked, sunglasses dropped into place, earpieces set. All of this activity sent the crowd cheering in mad anticipation. Beavenstock. *Beavenstock* was coming out to talk to them, moving from within that flying wedge of male Jersey meat toward a cluster of microphones and cameras at the top of the left stairs and on the other side of the Great Guillotine. The Changers knew how to frame a shot if no one else did.

Warren's mouth literally hung open as the Jerseys and the shortish man in their center came down the steps at the far right. It's like turning a corner and realizing you are suddenly face to face with the President, or Elton John. A completely involuntary "holy shit" face.

His first inane thought was, he's blonder than I thought. Then, he's more solid and stronger-looking than I thought. Then: He's also terrifying.

Indeed, at that moment, Jeff Beavenstock was terrifying. He looked like a man royally pissed at everything, and he wanted to let the world know it. He and his Jersey guard strode down the stairs, crossed in front of the guillotine, and moved with purpose toward the microphones and cameras. Even the press appeared to inch back, and why not? Jeff Beavenstock was a man with the blood of well over two hundred – maybe three hundred – people on his hands, and he had never once looked truly annoyed while going about such business. Now, however, he looked ready to explode. So who knew what that meant?

Once Beavenstock placed himself on the third step down to address the media and the world, however, a stronger emotion replaced Warren's wonder. Joy. No, stronger than joy. A sense of complete life fulfilment. Because Warren realized this was all going to work out. He had finally done the right thing in life. He had followed instructions and it had paid off. He wound up in the right place.

He knew this because the first camera that moved in on Beavenstock, shouldered by a pot-bellied bearded man offering a good degree of plumber's butt courtesy of his sagging and low-riding jeans, had a logo emblazoned on its side. And that red-and-white lettering was as familiar to Warren Potsburger as his own name. Maybe more so.

The camera read: CNN.

Warren had finally arrived at life's pinnacle. The moment was here.

32. *CNN*

1

Chase, the Reverend, and the Ambassador were in the Emergency waiting room, clustered together on uncomfortable chairs. The Harley Man had gone off somewhere but said he'd be back. Commander Holden returned with two of his own men and leaned down to whisper in Chase's ear. "I just wanted to let you know, it's been decided that Captain Duryea should be kept under medical observation."

Chase was baffled. "Who is Captain Duryea?"

Holden looked equally baffled. "Captain Duryea was in the car with you. He is your personal security officer."

"And presumably Dr. Hamer's as well?"

Holden hesitated just a fraction of a second. "Well, yes. Both of you."

"Well then, I would agree that Captain Duryea should indeed be kept under observation. For as long as necessary. Then I would suggest he never be used as anyone's personal security again. How is the driver?"

"Linnock? He is also being kept under observation and will receive counseling." Holden clearly was becoming uneasy under Chase's steady gaze. "Both of these men have been through a traumatizing event, Professor."

Chase said nothing.

Holden stepped back.

Chase's phone rang. He looked at the screen. Brueler. Chase got up and stepped away for privacy. "Thank God!" Brueler said when he heard Chase's voice. "How are you?! How is Hamer?!"

"We're waiting to hear," Chase said. "Two hours ago they told us they'd give us an update in an hour. The rest of us are all right. Are you at the State building? How are things there?"

There was a slight hesitation. "A lot of angry and pissed-off Reasoners. No, frightened. Ms. Pappason believes everyone is under attack and has demanded you all be airlifted to safety." Chase heard the weary impatience in Brueler's tone. "We're wading through the reports. Are you watching the news nets?"

"We have CNN here."

"Beavenstock's going to speak, apparently."

"Apparently."

"What can you tell me?"

Chase gave it as cleanly as he could. "It was clear sailing until we got onto the bridge. Suddenly there were a hell of a lot of angry people facing us. They were chanting. And they had signs. 'No reason to be reasonable with Reasoners.' The pun is obvious."

Brueler groaned. "Holy shit."

"Exactly," Chase said. "They knew exactly who was in those cars, just like they knew what route we were taking, and – according to cable news, anyway – where we were going and who we were going to see."

"That's a lot."

"It's everything. We were bottled up. Holden's car was in the lead, then the Ambassador and the Reverend, then Hamer and myself. I don't know but for some reason it felt like they focused on our car. Any idea who the shooter was?"

"Some no-name Changer supposedly. But then it was a Changer who brought the shooter down, wasn't it? Did you see him fall?"

"Yes," said Chase.

"He's never going to be talking to anyone again. Certainly not to tell who put him up to it."

"Convenient," said Chase.

There was just a fraction of a second before Brueler said,

"You're wondering about Sister Sheena's other accusation, aren't you? All that 'traitor in the ranks' bullshit."

"Maybe it wasn't bullshit after all."

"I think we need a lot more information before we jump to that conclusion."

"We may not have time."

"I think I'd better get down there," Brueler said.

"No," Chase said. "Stay there. Take care of the rest of them. It sounds like you've got your hands full."

Chase clicked off just as the Harley Man returned to the Emergency waiting room, carrying a cafeteria tray. He placed it on the table in front of the Reverend and the Ambassador. They looked at the three soups, sandwiches, and coffees in amazement, then back up at the Harley Man as he returned to his spot against the far wall. He popped a toothpick in his mouth.

Chase took one of the coffees. "Who is that man?" the Reverend whispered.

Chase glanced back at the Harley Man. "I don't know."

CNN trumpeted another "breaking news" interruption. They all turned.

CNN had shifted its focus back to the Capitol steps. A figure was grimly moving across the second level, past the guillotine, toward a cluster of microphones and cameras positioned on the north terrace. Even through all that security, there was no mistaking him. The hard-set jaw, the grim furrow of the brow, the blond hair, the blue eyes, but most of all the stocky build of a man who had been doing manual labor most of his life. Jeff Beavenstock. And he really did look mad as hell.

It took awhile to even get him to the microphones. His security had to shove away folks who had moved in too close.

Once the path was cleared and secured, though, Beavenstock didn't say anything. He just stood there in front of all those microphones, silent, as if gathering his thoughts. Or controlling himself.

He was staring down at them from giant screens all across the Mall. Slowly, under that gaze, they harkened to him; folks who were busy burning a couple of food trucks turned from the flaming wreckage; parents yelling at their kids stopped and pulled them close as they turned their attention to the screens; a bunch of teenagers playing very tough football stopped and watched from whatever position they had wound up in; four guys firing lethal lawn darts at targets erected alongside the Korean Memorial stopped in mid-shot. Everywhere along the Mall, all the way down to the Lincoln, people stopped and focused on the leader.

Chase, the Ambassador, the Reverend, Holden, the Harley Man, Holden's security team and everyone else in the Emergency waiting room were also holding their breath.

"I have a bad feeling about this," the Ambassador murmured.

As if picking up on the Ambassador's thoughts, Beavenstock raised his arm in a fisted salute and roared – not shouted, not hollered, but *roared* – into the microphone, "This is BULLSHIT!!"

2

He knew about timing, you had to give him that. Exactly where or how he learned it, who knew? But this West Virginia coal miner knew timing.

"Let me be really, really clear," he said. "We. Did. Not. Do. This."

Then he waited as the crowd gradually realized what he was saying and where he was going ("we are *not* the bad guys") and as they did, they started to shift. Silence became murmurs, murmurs became cheering, cheering became shouting and soon there was the chant of "Jeff! Jeff!" In the hospital, Chase and his fellow Reasoners glanced at one another uneasily.

"I'll tell you what we *did* do," Beavenstock said once the crowd calmed down a bit. "We made a deal. We made a deal with the people who once ran this country and we said, 'Hey, if you folks think you can work with us to get things to where they need to be, sure, let's talk. Let's reason. Let's work together *as equals*. You got a team of smart folks you want to bring in? *Absolutely* we'll see what they have to say! Long as you're being fair. We are not unreasonable. You gotta start somewhere, right?"

There was a half-hearted "YEAH" from the folks on the lower steps of the Capitol, but the enthusiasm only rippled a few hundred feet before it died. This crowd actually didn't want to hear about starting somewhere and being reasonable. Or fair. They wanted to know who was to blame for whatever had happened and who was going to die for it. Simple. Straightforward.

Beavenstock knew this. He could feel it. He shifted gears. "The deal was THIS!" he shouted. That brought them back to attention. "The DEAL was to operate in good faith and with mutual respect! We already showed them what you folks can do. We made THAT clear, didn't we?"

This got a better reaction. "Oh yeah, Jeff!" rang through the crowd. All Changers liked hearing that they were strong and that they had brought the government to its knees. It was a story that never got old.

"It cost!" Beavenstock said. "It cost, no question. But as the Wolf says, and remember this, 'When your leadership will not listen to argument, the only rational answer is to be irrational, and the most irrational act is the shedding of excessive blood.'"

"YEAH!!" *Now* the crowd roared its approval. Beavenstock didn't often quote the Wolf, mostly because a lot of the sentences were too long and he didn't want to be seen reading from a piece of paper, but he'd taken the time to commit some of it to memory. Changer crowds always loved Wolf quotes, especially if the word "blood" was in there. "So they listened to us, didn't they?" Jeff asked.

The crowd roared again.

"So we met them, we made an agreement, and we stuck to that agreement. And now *they* are the ones to break it! You know what they were doing, right? They were trying to go behind our backs and bring in the military to destroy us! To kill us all!"

Another roar from the crowd, good and angry.

In the Emergency waiting room, the Reverend took an unconscious step backward. "I think we should get back to the State building." Then, "Chase?"

But Chase was transfixed, watching Beavenstock as he waved his hands to get the crowd to shut up. "Let me be clear, let me be clear. So what's the first deception? Them sneaking off to try and get the military to destroy us was the first deception! Right out of the gate they broke the rules. Those people can't help themselves. You want to know the second deception? Because it's big! No fucking around!"

In the hospital, Chase looked back at Holden. "Where are they treating Dr. Hamer?"

Holden gestured with his head. "They're still working on him in the trauma room, but they're not letting anyone back there."

On the screen, Beavenstock was filling everyone in on the deception. "The story they're spreading is that yes, MAYBE they were trying to sneak out of the city, MAYBE they were going to stab us in the back, MAYBE they were up to no good, but then we – we! – attacked them on the bridge going out of town. We shot up their cars, we shot up some of their people, we behaved like wild animals!"

The crowd roared its approval for wild animals, before realizing that might be the wrong reaction. Beavenstock looked unhappy. Apparently, he had something else in mind when it came to the comparison to the wild animals.

"You know how you can be sure that story is a lie? I'll tell you. Do you think that if any of us here – " He pointed into the crowd indiscriminately. "I'm talking you – or you – or *you* – or certainly any of my friends up here!"

There was a big roar of approval for the Tacticals and the Jerseys surrounding Beavenstock.

"You think that if any of you wanted to stop a couple of cars on a bridge, or take out a couple of professors, you'd screw it up???"

A huge laugh and roar! Now they got it!

Beavenstock hit his point hard. "You think those were *Changers* on that bridge?? Believe me, if those had been real Changers on that bridge, no Reasoner would have left that bridge alive!"

"What is he trying to do?" the Reverend asked.

"No!" Beavenstock shouted from the TV. "They want to blame the Changers for trying to break the peace! So they put their own people out on that bridge and made them look like us! Then they can declare all-out war on us! They were never serious about our agreement in the first place."

"A very interesting tactic," the Ambassador murmured. "We attacked ourselves on a bridge while attempting a covert mission to gain military assistance in destroying the Changers?"

"It doesn't make any sense," said the Reverend.

"But that's not really the point, is it?" The Ambassador turned to Chase. "What do you think, Professor?"

But Chase was no longer in the waiting room. Nor was the Harley Man.

3

He was searching through the labyrinth of hallways which made up the Emerg and trauma unit. Pretty much every door said RESTRICTED TO MEDICAL PERSONNEL, but Chase ignored those warnings. The Harley Man was four paces behind him.

Since the arrival of the Reasoners and their security force, all of the other Emerg patients had been moved to the secondary ICU unit on the second floor, so Chase encountered empty beds and deserted nursing stations. He had to pass through three sets of doors and a darkened med-surg ward before he found the nexus of activity he was seeking. There was plenty of light and plenty of activity coming out of Trauma Room 3.

Chase peered through the glass portal. And gasped. What he beheld was an ungodly horror.

There was blood smeared on the walls and floor of the

trauma room, yellow and brown liquid puddles, bandages, bloody compresses, bloody surgical gloves, masks, and scrubs underfoot. In the center of the room, a medical team surrounded a surgical table and were subjecting some object to untold abuses from all manner of medical equipment: shock paddles for the heart, a craniotome for the brain, suction hoses, drills, saws and scalpels. Blue gowns and masks formed a barrier beyond which Chase could see very little. Then, as a nurse reached across to yank a tray closer, Chase got lucky: For one split second he saw the poor creature on the table, ancient in age, pale wrinkled skin stretched across brittle bone, the chest cut wide open, the top of its head exposed via a bone flap which gave air access to his dura. It might have once been a man, but now it resembled a brittle chicken being pummeled back into life by people who have been told to do everything they can when, in truth, there is nothing they can do. This was what was left of Dr. Tay Hamer, one of the finest minds of his time, two-time Nobel Laureate, lover of empire tarts or, really, honestly, any pastry covered in icing.

Chase stepped back in horror.

On their way back to the Emergency waiting room, they glimpsed one of the TVs over the deserted nurse's station. It was tuned to Fox. On the screen, Beavenstock was nailing his point home. "These people are trying to blame *us* for breaking the peace when their plan the whole time was to see us slaughtered like animals! And *that* we are not gonna allow!"

He lifted his arm in a salute. The roars that greeted the gesture were overwhelming. Beavenstock literally appeared to rock backward at the sheer force of the anger he had unleashed with his simple, unapologetic, yet easy-to-follow story. True or not wasn't the point.

Chase doubled his pace back to the Emergency waiting room. "We've got to get out of here," he said to the others. "Back to the State building."

The Reverend rose. "What about Dr. Hamer?"

"He's dead."

She looked truly shocked. "But no one has said that!"

"He was probably dead when he got here," Chase said. "He's certainly dead now." He gestured to the TV. "We have to go."

On the TV, Beavenstock was saying, "What we will not allow – "

And then he said no more.

Chase, it turned out, was too late.

4

Warren couldn't believe he was able to get so close. At first, when Beavenstock had started talking, Warren had been a good twenty paces to the man's left and at least ten paces behind him. But soon Warren was able to edge closer, till he was almost directly over the leader's shoulder. For sure this put him in line with the CNN camera. Warren figured if he could see the lens clearly, then the lens could see him.

He was thinking only one thing: Bella. Bella sitting on the couch. Watching TV. Maybe not paying a lot of attention at first, maybe snacking on a Dorito or two, fanning away the latest hellacious fart from the dog, but then, wait, what? "That can't be!" she'd say. She might get off the couch and get down on her knees, close up to the screen, pressing her face against it, and then – a whoop! A holler! "Holy shit! Warren! WARREN!" Then she would turn her head. "Mom! It's Warren!"

Warren didn't know how Bella's mother got into his fantasy, so he quickly went back and fixed things up. No mother. Just Bella whooping at the TV as she realized that right behind *the* leader of the Changers was Warren, looking like a badass and clearly part of the big picture. *Her* Warren, whom she had so clearly written off as a damned fool. Warren *("Warren, come home")*, whom she had not respected in any way you could call respect, Warren *("Baby, listen to me")* whom she hadn't really loved the way he'd loved her, Warren who ...

Warren's thoughts ground to a halt. The phone call with Bella.

She told him to come home. She had told him she loved him. She had told him that he could just come home and forget this whole revolution thing. So ... what the hell, Warren wondered, was he doing?

He realized that even at this point he could just take a few steps back, wait for this asswipe to finish up his bullshit speech which made no sense anyway, climb back over the rope when no one was looking, and wander back to the train station. If he was willing to cling to the side of whatever train was leaving town, by tomorrow he could be back on Cabbel Street and take up life again with Bella and the dog and even her goddamned mother, and why not? *Why the fuck not?*

It was suddenly so clear to Warren. He had been duped in some way. Conned. He started to edge toward the left again, toward the rope and away from this madness.

Except that's when he saw one of the big jumbo screens erected across the Mall.

This one was slightly askew from the Grant Memorial, showing exactly what the CNN camera was showing. What he saw was a big-ass closeup of Jeff Beavenstock – and, way in the distance behind him, Warren. Right up to his neck.

But his face wasn't visible.

For Warren, the idea that he had come this far, that he had got so close and in the end he would only be recognized if Bella could guess that it was Warren in the 49ers jersey – a jersey thousands of other guys on the Mall wore that day – was too much for him to take. It was heartbreaking is what it was.

He had to at least let her know he was there.

Warren stepped forward two more steps, then looked over at the big jumbo screen. Now, at least, his neck was showing. He took another step. The top of his chin now.

It took four more steps toward the steps and three steps to the right for Warren to even get his face into the shot. By this time Beavenstock was really ranting, so the crowd wasn't paying attention to Warren or any security dude. Some of the others up on the steps, however, *were*. They were starting to give Warren an odd look. And one of those people giving him an odd look was none other than Lowell Grange, the Viking who had let him over the rope. Lowell with the unusual love for his baseball bat.

How Lowell had got up this close was a mystery in itself. Warren had pegged the Viking as strictly a rope man, not a steps man, yet somehow here he was. Worse, he was giving Warren that mighty fishy look, like, "Maybe you *aren't* the important Jersey I thought you were and why are you moving around so much and so close to Jeff?" Warren decided to fix the Viking with one of his newfound stern "don't fuck with me" looks, just like he had done at the rope, but for some reason that didn't back this guy off this time. Worse, Viking leaned over and whispered something to one of the Tacticals. Then Tactical fixed Warren with a look. Then Tactical tapped a buddy. Soon Warren had three Tacticals and a Viking staring at him.

This was bad. There might be no trip back now. No clinging to the train. There might be nothing now but going ahead with what he'd been sent to do by that crazy bitch with the filthy tits.

Fuck! Warren screamed in his own head. Fuck!

Clearly, he had to make a decision. So he made it. Warren turned his attention to the jumbo screen, made sure he was clear and visible in the CNN lens, drew the bitch's gun, and made his move.

It took six steps forward and two to the right to get close enough to Jeff Beavenstock. Warren was fast – he had always been fast – so as the crowd roared in delight at something Beavenstock had just said, Warren was able to unload four shots in the man's back before anyone even knew what was happening, and certainly would have been able to unload the crucial fifth shot if someone with very big sideburns hadn't suddenly tackled him and crushed him to the ground.

As it turned out, he would have been better off if they had just shot him.

5

In the Emergency waiting room, no one knew at first what they were seeing. "Something's happened to him!" the Reverend shouted, "What's happened?!"

"He's sick," the Ambassador said.

"He slipped," Holden said.

"Shot," a voice said.

All heads turned to the Harley Man for just the briefest of seconds, then back to the TV. "Oh crap!" said Holden. "He's right!"

Utter chaos descended on the hospital in seconds. Cars skidded up to the sliding doors of Emerg, Holden's security people shouted across at one another, intending to put the three Reasoners in the same car. The Harley Man clearly had different plans. He yanked Chase by the arm and hustled him through the sliding doors and into the back of what looked to be an armored Jeep Grand Cherokee. The Harley Man ripped open the driver's door and said to the soldier within, "I drive! You sit in the back!"

The soldier complied instantly.

The small unofficial convoy booted it as fast as they could back to the State building.

6

Warren was just staring at pavement. Around him, chaos screamed in his ears. Literally. High-pitched screaming from women in the crowd, male shouting from up here on the steps. Warren just stared at all the blood on the concrete ground and tried to imagine what was happening, but he knew he didn't dare move his head even an inch or the boot that was holding his neck to the ground (Lowell Grange the Viking's boot? He couldn't tell) would almost definitely snap his spinal column. The blood was not Beavenstock's blood. It was Warren's — from where the last of his teeth had been smashed in when they threw him onto the ground.

If I stay still, Warren thought, they might actually maybe forget about me. If I make myself a small ball, maybe they might not even know I'm here.

But, of course, they knew he was there. That's why he couldn't move. In addition to the boot on his neck, there were more than a dozen heavily armed men kneeling on him and shouting to one another, as another two dozen heavily armed Jerseys hustled Jeff Beavenstock's body away from the microphones and cameras, first up the steps – presumably thinking they'd take him back the way he had come – then back down the steps toward whatever kind of medical care they could find on ground level. For the first time, the Changers discovered that they might have fucked up by not arranging a First Aid station near the base of the Capitol steps.

The TV cameras were trying to get right in there, but for the first time in their history, the Changers were shoving the cameras away. They even yanked a few from newsie shoulders and threw them to the ground. Jeff Beavenstock's bloodied body was just starting to convulse as they hustled it toward a Dodge Ram on Northwest Drive. Everything had changed in a second. All bets were off.

If Beavenstock's future was uncertain, the fate of Warren Potsburger was perfectly clear. Later, some Changers would point out that if any "of the morons" up on the guillotine level "had been able to keep their wits about them for even one second" they would have realized that finding out *why* Warren did what he did, and *who* put him up to it, was far more important than exacting revenge on the man who pulled the trigger. But in moments of extreme and violent crisis, guys in masks, tactical gear, and ammo belts do not usually stop and consider the most prudent and properly reasoned investigative procedures.

By the time they hauled Warren to his feet and dragged him toward the guillotine, the fix was in. Warren was about to get his wish. Big time.

Here's how it was going to go:

When Jeff Beavenstock had stepped in front of the microphones, more than seventy million Americans and maybe another forty million worldwide were following the events taking place on the Capitol steps live. That doesn't include Twitter feeds or livestreams of other forms of social media.

By the time Warren pumped his first bullet into Beavenstock, another five or six million added to that number, simply because word had spread that "Jeff was losing his shit" over whatever had happened on the bridge that morning.

But by the time they crushed Warren to the ground, viewership was going through the roof. Electronic word spreads fast. Beavenstock had been shot and they had the guy! On the steps!

By the time it topped 110 million views domestic, Warren was being dragged toward the guillotine.

Warren could not believe this was what was going to happen. Granted, he had not thought much about how he would get away once he had performed his duty – in fact, he hadn't thought much about the specifics of his duty at all until he was carrying it out – but he certainly had assumed he would get away somehow. It would be dicey, but he'd do it.

The first thing he told himself was that they were just trying to scare him. Putting on a show. They *knew* he was one of them – look at him! The wolf hat! The jersey! – so there was no way they were really going to carry out an execution on one of their own.

But when he saw one of the Jerseys move to unlock the stock, pull back the safety, and draw up the blade, Warren began to worry that there had been a hitch in his thinking.

What the fuck *had* he been thinking?

Horribly enough, none of it happened as quickly as it felt to Warren. In fact, by the time they dragged him over to the guillotine and told him to kneel – one of the Tacticals shoving the muzzle of his AR-15 into Warren's back, shouting, "Kneel, motherfucker!" – there had been enough time for another whopping twenty million viewers to tune in. This was beyond the Superbowl, which had pulled in 105 million domestic and less than 10 million foreign.

(What might have annoyed Warren, had he wanted to think about such things, was that even had he topped 200 million viewers, it was still a mere drop in the bucket compared to the London Olympics opening ceremony of 3.6 billion, or the Leon Spinks-Ali rematch, which was 2 billion.)

Dragged toward the guillotine, Warren looked out at the sea of people which stretched across the Mall and Constitution Avenue and as far as the eye could see beyond that, as far as Virginia in fact, and grappled with the sheer vastness of the human population, of the fury invested in the hearts of so many people, and thought, "It's possible this isn't going to work out for me."

That's when he started to panic. That's when he tried to stand up and that's when what felt like dozens of hands grabbed his head, his shoulders, his arms, his feet, and welded him to the spot. "You're not going anywhere, motherfucker!" was what he heard, and now they were moving his neck onto the terrycloth resting spot, and then someone deftly slid a blue recycle box under the other side of the guillotine.

Warren had never felt such helplessness. They had him in an iron grip. He was literally unable to move an inch on his own. Once, years before, in the back of a police car, he had felt such helplessness, but he had also been aware in the smallest recesses of his brain that he would somehow survive the event. In this case he felt the complete opposite. He had total surety that in the next few minutes – seconds?? – his life was going to be over, and everything he had ever known, or touched, or felt, or smelled, or tasted, or kissed, or laughed at, would be gone. He would see darkness (maybe) and disappear. Or would it be like when they put you under an anesthetic? You were there one second, and then you weren't, and you never even felt it. Just gone, counting backwards from ten.

Viewership was over 180 million by the time they placed the locking plate over his neck.

Warren looked out over the crowd, which was hard to do because of the angle of his neck. They looked so angry. They looked like they hated him. But what was really spooky was how many of them were laughing and smiling. Some gave him a cheery thumbs up. More gave him the 'slashed throat' gesture.

Then he thought he saw her. At first, he wasn't sure, but then a man in a Grim Reaper costume moved slightly to the left and there she was, grinning at him. No, not grinning. Laughing. With her gap-toothed mouth which often snagged him just a bit when she was going down on him, and that weird almost cross-eyed glare that suggested she wasn't entirely all there. Then she raised her hands above her head in a 'you're the champ' gesture. Tempo. But not Tempo. She had another name.

That's when Warren knew he was a goner. And that he had been fooled.

Warren crossed over 210 million viewers when they cuffed his hands.

213 by the time the Jersey guy yanked the rope free from its mooring pin.

Then, someone began to make a speech.

Now?? Warren couldn't believe it.

He didn't know who it was, but they were behind him, and they were yelling, and soon everyone was listening. The speaker really went at it. "You all saw it! This fuckin' asshole here did the worst shit you can imagine! We don't need any bullshit trial! We all saw it! This guy is so fucking guilty it's crazy! We're sending a message, okay? We're sending a message and everyone get that message! We don't want to be violent – no one wants to be violent – but we get attacked, we attack back! That's the law of the jungle! And this here is a jungle! And this asshole is like some animal we have to put out of its misery because that's the way it works … "

On and on the guy went, whoever he was. All Warren knew was that the crowd was getting pretty impatient. Even Warren wanted the speech to end, although clearly that meant they would be moving on to the main event, which Warren did *not* want.

Eventually the speech did end, if only because the crowd was yelling for it. The speaker yelled back, "Yeah, yeah! I know! You guys are fucking animals! But don't worry, we're gonna do this. Because this shit will not stand!"

There was a moment, some murmuring, and then Warren saw the Jersey man holding the rope step back.

At that second, Warren scrambled for something to look at. Anything good! He knew the blade was going to fall the second the Jersey man let go of the rope, and he wanted to see something. A beautiful girl maybe or a baby, even a kid with a dirty nose, maybe a fucking dog. He searched desperately, but he couldn't find anything, nothing, not a single thing in that crowd he wanted to see. Nothing but –

A woman. A woman in a big floppy hat. Like the kind ladies wear when they're gardening. She was looking at him. And she was the most beautiful thing he had ever seen. And at that second he could see, just out of the corner of his eye, the Jersey man let go of someth–

7

247 million people saw Warren Potsburger get his head chopped off. 247 heard the thunk as his head fell into the recycle box in front of the guillotine. Among the 247 was Bella, sitting in her little house on Cabbel Street.

She only recognized him at the last second, and only uttered one word.

"Warren?"

33. *Back at State*

1

The Reasoners who had survived the bridge debacle were not among the 247 million witnesses to Warren Potsburger's sad fate. While Warren was being taken to his end, Chase, the Reverend, and Ambassador Macomb were speeding through the streets of Washington back toward the State building.

This time it was a heavy escort, with no attempt at secrecy. Why bother now? There were sirens on the first two vehicles, and open windows on the two follow-up cars, out of which the muzzles of automatic weapons protruded. The message was clear: "Stay back." There weren't a lot of civilians on the streets, but the ones who were out – and paying attention – did exactly that, ducking back as the motorcade sped past, or even leaping for cover behind mailboxes or transit benches. And for good reason.

A Reasoner had been killed. The Changer leader, Beavenstock, had been shot and *probably* killed. Everyone understood that this was enough cause for the city to become even more unhinged than it had been thus far – if such a thing were possible.

The cars blasted through the front gates of the State building and past the Normandy fencing. Chase assumed they were just going to jerk to a stop in front of the main entrance, but the Harley Man shot the Jeep Grand Cherokee down the ramp into the underground garage. Chase reached for the Reverend and held her shoulder as the front of their car hit bottom and scraped out, then pulled to the right. "Holy shit!" she said, bracing herself against the door.

Brueler was standing waiting for them near the underground

elevators. There were three militiamen in full cammo standing beside him. The resemblance to the Tacticals who had stood behind Beavenstock was striking. They appeared to be one and the same.

The Harley Man brought the Jeep to a halt inches from Brueler and leaped out to open the doors. But Brueler beat him to it. "Let's go!"

The Ambassador, the Reverend, and Chase scurried across the back seat and out the passenger side. Brueler gestured them toward the elevators. "Let's go!" Then he snapped at the Harley Man, who clearly had every intention of going with Chase. "Who the hell are you?"

"He's with me," Chase said.

They went through the underground security doors and into the elevator vestibule.

"What's happened?" Chase asked Brueler.

"Do you know about Beavenstock?"

"We know he's been shot. That's why we got the hell out of there. Is he dead?"

Brueler shook his head. "No news yet."

"Who did it?"

"Some nut got him at the scene, so you can imagine what's probably going to happen next. They're animals." He tried to recover himself. "The rest of them are watching in the boardroom. Tell me about Hamer."

Chase shook his head. "No."

Brueler lowered his eyes and took a moment. The elevator doors opened, and they got off on the fourth floor. There were armed security officers in the corridor wearing full riot gear, complete with automatic weapons. The Reverend and the Ambassador headed straight for the boardroom and its opened double doors, but Brueler gave Chase the eye. Chase held back. So did the Harley Man, but he kept a discreet distance.

They found a private corner of the corridor. "All morning I've been trying to communicate with our friend in Virginia," Brueler said.

"Van DeVere?"

Brueler nodded. "First, to let him know what had happened and then – once the Changers started selling their alternative facts to the media – to make sure he knew *our* side of things."

"And?"

"I haven't heard a word from him."

They considered this in silence. Neither had an answer. Finally, Chase said, "Keep trying. There's something very wonky here."

"There sure as hell is."

"I mean something's in place that we don't understand. But I'm not sure the Changers understand it either."

2

The boardroom was set up exactly as it had been the day the Reasoners first arrived. Then, however, everyone had been milling about the tea table awkwardly, shy about introducing themselves. Now they were clustered together as a tight-knit group – nine of them staring at the flatscreen TV bolted to the side wall. They had just witnessed Potsburger's execution, repeated for what would be thousands of times. The news nets had all created a loop of it and given it its own graphic.

The Reverend and Ambassador Macomb, who were seeing the execution for the first time, were particularly shocked. The Reverend couldn't manage words. Finally, she swallowed and said, "Do we have any idea who he *was*?"

Vin Jansert had no problem offering his views. "Of course!" he shouted. "The lone crazed killer! The nutter. That's who he always is! Oswald, or James Earl Ray, or Sirhan Sirhan, or John Hinckley Junior, or Mark David Chapman."

Kirsten Pappason could barely move. "My God, they're going to kill us all."

CNN interrupted them.

"– truly astonishing news coming out of Washington," Anderson

Cooper was saying. "So we'll be going to Bridgepoint Hospital, on the Changers side of the line, or what the Changers call 'their' territory. It's hard to tell exactly where the divisions are, especially on a day when everything is coming in so fast and furious – but correspondent Mark DuVall is there and – "

The camera cut clumsily to a very confused Mark DuVall in T-shirt and baseball hat (was the idea to blend in with all those Changers?) standing in front of mud-colored Bridgepoint Hospital. Behind him was a tangle of cameras, reporters, lights, security forces in tactical gear, Jerseys, and wolf hats. Mark had his finger to his ear so he could hear himself better, but he still had to shout into the microphone. "– less than fifteen minutes ago, Anderson, and it's been chaos since then!"

The screen split to show us Anderson's cool and calm demeanor, contrasted nicely with Mark leaping out of his own skin. "Mark, I think we missed the top of that," Anderson said.

Mark cut Anderson off. "Yes, Anderson. She got here some – fifteen minutes ago – "

"– Mark, we're only getting every other word – "

Suddenly every electric light in Christendom turned on as the sliding doors behind Mark DuVall whispered open and a small figure emerged. Mark leaped out of the way.

On the fourth floor of the State department building, all eyes were rivetted to the TV screen. Only Brueler hung back. One of the PSLOs handed him a phone and he stepped into the corridor.

On the TV screen, Sister Sheena positioned herself perfectly in the center of the media scrum. She was back to her usual combat gear and black T-shirt that said SURVIVE, but perhaps in deference to the moment she had donned a new item of apparel never seen before, at least on her. Sister Sheena was wearing a 49ers baseball cap, the same hat Beavenstock often wore. Her ponytail fit neatly through the back.

The second she stepped into the light, CNN split their feed between the hospital and the hushed crowd at the Mall. They too were watching the transmission in real time on the jumbo screens, and every single one of them shut up in a matter of seconds.

This was going to be the Death Announcement, and everyone knew it. Sister Sheena's mere presence told it all.

"This morning," Sheena said, looking directly at the cameras and not at the reporters, "the elite patriarchy took a shot not once but twice. They dragged out their old playbook of deceit and double-cross and did what they always do. They lied. The movement of which I'm a part does a lot of things, but one thing it doesn't do is lie. The patriarchy also does a lot of things, but the one thing it doesn't do is tell the truth."

On the Mall there was hesitant applause and agreement. At the hospital, there were shouted questions, all about Jeff Beavenstock. Sheena held up a fist and lowered her head.

The reporters stopped shouting. Even the people on the Mall stopped clapping.

Sheena turned her eyes back to the cameras.

"For all of us who believe in the power of the people, there is good news: They fuck up. The power elites fuck up all the time. In fact, one of the reasons they *have* to rely on the boot on the neck, or the lie of the patriotic battle for nonexistent freedom, or the myth of their rugged individualism – which means dying alone without medical care – is because they can't get *anything* right. Ask the Vietnamese! Ask the Afghans!"

There was murmured agreement from the Mall, even if it was confused. Sometimes, people didn't quite get what Sister Sheena meant. Afghans? What about Jeff? Almost as if she could hear them, Sheena went on: "Remembering that fact, sisters and brothers, remembering this above all else, listen to me now."

She looked off into the sky.

She certainly knows how to own a moment, Chase thought.

She turned back to the lens. "Our brother was dispatched to die this morning. By a patsy instrument of the sons of money monsters. But truth is stronger than duplicity. And so, I can tell you, is Brother Jeff."

You could hear a pin drop. At the hospital. At the Mall.

"Brother Jeff was shot four times," Sheena said slowly. She focused her unblinking stare. "Yet he still breathes. He still thinks. And he still speaks."

Still *breathes*? Still *thinks*? Still *speaks*?

There was complete and utter pandemonium on the Mall. The press corps too. In the boardroom of the State building Kirsten Pappason grabbed Agniew's arm in shock. The Reverend looked directly at the Ambassador as if to say, "What the hell?"

Sister Sheena let the questions and shouting die down before she delivered her next whopper. "And what he just said to me, what he was going to say to *you* just before the pawn of the power elites interrupted him, was this … Are you writing this down?"

For emphasis, the CNN camera moved in on her. She looked right into the camera and delivered it perfectly. "He said to me, 'Why half a city instead of a whole? Why half a country instead of a whole? Why half the people instead of everyone?' In other words, TAKE IT ALL!"

The Mall erupted like a volcano.

At the hospital, the reporters crawled over themselves to get even closer to Sister Sheena. But she ignored them, turned and walked back into the hospital.

"Holy fuck," said Kirsten Pappason.

"He's alive?" Vin Jansert asked. "How the fuck can he be *alive*?"

They were so distracted by this turn of events that not one of them noticed Brueler as he leaned in to whisper in Chase's ear. "I need to talk to you."

The two of them returned to the corridor, with the Harley Man following.

3

The four military personnel stiffened as Brueler and Chase came out and went to the far end of the hall. The Harley Man hung back.

"I just received a communique," Brueler said.

"From?"

"Certain military personnel."

"The man himself? How did you manage that?"

"I didn't. He reached out to us."

That was surprising. It didn't feel right. "His initiative?"

"Yes."

"Why?"

"Well, he's been watching the events of today just like anyone else. And there's an issue."

"Which is?"

"He's in Missouri."

"That's fast. When did he leave Virginia?"

"He *didn't*," said Brueler. "That's why he wanted to reach out to us. He wanted to let us know that he hasn't *been* in Virginia."

It took Chase a moment to process that.

"Chase, he hasn't been in Virginia since *June*."

Chase and Brueler studied one another.

"The first time he heard about our meeting," Brueler said, "was on the news this morning. He knows nothing about any plan to meet us. Ever."

In one second, everything lit up in Chase's head. Everything was visible.

He rushed back into the boardroom, pushing past the Harley Man.

They were still gathered around the TV, talking worriedly amongst themselves, clearly grappling with the ramifications of what Sister Sheena had just said, and what she may have unleashed.

All nine Reasoners. Nine. Chase made ten. Hamer was eleven. One was missing.

Chase turned back to Brueler. "Where is General Williamson?"

Brueler started to answer, but he had no words. He looked pale. Finally, he managed, "I don't know if I've seen him this morning."

"Since the news broke?"

"No, certainly not since then."

"Where is his room?"

Brueler stumbled for an answer. "I'm not sure I – "

"Where's Tyler?"

4

There were four of them on the elevator. PSLO Tyler, looking very tense and clearly aware that something was up. Brueler, Chase, and the seemingly always silent Harley Man.

They got off on the fifteenth floor. There were two armed military up here. Both looked surprised by the group that stepped off the elevator and marched with purpose to the room at the end of the west corridor. Tyler knocked first. "General?"

No response.

"Just open the door," Chase said.

Tyler ignored him and knocked, timidly and politely, two more times. "General?"

No answer.

"Open the door," Chase said.

Finally, Tyler used his passkey as well as his keycard and his personalized code.

The moment the door was open, Brueler pushed his way in. Chase followed. The Harley Man followed Chase.

The room was an exact replica of Chase's room, one floor below. Brueler examined the living room. Chase went into the bedroom. The Harley Man went into the bathroom.

In the end, it was the Harley Man who slid open the closet door.

General Williamson was inside, hanging from a carefully noosed belt. He was in civilian clothes. He likely had been dead for a few hours.

"Fuck!" shouted Brueler. Then, he looked to Chase. "There *was* a traitor."

"Apparently."

"We got that wrong."

"Oh," said Chase, "we got a lot more than that wrong."

5

Later. It was just Chase and Brueler in Williamson's room. The body had been removed and Brueler was examining the closet.

"He removed the shelving and slid the door shut on himself," Brueler said. Then, he added thoughtfully, "When this happens in the movies, they always put their uniform on. You ever notice that? A sort of last noble action?"

"That's right, they do," Chase said absently.

"But he didn't."

"I suspect General Williamson didn't feel very noble."

There was a long silence between them.

"Do you need a drink?" Chase asked.

"Yes."

Chase went to the mini-bar and rooted around until he found one of the mini Johnny Walker Reds.

Brueler sat in one of the armchairs. "So, we were never in contact with General Van DeVere – the real General Van DeVere – at all. For whatever reason, Williamson set us up."

"It would appear so."

Chase handed Brueler his drink.

"But why?"

Chase went to the window with his drink. "That may take a little longer to answer. But one thing's certain. Once things went sideways, once the General saw Beavenstock shot, he realized he'd been used too. By someone."

"So what now?" Brueler asked Chase.

Chase just stared out the window. "That," he said, "is the only question that matters."

Book 3:

Wild Wings

"One must still have chaos within oneself to be able
to give birth to a dancing star."
– Friedrich Nietzsche

"Blood and anger purify everything. Only through
the shedding of blood do you find what you believe in,
and who you will follow."
– *Wolf Words* (pg. 255, Barnes & Noble edition)

34. *The Mallickey Plan*

1

In the face of everything that had happened, the Changers on the Mall were overcome with frustration, fear, and fury.

The Changer leader had been shot. That was almost impossible to take. The fact that he had been shot for trying to tell a truth, however, was the truly rage-inducing insult. And what was that truth? Clearly, what Jeff had been saying: While the Changers had been acting in good faith, the Government of Record and the Reasoners had not. This discovery, coupled with the realization that once again the governments and elites had hoodwinked them – those very assholes they had fought against and in whose name they had burned cities – was more than any Changer could bear. And whose dumbnut fucking idea had it been to even make a deal with those people on their terms in the first place?

But it's intriguing to track what creates smoke versus what actually lights the fire. That afternoon on the Mall, it could be argued that it wasn't the attempted assassination of Jeff Beavenstock which most affected the crowd, and it certainly wasn't the death of some foreign commie scientist in the back of an Escalade. Nor even was it Sister Sheena's exhortation from the front of Bridgepoint Hospital. No, many would say later that it was the killing of Warren Potsburger that really set things off.

Most of the roving TV cameras missed it because they were focused on what was going on with Jeff. But the second Warren's head hit the bottom of the recycle bin, there was a scream of joy and a spontaneous crush toward the Great Guillotine, almost as if the crowd needed to touch the big blade itself as confirmation that they hadn't, once again, been proven powerless. That smug Harvard fuckfaces hadn't duped their leaders.

As it turned out, getting to the guillotine wasn't as hard as it looked. With so many Tacticals and Jerseys at that point racing Beavenstock's bleeding body to Bridgepoint Hospital, security around the Capitol steps was weakened. Soon the rope came down and the crowd was able to surge forward onto the terrace. Warren Potsburger's headless body was lifted high for everyone to see. Those close enough began taking selfies with body and guillotine in the same shot.

Warren Potsburger was, for the moment, an icon.

2

As the Changers were expressing their anger, the Reasoners were also getting it off their chest – in their own way. In an almost eerie parallel of what the Changers on the Mall were experiencing, however, the Reasoners discovered it wasn't Tay Hamer's tragic death which set them off, but the announcement that General Alwyn Williamson was discovered hanging in his closet, the victim of an apparent suicide.

"Suicide bullshit!" Kirsten Pappason shouted. "How do you know he wasn't murdered too?!"

She was shouting at Brueler. The rest of the Reasoners seemed to be gathered in a pack around her. The exceptions were the Reverend and Ambassador Macomb, who sat at one of the round tables off to one side, self-exiled by their guilt-by-association with the Great Bridge Debacle. Chase sat alone.

Brueler said slowly and quietly, "There is no *reason* to suggest he was murdered."

"Bullshit!" Vin Jansert shouted, throwing his hands up in frustration.

"Tragic," Brueler conceded, "but not bullshit."

"But why the hell would the General kill himself?" Vin demanded. "Give me one good reason!"

It took a second for Chase to realize this question was directed at him. He looked at his fellow Reasoners. The real answer ("because he was some sort of double agent for someone trying to destroy what we're trying to do here") opened a can of worms that Chase didn't think should be opened. At that moment. So he decided to do something he had not yet done: He decided to lie. It was wrong, it was against his very code, but he had no question that it was the most efficient thing to do. "Look," he said. "When we realized we needed to meet with General Van DeVere – "

"We?" Agniew barked in surprise. He pointed at Brueler. "I thought contacting Van DeVere was his idea!"

As if by divine intervention, they were interrupted by the double doors opening. Commander Holden. The timing was ideal. "We have a very unscheduled visitor on his way up," he told Brueler.

"Now?" Brueler asked in amazement, looking between the Reasoners and the TV, which was still playing all the assassination attempts all the time. "Who?"

"Secretary Mallickey."

Vin Jansert laughed. "*Secretary*?"

Holden nodded. "That's how he announced himself."

There were a few flashing glances. "Pray God don't tell me he has his full staff with him," Brueler said.

Holden shook his head. "Two aides."

There was an awkward silence, finally broken by that warm Texas drawl. "If I may, I would suggest that at this moment of crisis we all need to work together." They all turned. The Ambassador was stirring his tea. He carefully placed the spoon on the saucer. "This is statecraft. No time for division amongst allies."

Brueler nodded at Holden, who went to fetch Mallickey.

Chase asked, "Is it possible he already knows about General Williamson?"

Brueler sighed. "I'd be shocked if he didn't." Suddenly Brueler looked very tired. The expensive suit looked particularly rumpled. "The PSLOs certainly know. It won't be long now before everyone knows. And now Commander Holden will insist on individual security for each of you. That will trigger talk."

"It appears some of us already have our own individual security," Jansert said with a sneering glance toward the corridor, where the Harley Man waited.

Eyes turned to Chase. He responded simply, but with a cool indifference. "We'll argue about that, Vin, after you've been shot at a few times and had a mob try to literally pull you apart."

Vin shut up.

Mallickey didn't enter so much as burst through the doors, two aides with him. "Well, we've certainly got a shitshow on our hands now!" he bellowed almost happily.

"Congressman," said Brueler.

"Or should we say 'Secretary'?" asked Vin Jansert.

Mallickey gave him a dark look. "Congressman is fine." He put his briefcase down on a table. "Cards on the table! I know about Dr. Hamer and I also know about General Williamson."

Brueler and Chase exchanged a look.

"Now *that's* a murky situation, isn't it?" Mallickey said. "But that's not why I'm here. I'm here to share information. Unfortunately, I feel I am only able to share it with specific members of this panel."

"Is that a joke?" asked Pappason.

"No joke. I would like to speak to Director Brueler and Professor Chase alone."

The Reasoners looked at one another. In light of what had just been said about some of the panel being more equal than other members of the panel, the pause was particularly long, awkward, and ugly. Finally Agniew said, "So you're serious."

"If I'm not joking, obviously I'm serious," Mallickey said. He clearly read the tension in the room. He also, just as clearly, enjoyed it. "Perhaps the free flow of information has been something of an issue inside the Reasoners? Well, that's your problem, not mine. But

I'll offer this up. If Director Brueler or Professor Selby wish to share what I tell them, I have no objection. That's their business. After the fact, of course."

Before anyone could say anything, Chase stood up. "And we will definitely share. After the fact."

"Your choice, then," Mallickey said, and left the room.

Brueler and Chase followed Mallickey and his two aides. As they headed toward the elevator, the Harley Man joined them.

3

They chose Chase's suite, with the Harley Man waiting in the hall. Mallickey's two aides were present but at least tried to make themselves as unobtrusive as possible, sitting at the table against the far wall. Chase was learning that one thing all government aides were good at was sitting against walls and keeping silent.

Mallickey clearly had a few things to get off his chest before getting to his true purpose. Primarily, he wanted to gloat, even at the expense of a dead American Medal of Honor recipient and one of the world's greatest minds, to say nothing of a wounded Changer leader.

"Boy, did you folks fuck up! I don't know what you thought you were trying to pull off, but it's amazing the chaos you've unleashed. Two dead and Beavenstock shot! And have you looked outside?!"

This was unnecessary. Everyone was aware of the groups that had started to come up from the Mall and crowd the streets. Chase, standing at the window, was looking down at them now. The rabble hadn't done anything particularly violent as of yet, but they would soon.

"We're all aware what's going on outside," Brueler said. "Just as you were perfectly aware of our covert mission. You even passed on information to me about El Paso, Colorado. Or have you forgotten that?"

That yanked a little wind out of Mallickey's sails. He seemed annoyed. Convenient memory lapses and plausible deniability were part of the D.C. game, and Brueler wasn't being fair bringing up real facts now. "I'm telling you there's going to be chaos," Mallickey persisted. "My question is, what did you think you were doing?"

"How do you know we weren't fulfilling your initial request?" Chase asked. "Following the orders of Congressman Miles Mallickey, speaking for the U.S. government?"

"I didn't mean to do it like this! Your actions have effectively threatened any written understanding we have with these maniacs. Now they think we shot their leader! And I don't for one second believe you were doing what I wanted you to do!"

"Of course not," Brueler said. "If you must know, it was a fact-finding mission."

"Which went very fucking wrong," said Mallickey.

"Which went very fucking wrong," Brueler agreed.

"Look," Chase said. "Why don't we focus on the real issue at hand? Isn't the question what we do if Beavenstock dies? If these people become leaderless?"

Mallickey laughed. "Leaderless? Are you kidding? If Beavenstock dies, that's the last thing they'll be!"

Mallickey could see Brueler and Chase's confusion.

"Obviously *she's* responsible for shooting the Beav!" Mallickey practically shouted. "Who else could be behind whatever that poor bastard thought he was up to?"

Chase was surprised. "You're saying Sister Sheena set up a hit on Beavenstock so she can take power?"

Mallickey nodded. "Of course. Those two don't have the same goals, just an ability to inspire people to crazy-ass insane violence. He's just a brute. She has ideals. And plans."

In fact, nothing less than a new American constitution, Chase thought. He hated to admit it, but Mallickey might be onto something. He wondered if Mallickey knew about Sister Sheena's new draft of the American Constitution. He doubted it. Then he began to doubt the Mick's theory. Sister Sheena was a lot of things, but Chase doubted she was someone who wanted to lead that rabble out on the Mall. Those were Jeff's people, and everyone knew it.

Still, it was worth hearing what was in Mallickey's mind. "So you think she's also behind the setup that put us on the bridge?" Chase asked.

"If that *was* a setup – sure."

"What about her appearance at the hospital?" Brueler asked.

Mallickey shrugged. "Theatre. What else was she going to do once it was clear he wasn't dead? She played it perfectly. Still, her best hope is he dies. So maybe she's lurking around waiting for her chance to hold a pillow over his face. Like in *Godfather II*."

Brueler glanced at Chase. "Chase, you look doubtful."

Chase nodded. "Because it feels incomplete."

"There's nothing else here," Mallickey said. "She's Brutus and Cassius put together. That's it, cut and dried."

Brueler and Chase exchanged a raised eyebrow. Shakespeare? Mallickey?

Brueler switched gears. "I'm sure you didn't come here to talk to us about conspiracy theories."

"Actually, I did," said Mallickey, his tone altering. He was shifting to government committee mode. "Just a different one."

He reached for his leather folder, withdrew some papers, then sat down in the big armchair. He flipped through the files on his lap. "I've decided I have a duty to share this. In light of everything that's just happened."

Brueler sat in the chair opposite Mallickey. "About El Paso?"

"I have no new information about El Paso beyond what I told you already," Mallickey said. "But as you know, under the Compromise, the Government of the United States and the Changers guarantee the Reasoners' safety, with the government doing the actual management." Mallickey cleared his throat. "Obviously, no one thought it was necessary to impart all details of security management to the Reasoners themselves or their Director. After all, you people are supposed to have a hell of a lot more important things on your mind. This thinking included such things as individual threats to safety."

Chase could feel Brueler stiffen. He didn't know why. Yet.

Mallickey looked at Chase directly. "Obviously, in the climate we're in, physical threats are common as dirt. In the case of the Reasoners, however, we couldn't take any chances. In fact, we assembled a specific team to review all threats against the Reasoners – minor, unlikely, or irrelevant."

Now Brueler was annoyed. "Why wasn't I informed whenever threats were made?"

Mallickey almost laughed. "Because there were so damned many! And you know what they meant? Fuck all!" He flipped through his papers to a specific sheet and read out loud. "'The Reasoners are going to die!' 'We're going to make sure the Reasoners are going home in a box!' 'The only good Reasoner is a dead Reasoner!' Then a variety of lurid threats focused on the women, with particular attention to Hydy Horvat." Mallickey looked back up at them. "But we looked at them all. That's the point. Chat groups and social media. And you want to know why? Because I've got news for you people! There are actually some things the federal government *can* do!"

"However," said Brueler.

"*However.*" Mallickey returned to his notes. "We did receive some very specific threats the day before yesterday, and then two more the day after. These, I confess, did slip through the stream."

"How specific?" Brueler asked.

Mallickey looked at both of them. "They named the bridge."

Chase and Brueler both drew in a breath. Finally, Brueler said, "Jesus."

"And the target."

"Good God."

"It literally named Hamer?" Chase asked.

"No," said Mallickey. "It named you."

There was silence between the three men. Finally, when Mallickey spoke, his words were sharp, but his tone was almost mournful.

"So ... whatever happened out there, it looks like everything was planned. But the plan was to kill you, Professor. Not Hamer."

Chase's mind was racing to put this together. To hold reason. "But why ... What could possibly ...?"

"I was hoping you would tell me."

"I have no idea."

"Perhaps General Williamson?" Mallickey was fishing.

"I don't believe that," said Brueler quickly. Too quickly. "In fact – "

But Chase caught his eye. A silent caution. Brueler returned to Mallickey, "We don't know precisely why General Williamson killed himself or if there's any connection to the bridge."

"But he was the one who contacted Van DeVere to set up the meeting, wasn't he?" Mallickey asked.

Chase answered before Brueler could. The lie came out perfectly smoothly. "That was me."

Mallickey looked doubtful. "Really!" An exclamation, not a question. "And how did *you* get to the Chairman of the Joint Chiefs?"

"I'm a Princeton academic, Congressman. The link between American universities and the military complex is long. It wasn't that hard."

"I don't believe you."

"Believe what you want."

Mallickey studied Chase a moment and then appeared to decide he wasn't going to get anything more. He tossed his papers back into his leather folder. "Okay, but whether you tell me or not, there's still something clearly rotten in the state of Reasoners. You're fractured, maybe fatally, there really was a weak link your ranks, and some of you have made some truly idiotic decisions. Fortunately, I have a plan to fix all that."

"What's your fix?" asked Brueler.

"I will join the Reasoners."

If anyone had told Chase even twenty seconds before that he would be struggling to fight back laughter, he would have told them they were insane. Yet it took everything he had not to burst out in

Mallickey's face.

Clearly, Brueler felt the same. His eyebrows simply went up and stayed up. He looked like a man who had just seen the dog driving the family car. Then he stifled a guffaw as a cough.

Mallickey was not amused. "I don't see what's funny! You're down two Reasoners, correct?"

Brueler sobered some. "That's correct," he said. "But surely you recognize that the purpose of the Reasoners is to … well, stand outside of existing governmental structures. To counsel. Untainted by partisan or special-interest considerations. In the view of many – well, most Americans – government simply ceased to work due to partisan warfare and corruption. So even if you were to resign your position with the GOR and take up a role as a Reasoner – "

"Wait, wait, wait," said Mallickey. "I never said anything about resigning my current position. I'm talking about in addition to."

Brueler stared at him.

They were now entering the land of the absurd. Chase got up and resumed his study out the window.

"In addition to your government duties you would be a Reasoner?" Brueler asked.

"Sure," said Mallickey.

"Filling both Dr. Hamer's slot and General Williamson?"

"No," said Mallickey. He pointed to one of his aides. "Trevor will make an excellent second Reasoner. That would bring you back up to twelve, and twelve is what you're mandated for. Not ten."

Brueler and Chase looked over at the handsome young man with the Ken doll haircut sitting against the wall. Trevor was busy brushing an invisible bit of carpet lint off his perfectly polished shoe. He didn't look more than twenty-five.

"Trevor," Brueler said.

Trevor looked up when his name was called, confused.

Brueler looked back at Mallickey. He seemed genuinely surprised there was any question about this terrific go-forward.

What followed was a very direct and heated explanation of what the word 'impartial' meant, as well as Brueler pointing out just how unlikely it was that Trevor would be able to fill the shoes of Nobel Prize winner Tay Hamer, or Medal of Honor recipient General Alwyn Williamson.

Chase didn't bother with any of it. He was distracted. Something odd was going on at the far end of the Mall down near the Lincoln Memorial. Even though there were others in the room, he got out the binoculars and adjusted them for the tightest view he could get.

At first, he thought the crowd was listening to music. Indeed, they were standing together in a semi-circle as they did when a band started up. He realized they were watching a group of men setting up a series of posts of some kind. Supports for a sound system? Something stronger than the wheely basketball nets they had used so far? No. Chase suspected he was looking at something very different.

They were placing broad-based wooden platforms maybe twelve feet or so apart across the lower steps of the Memorial. They looked like immense Christmas tree stands. A number of men wearing tool belts who looked to have put these things together off four identical Black & Decker 426 work benches were now struggling with what looked like a twelve-foot telephone pole, the old wooden kind. Or maybe an immense Scottish caber. Whatever it was, they were struggling to slide the end of the pole into one of the wooden tree stands. It wasn't easy – clearly the pole was heavy and clearly there were too many cooks in the kitchen shouting orders at one another – but they were going to get her done. These people always got things done.

Finally, cocked at the right angle, the giant wooden pole slid into the opening of the tree stand and the four men "walked" it upright. In seconds, this first twelve-foot mast was towering over the Lincoln steps. But it wasn't a mast, was it?

The door behind them opened abruptly. A voice said, "I'm very sorry to interrupt."

The Romanian, Albert Calinescu, stood in the open doorway.

PSLO Tyler and the Harley Man stood behind him.

Brueler asked, "Can I help you, Doctor?"

Calinescu addressed both Chase and Brueler. "Tay Hamer was my friend. But if his death has caused what is happening, I want no part of it. But I felt you should know."

"I'm sorry," said Brueler. "I don't know what you're talking about."

Calinescu stepped into the room, holding his smartphone out like an offering. "If we succumb to the fracture of our parts, we defeat ourselves. But it's the comments about Tay that I don't like."

Confused, Chase took the smartphone. He realized it was streaming something.

At first Chase thought it was a commercial broadcaster, but then he recognized the host. It was Andy Young, a blowhard populist who for the past ten years had made a fortune selling conspiracy theories. He called his homegrown network ABT, which sounded like an actual channel, but it really only stood for Andy Broadcasts Truth.

Calinescu reached over and turned up the sound for Chase and Brueler. Andy Young was shouting. "It sounds to me like some sort of coup!"

Then the voice of Andy's guest rang out, clear, crisp, sounding slightly harried yet clearly experienced in broadcasting. "I wouldn't say it's a coup!" said the guest. "But I would say that there's a clear division within the Reasoners, and *that* has to be recognized."

Then they split the screen, Andy on the left side and Vin Jansert on the right. Vin Jansert – clearly calling in from within his own room in the State building. The camera – likely on Vin's laptop – was cheated to be looking down on Vin. The positioning made him look a good ten pounds thinner. "Whatever happened at the bridge this morning did *not* involve all Reasoners," said Vin. "That's what I want to be clear about. It was just a rogue element. But not me, nor most of the others."

"You think anyone's going to believe that?" asked Andy.

"Why not?" Vin shot back. "There weren't twelve Reasoners on that bridge. There were four. That's what I'm saying: Some of us came here to do our job according to the rules everyone agreed to, and clearly some had other ideas. You can't lump us all together, Andy!"

Brueler went pale. "My God! What does he think he's doing?"

Chase turned to Calinescu. "When did this broadcast start?"

"A few minutes after we broke our meeting," Calinescu said. "Maybe fifteen minutes ago? Professor Pappason brought it to me."

"And what did she say?"

Calinescu hesitated just that extra second. "She … did not entirely object."

"What the hell!" Brueler threw up his hands.

"You see?" Mallickey said, grabbing Calinescu's phone. "If there ever needed to be greater proof of how the Reasoner setup needs to be altered …"

Brueler was looking around the room. "If he's using the building's Wi-Fi, we can just shut him down."

"No," said Chase. "This is Free-Fi. Look at that picture quality."

"Then forcibly pull him," said Mallickey, handing the phone back to Chase. "Then call everyone back together and make the announcement that Trevor and I will fill Dr. Hamer and General Williamson's spots."

"You mean pull Vin Jansert off the air in front of the country?" Chase asked. "Followed by an announcement that we're filling two vacancies on the Reasoner panel with government officials? If there's any way to create even more chaos, Congressman, you've found it. No, we should leave him on."

Brueler's eyebrows went up. "Chase, everything that clown says is going out across the country – the world – "

"Then let it. In truth, he probably *is* only doing it to protect the Reasoners who weren't at the bridge. Which might, actually, be a worthwhile cause. So let him spout as much as he wants."

"And throw three of you to the wolves?"

Chase shrugged. "We're not winning any popularity contests right now, so what's the loss? Besides, Beavenstock is the day's headline. No, the thing for us to do is nothing." Chase handed the phone back to Calinescu. "Although, once Vin is finished, we might tell him and the rest of the Reasoners that there's a breakfast meeting planned for tomorrow to sort through all of this, including Congressman Mallickey's security report and his proposition for filling the missing slots on the Reasoner panel."

Mallickey seemed truly shocked that any of his ideas would even be tabled. They had taken him seriously. Somewhat. It was an unusual thing for him.

Chase went on. "Then everything is laid on the table. We might also suggest to everyone the wisdom of avoiding impromptu interviews with the populist press. Or any press. In the meantime, everyone is extremely grateful for Congressman Mallickey's report, and we'll take him up on his offer of sharing it with the others at our discretion."

Mallickey smiled at the compliments but then his expression darkened as he realized –

"Thank you, Congressman."

– that he was being dismissed.

Mallickey had no intention of looking or appearing diminished in front of his aides – and certainly not in front of the perhaps-overvalued Trevor. So the man who spoke for the U.S. government reached for his zippered leather folder and explained that he couldn't spare another second.

Miles Mallickey and the two aides were gone in a matter of minutes.

When Calinescu left, Chase and Brueler were alone. Brueler fell back into one of the armchairs. "I don't know whether to laugh or cry."

"There's a lot to unpack there," Chase agreed.

"Yes there is," said Brueler. "The threats about you, for one thing."

"I don't buy that."

"You think Mallickey would make that up?"

Chase shook his head. "No, but why me? I'm nobody in particular. Part of a group." (Except he could still smell Senator Sofia Puccelli's perfume, couldn't he? As she leaned in and asked him, "Why you, Chase? You tell me.")

"Perhaps someone thinks you're more than that," Brueler said.

"Who?"

"I have no idea."

Chase didn't like where this was going. "We have a lot to do before tomorrow morning."

"What do you have in mind?"

"Reaching out to General Van DeVere."

Brueler sat up slowly. "Excuse me?"

"Of course."

"Chase – Professor – excuse me, but making contact with General Van DeVere is what's caused all this shit in the first place. We're in this nightmare *because* we – "

"No," said Chase. "We're in this nightmare because we made contact with someone who *wasn't* General Van DeVere. Fortunately, as a result, the real general did reach out to us. Why shouldn't we pursue our discussion as planned?"

"How are we going to manage that?"

"I don't know."

"You alone?"

"Of course not."

"Then you and who?"

Chase thought a moment. "Let me think about that. But let's make the request. And if the General hesitates, just tell him where the Reasoners think we are."

"Which is?"

Chase glanced out the window at the crowds in the distance. "At the precipice."

4

Once Brueler had gone, the Harley Man asked, "You want I should check the room?"

Chase held open the door, stepped back, and welcomed him in. He watched as the big man disappeared first into the bedroom, then crossed to the bathroom, then came out and began to run his hands under every lamp and along the curtain rod which spanned the picture window.

"Now would be a good time for me to ask the obvious, I suppose," Chase said. "Why?"

The Harley Man looked up at him. "Why what?"

"Back at the bridge. Why save me?"

The Harley Man returned to what he was doing, feeling the underside of an end table. "What was going on there wasn't right."

"Are you a Changer?"

The Harley Man nodded. "Sure was."

"Were you part of what happened?"

The Harley Man shook his head.

"So how …?"

The Harley Man shrugged. "Some of us heard something was going on up there. No one knew what. Then we saw the school buses. We followed them." The Harley Man hesitated. "I didn't recognize those people at the bridge. They might have been Changers, but I don't think so. The only thing I know is someone was looking for a fight. Whatever it was, it wasn't right."

Chase studied him. The Harley Man was now reaching under the radiator. "When did you decide to stop being a Changer?"

"Awhile."

"And yet you stayed here. In the city."

The big man shrugged. "I figured I might be needed."

"So, if you're not a Changer, what are you now?"

"Just me."

The biggest question. "Why are you taking care of me?"

The Harley Man finished checking the undercarriage of the radiator and pulled himself up. "I've watched you," he said. "I got you figured."

"As what?"

"Something that's needed."

"And what happens to me the moment you figure out that I'm not something that's needed?"

The Harley Man thought about that a good time. "I guess I would just go. But I wouldn't turn against you."

"Is that a promise?"

"That's a promise."

Chase considered that. "Okay. Fair enough."

5

When it came time to figure out sleeping plans, Chase was surprised to learn that the Harley Man expected to sleep on a chair outside in the hall.

"No," Chase said. "That's impossible. If you're okay with it, you should sleep in here." He pointed to the couch. "There, if that's all right, or we could have something brought in."

"I'll make do," said the Harley Man.

Then, before he went to bed, Chase realized he hadn't asked. "What do they call you? What's your name?"

"Hog."

"Hog?"

He nodded.

"Okay then. Hog."

Chase went to bed and Hog checked the room again before he lay down on the couch. He slept with his back to the window. He always had an eye on the door.

35. *On the Wall*

1

The day had been cloudy on the Mall and the evening was no different, so there was no moonlight to speak of. Add to that some sort of screwup with the power grid which usually lit the lamps around the perimeter – rumor said that someone had purposefully messed with it, which was a vandalism first – and you wound up with an almost medieval darkness which spread like a blanket all the way from the Capitol to the basin.

It also *felt* dark, as it never really had before. Even in the most violent days of the culling, after 5/22, life on the Mall had a sense of jubilation and celebration about it; a feeling that a new day was dawning, and even the ugly things were at least part of a greater good. Those were the days of a hundred thousand people singing or chanting together.

But that first night after the Beavenstock shooting was the beginning of some sort of shift. That night – and the night after and the night after and the night after – dark forces seemed to slither their way in, like smoke or a midnight fog.

Men traveled in packs in the darkness, some to protect, yes, but it seemed others had developed a mind to disturb. Everyone was on edge. Families zipped up tents soon after dark, and dads slept closest to the zipper, firearm at the ready. Tonight, with their leader having narrowly escaped an assassination attempt, the fear of the near future was palpable.

Fortunately, the Jerseys and Tacticals had at least retaken the Great Guillotine. Capitol steps security wasn't up to full force, of course – a good number of them were still stationed around Bridgepoint Hospital – but the rope was back and there were enough of them to discourage anyone who was thinking of challenging their authority again, at least up here. The cause of law and order was further helped when word spread – true or not – that when some of the Tacticals returned from Bridgepoint and came face to face with the yahoos who had assumed possession of the guillotine after Warren's death, they simply shot them.

Now the Tacticals and Jerseys roamed their wall like new centurions looking out over a spread of humanity which even they could tell was spoiling for some kind of fight. Most would chalk it up to the madness of the day, and not unprecedented in American history; most Changers viewed the assassination attempt as yet another assault on a great American leader, no different than MLK or JFK or Bobby.

What the guys up on the steps didn't know were the particulars. There's only so much you can see from the mountain. Had they decided to step down and actually mingle with their fellow Changers, they might have been surprised, even concerned, by some of what was happening on that moonless night.

How about a bunch of young white nationals trolling around in their pseudo-Nazi uniforms, acting like a sort of militarized gang-rape party, drunk and full of power? Their favorite trick was slicing open zippered tents and dragging women out for sport. Fortunately – or unfortunately, depending on whose side you were on – a whole lot of shitkickers who called themselves Satan's First were also pack hunting that night. Soon the Satans zeroed in on these same white nationals and, when they caught them, tied them to trees and used them for knife-throwing practice.

The Good Dads group, who up until now had acted as a sort of general security force across the Mall, seemed to have also lost their way, in purpose if not geographically. They were now rounding up and "arresting" teenagers they deemed out of control and forcing them into cages they had slapped together on the west side of the Smithsonian.

Then there were the fires. There were a lot of them. Nine bonfires in total, some built around a white stone cross. And while no one knew who the robed folks surrounding the fires *were*, you could tell they were armed, and really liked chanting, even if what they were chanting sure didn't sound like English.

Then there were the mysterious dozen poles erected earlier in the day on the steps of the Lincoln Memorial. These were the ones Chase had seen from his window. A lot of work had gone into them, but now they were abandoned, almost as if waiting their turn. A few people stood studying them, as folks will gather around newly planted modern art in a city park. There was a lot of head scratching.

"Whaddya think?"

"Can't be anything but."

"You don't think?"

"No."

"What then?"

"Burning."

2

It wasn't just at the Mall, either.

By nightfall, all sorts of towns and smaller cities across America – places that had convinced themselves the bad days of the insurgency and violence were over, at least as far as their communities were concerned – discovered just how easy it is to rekindle a flame. The problem was just where and how to focus your fury when a lot of fury has already been spent. Yes, some towns had rebuilt, but not all. So if you spent the day watching perpetual cable coverage of Beavenstock being shot and the craziness that had started it all, and if you got yourself riled up enough to go downtown and light City Hall on fire, chances are you'd discover that City Hall was still just a ruin. So was the Chase Manhattan bank. The local Verizon office as well. Options were limited.

But refrigerators which seem empty of any real food can often yield some really satisfying meals if you just get creative. That was the case in a lot of places, where truly dedicated shit disturbers discovered that somehow, they'd missed a lot of juicy targets in the first go-around. As a result, storefront operations like Mortgages-2-Go were blasted into non-existence courtesy of Molotov cocktails, while other operations, such as Money Marts, were simply robbed and trashed. And there developed a strange bias against certain companies – Cash For Gold was one – which led to ex-customers literally shitting and pissing all over the premises, and any healthcare billing agency – any – found itself the victim of wholesale demolition.

What this had to do with the shooting of Jeff Beavenstock was hard to tell, but what are you going to do?

Clearly, a lot of people took "take it all" to heart.

36. *The Night Call*

1

Chase was dreaming of Rin. One of those dreams where you miss someone so much that waking is painful.

He could sense not just her, but *them*, as a couple, clearly and in such high definition it was hard to believe he hadn't been transported back in time.

It wasn't just their physicality which consumed Chase, but their humor. In a way, that was worse. Because he and Rin had laughed in bed the way only people in love can. They had made crude jokes and confided things never whispered to another person on earth, intimacies shared as no two people had ever done before.

Almost from the beginning, each day became a matter of getting through whatever business needed to be done with "real people." Then they could race back to partake of the drug of each another. When they were able to avoid "real" things that needed doing, they spent endless afternoons, somehow always rainy – or at least in memory – when the rest of the world went about its responsible business and they lingered in bed until the streetlamps came on and the whole day was lost. Wonderfully lost.

So, when the flaws started to appear, Chase did everything to convince himself they weren't there. And certainly that they weren't fatal.

There were rage issues, for one. Mostly the world against her. The charming battle with the subway train and the suitcase turned out to be the way it always cut, although often without the charm; she railed against late buses or people on sidewalks who didn't move fast enough or children who made too much noise on residential streets. Waiters were rude and their rudeness meant Chase and she had to leave restaurants abruptly, untouched meals sitting forlornly on still-warm plates. Anyone she had to work with for more than a few days was incompetent, so she characterized leaving a job as deciding that "enough was enough," rather than her being let go – which he began to suspect was the truth more often than not. That probably (almost surely?) explained the loss of the incredible gig she finally *did* pick up with a small production house which produced feature pieces for Sky. They fought for an hour on the street about that one, and never entered the restaurant where they had reservations.

These frustrations with the world's operations would almost always send her into a tailspin, and during those times, sometimes for days on end – even a week or two – she couldn't get out of bed because she was "feeling rough." He tended to her as best he could. She would turn on him then. "I guess you feel I'm just this ugly toad you've been saddled with!" (*Everything* was a toad. "That toad of a toaster should be strangled it's so useless"; "My friend Frieda gave it to me. She's a toad too.")

When his insincere and genial comfort became oppressive, she would turn on Chase himself. "You think looking at me like *that's* going to help?" He found himself backing away from any attempt at reasoned talk and just agreed with everything she said. He let her hammer away at him, figuring she would eventually clue into the insincerity of his equanimity. But she didn't. She was way down the rabbit hole.

Eventually, on a day when she was railing at the news and how insane the politicians were ("Don't they see? Don't they have eyes?") he realized he was just sitting staring at her having these conversations with no one, and for the first time he thought to himself: "She is actually not right."

The thought was so awful and felt so traitorous that he had to yank open the old glass door and step out onto the balcony and lean over the tiny iron railing, literally gasping for air.

"Not right?" What the hell did that mean? He imagined it meant he thought she was clinically ill, beset by any number of physical and emotional ailments, like an alcoholic bedeviled by the family gene.

No. Because that wasn't it. Right diagnosis or wrong, he realized he had started treating her – sometime before, at some indistinct or unmarked moment – like someone who simply couldn't function in real society. He began to wonder if their days of lovemaking – soft or hard – had really been a disguise for those times when the challenge of getting up and bathing and getting dressed and going out had become too much for her – when she was simply unable to function. "A rough day full of toads," she would say mournfully.

She was too smart, though – smarter than him, certainly – not to recognize what was happening. She always knew everything. So, some left side of her brain saw him gasping for air on their tiny balcony in Earl's Court and a transformation would take place. She went to him and made sure he understood that her love for him was infinite and superseded all. And he was grateful for that. And then, just as quickly, she could sense his concern for her, and realize the concern was for her mind.

"You want to go away? You want to make a break for it?"

The way she said it wasn't threatening. It was pitying. As if she knew what a strain she placed on him.

A waking dream began to overtake him toward the end of their being together. A terrifying dream, in which he did not press the red STOP button in time, and instead she ran straight into the steel girder at the end of the subway platform. There was a horrific crack. Her face was destroyed, and she fell to the ground in a completely unnatural way. But her hand didn't let go of the suitcase, so as the train kept going she jerked alongside it until they came to the tunnel entrance, where she was destroyed against the brickwork, a human explosion of blood and bone and yellow tissue.

2

Chase woke with a start.

It took him a moment or two to understand where he was, but the paneled wall and the acoustic ceiling tile brought things into focus. Still, all he could smell for a few seconds was sugar and bread and incense and her perfume and the Earl's Court flat. It was so painful that all he could do was gasp for air, as he had on the balcony, like someone punched in the stomach. Then he slowly, in pain, got up.

In the bathroom he ran the tap for cold water to drink, but then he heard something. He turned the water off and listened. A murmuring? Perhaps chanting?

He returned to the bedroom and opened the blinds.

His binoculars were in the other room, but even with the naked eye he could see distant fires out on the Mall. A lot of them. He imagined he could hear some element of the crowd chanting, but of course that was impossible from this distance. From the loudspeaker system? God help us, whatever they were doing. Except, of course, a Reasoner doesn't believe in gods or visions, does he? A Reasoner, after all, was reasonable.

Except for Rin.

His phone rang.

It was on the bedside table, alight and vibrating insistently.

At what? Maybe three in the morning?

He picked it up. It was 2:21 a.m. and the caller had blocked their number. Chase took a second to make a decision, then pressed "Answer." He held the phone to his ear. "Tom?"

But it wasn't Brueler. Instead, a woman: a strident, challenging voice. "Do you limit your history to the nineteenth century, Professor?"

There was no mistaking her voice.

"Try me," he said.

"There's a garage in Rosslyn," she said. "It's still there. Level 3. In two hours."

"Is this a joke?"

The woman erupted. "We all know the joking's over and this shit has to stop."

"Which shit?"

"This fucking runaway train"

The reference stopped Chase cold, his dream too fresh. A runaway train?

And then, as if reading his mind and plucking out the image, she said, "And someone has to hit the red button, don't they?"

He wasn't sure how long he stood there with the phone to his ear.

"You can bring your friend," she said. "But no one else."

After a second or two, he realized the connection had been cut.

He pressed "END," then accessed the search engine. He typed in "famous garage" and "Rosslyn." He stared at the results. Somebody, he realized, had a sense of humor after all. Maybe.

3

Hog woke up instantly.

"Can you take me somewhere without anyone knowing?" Chase asked. "Away from this building?"

Hog looked around, as if making sure he was where he thought he was. He was groggy. "Tonight?"

"Right now."

"Where?"

Chase told him.

Hog thought a long time as he woke up. You could almost see him calculating the variables. "Yeah," he said, now fully awake.

"How?"

Hog pulled his blanket off. "I'll text you when to come down. Out back. I'll be there."

"What about the soldiers in the hallway?"

"I'll deal with them. You'll be able to walk right past them."

Chase returned to his bedroom. He put on his dark blue jeans and the black Princeton hoodie. He thought of a ball cap but that seemed excessive. He slipped all the money he had with him in the front pocket of his jeans but decided to go without any identification. Once Hog texted him with final instructions – a good twenty minutes from when he'd received the call – he left his room.

The two armed soldiers were still on duty in the corridor, but Chase simply gave them a nod and they nodded back. He pressed the elevator button and stepped in when it arrived, and to his amazement they made no effort to stop him or ask him where he was going. Whatever Hog had told them worked.

Chase pressed 1, and then R for "Rear" – as instructed.

Hog was waiting for Chase in the service area on the ground floor of the building, at the back, where deliveries were made. "Always six paces behind me," he told Chase, and pushed through a crash bar door. Chase looked around in amazement as they emerged into the heavy night air. There were *no* armed personnel out here. How was that possible? Especially after the events of today.

It was an old orange Dodge Caravan with Florida plates, sitting by one of the service bays with the engine running. Chase noticed a tiny lime green flag hanging from the tip of the radio aerial. Hog yanked open the side door and Chase hopped in. Hog slid it shut with a whoosh and then hopped in the passenger seat. They pulled away.

The guy driving the caravan could have been Hog's twin brother, only he was gnarlier, uglier, older, and much shorter. No leather Harley jacket for him, either. Just a jean jacket with SKULLS painted on the back in bright paint. Hog made the barest of introductions. "Neil," he said.

Neil looked in the rearview mirror at Chase. "Stay down and out of sight, Governor."

Governor? Chase stayed down and out of sight.

The guards at the back gate of the State building had very few questions, but Neil answered everything smoothly. He handed them something; whether an ID card or money, Chase couldn't tell from his position in the back seat, but it seemed to satisfy the guards, and out they went.

Was this really the true state of the Reasoner's security?

The Caravan circled around a few streets before heading northwest.

From the floor of the back seat, Chase asked, "How did you do that?"

"Do what?"

"Get through so easily."

In the front seat, Hog and Neil exchanged a quick glance. Finally, Neil shrugged. "There's security and then there's security."

"What does that mean?"

"Have you ever tried to get a gun onto an airplane?"

"Of course not."

"Try it sometime."

After a while, Chase asked, "Am I safe?"

"Oh, you're safe."

"How can you be so sure?"

Neil gestured to Hog. "Him."

After another minute or so, Hog signaled that Chase could sit up. When he did, Chase was shocked by what he saw. Had all this happened in one *day*?

This side of the city was technically government territory and up to now had almost – pretty much – resembled a normal working D.C. Tonight, however, a transformation had taken place. Now there were tents along many of the sidewalks, as well as cardboard shacks and lean-tos made of corrugated tin. Open campfires burned curbside, and people wandered back and forth, armed. Perhaps just visiting with one another, perhaps on some sort of patrol.

Neil drove on, circling around islands of debris.

A few blocks north of Woodley Park they passed a small fight.

Three enormous men broke it up easily, if brutally. As they passed, Chase turned his head to get a better look, and saw streaks of lime green paint on the sleeves of their jackets. It was the same color as the flag on the aerial of the Dodge Caravan. The same color as the word SKULLS on Neil's jean jacket. "What's with the green?" he asked.

"Law and order," said Hog, looking straight ahead as Neil skillfully snaked the Caravan around trash and tents dotting Connecticut Avenue.

Weren't there supposed to be real cops up here? Chase hadn't seen a single one. Instead, it appeared a self-appointed street force had risen up to manage these folks. And from where? Were they Changers who had decided to give up the battle and cross back over into GOR territory? Then a darker thought struck Chase. Perhaps they were folks who no longer wanted to be part of whatever was going on down at the Mall tonight. Which begged the question … What *was* going on down at the Mall tonight?

The streets cleared up the farther north they went, until eventually it looked like Washington again. But they were still heading in the opposite direction of Virginia. Chase leaned forward. "Where are we going to cross?"

"The chain bridge," said Neil.

"Why aren't we taking the Key bridge?"

"Gone," said Hog. "As of three this afternoon."

37. *The Parking Garage*

1

The historian in Chase couldn't help being intrigued. Then, as it appeared up ahead on his right, he was surprised to discover that it looked like any other parking garage. What else would it be, though?

Neil wheeled them around to a side street and pulled up to the curb. The contrast with D.C. was total. No tents or fires here in Rosslyn. In fact, nobody on the streets at all.

Hog hopped out first and told Chase to stay where he was. Hog went up the street to the corner, looked around, then crossed and went in the opposite direction, standing on the far corner and looking both ways and back. Eventually he returned to the side door. "All right."

Neil stayed behind the wheel as Chase got out and followed Hog, making sure to stay six paces behind as instructed. The big man took them halfway up the block, seemingly past the garage entrance, and then suddenly turned right into a recessed doorway. He opened an industrial metal door that said P-1, holding it ajar with his foot. He gestured that Chase hold up. As Hog peered into the parking garage, orange fluorescent lights fell on him. Chase saw that somewhere along the way, Hog had slipped the silver cannon out of its holster. He held it low. Chase had never imagined in his life that he would be so comforted by the sight of a gun.

Hog reached back for Chase and drew him by the shoulder into the garage.

It's possible, Chase thought, that this man has set me up. From the beginning. Yet while this idea struck him as perfectly reasonable, he also discounted it immediately. Call it instinct. Another strike against reason from a Reasoner. 'Instinct.'

There were very few cars in the garage. Maybe thirty. Chase's intention was to walk out into the middle of the space to make himself seen. Hog, however, clearly had other ideas. He held a tight grip on Chase's upper arm. He wanted to keep the two of them back here by the door. In the gloom.

Finally, a voice called out from nowhere. "All right?"

Hog and Chase turned at the same time. In a very dark corner by a massive ventilation duct, there were two figures. They were almost parallel opposites: a large, imposing figure wearing a leather jacket and ski cap, and a much smaller and slighter figure, wearing blue jeans, Adidas sneakers, and a hoodie. "Over here."

It was the bigger man calling them. The smaller figure was silent.

Hog looked at Chase. "Are you good with this?"

Chase nodded, although he wasn't sure if he was good or not.

Perhaps reading Chase's doubt, Hog led the way across the garage floor toward the dark corner and the two strangers. He held the silver cannon out in front of him for all to see. "Don't – even – think – about it," he said to the duo in the corner.

The person in the Adidas and hoodie finally spoke. "I didn't think you'd come. You've got balls. I'll give you that."

Chase and Hog stopped twenty feet shy of the corner. "We're close enough," said Hog.

It was a standoff. Then the person in the Adidas and the hoodie stepped out into the light. "Professor," she said to Chase, "you and I are going to talk alone."

It was her appearance. Without the pulled-back hair and what he now realized was a good amount of makeup, the cammo pants and the SURVIVE T-shirt – or the haute couture of the Reasoners meeting – she looked like what she had probably been only a few years before: a teenager from northern California.

Her hair was hidden under the baseball cap. Gone was the 49ers;

this one read "Safe Space Security" and Chase remembered reading in his big briefing book that her father, back in Oakland, owned a small security consulting firm which specialized in strip malls and chain restaurants. The Adidas jacket made her tiny.

Still, Sheena had a swagger no matter what and she showed it as she led Chase away from their protectors toward the dark alcove by the elevator doors. "They told me this is where all that Watergate shit went down."

"Yes," Chase said. "Where Woodward met Deep Throat."

She gave him a funny look on that, as if she wasn't sure if he was making a joke or not. She decided to let it go. "I figured all that history would bring you here even if I couldn't."

Bullshit, Chase thought. It was the reference to the runaway train that brought me here and you know it. That and a day from hell.

They were far enough from Hog and Sheena's protector that no one could hear them. Sheena turned to him. She was rolling a small piece of chewing gum around under her tongue. "I want to tell you something right off."

"Okay."

"We didn't know anything about the goddamned bridge. Not a fucking thing. And we sure didn't have any plans to get rid of your Nobel man."

'Nobel man.' An odd way to put it. Did she really not remember Hamer's name?

"Why should I believe you?" Chase asked.

"It didn't come from me, and it didn't come from Jeff. Or anyone close to us. You'll just have to believe me."

"But someone planned it."

"But that's what I'm saying. Not us."

"So someone as powerful as either of you."

She flashed at him. "And who the fuck would that be?"

He was pleased to see how quickly she was rattled. "Obviously someone with enough nerve to infiltrate the Reasoners as well as pull that whole demonstration together," Chase said. "And with enough nerve to try and kill a bunch of us."

"Yeah, *but not us*," she said.

Chase was watching her carefully. He had used the phrase 'infiltrate the Reasoners' strategically. He was acknowledging that there was a traitor amongst the Reasoners. How would she read that?

The answer was, she didn't care. Instead, she jammed her hands into the pockets of the Adidas jacket, rolled her gum around her teeth, and looked first to the left and then to the right, reassuring herself they weren't being overheard. Man, she was nervous. "Here's the thing, though." She looked back at him. "I lied. About Jeff."

"Lied to who?"

"Everyone. He's *very* fucked up. Very. He didn't say any of the things I gave him, because right now he's not saying anything. You hear me?"

"I hear you." Chase hoped he looked calm and unmoved, but inside he was holding his breath. "So why are you telling me?"

"What I'm *giving* you is that he's vulnerable, you hear what I'm saying? I'm trading."

"What for what?"

Again, she rolled her gum around and looked first right then left. "He could go any number of ways. You could probably dream up about twenty. But if he goes, I won't do anything about it. If you need it, I can even tell you how to get in there and do it."

He just took it in what she was saying, as unbelievable as it seemed.

So Mallickey was right. She did it. She set Beavenstock up. The only problem was it hadn't worked. For some reason.

"Let me get this straight," Chase said finally, keeping his voice even. "You want us to finish off what you started and couldn't get done?"

She took an involuntary step back from him and offered a small laugh. "What??" Her expression of stunned disbelief – mixed with what? Amazement? Insult? – seemed absolutely genuine. "You fucking morons think I had a hand in this shit?"

Now Chase was confused, but he kept on. "Beavenstock out of the way puts you on top. You tell us or the GOR how to finish off Beavenstock and in exchange you get complete control of the Changers."

She took another unconscious but immediate step back. "Man, you are fucking stupid! You think I want to manage *those* fucking crackers and toothless hillbillies? Those aren't my people. This isn't my shit. Those jokers don't even know what the cause *is*!"

Chase was confused. "What *is* the cause?"

She shrugged. "Tear it up. Start again."

It was the shrug that hit Chase. Not the shrug of a revolutionary, or a despot, or even a leader. It was the shrug of a kid.

Chase decided to test her. "By 'it' you mean the whole system? Because that's what your new American constitution seems to be saying. You even got rid of higher courts."

"Higher courts?"

"Tell me about that idea."

She just stared at him, a blank. She was unaware that he had just tested her, and she had failed. "Except you don't know about your new American constitution, do you?" he asked. "Because you never wrote it. Maybe you haven't even read it. So where'd it come from?"

She shrugged again. "Some miner of Jeff's. I don't know who."

"So tell me about the traitor within the Reasoners. Tell me about the nukes."

"What about them?"

"What do you really know about Russell, Kansas?"

"I don't know him."

He would have laughed if he'd been able. But Chase believed her response and was trying to sew it all together. Sheena was looking back over her shoulder every second now.

"And the traitor?"

"Yeah, a traitor," she said, but she wasn't paying attention to what she was saying.

An actor, he thought. She knew her part, she knew her lines, but once she delivered them she couldn't remember what they'd been about or where they came from in the first place. He tried again. "So you can't tell me about traitors and you can't tell me about nuclear weapons. So why are you even here?"

"Like I said, we're trading."

"No," he said. "I don't mean that. I mean here." He gestured to the world. "I mean all of it."

"You don't think this whole system needs ripping *up*?"

"Some of it. Not all."

She stepped forward again. The fire. The anger. "Look," she said, and now he could smell the spearmint on her breath. "Let me tell you how it works, because you don't know shit. So for about four years my uncle moved into our house because he and my aunt were splitting up." She said 'aunt" as 'awn-t.' "He lived in the place at the back. And for about four years that cocksucker put his hands on me every single second he got a chance. And I'm not just talking whatever perverse dick shit was in his head, I'm talking about taking a swing at me whenever he felt like it or whenever he was juiced to the gills, which was pretty often. You hear me?"

"I hear you."

"Now ask me what he did for a living."

"What did he do?"

She blurted it out with glee, as if it were the greatest punchline. "A mailman! A fucking postie! You get it, don't you?"

"I'm not sure I do."

"A federal employee, brother. He worked for the government. During that whole time, he collected a paycheck with the eagle on it. So ask yourself, how could they let a sack of shit like that work for them? Obvious answer: because the government is already full of sacks of shit!"

Chase wanted to run. Or shake her. A kid, he thought. But he stayed where he was and stuck with it. "So, what are we talking about?"

"I want out," she said. "I'm not doing this shit anymore, and I'm sure not sticking around until someone pumps one in my head and three in my back, okay? I didn't sign up for this shit."

"You're worried you're next." If that were the case, then she was telling the truth: She had nothing to do with what happened to Jeff.

"Oh, I know I'm next."

"So what do you figure?"

She thought about that. Her answer simply amazed him. "I was thinking I might get a job in journalism. Maybe be a pundit. Like Alex Wagner."

Chase knew he was openly staring at her. He wasn't, however, actually seeing *her*. What he was seeing was the dead. The endless stream. And the violence. The burnt and destroyed lives and buildings. The poor dumb bastard who had shot Jeff Beavenstock, executed on live television for everyone to see, his head falling off his body and blood shooting into the crowd over the usual shouts of revulsion and joy.

Death, everywhere.

He had to shift tactics. He was letting this opportunity get away from him, letting his astonishment keep him from doing what he needed to do. He looked down at the floor and gathered his thoughts as efficiently as he could. "Our world," he said slowly, "is about to burst open even wider, and if I'm reading you right, you're talking about leaving all those people leaderless."

"Well, if you're looking for leaders, the place is crawling with leaders. That's the fucking *problem*."

"Okay," said Chase. "So there are plenty of leaders everywhere and a new one steps up to manage the Changers. But who is to guarantee that this new leader will behave? What if this person has revolutionary ideas of their own?"

She laughed in his face. "What do I care? I'm just saying whatever's going to happen is going to happen without me. I didn't sign on to be leader of yahoos and I didn't sign up to be a dead woman on a postage stamp. I could put up with them as long as they kept the flame turned up – and they know how to run things – but clearly that isn't the case."

She was becoming irritable. Chase was out of time. "Why did you tell them to 'take it all down' if that's not what Beavenstock actually said?"

"Wouldn't you? If you had a chance? Just to see what would happen?"

Chase thought. Hard. "Okay, Sheena. I'll make a deal with you. But nothing to do with Beavenstock."

"Beavenstock *is* the deal."

"No, not yet. Later. For now, don't say anything to anybody. Let them think you're the leader – "

"Do you fucking listen or not? I just said – "

" – or leader-in-waiting for *now*," he said. "And, as leader, or leader-in-waiting, when we come to you, make a deal with the GOR, under recommendation of the Reasoners. Then, after, if you want, you can step down."

She looked at him and seemed about to say something when there was a sudden loud clatter on the other side of the garage, opposite from where Hog and Sister Sheena's security guy were standing. Everyone spun around. Someone dropping their keys? A weapon cocked?

Chase grasped her arm and steered her farther into the darkness, inches from one another. Her eyes were electric in the darkness. She peered up at him with a mixture of fury and fear.

"Look," he said. "That's the deal. Say nothing now – to anyone – and I'll get you your deal, maybe even talk to MSNBC."

"You sure?"

Once again, there was the sound of keys on the other side of the garage.

Then, out of nowhere, Hog was behind him, a hand on his arm. "We're going."

Chase turned and looked back at her as Hog led him away. As

Sheena spoke she seemed to diminish in size. "My plan really isn't as crazy or unhinged like you think," she said. "Nothing can stay the way it is forever, not even a revolution. This is gonna change. And when it does, they'll do what they always do."

Chase and Hog were at the exit door to the outside. Chase shook Hog off for just a second. "What's that?" he asked.

She shrugged. "Fuck."

Chase couldn't help himself. He laughed.

But Sheena never liked people laughing. "Don't make me your punchline, Professor. I mean literally fuck. Have children. Buy more crap. Argue at night. They'll place all this shit in the memory box. Their fight at the revolution. Like Woodstock, or Live Aid. Everything disgusting put aside. Rewrite the story. They'll have more kids and order up more cable."

"This is one that can't be sanitized, Sheena."

"Really? I bet I'm on TV as a good regular before you know it."

Hog tugged him again and Chase followed.

The double crash bar let out into an alley. They were behind an office building. Hog led him around the corner, then another corner. Chase was turned around and confused, but then suddenly they were back on the deserted main street. The Dodge Caravan's headlights lit up.

"Did you get what you wanted?" Hog asked.

"It isn't her," Chase said. "She knows nothing. Maybe never did."

The van pulled up within inches. Neil was at the wheel. It was starting to rain. They got in quickly and Hog slid the side door shut with a thunk. He hopped in the passenger seat.

The three of them drove in silence. Chase was looking out at the deserted streets of Rosslyn but he wasn't seeing them. He was turning over everything that had been said. It was almost too big to manage.

Her initial message was very clear, though: You find a way for me to get out and I'll give you a clear shot at killing Jeff Beavenstock.

Chase turned it over in his head. Again. And again.

Finally, he sat forward. "Hog." Hog turned his head so Chase could speak quietly into his ear. "How do we get to Beavenstock?"

Not even the slightest ripple of surprise. Hog waited.

"Because I want us to do everything we can to keep him alive," Chase said. "No matter what."

Hog didn't flinch or express any surprise. "I can make that happen."

"Okay then."

Chase sat back. They rode in silence as they approached the city. In the distance, he imagined he could see activity on the Mall.

He knew what he had to do the minute they got back. Unbelievable as it seemed.

38. *The Virginia Plan*

1

Vin Jansert held open the door and almost laughed, or maybe sneered, in Chase's face. "I guess I've been expecting you!"

"Too late for breakfast?"

On the contrary. Vin held open the door.

Chase nodded to Hog that everything was okay and stepped into Vin Jansert's suite. Hog stayed in the hall. Vin closed the door on him, too loudly.

The suite was plainer than any Chase had seen so far, certainly plainer than his own. Instead of American corporate luxury, there was a sense of desperate Soviet elegance. Perhaps they had simply run out of the good furniture, or perhaps someone was mocking Vin and his pretensions?

Because Vin certainly had those. At the moment he was downright flamboyant in a flowing silk yellow robe with a Chinese dragon embroidered on the back. He wore velvet purple slippers and red silk pajamas. He was pouring himself a goblet of orange juice from the silver breakfast tray they'd rolled in.

It was only just after seven, but Vin was clearly already game to engage. "I'll listen to you, but you're not going to lecture me." Clearly he assumed the purpose of Chase's visit was to talk about yesterday's appearance on Andy Young's show. "I was protecting the rest of us."

"And thereby putting us all in danger," Chase said calmly.

Vin shot back. "Hey, if I wanted to put you in danger, I'd make the case that you killed Hamer! You push me any further, I'll do exactly that."

The charge was so ludicrous that Chase didn't even bother with anger. Instead he moved toward the coffee. "Is that fresh?"

"Just brought up."

Chase tried to open the carafe. "Really? I killed?"

"*Had* him killed then. Got him in a situation where they were able to kill him."

"How'd I do that?"

Vin downed half his orange juice. "What matters is that everything's out of control now and that's largely because of you and your half-cocked plan. By the way, who gave you this special role in the Reasoners? When did that happen? And where the hell was I?"

Chase was having trouble figuring out how to open and pour from the coffee carafe. He noticed that while he was given a brushed-steel carafe in the morning, Vin's was real silver. A luxury he insisted on? "You're not the first person to notice that everything's out of control here," Chase said, ignoring Vin's question. "What I suggest you do, however, is just shut up, relax for half a minute, and listen to me."

"You talk to me like that again and I'll sock you in the goddamned jaw."

Chase smiled. "William F. Buckley to Gore Vidal. 1968. Which one am I?"

Vin was so surprised Chase got the reference that he stopped in mid orange juice and laughed. Some of the tension cleared the room.

Vin snatched the carafe from Chase, twisted the top, and poured him a coffee. Chase accepted it graciously and sat in one of Vin's armchairs, which felt too low. "I've just had a truly interesting meeting," Chase said. "I haven't told anyone else about it because I wanted to tell you first. In fact, I'm not sure who else I'm going to tell, if anyone."

"Meeting with whom?"

"Sheena."

Even Vin couldn't hide his shock. Finally, he said, "Bullshit."

Chase certainly had Vin's full attention. Every inch of it. He gestured Vin to sit in the opposite chair. Vin chose the couch. It put him closer to his guest.

In the Dodge Caravan coming back from Virginia, Chase had rehearsed his explanation of how Sister Sheena had reached out to him, choosing which crucial details to leave out. As a result, he was able to be as brief as possible with him. When he got to Sheena's offer about Jeff, however, Vin whooped in delight. It wasn't the reaction Chase had been expecting.

"That's it, then!" Vin said. "They're done! They're falling apart. Already!"

Chase tried to interrupt.

But Vin was only listening to Vin now. He was up. And pacing. "She's telling you she's terrified, so she wants out and she's okay if we take advantage of the situation and literally *kill* Jeff Beavenstock?! Trading for her own safety! That's what she's doing. There's no other way to read it. They're done."

"Okay," said Chase, amazed by the simplicity of the interpretation. He didn't have time for *this*. "Imagine for a second that's true. I'm not saying it is, but imagine it is. And for a second let's forget whoever did set us up on the bridge and whoever did manage to convince some poor slob to try and kill Beavenstock in the first place. And let's presume that Sister Sheena is out of the picture and someone 'accidentally' turns off Beavenstock's life support. What then?"

"*What then?*"

"Yes. What then?" Chase put down his coffee, went to the window, and pointed in the direction of the Mall. "What about them? I have a pair of binoculars upstairs. They let me see a lot … And I can tell you, those people don't look 'done' to me. In fact, I think they're starting to come up with some new ideas." Chase turned back to Vin. "Do you know that at the Lincoln Memorial there are now huge poles up in front, on the second steps? They put them up last night."

"Poles to do what?"

"My guess is either for lynching or burning people alive."

Vin went pale. His mouth hung open.

Chase continued. "We'll know soon enough, especially if those people find out there's no longer anyone piloting their ship – or worse, they get a new pilot."

"What are you saying?" Vin asked. "You can't possibly believe that we're better off with the leaders they've got now – *leaders who have cut people's heads off* – than with a new setup. Any new setup."

"That's exactly what I believe."

"Then you're not just an academic prig, you're insane. Let me see if I get this. A self-appointed leader of the Reasoners – that's you – wants to convince the mob that everything is still status quo, even though their head-chopping leader might be at death's door and their thinking leader – the only one other than the miners with any brains – is possibly at this moment scampering back to Mom and Dad's house in California?"

"No," said Chase. "It's a tougher sell than that."

"*Tougher?*"

"I want to convince them that they're winning. And I want you to do it."

Vin just stared at him. He sat down again. "You know, I don't know who you are really, or who you think you are, but I don't think you are who you *think* you are."

Chase ignored this. "I want you to go back on Andy Young's show. I want you to do exactly what you did before, but more so. Let everyone know just how fractured we are. And then I want you to tell the story that Miles Mallickey told us."

Vin reached for his cup of coffee. "What story?"

"About Russell, Kansas."

Vin's coffee paused on its way to his mouth. "What could the possible point of – "

"It will give them something to think about."

"It sure will. And inspire them to even greater violence."

"Not if you also hint that one of the Reasoner's greatest fears
— and the reason we were crossing the bridge in the first place — is
that the Changers might soon have access to the weapon that will
make the mere idea of Reasoners, or any other kind of compromise,
pointless."

"And that weapon is?"

"The United States Armed Forces."

Vin Jansert just stared.

Chase's phone vibrated in his pocket. He checked it. It was
Brueler. "SEE ME," it read.

"Trust me on this," Chase said.

"I don't trust you at all."

"Then stab me in the back. But do it later. Meet me halfway."

He left Vin Jansert sitting holding a mostly full coffee cup that
he'd forgotten he was holding.

2

Brueler was sitting at the big table in his own suite, surrounded
by his papers, books, and calendars. He looked freshly shaved and
showered, but the rolled-up sleeves suggested he'd been working for
a few hours already. "Close the door."

Chase did.

Brueler twirled the pencil in his hand, clearly unsure where to
start. "A meeting has been set up."

"With?"

"Van DeVere."

"The real one this time?"

"The real one this time."

"Okay."

"But there are issues."

"Such as?"

"The plan is practically a repeat of what didn't happen last
time, and what put you all on that bridge in the first place. The only

difference is that this time he's proposing three of you plus me. It's a good negotiating number."

"Why?"

"Three people can't be split. I'm a good addition because I'm administrative, but I don't have the power of a Reasoner. So three is smart."

"Did he name which three?"

"He left that to us."

"What do you think?"

"Well you, obviously. Then I was thinking Calinescu."

"A replacement for Hamer?"

Brueler nodded. "He watches. Thinks. He decides later. He's not obsessed with the sound of his own voice. Also, everyone likes him. I'm afraid that means the other Reasoner should be …"

"Pappason," Chase said.

Brueler sighed unhappily. "Everything is politics, isn't it? She's loud, she's no fan of yours, and she cuts to the quick. The problem is, she has no background in this kind of thing. So in terms of substance, she adds no advantage at all."

"But I agree. She should be the third."

"Which brings us back to our key problem: how to get everyone out of here without a repeat of our previous debacle. I don't have a plan for that yet, but I'm going to sit down and talk with Holden – "

"No Holden."

Brueler stopped in mid-motion. He gave Chase a look.

Chase didn't want to reveal to Brueler his meeting with Sister Sheena. At least, not yet. Instead, he said, "I have reasons to believe it can be done – possibly the Chain Bridge – but I want my new friend to oversee the details."

"The *Harley*?"

"The Harley."

"You trust him that much?"

"I do."

Brueler looked at him over the rim of his glasses. "You can

hardly blame Holden or the security force for what happened at Scott Key. That was Williamson's betrayal – probably – which means no one could have avoided – "

Chase shook his head. "I was in that car. I saw how they reacted. I want it to go this way."

Brueler sat forward. "Look, I know I'm just the cruise activities director here, but despite what Mallickey says your security is partly my responsibility as well. You want me to trust your safety entirely to some biker dude and his friends? You do not technically have say over your own security. That was never part of the arrangement."

"No, but what *is* part of the arrangement is that any Reasoner can quit at any time."

The threat shocked Brueler. "Jesus, Chase."

"Where is the actual meeting place?"

Brueler tried to recover. "Well, that's also a bit of a surprise. The General was very specific about that."

"Fort Belvoir? Vernon?"

"Neither."

"So?"

39. *Van DeVere*

1

Once Chase saw the Buffalo Wild Wings location, it made perfect sense, in a strange, practical way.

For one thing, this franchise stood on its own; it was just a square box in the middle of the eternal vastness of the parking lot which served the Fashion Center, a mall in southeast Virginia which had seen better days. The second advantage was that there were no windows – in deference to the need for minimal glare on TV screens – which meant the place was an almost perfect cinderblock bunker. Then there was the roof: a perfect flat square, mighty helpful when it came to landing the VH-3D Sea King helicopter – which looked like a squat khaki iguana up there – or the CH-53D Stallion chopper which sat beside it. (Contrary to its name, the CH-53 actually looked like a grasshopper.)

The final advantage was obvious: Who would suspect that the highest-ranked career officer in the United States Armed forces, four-star General Rasimus Collier "Bud" Van DeVere, would use such a screwy location for a covert rendezvous?

Not that there was anyone around to admire Bud's military cleverness. They'd cleared the entire area for a three-mile radius. The Fashion Center had been shut down before even that.

Four cars approached the mall. They were about as far removed as you could get from the black luxury SUVs which had been used previously. The orange Dodge Caravan which had taken Chase to Rosslyn was in the lead, followed by a late-model green Crown Victoria, and behind that an already gone-to-seed Dodge Charger, and a Ford F-150.

As the four-car convoy containing the Reasoners and their security detail pulled into the Fashion Center lot, Chase bent down to look out the back window of the Dodge Caravan. "Holy shit," he said. And why not?

There were a half-dozen combat vehicles parked strategically around the Wild Wings, with armed infantry in behind those. Along the roofline of the stores that encircled the restaurant there were silhouettes of sharpshooters, maybe one every twenty-five feet. This setup was tight. "Like Arafat," Chase said.

Brueler, in the seat beside him, glanced over. "What?" He had been distracted and silent from the moment they had left Washington in the pre-dawn light – waiting, no doubt, for the inevitable gunshot or explosion. A repeat of the Key Bridge.

Hog, up front in the passenger seat, pointed. Neil, driving, took direction: The car circled around the combat vehicles and pulled right up to the main entrance of the restaurant.

Hog got out first. He spoke to the armed infantryman who stepped forward to meet the vehicle. Once they got through whatever they had to say to one another, and all seemed in order, Hog gestured for Chase and Brueler to get out.

Kirsten Pappason and Albert Calinescu were in the Crown Vic behind them. Seeing Brueler and Chase step onto the sidewalk in front of the restaurant, they also clambered out. Pappason blinked in the morning sunlight.

Chase wasn't sure which emotion was stronger: relief at having survived the journey from Washington, or curiosity about where they were and the man they were about to meet – Chairman of the Joint Chiefs, Supreme Commander of United States Armed Forces, winner of the Defense Distinguished Service Medal, the Army Distinguished Service Medal, the Bronze Star, the Legion of Merit, the NATO Meritorious Service Medal, and the Joint Service Commendation Medal.

As it turned out, Rasimus Collier "Bud" Van DeVere didn't disappoint. He lived up to all that. And more.

2

The first surprise: Even though there were no customers or staff, the sports bar was operational. The air-conditioning and all of the TV screens were on. Once they stepped into the vast main room, however, the Reasoner team saw the logic – and maybe the other reason Wild Wings had been chosen as an ad hoc command center. Instead of football, baseball, basketball, soccer, and hockey games, the screens were running all the cable news all the time. It was the same thing the nets had been running for two days – Jeff Beavenstock telling the world that there was now a conspiracy to frame "his" people for the murder of one of the Reasoners, followed by Beavenstock taking four in the back. The thing was, though, that what with the different broadcasts, the variety of screens in the room, and the way the channels fragmented the images, it seemed like Beavenstock was getting shot over and over again from inside a sort of cubist nightmare: different-sized shots, angles, and perspectives, but the same man, same speech, same bullets, again and again and again.

General "Bud" Van DeVere was sitting at the immense center table, the one usually reserved for parties.

Surprise #2: He was utterly alone, studying an open Dell laptop, with a positively immense coffee mug at hand. He wore full fatigues, complete with sidearm.

The thing that struck Chase was a sensation of cleanliness. The man seemed outrageously tidy and well groomed. Then, as the Reasoners entered and the General stood up, Chase was struck by how stocky he was. The General couldn't have cracked five-eight, yet the build made up for it. This was someone who had overbuilt himself to the point where he resembled a bear. The close-cropped hair, just starting to go grey, helped. Only when he smiled and he turned those blue eyes on you did you glimpse the corn-fed farm boy.

Yes, Chase, thought, a boy – but a dangerous boy. Dangerously ambitious (he'd made Commanding General in his thirties) and dangerously smart; there were two PhDs in two entirely different disciplines – one in cognitive sciences, the other in medieval history – and a string of published works stretching back into his twenties. It was rumored he spoke more than ten languages; he legendarily communicated with his desert opponents in conversational Farsi. He believed in nothing but practical ends. In one case he bombed an ancient city into dust to destroy a safe haven; in another case he merely bought dozens of warlords off with bundles of American cash wrapped in rubber bands and dispensed in organized lineups, complete with receipts from pads purchased at Office Depot.

Now he turned the blue eyes and charm on, and came around from behind the big table, greeting them by name. "Thank you for coming to me," he said, as if there had been any other option.

He gestured to a refreshment station near the entrance to the kitchen. There were fountain drinks as well as urns from which wafted the scent of freshly brewed coffee. "Help yourselves."

As Calinescu, Brueler, and Chase did, Kirsten Pappason plunked herself down on the other side of the party table, dead center; ready, presumably, to do battle with America's great military leader.

The General nodded at Hog and the two military men who had escorted the group in. "We're fine for now," he said. He seemed to accept Hog, despite the Harley gear, as just another soldier.

Hog shot a quick glance at Chase. Chase sipped his freshly poured coffee, nodded imperceptibly, and Hog left, but not without a dip of the head at the General. Had Hog served?

"Forgive the unusual location," the General said. "But this works for us for right now." He looked at Brueler expectantly.

Brueler knew what the General wanted. He put down his coffee and reached in his leather file folder. He withdrew three papers stapled together and handed them over to the General. The General reviewed them carefully, then looked at Brueler. Brueler nodded. "Your copy," he said. The General slipped them into a file folder sitting beside his laptop.

Chase knew that these were copies of the original articles of authorization of the Reasoner Compromise, signed by the GOR and Jeff Beavenstock himself (using a fading Sharpie). The very fact that the General wanted to have his own copy reminded everyone that no matter what, he was very much a "cover the basics" man.

He gestured everyone should sit. Calinescu chose a chair beside Pappason, while Chase chose one along the side of the table, closer to the General and perhaps less confrontational than where Pappason had parked herself. Brueler, in keeping with his view of his role, sat at a smaller table, removed. He brought out a pad of paper and pen to take notes.

General Van DeVere clicked a remote control and all of the screens went silent. "Distracting," he said. He took his big mug and drew himself more coffee from the biggest urn. "I was very sorry," he said, "to hear about Dr. Hamer." He looked at each Reasoner. "I knew his work. I was even foolish enough to write a piece on him years ago."

"I wasn't aware," Chase said. This was a lie.

"Nothing valuable. But what a mind."

Two pieces, actually. One was for *American Scientific Mind* – about the possibilities of remote underwater mapping technology – and the other for a *British Economics Journal* on the efficacy of crypto-currencies. Like Hamer, the General was a man of many sides and talents.

"It looks like someone took you from behind on that," the General said. "The bridge, I mean."

"Yes, they did."

The General settled himself behind the table once more. "But the question is who. Such an attack is certainly more sophisticated than anything they've sprung so far, at least in my estimation. Not Jeff's style. I haven't had any direct dealings with him, of course, but we've studied all of their tactics and methodology, and they've shown true consistency: 'Hit you over the head and steal your wallet' is pretty much the size of it. Subtlety and the double-cross don't seem to be in their wheelhouse. No long-term thinking."

"Some suspect there's another party at play here," Chase said. Yes, he was fishing.

The General nodded. "Pay attention to what Beavenstock said in the minute before he was shot. He said, 'We didn't do this!' Take him at his word. So, if he didn't do it – and it's likely you didn't set yourselves up or kill one of your own Reasoners – then by definition, yes, there's another party at play. Someone smart enough to kill Hamer and smart enough to almost kill Beavenstock and smart enough to have followers and smart enough to turn the temperature up on the whole damned country without being noticed. That's plenty smart."

"It certainly changes the nature of our role," Chase said. "Perhaps yours as well."

The General shook his head. "I know my role."

Pappason couldn't hold herself in any longer. "And what *is* that role exactly, General? Sitting and doing nothing while Washington and whole swaths of the country tear themselves up even further?"

The General pivoted his attention to Pappason and studied her for a moment too long. Those nice blue eyes turned cold. "With all due respect, Doctor Pappason, as unbelievable as it sounds, everything that the country has seen so far has been – comparatively speaking – nothing more than a fistfight outside a bar."

The three Reasoners and Brueler looked at one another. No one knew what to say to that. Finally, Calinescu spoke in his slightly halting way. "With all due respect to yourself, General, people have burned down cities. Washington is now divided by a mob, and many people – our leaders – have been kidnapped and systematically and publicly murdered. Our government has been split. And if I may add, a friend of mine, one of the finest minds on the planet, has been murdered. We are living in a new Reign of Terror. That is not a fistfight."

"I said, comparatively speaking."

Pappason was angry. "That's insane!"

The General turned back on her. Chase could practically see the gloves coming off. "Is it? Perhaps I view your description of what

I've been doing – 'sitting and waiting' – as insane."

They were off to a rollicking start.

"But that is what you've been doing!" Classic Pappason. "Hiding behind the court's decree and an outdated parsing of the 25th Amendment."

"Only if you call protecting the planet sitting and waiting."

That shut her up. Chase saw his moment. "Perhaps, General, you can detail some of the reasoning behind your actions or inaction. That might help us tremendously."

Van DeVere got up, went over to the coffee station again, and topped up his cup, which didn't need topping.

The General said, without turning, "Let me ask you a question, Dr. Pappason. What do you think the rest of the world does when the United States decides to have a civil war?" He turned. "Sit back and wait? Watch with bemusement? You think our enemies just press the 'pause' button and wait for us to get back in the game?"

Pappason said nothing.

The General made his way back to the table. "I don't believe our foreign friends or enemies would agree at all that I've been sitting and doing nothing. I think they would say I have been on the wall. With my gun. Fully loaded. Making sure our enemies know that there are incalculably strong forces ready to destroy them if they even consider trying to take advantage of this situation, or interfere in any internal strife or civil war in any way."

He turned his laptop around so they could see. He hit "full screen" and revealed a surprisingly rudimentary map of the world.

"And I'm not just talking about making sure that our ships are roaming the Persian Gulf or the Strait of Hormuz, or the Black Sea. I'm talking about the battle against cyber warfare, bio-technological threats, AI, you name it. And my intention has not been merely to maintain status quo, either. I'm talking about ratcheting up the threat so everyone knows – *everyone* – that while we are sorting out our problems at home, no one dare take a potshot. That includes Russia, China, North Korea, and certainly our old friends in the desert."

Pappason was silenced by the directness. At first. But she recovered quickly. "Perhaps we wouldn't have to be so aggressive if you'd interceded in the first place, when this crisis erupted."

"As the court made clear, the military only takes its orders from the duly authorized Commander in Chief, Doctor," said the General. "And that's what I did and am doing."

The Reasoners exchanged confused glances. Finally, Chase spoke. "Excuse me?"

"Do you people think I've been operating strictly on my own judgment? You're a historian, Professor Chase. Do you believe that's possible? Even likely?"

Chase searched for an answer. "Everyone has assumed ... "

"Yes, everyone has assumed. But don't assume. Everything I've done and am doing I have done and am doing on standing orders received from my Commander in Chief. And that order was to not engage with insurgent Americans under *any* circumstances."

The shock that greeted this statement was complete and total. From all Reasoners. From Brueler. Pappason's fury simply disappeared. But she pulled herself together enough to ask the most important question. "Which President are you talking about?"

"The last one elected by the American people."

It took Pappason a moment to realize what he was saying. "President *Drury?*"

The General nodded. "He was very clear."

"But when was this?" Calinescu asked.

"May 5."

Chase wondered if his fear showed. The ramifications of this, if true, were inestimable.

Pappason rallied again, though. Brueler and Chase had been wrong. She was the perfect choice for this mission. "He told you this? You talked to him? This was verbal?"

"Verbal, and emphatic," said the General.

"Define emphatic," Chase said.

"Yelling."

"What was he yelling about?"

General Van DeVere shook his head. "No. Even now – perhaps particularly now – I'm not going to recount word-for-word private conversations I had with an American President."

"The man is not the President now, General," said Pappason.

Van DeVere raised an eyebrow. "Are we sure of that?"

Oh shit, thought Chase.

The General clarified. "Let's be clear," he said. "He was in favor of them. Right up to the end."

"In favor of what?" Kirsten Pappason asked.

"The insurrections."

The room was silent.

Eventually, it was Calinescu who spoke. Clearly and directly. "You are saying that the President of the United States approved of the Uprising? The burnings of the cities? The chaos? The violence?"

The General nodded. "Again, without getting into a word-for-word, he expressed a theory – at least I think this was his theory – that all the trouble could be blamed on his political opponents. He was determined to win back the House. He knew the public perceived him as weak – very weak – and he wanted to be seen as strong. Law and order. Crushing an insurrection at the last second might be just what the doctor ordered. Unfortunately – and now we get into mere speculation – things went much further much faster than perhaps he ever imagined. So, once he saw it had turned on him and that he couldn't control it – that not only was he in physical peril but that he would be found to have a *role* in these matters – "

"He freaked?" Calinescu asked.

The General smiled, liking the word. "Yes, Doctor. He freaked."

"Which is when the Vice President decided to invoke the 25th Amendment," Chase said, filling in the rest of the story.

Van DeVere shook his head. "No, I don't think he decided anything."

"What?" Pappason asked in amazement.

"He was acting on the President's orders. The last thing I understood – from the President – was his belief that the 25th Amendment might protect him."

There was a long while as they all tried to absorb what they'd just heard.

("Let us be clear," Senator Sofia Puccelli had said to Chase. "He is a very, very weak man.")

"Okay," said Kirsten Pappason, slowly, clearly measuring out her thoughts. "Okay, okay, okay. But you have a new Commander in Chief now. In fact, you've had two since then."

The General's eyebrows went up. "Have I? And do I? Oh, I understand the narrative. After the Vice President and the Cabinet invoked the 25th Amendment, the Vice President changed his mind – by then the culling had started and he wanted nothing to do with that – so things bounced down to the Speaker of the House."

"She's your new Commander in Chief," Calinescu said. "Emmeline Jones. And the Constitution states – "

"I believe everyone needs to read the Constitution much more carefully, Doctor," the General said. "My copy quite clearly states that in the event of the Vice President assuming the President's authority, the VP and the Cabinet have to transmit their declaration within *four days* to the President pro tempore of the Senate and the Speaker of the House. Did that happen? It didn't. Then the Constitution is even clearer: The House is supposed to assemble within forty-eight hours and put their stamp on the whole thing. Did that happen? No, that didn't happen, either."

Pappason practically pounced on him. "Perhaps because members of Congress were imprisoned in the basement of the Capitol!"

The General nodded. "That they were. And for all I know, the new 'President' took a hand in making that happen. After all, she was the beneficiary."

This was too much for Pappason. "Oh come on! Do you honestly think – "

Finally, the General lost his composure. It was as Chase

suspected. Zero to sixty. "That's the point, Doctor! I'm not *supposed* to think. I'm supposed to follow orders from the Commander in Chief. Congress has not met the standards of proving to the satisfaction of this command who that is. Did we have a real transition of power or are we engaged in an overthrow, one party over the other?" He stopped a moment and looked down at the floor. He was clearly doing whatever he'd learned to do to tamp himself down. Eisenhower. Washington. MacArthur. They all had the same temper.

When he looked up, Van DeVere looked like the most tired man in the world. "I know what everyone wants. You think I don't know?" He reframed his thoughts, then sat forward, his elbows on the table. "But let's just talk it through. Imagine I go into Washington with a Division or two – and it's going to take a lot more than that, but let's say a Division or two for starters. So, we go storming into D.C. and start blasting away. Like MacArthur and the bonus army in '32." He nodded politely at Chase. "That'd be your area, Professor."

Chase nodded back.

General Van DeVere continued. "Now, to avoid this being some sort of coup, I'd have to be doing so at the behest of the Commander in Chief, whom everyone is satisfied – let's say, for the sake of no argument – to be the ex-Speaker of the House. She has approved everything we do. So we go in, guns blazing. Well, Doctor, we had trouble in Fallujah. We had trouble in Kabul. We had trouble in Mosul and Baghdad, and that was with air support. I'm telling you that ground wars are not a piece of cake, and we're not facing six hundred ISIS fighters here, we're facing six hundred *thousand* Americans, many of them loaded to the tits before they even got there. And that's forgetting those trucks that have pulled up and unloaded weapons day after day since then. God knows how powerful they are now, but for sure they are a hell of a lot stronger than six hundred ISIS fighters. Worse, they have fortressed themselves in historical sites and they are convinced that they are fighting nothing less than a second American Revolution – and they *are* American citizens. Now, to turn this thing around, we'll have to kill them – most of them – and reduce much of the area to rubble. And that's just for starters."

He stopped. The Reasoners were silenced. Overwhelmed. It was a safe bet that none of them had thought this through quite this way. For sure Miles Mallickey hadn't.

Calinescu tried his best, grasping for rosier options. "Surely," he said, "there must be another way … "

The General shook his head. "This is not going into a park to break up a knife fight, Doctor. This is armed street combat. With artillery. Heavy artillery."

Pappason chose a new tack. "You're saying you can't win."

The General shook his head. "Of course we can win. What I'm saying is that no one could tolerate the way we would have to win. And how in the world you'd stitch back a nation – little less a government – after that is beyond me. Wars are about killing, Dr. Pappason, not about converting and bringing people back together. For that you need political leadership and in case you missed it, that's been severely lacking in this country not just for the past six months but for decades. And what decent leadership we might have is probably locked up in the Capitol basement."

Finally, he sat back and crossed his ankles. For the first time he seemed vaguely relaxed. He had said what he needed to say, possibly for the first time since the whole mess started. "So, we're sitting tight right now. Because, as awful as it sounds, whatever happens out there now – even with that Great Guillotine on the scene – is nothing compared to what *we* would unleash. And we're supposedly on the side of the good guys."

There was silence. Everyone was gathering their thoughts. Finally, Pappason spoke. "I'm listening to a U.S. soldier – a general – unwilling to do his job."

If she was trying to land a punch, it didn't land. The General shrugged, taking the insult in stride.

"And what about *your* job?" he asked. "Didn't you sign on as a Reasoner, whatever the hell that is? Isn't your job to 'reason' us a way out of this so that I don't have to blow the Capitol and country to kingdom come? Didn't both sides even sign on to that? And yet, to my eyes, it seems like you've done nothing much beyond having meetings and messing up to the point where we've got an assassination attempt on our hands and two dead Reasoners, if some of the rumors I've heard are true. And now you're pissed that I won't just come in and turn the nation's capital to rubble to fix what you refuse to do. Where's the reasoning in that?"

Voices started to speak at once. Chase cut them off. All eyes turned to him.

Chase chose his words carefully. "Maybe we can explore messing up at a later time. There's something else, I think, we do need to explore ... "

The General knew what Chase was going to say. "You're going to ask me about Russell, Kansas."

"I am."

The General shrugged again. "Well," he said. "Likely everything you've heard is true."

"Jesus!" said Pappason, throwing her hands in the air. She got up off her chair and paced to the back of the room.

The General looked from face to face, like a good prosecutor clarifying things for the jury. "Let's be clear. The NNSA is responsible for nukes, not the U.S. military. And the Department of Energy. Again, not us."

"So who is manning that facility?" Chase asked.

The General took a moment before answering. "On August 6, one of our squads came across a nuclear silo base that was totally – I mean totally – deserted of all United States government personnel. The only people on the base were a bunch of yahoos who said they were taking over the weaponry in the name of this thing called the Wolf."

"The *Wolf*?" Chase asked.

"That's what they said."

"The Wolf specifically? Not the Changers?"

"The Wolf."

"And what happened to those people?" asked Calinescu.

"Well, Doctor, we killed them."

It was the bluntness of the statement.

"You *what?*" Pappason said from the far end of the room.

Van DeVere could have been talking about taking down a coyote that had invaded a chicken coop. "They barricaded themselves in a nuclear weapons facility and were making it very clear of their intention to try and launch the thing. Now, as I understand it, they all seemed pretty drunk, so the odds of them pulling that off were pretty much up there with flying to the moon on a waffle maker. And maybe they'd already been there a few weeks with no luck. Who knows? Who cares? Also for all I know, despite evidence to the contrary, they might very well come up with a couple of geniuses from the pack who could launch the thing. So, we removed all possible threat."

"You killed them all?" Chase asked.

"Yes."

"No witnesses left?"

"We secured the facility."

"And who's in control of it now?"

"We are. U.S. military."

"With no possibility of that situation changing?"

"None."

"And El Paso, Colorado?"

"We took no risks there. We heard there was the potential for an assault, so we secured that facility as well. You better tell me what you're getting at, Professor."

"Just this." Chase sat down in the chair opposite the General. Pappason's. Finally, the two men were looking at one another directly. "We could be heading into a crisis that makes everything we've just talked about look like child's play."

"Yes, there's always that possibility."

Chase nodded. "But I believe it's also possible that all that could be avoided if we can simply convince the Changers of what we might call … 'alternative facts.'"

The General smiled. "And what 'alternative facts' would those be?"

Chase looked at the others. For a mad second he was tempted to tell them about his breakfast with Vin Jansert, but reason prevailed. He kept it simple. And direct. "That rather than being weak, the Changers are much stronger than they think. That they actually *did* gain control of a nuclear facility and in fact they hold it now. Maybe more than one. Maybe El Paso, too. That they did actually repel an attempt at bringing in the U.S. military into Washington, and yes, they did kill a Reasoner without any repercussions."

Pappason erupted. "Why in the hell would we tell them that?"

Chase looked back at her evenly. "Because we can't fight these people," he said. "We can't win. We have to admit that. So clearly we need to tell them that we've lost."

There was a prolonged silence as they all weighed this.

Finally, the General laughed. "Apparently in coming here, Professor Selby had much more important things on his mind than a mere status report from the U.S. armed forces and its very tired and grey nominal leader."

There were a few weak smiles.

"I did and I do," said Chase. "But first I needed to know two things. The state of our WMD facilities as well as just how bad a full attack from the U.S. military would be. You have informed us of both. I, for one, believe you. Unfortunately, the events of the past few days, as well as what you just said, also mean we can forget about the time-honored tradition of bad guys coming together with good guys to create a peace." Chase looked at the General. "Someone has to win here or we're going to utterly destroy ourselves."

"And you've decided it's got to be them who wins."

"Yes."

"With the ultimate objective being that they *don't* win?"

"Of course."

"And who," the General asked, "is going to convince all those Changers that they've actually been winning all along? That they're not just a rabble of deplorables? Who is going to convince them the government couldn't, in the end, stand up to them?"

Chase checked his watch. It might be over by now, or it could still be on. Either way, he knew he could find it on social media.

He asked if the General could find him a Google page on his laptop. The General, puzzled but intrigued, toggled a few keys, then spun the laptop around for Chase. Chase leaned in and typed. In seconds, he found a site that was streaming it live. "Watch."

The others leaned in and watched. "Oh my Lord," said Calinescu.

For there he was. Vin Jansert. Broadcasting from his room and chatting once again – via split screen – with shock "news" commentator Andy Young.

If he had looked somewhat guilty in his first broadcast, or even, being unkind, like a hostage making a ransom video, Vin seemed downright perky today. You could almost see his tail wag. "I'm saying it's time to stop the bullshit, Andy! We got it straight from the horse's mouth – Miles Mallickey – that this thing in Kansas actually happened – "

Pappason's hand went to her mouth. "What does he think he's doing?!"

Chase was expressionless. "Telling them a story they'll like. That they'll believe. A story we can use." He looked back at Van DeVere. "Which means you're wrong about one thing, General. You *will* be going into D.C. But not with guns blazing. With them cheering you. Because they'll be convinced you're *their* military now."

The General was stunned. "And then what?"

"We'll take it from here," Chase said.

"Take it from there how?"

"No," Chase said. "That's your message. 'We'll take it from here.' Isn't that the usual phrase? You'll take over the cells in the basement of the Capitol, and you'll take over the business of the executions. In short, you've got this one. And they can all go home."

The General smiled. "And how exactly does that happen, Professor?"

"Call me Chase."

<h1 style="text-align:center">3</h1>

Chase and Brueler were silent in the Dodge Caravan heading back to Washington. Brueler looked like a man who had been in a traffic accident and was just starting to clear away his shock. Finally, he said, "Do you think it's even possible?"

"Frankly? I don't know."

Brueler slowly turned his head and gave Chase a puzzled look. Then he clarified what he meant. "About *President Drury*. Do you believe what the General said is even – at all – possible?"

"Oh, that. Of course. Don't you?"

"It just doesn't seem – plausible."

"I think it's the most plausible thing so far."

The two men studied one another as if across a vast gulf. "You can't be seriously thinking of Vin Jansert playing a major role in – anything," said Brueler.

Chase shrugged. "We need a messenger, and he's a professional messenger."

"He's a clown!"

"Yes," Chase said. "Precisely because he's a clown. The nation listens to clowns. Vin Jansert, however, is not what concerns me."

"The General?"

"Not that General. I was thinking about Black Jack Pershing."

"Excuse me?"

At first, it was only a half-formed thought in Chase's head. But as he looked out his window – they were about to cross the chain bridge now, so far so good – his thoughts became clearer.

"Pershing was against the Armistice in World War I. Did you know that? He thought we should keep fighting until the battle was literally in the streets of Berlin and every German village. Do you know why?"

"No," Brueler said. He was confused by this sidetrack.

Chase went on. "Because, without such proof, the General said, he feared the German people would never truly accept that they had lost. And if they believed for even a second that they hadn't lost fair and square, they would always chafe at the Armistice. Which, of course, turned out to be true. Hitler rose to power by referring to the Armistice as the 'knife in the back,' and in almost every way, the Second World War was about retribution for the First World War."

Brueler was impatient. "I'm sorry, Chase. A lot of things have just been thrown at us. I'm not sure what Old Jack has to do with where we are now."

"Because however this resolves itself," Chase said, "the Changers have to believe that they won, that their anger was not sacrificed. Otherwise, they'll be back."

Brueler took that in. Then, finally, arched a brow. "And you think *Vin Jansert* can convince them of that?"

Chase smiled. "Sure. But don't get me wrong. Vin is just a messenger. Just as the General is and the military he represents. In the end, we're going to need a voice that can control literally millions of minds of fury and convince them they have won their revolution."

"You have someone in mind for that role?"

"I do, actually."

"Who?"

"The only possible entity that binds all of them together."

Brueler looked at him in amazement, as if seeing for the first time that Chase was truly, utterly, off his rocker. Finally, he said, "The Wolf isn't real, Chase."

Chase smiled. "I know that. But hear what the General told us back there. Even before identifying themselves as Changers, those people believe in the Wolf, or at least the *Words of the Wolf.* And Black Jack Pershing would say we need the people to be convinced."

"But how do you bring on board something that doesn't exist?"

"We make one, Tom."

"One what?"

"Wolf."

Brueler thought about that and nodded, finally. "That's very clever. Except for one thing."

"What?"

"What if there really *is* a Wolf?" He ignored Chase's startled look. "And it bites back?"

40. *The Attack*

1

Chase would later play events over and over in his head and always wind up asking the same question: How could he not have seen what was so obvious? What lives could have been saved if he had?

The problem was in the planning. They had left D.C. in the pre-dawn hours when the streets were largely deserted, which was essentially a replay of Chase's trip to Rosslyn to see Sister Sheena. The distance to the General and the time spent with him at Wild Wings, however, meant that no matter what, they were returning in the late morning, which meant the streets had filled up with traffic and pedestrians. Although they always kept to the Government side of the city, Chase estimated that half the sidewalkers were now Changers, just going by wolf hats and sports jerseys. These were possibly Mall migrants, as he'd begun to think of them; folks trying to distance themselves from some of the darker things that were starting to take place down there.

Trouble, however, was not in the ride back. Trouble appeared as they made that last right-hand turn.

The first surprise was that there were crowds outside the gates of the State building. Changer crowds. Angry Changers. And they were singing.

Brueler sucked in his breath the second he saw them. Chase leaned forward between the two front seats for a better view. He sensed Neil hesitate at the wheel for just a fraction of a second. Hog didn't hesitate at all. "Go in! Go in!"

Neil nudged the gas just that extra bit.

The second the crowd realized that the approaching orange Dodge Caravan was intending to pull into the State building – along with the three cars behind it – they set upon the hood and windows, banging and singing. The folks inside the vehicles were treated to the ugly contorted faces of the truly pissed-off.

"What are they singing?" Brueler asked, a tight grip on his arm rest.

Chase tried to make sense of it. "We don't need no … patrol?"

"Thought control," said Hog.

"What??" Brueler asked. The crowd was now rocking the car.

"Thought control," Hog repeated.

He was right. Rather than chanting, "You don't tell us, we tell you," the Changer crowds had chosen to sing, "We don't need no education, we don't need no thought control," over and over again. Not quite with the gusto of the fellows in Pink Floyd, but pretty close. The question, of course, was what were they *doing* here? The Reasoner location hadn't been exactly a secret – if you really wanted to know, you could find out – but nor had it been the focus of Changer ire. For one thing, it was on the wrong side of the dividing line. For another, everyone knew that Reasoners were hands-off. But things, clearly, had shifted, hadn't they? And so, the State building was now a target.

Chase turned to ask Brueler about this, when a shot was fired.

In a repeat of what had happened on the Key bridge, the crowd scattered instantly. That was enough time for the security team working the State building gate to run out and form a cordon around both sides of the car, automatic weapons at the ready. One of the watch commanders – Chase had never seen him before – was standing at the gate entrance, holding his pistol in the air. Clearly, he had been the one who fired the shot; a warning, most likely, but he certainly looked like he was ready to make good on the threat if anyone wanted to take him on.

They waved the cars through quickly, bumper to bumper.

Neil did a half-circle around the driveway and bumped into the underground parking garage.

The sudden change from sunlight to the dark of the underground blinded them, and Neil slowed as they drew up to the elevator entrance. Five security soldiers in full cammo stood armed and ready to escort the Reasoner team upstairs. The moment all four cars were safely in the underground, the big garage door closed behind them. Visibility improved.

And yet Hog seemed concerned. He was peering in his side mirror, studying the closed garage door. "Has it ever done that before?" he asked.

Neil brought the Dodge to a stop in front of the soldiers. Still keeping an eye on the garage door behind them, Hog got out. He opened the back door for Chase and Brueler. The cars behind them started emptying as well.

As Chase clambered out, behind Brueler, he was focused on the strange expression on Hog's face. The big man was still fixated on that garage door. "What?" Chase asked.

"The guy at the gate," Hog said. "Have you ever seen him before?"

Which, of course, is exactly what Chase had been thinking mere seconds before. Chase had time to furrow his brow and start to turn his head when Hog suddenly fell at his feet, two hundred and eighty pounds of meat hitting the pavement.

Chase stared down at Hog just one stunned second, then turned to the left just in time to see the nearest soldier pivot his gun away from where Hog had been and aim directly at Kirsten Pappason, who was coming up on the driver's side of the Crown Vic. He fired twice and she went down, hit (Chase was sure) squarely in the chest.

Calinescu was also hit, or he ducked adroitly behind the rear of the Caravan.

Chase turned back in time to see Brueler also hit the ground, clipped in the shoulder. Another shot took a chunk out of the pavement.

Eventually, finally, after what seemed an eon, there was returning fire.

From somewhere within his jean jacket, Neil the driver had pulled out the cousin to Hog's silver cannon; a massive Glock with a wide barrel that seemed to poke out a good six inches longer than it really needed to.

The first shot was perhaps the loudest noise Chase had ever heard. Instantly, the soldier who dropped Hog was blasted – literally blasted – against a cinderblock wall in a spray of red goo. Like a paintball hunt gone seriously wrong, Chase thought. Then the soldier who had been beside him, the one aiming to finish the job on Pappason, simply lost his face. He stumbled around for a second, as if wondering where it had gone, before finally executing a kind of elegant pirouette and falling head first onto the concrete.

Hog's security people, the ones in the last two cars, took cover behind the third car, the Dodge Charger, and returned fire on the remaining three soldiers. They in turn took cover behind the nose of the Caravan.

Chase was yanked down to the ground. "Go!" Neil screamed in his face. "Go!" He was pointing. Chase saw what Neil was thinking. If Chase could scramble the ten feet to the elevator vestibule, the cinderblock wall that jutted out would protect him, and enable his escape in the parking elevator.

"GO!" Neil shouted again, waving his gun, and for a second Chase thought he was going to aim it at him.

Chase looked at Hog's inert mass lying on the concrete.

Ten feet?! How??_

Chase looked back at Neil, ready to tell him that he was insane, but the second Neil began to return fire across the Caravan, Chase made his move.

He had run track in school, and he had been pretty good, but he had never run the four hundred like he ran the ten feet to that elevator vestibule. Pure animal force pushed him. He thought he was going to smash into the cinderblock wall, but at the last second his left foot did the slide it needed to, and he was able to pivot around the wall a micro-second before two shots made huge gouges in the wall.

He pounded on the elevator button, but it didn't light up. "Shit!"

Then the mental image of PSLO Tyler using his keycard, his key, and his entry code came into Chase's head. That's right: The elevators opened only from multiple security systems. He was screwed and trapped.

Then the elevator doors opened.

Chase threw himself in. He hammered at the CLOSE button with his fist until the doors slowly – agonizingly slowly – drew shut, muffling the sound of gunfire.

He stared at the panel stupidly. It took him a second to remember that this elevator only went up to the main lobby. That probably explained why they didn't require the same security protocols as the rest of the building. He pressed L.

As the elevator rose slower than any elevator had ever risen before, the sound of gunfire from the parking garage grew fainter and fainter. Chase had the sensation of being lifted by some benevolent deity from the Land of Complete Fear into the Land of Upper Safety.

The elevator slowed to a stop. Chase looked at the doors expectantly. Eventually they opened.

Unbelievably, it was business as usual in the lobby. Almost. The glass wall at the front gave you a clear view of the mob on the street still offering their rendition of *The Wall*. Tyler was slouched casually at the security desk, chatting with the soldier who manned the security controls. It looked like they were maybe laughing at the rabble outside. Two other soldiers were slouched in chairs by the front door.

"Tyler!" Chase shouted as he jogged to the front security desk. "Hit the red button! We need security support right – "

Chase never finished the sentence, because by the time he got close enough to spin Tyler around, his foot slid on a single smear of blood on the marble floor. He stared at it stupidly. Everything clicked into place when he reached for Tyler.

Tyler neatly folded into Chase's arms. He hadn't been slouching at all, nor had he been chatting; he had been perched at the security desk as dead as dead could be, a big fat hole in his head and a look of complete surprise on his face.

The soldier manning the security desk, who had appeared to be intently studying something on one of the security screens, had also left this world, and apparently some time ago; the bloody hole in his throat had already started to congeal. Chase didn't need to cross the floor to determine the truth about the two soldiers slouched in the chairs by the window; a second glance at their posture told it all. They were also dead.

For the first time since Hog had fallen at his feet, Chase allowed himself a second to consider exactly *what* might be happening and why. The most important thing to accept, he decided, was that he probably wasn't going to come to any grand conclusions in the thirty seconds he had at hand – thirty seconds if he was lucky. What he probably most needed to do was get to safety, assess how bad things were, and *then* do the big thinking. He also needed to find the other Reasoners.

His attention returned to the dead guy hunched over the security screens.

Chase nudged the dead man to the side. Everything on the security control panel, it turned out, was neatly laid out, and the security screens were still on. Chase toggled buttons P1 and P2, and suddenly over-bright images of the parking garage appeared. He was now looking at a pretty clear view of the entrance to the parking-level elevator, and a very wide shot of the entrance from the far side of the garage. That meant he could see the Caravan and he could see the Crown Vic and part of the Charger and the F-150 parked behind them. There was a body on the ground that he couldn't identify, but the boots suggested Chase was looking at the dead soldier who had fired at Calinescu. But that was it. No one popped up from behind the Caravan to fire a weapon, and no one scurried around to take protection behind the Crown Vic. Everything was eerily still. Where had they all gone?

Chase frantically toggled "Corridors." The second-, third-, fourth-, and fifth-floor corridors all came in, but were empty. The fourth-floor boardroom was made up for what looked to be lunch, but there was no one in that room either.

Which, of course, was impossible.

This building was pretty much the equivalent of a fully operational hotel. Forget finding his fellow Reasoners, Chase should at least be seeing cleaning staff, catering staff, or security. Or, considering Tyler's current status, their bodies. Instead, he saw nothing.

Then, suddenly, out of the corner of his eye, he saw movement on one the screens. A fleeting glimpse of someone crossing the lens. Then they were gone.

This view was from the camera mounted in the elevator vestibule in the parking garage.

Chase hit "ENHANCE." The camera zoomed in to show the parking garage elevator doors just as they were closing. Someone was coming up to the lobby. But good guy or bad guy?

Chase looked around frantically. Then he saw it.

Tyler was hanging in a kind of odd limp pose off the security desk, but his belt was exposed and his key card was prominently displayed, attached via a wispy little garishly purple plastic coil that said "disco disco" on it. Chase ripped it off. He searched Tyler's pockets for the key itself, which he knew was a big silver thing with an almost paddle-like end. Tyler's body began to slide down the side of the desk on its way to the marble floor, but Chase held it up with his knee until he found the key in the left front jacket pocket. With these two items in hand, he raced to the tower elevators.

He also needed the ID code, of course, but Chase had long ago memorized that, just from Tyler escorting him around. The code was 070476. Keener that he was, Tyler had chosen the numerical value of the signing of the Declaration of Independence.

Chase punched in the code, swiped the card, and turned the key just as he heard the elevator door from the parking garage opening onto the lobby.

He heard footsteps approaching, but just in time his elevator closed.

He pressed four. He knew that up there he would learn – pretty much within a good margin of accuracy – *when* all this shit had happened.

2

As the elevator moved, his mind moved. Cogs and wheels were crunching together and keys were turning. If he couldn't see the answers, then at least he was seeing the pieces of the puzzle which needed to be assembled in order to find the answers.

Timing was everything.

The expedition to General Van DeVere had set out in the pre-dawn hours and they had returned just after 11. So, there was a good five-and-a-half hours for whatever happened here in the State building to happen. It was a hell of a broad window, but Chase was pretty sure he could narrow it.

That's what he needed to do if he were going to understand certain things. The crowds outside, for one. When had they appeared? Surely, they were tied to what had taken place inside. Were they cover? They certainly weren't a coincidence.

The elevator stopped at four, and as he stepped off, he felt extremely empty-handed. He had seen a lot of violence in the past few days, but up until this second, he had felt no urge to engage in any himself. Now, however, stepping into a too-quiet corridor on a too-quiet floor, Chase imagined a gun would feel very good right about now.

The corridor being empty was a big flashing "wrong." In so many ways. Every time the Reasoners had come to meals or held meetings on this floor, there had always been two, sometimes four, heavily armed soldiers. Where were they now?

Boardroom 4 itself told him even more. Their dining room was deserted. He went to the buffet table.

It was set for lunch: trays for sandwiches, hot chafing dishes for the two soups, and the round serving platters for fruits and vegetables. It had never been an overabundance of plenty – no cruise ship was going to ape the State department building – but it had been very good. The most important thing for Chase, at the moment, was the soup.

Carefully, he lifted the stainless-steel cap on the canister. A waft of steam escaped, along with the smell of vegetable and barley, which reminded him faintly of old socks.

It was piping hot.

Chase turned to the coffee urns. He grabbed a cup and placed it under the spigot. He released a quarter of a cup. He put it to his lips. Hot. Fresh.

Okay, he told himself. Whatever had happened had taken place within the past hour at the very most. More likely within the past half-hour.

He studied the three round tables. Everything was as it should be. The tables were neatly set. The tablecloths were smooth and unstained. No chair was out of place.

Which, of course, in itself didn't make sense.

Only Brueler had a guest room on this floor. Brueler, who, presumably, was lying dead on the cold concrete of the parking garage six stories below. Chase needed to check his room. If whatever happened had taken place during the setting-up of lunch, then it was possible the serving staff and Reasoners had sought Brueler's room for safety.

Chase was pretty sure that Tyler's key was a skeleton key. He had seen him open many doors but had only seen him dealing with the one key. But the business of the security code was another thing. If Tyler had a different code for different doors, then Chase was screwed.

Chase slid the physical key into Brueler's door. It slid in easily. He turned it. Easily.

A light on the electronic panel to the left of the door suddenly beeped a very unpleasant red, while emitting a sound like a truck's backup signal.

Chase wasn't sure what to do, so he did what made the most sense. He waved Tyler's plastic card in front of the electronic panel.

Almost instantly the red light changed to green. It offered up an electronic keyboard. Chase typed in the patriotic code. The door made a click. Chase turned the key again. It turned. He was in.

Brueler's room was exactly as he had last seen it, minus Brueler. The books, the papers, the tabletops covered with calendars and maps. Unfortunately, what wasn't there was a cowering group of caterers and wait staff, or nine Reasoners hiding behind the drapes.

He went into Brueler's bedroom. The bed was made. On the sixteenth floor, housekeeping usually came around ten a.m. So earlier or later down here? The bathroom was immaculate, with fresh towels. Again, not a chair out of place or any sign of disruption.

As he left the room, closing the door quietly behind him, Chase thought he heard something. Downstairs. Someone shouting in the lobby of the building?

He didn't take the elevator up. He discovered that a single swipe of the key card gave him access to the industrial stairwell. He took the stairs two at a time. He chose the sixth floor. Pappason and Hydy Horvat. The same routine – key, key card, code – gave him access to each room.

And each room was utterly unremarkable, except for the fact that Kirsten Pappason turned out to be a secret slob. Even Housekeeping couldn't keep up with her. There were clothes everywhere and every inch of the bathroom counter was covered. Contrast that with Hydy Horvat, who apparently lived like a monk and had only three outfits, albeit of exceptional quality, along with an extra supply of pillows and a small bag of Flamin' Hot Cheetos.

But not a sign of any violence or forced entry.

Chase went back into the hallway.

He was starting to wonder if it was possible that whoever

gained access to the building and finished off Tyler and the main floor security team – to say nothing of the real front gate guards and the real security team which was supposed to meet them in the underground – had failed to breach the floor above the lobby for some reason. But if that were the case, then where the hell was everyone?

Suddenly, there was a loud thrum in the wall behind him.

Chase's heart shot right up into his mouth. There was no questioning the sound. One of the elevators was moving. He looked up at the numerals, but of course they'd been deactivated for security reasons, something he'd noted the first day. So was the elevator coming up or going down?

He ran to the end of the hall and the stairwell. He almost cracked his wrist trying to push through the crashbar door, forgetting that the security system locked the doors as well as the crashbar. So, another swipe of the card, a half-second wait, and he was through.

He vaulted two more floors up to the eighth.

Another two rooms up there. Agniew and the Ambassador. But before he tried either one, he went to the elevator door and put his ear to the cold metal panel.

The thrum was much farther away. Maybe five or six floors. Maybe more. Then it stopped. The top floor? His floor?

If that were the case, then someone was looking for him specifically. The only other person in residence on the sixteenth floor was dead.

Chase needed to hide.

He breached the Ambassador's room in a matter of seconds and locked the door behind him. There was no chain, however, and that gave him a moment to almost laugh at himself. What would the point of a chain be?

The Ambassador's room was also utterly unremarkable, but for a stack of books on his bedside table. *A Case for Christ*, *God's Life*, *A Search for Meaning*, and something called, *The Temptation of Disbelief*. Who knew?

Stepping close to the window struck Chase as an unreasonably dangerous thing to do, but he was right over the front entrance to the building, and that which might be learned seemed worth the risk.

Carefully edging his back against the drapes, he peered out cautiously, exposing as little of himself as possible.

Oh yes. They were still down there. Still singing, although by now they had switched from *The Wall* to *American Pie*. Why that particular song was anybody's guess, although Chase couldn't help noticing that, unlike *The Wall*, every single member of the crowd seemed to know all the words to *American Pie*.

When the jester sang for the King and …

And that's when Chase saw it. The wooden chairs placed around the Ambassador's little dining-study table. Three were pushed neatly up against the table edge. The fourth chair was knocked over and its wooden cross brace snapped in two.

Chase moved toward it slowly, circling the room so he wouldn't expose himself at the window. He bent down and righted the chair. He studied it. Yes, the brace had been kicked in. But by whom? More importantly, when? Had the Ambassador done it in a fit of anger or frustration, or had someone else done it, more recently?

Chase was ready to convince himself that this had been done days or perhaps even a week before, that there was no connection between this chair and the carnage downstairs, when he noticed a hole in the wall just three inches above the flatscreen TV.

He moved toward it, unaware he was still holding the chair. The hole was a neat, perfect little round dot of darkness. It could only be one thing. A bullet hole.

As that reality sank in, he looked around, frantic. Suddenly he wanted to get the hell out. Not just out of the room, or out of the building, but out of this city and the entire situation. What kind of world was it where you convinced yourself that danger – mortal danger – was worth something as nebulous as a land, or a country, or freedom, or fairness? Bullshit.

Chase put the chair right and made for the door. He opened it quietly, careful to ease down on the handle, and stepped out into the corridor. He made sure he locked the door again, then turned back toward the stairwell. He jumped a good two feet out of his skin – or thought he did – when suddenly he found himself face to face with the Reverend.

3

She shoved him back against the door, shifting the smartphone in her left hand to her right. "Get back inside!"

"Reverend – "

She looked back over her shoulder, terrified. Now he heard it too. The thrum of the elevator starting up yet again. Getting louder. Coming closer. Clearly someone was searching for something, and almost surely it was them. "Come on!" she said, but this time there was a catch in her voice. Fear. Absolute and all-encompassing fear.

He swiped the card in a blinding flash and managed to punch in the code but fumbled with the key. "Hurry!" she said. Finally, he got the key to fit the hole.

Back in the Ambassador's room, she locked and double-locked the door behind them. "They've already been through here," she said. "So there's a chance they won't come back. But I wouldn't bank on it. Come on."

She pushed him into the bedroom. As she reached to pull open the sliding closet door, he realized that the object in her hand, which he had taken to be a smartphone, was actually a gun. A small one, a .22 or .32, but a gun nonetheless. She carried it like a person who had never carried a weapon in her life.

She slid back the closet door and gestured for Chase to get in first. He was confused. "For love of Pete!" she said, and stepped in. Realizing what she had intended, he followed her.

She pulled the door closed after him, then sank to a sitting position with her back to the side wall. For the first time Chase realized she was wearing Converse sneakers, sweatpants, and a hoodie that said VANDERBILT. She was breathing so hard she was almost hyperventilating. She laid the gun on the floor right by her left foot and began searching her pockets. "I have a flashlight somewhere," she said, then repeated it. "I have a flashlight. I've got a flashlight."

With Chase's back on the opposite wall, they were feet to feet. "Stop," he said. "Just tell me what's going on. Who are 'they'?"

She looked terrified. "I think I lost it!"

"We don't need a flashlight." This was true. There was good enough light coming through the cracks around the closet door. They could see each other clearly. "Just talk to me."

She patted the hoodie's tummy pocket with relief. There was a round bulky bump there. "I found it."

"What's going on? Tell me about 'they.' Who are they? And where are the others?"

"I don't know!" She practically shouted this, then seemed to realize where she was. She pulled herself together. Slightly. "I don't know," she repeated in a whisper. "They herded some of us onto the elevator and when the rest of us ran, they split up to chase us. I wound up in one of the supply closets with Alyssa and Mr. Agniew."

"What happened then?"

"We made a break for it and got separated. I heard gunshots and got in the elevator. I got up to the fifteenth floor and hid in Dr. Hamer's room – I figured no one would expect anyone to be up there – but then I heard them in the hall. I got under the bed. They searched the room but missed me. Once they were gone I came down and tried to find a way out. Then I heard more shooting and came back up. I've been hiding in the east stairwell for – I don't know – a half-hour maybe? Maybe less."

"What happened to the others?"

"I don't *know*."

"And who are 'they'?"

"I don't *know*," she repeated. Then, "Chase, I can't do this. I can't do this."

"Well, what do they look like?"

"Two of them had those weird haircuts. From the eighties. Mohawks."

Chase was confused. "Mohawks? Like a street gang?"

She shook her head. "Soldiers. Military. Not Changers. No jerseys or wolf hats. They just – I thought they were relieving the ones in the corridor. We were all about to eat lunch. We'd just gathered. Mr. Agniew was pouring a coffee – and then we heard gunshots. Right there! In the corridor! And suddenly they stepped in and told us all to line up at the door or they'd kill us."

"Were their faces covered?" Chase asked.

She shook her head and swallowed. "No. They looked – I told you – they looked like – we thought they *were*, soldiers relieving the ones in the corridor. They were perfectly normal!"

"Okay," said Chase, trying to calm her down. "Okay."

"They didn't say anything! What they wanted or what they were doing! They talked to each other through walkie-talkies. I heard one of them saying 'everything is all right belowdecks.' I figured that meant downstairs. Then some of us ran. I wound up in a closet with – "

Chase cut her off. "Okay, I got that part. And when did the people outside show up?"

She looked utterly baffled. "Who?"

"The people outside. When did they show up?"

She struggled to find an answer. "I don't know … they … Before. I think."

"Okay. Before."

"Chase, is it possible they've killed everyone?"

"Not if they lined you up and were planning on taking you all off on the elevators."

That gave her pause. "Oh my!" she said. "You're right! Why didn't I think of that?"

"Because you're in shock."

"Am I? But what's happened? We were supposed to be perfectly safe here."

He thought to remind her of the Key bridge, but he didn't – for a whole bunch of reasons, not the least being a cup of coffee. The perfectly obvious cup of coffee.

"Someone said they were looking for you," she said.

"Me?" This took Chase by surprise. "Why me? And who said it?"

"One of the soldiers. But I didn't hear him explain why."

"Did anyone tell any of these soldiers where we were? Pappason and Calinescu and Brueler and I? Where we'd gone? Who we were meeting?"

She had to think about that a minute, then shook her head.

"Was Vin with you?" Chase asked.

She shook her head again. "He wanted to eat in his room. It was just as well. Everyone is royally pissed about him doing those broadcasts. Well, most of us. I don't know if Gleeber was as upset as me. Or Dr. Horvat. Hydy told Agniew that it was possible Vin was looking out for our safety."

"But Vin wasn't in the boardroom with the rest of you?"

She shook her head.

"Did you see him later when these guys were rounding people up?"

Again, she shook her head.

"And you're sure no one asked where *we* were?"

She shook her head, but then she seemed to remember the importance of the mission to meet Van DeVere. "How *did* it go?"

But Chase was busy listening. Had he heard a door open? Or someone fiddling with the front door lock in the other room? Was it possible they – whoever they were – were about to burst in on them?

"What did he say?" the Reverend persisted. "Van DeVere."

"A lot of things."

"Did he talk about missiles?"

Chase was surprised by the question. "You mean Kansas?"

She nodded.

It was so awkwardly phrased. It took Chase a second to respond. "Yes, we got the real word on that. At least I think it's the real word."

"Which is?"

He looked at her. After a moment he said, "He told us he didn't know anything about Russell, Kansas. Or the state of the nuclear arsenal in general."

"That's ridiculous."

"Why is it ridiculous?"

She looked around on the floor, as if the answer might be found there. "He has to know something. Mallickey himself said – "

"Miles Mallickey doesn't know jack shit."

"Did the General say that? About Mallickey?"

Chase looked at her. The strange way she was leaning forward now, the way she was holding her belly. Finally, he knew it was time. This had gone on long enough.

"Reverend, Tay Hamer's room is on the sixteenth floor."

She looked confused. "What?"

"I know, because I'm on the same floor. So, were you on the fifteenth or the sixteenth? Maybe you were in someone else's room?"

The Reverend stared at him. Something inside her seemed to wilt. "Chase, I can't do this."

"And how did you get in, anyway?"

"Chase … "

"How did you get into *any* room?"

She literally stuttered. "I – I – "

"And Mr. Agniew couldn't have been pouring coffee because not a cup has been touched in the lunchroom and certainly no one left a half-filled coffee cup. Did he take it with him while everyone was being herded into elevators by these bad guy soldiers you're talking about? That seems unlikely."

She seemed ready to explain. But instead, all she did was repeat, "Chase."

"Reverend."

"Please understand this."

"What?"

She withdrew the flashlight from the belly pocket on the hoodie. "I am so sorry."

But it wasn't a flashlight at all. It was some sort of aerosol can. She closed her eyes and pointed the can at him, spraying him right in the face. He didn't even have a chance to blink, let alone cover himself. And then, without realizing it, he was in blackness and silence.

Book 4:

Tracking the Wolf

"I, John Brown, am now quite certain that the crimes of this guilty land will never be purged away but with Blood."
— Final words of John Brown,
leader of the Harper's Ferry Rebellion, 1859

"By covering our good work with the blood of our neighbors, we make sure that we awake each day to the bright dawn of national happiness."
— *Wolf Words*, pg. 91 (free ebook edition)

41. *The New Voice*

1

There was no news. None. Zero. Not from the Bridgepoint hospital, where Beavenstock was – recovering? Dying? Directing his forces? – not from the doctors, not from the Jerseys who had set up a twenty-four-hour guard around both Beavenstock's room and the ICU, and, most notably, not from Sister Sheena.

This puzzled and frustrated everyone the most, especially the news nets. After her appearance at the hospital, just about everyone assumed Sheena would pick up the battle banner and run with it. After all, Jeff had been *shot*. Some people said she was hunkered down planning colossal acts of retribution, or that she was directing some of the chaos which was, once again, breaking out across the country. Cynics said she was covering her tracks for her own role in Jeff's shooting. None of these options, however, explained why she was entirely missing from view. At the very least, Sister Sheena had always been about cameras, right?

The darkest rumor on the Mall was that they'd been lied to, and Jeff was in really bad shape. Brain dead, some said. Being fed by a hose or, worse, that the GOR had him.

An idea like that can take hold quickly, especially with no one around to contradict it. Questions arise. Conspiracy theories grow. As a result of this, the speakers soon appeared on the Mall.

They were self-appointed, but they had a captive audience, so they had plenty of opportunity to hone their message. In time, there were quite a few of them. If you wanted, you could wander from one to the other to the other and kill a whole day just taking in the theme of deception and planned retribution. But some began to attract bigger crowds than others, and some became downright objects of fascination in their own right.

2

Everyone called him Five-by-Five Bob. Five-by-Five had parked himself right beneath the Washington Monument, or as close as he could get. To compensate for his height, and to make sure folks could see him, Five-by-Five stood on a three-shelf stainless steel serving table on rollers, which he had almost surely swiped from one of the cafeterias in one of the government buildings. The serving cart gave him that much greater visibility, but so did the red firefighter's hat, which may or may not have been a kid's thing. The fact that the table was industrial grade was important, though, because Bob seemed as wide as he was tall (hence the name), so he needed the extra support.

The real appeal of Five-by-Five Bob, however, was not his appearance. It was his voice. He had a big, loud honker with a rumbling gravel in it that sounded like he was just getting over the plague. Add to that the things Bob *said*.

"We have been forced to ingest the pablum of deceit!" And that was Five-by-Five starting out. When he had first set himself up, folks had just stood around watching with bemusement, laughing at the idiot in the red fire chief's hat standing on the food table. They always intended to move on, but they never did. "We have been hoodwinked by the agents of fabrication!" If you chose to spend the whole morning listening (and eventually most did) you would clue in that Bob's message, pretty much, was that Jeff Beavenstock was dead, and that no one was giving the folks out on the Mall this news because they figured that A) they were too stupid, and B) their stupidity could be put to uses that would only feed certain elites. "Once again the old song sings itself!" Bob honked. "We're going to press-gang the deplorable rabble into means of production that will make the Monopoly Man rich! He's had his little revolution, but now it's time for Monopoly Man to take back Park Place *and* Boardwalk!"

A lot of the things Bob said were lost on his listeners, but his diatribes about the Monopoly Man went over extremely well. Everyone understood this stuff. What American hasn't played Monopoly? The Monopoly Man was the rich guy with the mustache. He had a rich guy's suit and watch chain and controlled the game, kicked you in the pants, and decided if you did or didn't go to jail. Oh yeah, folks on the Mall knew plenty about the Monopoly Man.

It wasn't long before the once-gawkers made a point of showing up early in the morning specifically to hear Five-by-Five, get a good seat, and munch on the Cinnabons or breakfast burritos which the food trucks supplied.

Not everyone was happy with the message, though. The suggestion that Beavenstock was dead and in fact there may be no point in being out on the Mall at all – and probably no point to the whole Changer movement itself – might have been thought-provoking, but there were a lot of people who didn't cotton to the general gist of pointlessness and everything being a lost cause.

"Bullshit lies!" they shouted.

"Lock this nutfuck up!"

"This is crap!"

The folks who spouted this were the few who moved on after a half-hour or so, having heard enough. Some stayed, though, and stewed in their anger. Three days after Chase sat in a darkened bedroom closet with Reverend Sarah Campbell, one such imposing figure was paying a great deal of attention to Five-by-Five Bob. He'd been there all afternoon. He looked like a biker but was wearing a Minnesota jersey. He had enormous red sideburns that practically met his mouth. To some, he might have been vaguely familiar, but they weren't sure why. Yet.

By the time Bob had intoned "we're back to working for the man and punching the timecard of defeat," this big guy had clearly had enough. "Okay!" he said. "No more of this shit, fat guy!"

Five-by-Five Bob was used to interruptions and hecklers, so he just plowed on. "Engage in personal self-examination, friends, and ask yourself if we would be where we are – if this is the natural juncture of events – if there were a firm hand at the tiller! Ask yourself if it's possible we're holding the upper hand when all around us we see – "

"Stop!" said Sideburns Man. "Just fucking stop."

Bob hesitated for just a second, assessing Sideburns out of the corner of his eye. Just another heckler, he reassured himself. Inaccurately. He kept on going. "All around us we see – "

Two enormous hands reached out and violently shook the cafeteria cart Bob was standing on. "Hey!" Bob, about to fall off his perch, shouted at Sideburns. "Knock it off!"

Bob struggled for balance, but when Sideburns did a double jerk at the last second, Bob comically fell off the back of the cart. There were both gasps of surprise and laughter from the crowd. A few stood up to get a better look.

Sideburns ignored Bob's plight. Instead, he stood in front of the cart and addressed the crowd. "What are you doing listening to this shit? You don't realize who this guy probably is? Are you fucking stupid?"

There were shouts for Sideburns to sit the fuck down and shut up, but some were willing to listen. For his part, Bob popped back up from behind his cart, dusted himself off, and started to climb back up again.

"This guy's a plant!" said Sideburns. "All that shit about Jeff being dead! You don't see that's exactly what they *want* us to think?"

A few more stood up to protest, but Sideburns went on.

"That's what's gone wrong here! Our enemies have put all sorts of assholes in with us to make us doubt what we're doing. Hundreds! Maybe thousands! You know what this guy is really giving you? Bullshit they've told him to say to break us up!"

There was an awkward silence as everyone chewed on that idea. Even Bob, on top of the cart, could tell that something had suddenly shifted; his crowd was slipping away from him, distracted by this intriguing new idea. Or new for them.

"We gotta pull this shit together," Sideburns said. "And we gotta pull this shit together *yesterday*! Look at all the weird crap that's started happening here on the Mall, at night especially. Where did that shit come from? Didn't used to be here. The Mall was safe. Now it's not. You wonder why? Walk around, asshole! Listen to these people telling all sorts of lies. Lies about Jeff. Lies about what we're doing here, lies about why we all started this in the first place. Who are these people? Where'd they come from? You know who they sound like to me? They sound like …" He looked for somewhere to point. He finally pointed north, toward the city. The Government side. "Them."

A chubby middle-aged man stepped forward. He was maybe in his forties and had the soft features and 1970s haircut of a math teacher, or maybe your mail carrier. What he didn't look like – in his X-pander-waisted pants and his George polo shirt and the sunglasses that fit over his normal glasses – was a revolutionary. But he must have figured himself something like that, because not ten seconds after the sideburned man said the word "them," the chubby man hefted the hard metal end of a lawn umbrella and smashed Five-by-Five Bob in the head with a perfect connect that killed Bob instantly with an incredibly loud crack. That sound was both Bob's cranium caving in and his spinal column detaching itself due to the force of his head spinning around.

The brutality was so extreme and so sudden that the people in the crowd – and these were people who had become used to beheadings – alternatively shrieked and screamed as they got to their feet. The chubby man uttered a satisfied "Lying cuntlicker!" at his handiwork, then considered his lawn umbrella, which was bent like a paperclip. The two most shocked faces, however, belonged to Five-by-Five Bob – who certainly hadn't seen it coming – and the man with the sideburns, who gaped with an expression of slack-jawed amazement as Bob's body did a little dance and then fell to the ground face first. Sideburns just stared and stared at that inert body, while the crowd continued to lose its mind. Sideburns didn't move.

History often *doesn't* turn on a dime. A lot of the time it turns on a whim, a moment of decision which usually surprises the decider as much as those around him.

Sideburns could have done a lot of things. For a second there it looked like he was going to grab the baseball bat he carried and say, "What the fuck did you just do, fuckface?!" But he didn't. Instead, he slowly turned, looked at him, then at the crowd on its feet. Some of them were starting to back away but most of them were staying, staring at Bob's lump of a body with its misshapen lump of head. Then, in a strong, hard voice, the sideburned man shouted, "He deserved that and every single one of you fucking knows it!"

All eyes turned to Sideburns. Some eyed the baseball bat in his hand.

"Not just because he was saying those things," said Sideburns. "That's bad enough. But because it's obvious to anyone that he wasn't one of us. He came here – they sent him – and tried to split us apart. And we're not going to put up with that!"

He had them. He didn't know why or how he had them, but he had them. He had never felt anything like this before in his life. Up to now, in fact, it had been a life of being a complete fuckup and disappointment to everyone who ever knew him.

"I bet there are fucking traitors like this all over the Mall! I bet they've sent in hundreds of them. Maybe thousands. Trying to split us apart. Destroy us. Well, the joke's on them. *We'll* be the one's doing the destroying!"

3

Were his head not currently occupying a plastic Safeway grocery store bag sitting out in one of the dumpsters behind the Capitol building alongside a tremendous amount of fast-food garbage crawling with flies and maggots, Warren Potsburger could have told you all about the sideburned man who had inspired a stranger to murder Five-by-Five Bob in cold blood. Warren could tell you about the tussle the two of them had at the rope line before Warren had buffaloed the guy. Warren could tell you he'd been spooked by the guy. There had been something strangely dangerous about him, even in this most dangerous of places.

Sideburns' name was Grange. Lowell Grange. But in time everyone would call him by the same name Warren had chosen based on the guy's jersey and his facial hair.

Viking. And, Warren might have warned from within his plastic bag, you gotta watch out for goddamned Vikings.

4

Word spread that one of the speakers had been "caught" for conspiracy against the Changers and been put to death by the guy called Viking. Which meant, in short, that there really were traitors amongst them, and if you didn't believe that, who the hell do you think had Beavenstock shot in the first place? It obviously wasn't Sister Sheena, or she would have shown up by now to claim her leadership. And wasn't this what Jeff had been warning everyone about at the very second he was shot?

Those who had clearer memories and argued that at the moment he'd been shot Jeff Beavenstock had actually been making a case that the Changers were set up by the Reasoners and the GOR, suddenly found themselves in the minority.

Viking was the one everyone wanted to hear, because his message was so much simpler. Add to that the realization that this was the guy who had technically saved Jeff at the last second and presto! A lot of people determined that Viking was Jeff's anointed successor. The fact that Viking was only a rope-line security thug who just happened to stumble into being at the right place at the right time, and that Beavenstock wouldn't have been able to pick Viking out of a police lineup, was not something anyone wanted to hear. They needed a hero, and all those TV replays made it clear that this was the guy who had pushed the assassin aside so that last bullet couldn't perform its no doubt inevitable and fatal deed. Now *that's* a hero.

At first, they set Viking up at the same spot under the Washington Monument where Five-by-Five had formerly held sway, but that soon proved to be awkward for larger crowds. Finally, they moved him over to the Sylvan, the outdoor amphitheater just east of the Washington Monument. Seating was much more comfortable there, and they had a stage, so Viking could stand over them and impart his message with elevated authority.

That message was pretty crude, but it got refined with repetition.

It usually started with a statement of allegiance to the man who wasn't there.

"I'm not Jeff!" Viking would start off. "And I'm sure not Sister Sheena. So I don't know anything. I'm just some guy." Now came the part where the guy who didn't know anything told the crowd that he knew a shitload of things with absolute surety. "There are traitors out here with us. I'm not fucking around. They've been put here to tear us apart. To turn us against each other. We don't have to put up with that. I say, let's find them, let's round them up, and let's send them back where they came from!"

A chant started up. Simple and direct. "Send them back!" they would shout. "Send them back!"

Except no one really meant send anyone back. First off, no one knew where "back" was, and secondly, what was the logic in sending traitors "back" where they came from? None. Traitors had to be dealt with more harshly than that.

Eventually, as Viking's popularity grew, the news networks, parked at the east end of the Mall in front of the Capitol steps and a very dormant guillotine, clued into the possibility that there was something new on the horizon that might keep their ratings up. After Beavenstock's shooting, they needed a fresh story. Might that story be the new guy everyone said was "cleaning house" within the Changers? This was now must-see TV – except, of course, they didn't want to lug all their crap over to the Sylvan theatre, which was buggy at best and at worst facing the wrong direction for the cameras. Instead, the news nets managed to convince Viking and his ever-crazy followers to move over to the Capitol steps. This meant that Jeff's followers, who had been patiently guarding the steps, had to give some ground. They eventually and grudgingly did. Press play, after all, was press play and without any direction communication from Jeff, they decided it's what Jeff would want.

So, in less than two days the pool cameras CNN, MSNBC, and Fox all used were still pointed at the Capitol steps, but finally, thank God, there was something to show: a crazy-looking dude called Viking who had a lot to say that the people wanted to hear, and who cared what it was?

"We have to get back to full culling!" he shouted. This was on Friday night, a week after Reverend Sarah Campbell had sprayed Chase in the face with God knew what. "But we're not going to do that until we've done a little house cleaning of our own!"

That brought the crowd to its feet. Yes! Exactly! They all knew what this meant.

Viking paused as he looked across the crowd. "We have to show the country we're willing to keep the Changer cause pure!"

There were huge cheers now and shouts and whistles. Feet stomped and chants of USA, USA, USA! began.

A record number of Americans saw this broadcast. A new Changer leader was something everyone had to check out. But what, the network heads – and even YouTube TV – wondered, would keep them watching?

It didn't take long to find the answer.

5

Hector Ganz was one of the first to set the tone. Hector lived in Carson, California in a two-bedroom bungalow not three blocks from what used to be the StubHub Center – before they renamed it the Touchy Feely Hot Tub Center, or whatever they'd changed it to. He'd almost paid the house off when Hector's neighbor's property had suddenly flooded. It amounted to property damage to Hector's place estimated at about $33,000, which of course the asshole neighbor's insurance company refused to pay, because the asshole neighbor had decided a good six months before to stop paying his premiums, apparently because his wife had gotten sick and it was either medical bills or insurance, right? There followed a lot of arguments about this, and talk of lawyers, but then Hector and the neighbor discovered they were both Changers, so there was some weird commonality that Hector wasn't sure he could breach – after all, if you resorted to rich man's court and rich guys in suits in order to get back at your neighbor, how were you any different than the assholes you were both fighting in the first place? The two men had even spotted one another at the Long Beach protest, and both had taken part in the torching of the Tri-Star building – the event which had brought Sister Sheena to national prominence – so that had to mean something, right?

That was then, though. Nowadays, Hector's idea of political action consisted of watching events unfold on TV. Which was what he was doing on that particular Wednesday afternoon. He was parked in front of the tube eating a large mixing bowl of Trix and milk and watching CNN's report about a guy named Viking, who was stirring up interest all across the Mall in Washington. Hector couldn't quite take in the whole Viking story, because he got distracted by the infuriating sight of the construction crew which had taken up residence on his lawn since Monday, with Bobcats and diggers, ready to repair the damage the flood had caused to his neighbor's property.

Repair. So somehow that fat fuck had the means to repair the damage to *his* house – this guy without any insurance – whereas Hector was looking at a $33,000 bill while sitting in an ever-more-lopsided TV room, the result of a shifting foundation that threatened to crack his house in two if he didn't do something super quick. No insurance? My ass.

Eventually everything this guy Viking was saying began to sink in to Hector. Whatever Hector hadn't understood, the pundits who came on afterward parsed out for him. Soon Hector saw the light. Viking was talking about the fact that within the Changer movement itself, there were traitors. To Hector, that made things super clear.

The work crew finally knocked off just before five and disappeared in a ramshackle Toyota pickup, leaving behind a partly dug-up lawn for the start of tomorrow's shift. The neighbor himself appeared just after dark with a dry-cleaning bag (dry-cleaning!) and a bucket of KFC. Hector didn't see that as the healthiest meal you could feed a sick wife. So maybe she wasn't so sick at all. So it was just more bullshit from this guy.

By nine o'clock, Hector had watched a good four hours of cable news, and it had helped him make up his mind. Just after nine, he used his cellphone flashlight to guide him across his neighbor's lawn. Hector figured there was no way he was going to find the gas line in the dark, but actually it turned out to be easier than he thought. The workies had spray-painted the line and even secured plastic ties around it to identify for safety purposes. All Hector had to do was yank a good chunk of it out of the ground, cut it with his garden clippers, and slide the open end under asshole's closed garage door. What happened after that was not his responsibility or his fault. $33,000 my ass.

The explosion which rocked the neighborhood at 2:32 a.m. – the result of Hector's neighbor getting up to light the gas and make some Cozy Bear tea for his wife, who suffered from insomnia as well as multiple sclerosis – was much bigger than anything Hector could have anticipated. It almost took half of Hector's house with it. Hector could have used that as a defense when the L.A. County Fire Inspector, no fool, questioned him about the cut gas line, but he didn't. Instead, Hector decided to dive in deep. "He betrayed the cause!" Hector told everyone and all, in particular the KTLA truck which had parked itself behind one of the pumpers a few houses down.

6

Someone, somewhere on social media, came up with the name: Purity Squads.

After all, *something* had to be done.

The idea was that they would roam through the mid-sized cities and smaller towns at night setting ablaze businesses deemed to be owned by what were now called Change Traders (the misspell had been an accident at first, but it stuck), or spray-painting houses and cars with a backward "C."

On the Mall in Washington, of course, the wages of purity correction were even more severe. And promised to get more out of hand.

42. *The Belly of the Beast*

1

Chase didn't wake up so much as pull himself out of a kind of sludgy sleep soup. There were disturbing images in that soup, people he didn't want to see again doing things they shouldn't be doing. His sister, for instance, still alive, was all tarted up as she had never been in life, telling him she needed sex at least once before she took her own life, and she was going to get it down on the Mall; his father, putting up traps on the back forty of a farm he had never stepped foot on, telling Chase he was determined to catch all the animals and bleed them to death and then eat them raw because it would make the cancer go away. Then Jeff Beavenstock, apparently fully recovered, driving by and waving from the driver's seat of a 1953 Cadillac convertible and saying he'd see Chase "at the hop."

It was the cold which finally made Chase open his eyes. He was freezing. He pulled the blanket tighter and reached for the bedspread down at his feet, except there wasn't a bedspread, just the blanket. That's because he wasn't in his room in the State building and he sure wasn't here in Princeton. He was somewhere very, very different.

There were no actual lights on in this room, but enough illumination was seeping in from under the door that he could make out a few important details.

The ceiling was acoustic tile, and below this were drop-ceiling fluorescent lamps, three across, the kind you found in every office across America. The walls were cinderblock, painted eggshell white, although there wasn't much on them but two blank whiteboards, the kind you use a dry-erase on. There were two doors, one to his left and another on the other side of the room. The far door had exit and fire instructions posted on the back. There was a plastic litter basket in the corner which smelled like someone had been pissing in it. Otherwise, the room was empty.

Chase had awakened on a mat in the corner, shivering under the thin blanket someone had placed over him. He was glad for the mat, though, thin as it was. It wasn't really a sleeping mat. Maybe a Pilates thing? A wrestling mat like they used to use in high school? Whatever it was, at least it kept him off the linoleum floor, which looked even colder.

A classroom, Chase thought. Or a meeting room of some kind. Or an office, circa 1963.

He couldn't think past that, not just because he was trying to haul himself out of whatever dangerously deep sleep had felled him, but because he was dealing with what felt like the kind of crushing hangover most people don't really feel past the age of nineteen.

His tongue felt as if it would crumble into dried particle board if he rubbed it against his teeth any more, and he had the sensation of his brain pushing directly against his cranium with no fluid interface, which gave him the very creepy sense that he could feel his heartbeat through his skull. And he couldn't splay his fingers without pain.

Gradually, he began to grapple with where he might be and how he got here.

The Reverend. "I am so sorry," she had said, before spraying him with something.

He could perhaps work at convincing himself that she was involved in an ornate plot to protect Chase and get him to safety, one that necessitated also knocking him out against his will, but that was a mighty big climb. It was a lot easier to imagine she had become some kind of bad guy – or maybe had always been a bad guy – and he had simply been too stupid to see it. From the beginning.

No, he thought, remembering the Reverend leading the other Reasoners in a group prayer on that first day, or how angry she had been that night in his room after the first meeting with Sister Sheena.

Not from the beginning. In both his head and heart, he knew the Reverend was, or had been, a good guy. Whatever had happened to change her had happened recently.

And yet. And yet … There's always 'and yet.'

And yet, in that first meeting with the Reasoners, Sister Sheena had accused them of having a traitor within their ranks who threatened the entire project. Obviously, considering how they'd found him, they supposed it was General Williamson. But what if they had been wrong?

"Why would he commit suicide?" Kirsten Pappason had demanded of Brueler when the other Reasoners learned of General Williamson being found dead. Why indeed?

But still. *The Reverend?*

"Shit!" It was a sharp, guttural expletive, a man's voice, frustrated, impatient, annoyed. And it came from very close by. The next room?

Chase got up on to his knees very slowly and very carefully, bracing himself with his left arm, which was hard to do if your hand shot rockets of excruciating pain when you put even the slightest pressure on it. As he adjusted his balance, his head felt like it was going to burst. As he turned it, his vision felt wobbly, like a film slipping its sprockets. He blinked and things evened out a bit. But only a bit.

The door to his immediate left didn't have any exit or fire instructions on the back and there was no lock on the knob. So likely it was a connecting door. Connecting, he imagined, to – what? Chase tried to stand up and reach for the knob, but his head decided this was a bad idea. So he crawled on hands and knees over to the door and put his head against it. It was cold.

"Oh fuck!" said the voice on the other side. There was a strange thud and the scrape of a chair. A groan and a sigh followed.

Slowly, carefully, mustering every bit of strength in him, Chase grasped each side of the doorframe and slowly pulled himself up, inch by inch. It seemed to take forever, and for a second he wondered if his knees were going to buckle, but once his spine was more than halfway up, things got a little easier. He heard a crack. Was that him? Then he looked around from this new, unusual standing height, like a kid on his dad's shoulders.

His room was smaller than his position on the floor had led him to believe. It couldn't be more than twelve by fourteen, if that. Maybe a storage room which had been turned into an office or classroom? Either way, the building was old, and the acoustic ceiling was unusually low, which suggested a lot of piping up there somewhere. So, a basement room.

Another grunt and groan and another expletive from the other side of the door, this one a "fucking hell."

Chase looked down at the doorknob. You never know. He gripped it tight and slowly, very slowly, inched it into a turn, expecting to find almost immediate resistance.

But he didn't. The knob gave only a slight welcoming click, then turned all the way. It was unlocked. He nudged just slightly and opened it no more than four inches.

The connecting room was not as dark as his own, and by no means as empty. He could make out a cot of some sort – Ikea special, by the looks of it – a stack of books and a cheap little plastic bedside lamp resting on a liquor store box of books. This was the room's only source of illumination. There was an office chair with clothes loaded on it and – hanging on the door marked "Exit," with fire instructions – a man's suit of clothes, which looked immaculate.

Someone was moving around in the room. Someone Chase couldn't quite see unless he nudged the door open wider. He decided to risk it, going another three, then four inches. What he saw made him forget all about his throbbing head.

A stubby brown man in his sixties appeared to be trying to hang himself. And he was having a hell of a time doing it.

43. *Gabriel*

1

Part of the problem was the chair, which was wobbly. It was an old wooden office model which had clearly seen better days. The other problem was the man's height, which was insubstantial; if the guy cracked five seven it would be extreme optimism. The third problem was that he was trying to hang himself with cheap kitchen twine. The fourth problem was that he was trying to link the kitchen twine to something up inside the acoustic tile, one panel of which he had pushed up and slid aside, presumably because there were pipes or joists of some kind up there to which he could attach the twine. This was tricky business and it wasn't going well.

"Fucking shit!" the man said as his latest attempt to attach the noose failed.

This was presuming, of course, that suicide *was* the purpose of the operation. Further examination suggested it might not be. The old man was holding something in his other hand which suggested Chase might have the wrong idea all the way around. It was an Extra Value Size can of Bush's beans. Vegetarian.

Suddenly, the man's stocking feet slipped on the chair, and the shift in balance almost sent him careening to the floor. Fortunately, he straightened himself at the last second, holding his arms and the can of beans out wide, like a surfer catching the wave. That's when he looked over and saw Chase staring at him through the partly opened connecting door. The man stared back and the two stood that way for a while.

"Oh there," the man said finally.

Chase slowly opened the door further. "Oh there," he said. Chase was surprised to hear his own voice. It was deep and scratched, as if he had spent a lot of nights drinking.

"You're up! Maybe you can help me."

Chase started to say "what," but his throat was too scratched. He cleared it. Finally, he managed, "What are you doing?"

The man got down and came over to Chase, holding out the can of beans. He wore dress suit pants, Chase noticed, old-fashioned suspenders, and a white shirt that had also seen better days, but no tie. The left sock had a big hole in the toe. Chase amended his gauge of the man's age: seventy at least. And he thought he knew him or had seen him somewhere before.

The can of beans, it turned out, was empty, and the lid removed. There was a hole in the bottom of it and coming out of the hole was one end of the twine. "You've got a good six inches on me," the man said. "So you might be able to make it work better than me."

"Make what work?"

"If you can get it between the two pipes, it receives well. I've done it before, but it's hard to do on tiptoe."

Chase had no idea what the old guy was talking about, but he went over to the chair and looked up into the cavity. Sure enough, a second empty bean can was clumsily lodged between two ancient copper half-inch pipes, part of a tangle of new and old plumbing which probably ran the length of the ceiling – the building, most likely. A line of twine was looped through the bottom of this can as well. Chase followed it until his gaze rested on, yep, the first can, which was in the man's hand.

The old man looked only slightly embarrassed. "Obviously it seems ridiculous," he said. "But it actually works. The sound sometimes goes all the way through those pipes. But of course I have to take it out every morning so they don't see it."

"What are you trying to hear?" Chase asked. "And who are they?"

The older man smiled. "They? They are they. The ever-present 'they.' What I'm trying to hear is if they're going to put the flag up again or not. Because I get a sense they are. Soon."

Chase wasn't sure what any of that meant, but he got up on the chair, steadied himself (the chair really was wobbly) with one hand on the acoustic ceiling and another reaching into the cavity to readjust the bean can. There was a real lath-and-plaster ceiling up there. Just giving it a glance, Chase corrected himself; wherever they were, this building wasn't just old, it was ancient. "You want it flush against?" he asked.

The man moved beside Chase and looked up. He steadied the chair, which helped. "Yes! If you can manage it."

It took some maneuvering, but Chase was able to position the bean can so that its open mouth was flush against the lath and plaster, held in place by the pipe closest to the ceiling. It wasn't snug, but it was tight enough so that the can wasn't going anywhere. "Why not just put the whole contraption up in the ceiling at night, cover it with the tile, and then bring it down in the morning?" Chase asked.

The old man stared at him for a moment or two, then burst into a very pleasant laughter. "You know, I never thought of that!"

Looking down at him from the chair, Chase realized that the height wasn't helping his head. He gingerly got down.

The old man had already put his ear to the open end of the can in his hand. He seemed thrilled with the result. "Oh my!" he said. He handed it to Chase.

Chase cautiously put the can to his own ear. It smelled bad. At first, he couldn't hear anything except the sound of the can against his skin and hair. Then, once he calmed his own breathing, he could hear something other than himself.

It sounded like water at first, but then he heard a thin reedy whine. Then a big wave. Then more of a whine.

"You get it?" the older man asked, grinning. He wanted Chase to be as pleased as he was.

"No."

"They're getting stoked up. Getting ready to put the flag up again, like I say."

"What flag is what?"

"The only flag there is, brother. I don't know who he is but whoever he is he gets them good and stoked these days. I haven't heard them stoked like that for a long time. So, I figure, the flag isn't far behind."

Then Chase realized what he was hearing. The reedy whine was a human voice. Someone making a speech. Or screaming a speech. And the wave of sound which followed it was cheering, or shouting. He knew that rhythm. He knew that sound.

The old man saw Chase wobble as he lowered himself from the chair, For a second it looked like he might hit the ground or faint. The old man eased him into a sitting position in the chair. "Okay, okay," he said. "I shouldna asked you to do that." He quietly took the can-and-string setup away from Chase, winding it very carefully. "It's not Marconi, but I'm proud of it. See, my idea was we're dealing with one of the oldest parts of the building – perhaps even going back to 1799. Certainly the most solid. So I figured some of those pipes are still copper, going back to the 1930s. Might be a good conduit of sound, I thought to myself. And situated where we are – " He pointed to the far end of the room " – west is there – it might all work out just fine. And, in a way, it has. Except, of course, when you realize what you're hearing. You know, for a few weeks there it looked like they were going to give up, it was so quiet! But then, the last week or so, all hell seems to have broken loose. I know one thing for sure: Five days ago the place was on fire. I thought they were going to shake this building to death. Do you have any idea what's going on out there?"

It took awhile for Chase to realize the old man was waiting for an answer. Unfortunately, at that very moment Chase was more concentrated on trying to refocus his eyesight and get rid of the wobblies than anything else. Finally, when he thought he had that a bit under control, he looked up at the old man. "I don't know anything," Chase said. "Why don't you tell me?"

The old man nodded. "Sure," he said, but it came out "shore." "I'll tell you anything."

"Where we are?"

The old man stared at him in amazement, then sighed. It was an incredibly sad sigh, and it didn't bode well for Chase's situation. The old man went over to the cot and reached far under, pulling out what appeared to once have been an executive messenger bag. It had a Capitol seal on it. He reached in and withdrew, amazingly, a can of Starbucks doubleshot. He held it out to Chase. "You want one?"

Chase could not have been more shocked if the guy had pulled out a magnum of champagne and a charcuterie board. He nodded slowly. The man tossed one can to him. It took everything he had to catch it, but Chase caught. Unfortunately, when it landed in his hand a thrum of agony went right up to the point between both his eyes.

"So?" he asked after a moment of recovery.

The old man cracked a can for himself. "You, my son, are in the last place any sane man on this earth wants to be, unless he has an eye for the historical moment and prefers infamy to his own skin. You are in the United States Capitol building."

Chase stopped in his sip from the can.

"Specifically," the old man went on, "the north basement wing, ST 18 and ST 20, which puts us pretty much under the west portico, or thereabouts. The stairs should be two doors over on the other side of your room. Not the stairs they use, of course, because they know how to make an entrance. They prefer the south stairs, on the House side."

"And the flag?" Chase asked. "That's your word for the blade?"

The man nodded quietly. "The flag is the blade."

Chase tried to pull it all together, but he couldn't. The Reverend. The closet. The spray. "There's been a huge mistake," he said.

"There sure has."

"What I mean is, I shouldn't be here."

"Well, shit, brother, neither should I."

"And how long have I been out?"

The old man thought about that for a second. "Frankly, I don't know," he said. "A couple of days at least. Maybe more. I'm ashamed to admit it, but you lose track of time here. Badly. Three of them brought you in here. One Jersey, and two I'd never seen before. One had one of those Indian haircuts. I haven't seen those in thirty years. It was a surprise, I'll tell you. They've never put anyone beside me before. Almost no one else has a room alone, you see. So I'd say – "

"Please," Chase said, although it came out more as a snap. "Two days? Three?"

The old man backed off in his warmth just a little bit. Something suggested he wasn't the type who got snapped at much.

Chase tried to even out his tone, but he couldn't tamp down the desperation, or the fear. "Four …?" It couldn't be four, he thought. A person doesn't just lose four days.

"Could be five, son."

Five?

The old man saw Chase's look. "But like I said, it's hard to keep track of time here now. One day flows into the next, and there's no real light down here … "

Chase interrupted him, rude as it was. "I have to speak to someone in charge."

The old man smiled an indulgent smile, but at least had the decency to hold back the laugh. "Well, that's going to be something of a challenge, son, as I don't know of anyone who knows anyone who is truly in charge of anything. The irony in that is thick, isn't it? Perhaps you could have said the same thing for this building since it was first put up." That seemed to amuse the old man, and this time the laugh did come out. He took another sip from the Starbucks can to clear his throat.

"No, you don't understand," Chase said. "I need to speak to someone in charge. I was making plans to … Let's just say I have to continue what I was doing, and there are people that I have to talk to. I shouldn't be in here."

"*None* of us should be in here."

"What I mean is … " Chase looked around. For the first time he wondered if the walls had ears. No, almost surely not. Not with the bean cans. "I'm a Reasoner."

The old man looked at him a good long time. Then he looked down at the floor, almost shyly. He nudged the linoleum floor with his stocking foot. "I know who you are, Chase. But I have bad news. It's possible being a Reasoner suddenly doesn't mean jack shit now. In fact, I got a sense from some of the rumblings I've heard lately that a lot of things might not mean jack shit anymore. The very fact that you're even in here says it all, doesn't it? I heard someone say they're starting to turn on each other. I've always suspected that they would. No man can put a chain around the ankle of his fellow man without finding the other end fastened around his own neck."

It wasn't just the ease with which it glided out, it was the stern conviction with which the old man used the quotation. Douglass. At that moment, Chase realized this man wasn't familiar, he was *known*. Chase felt he had even studied him in some way.

The old man could see Chase struggling to work it out. "Gabriel Soames," he said helpfully.

"*Gabriel Soames?*"

The man laughed. "Well, I like the way you say that. I haven't heard any regard for my name in a long, long time."

"The House Judiciary Committee."

"Not so glamorous. Ways and Means."

"But a lot more than that. You were once South Carolina SCLC. You marched with King."

"A lot of people marched with King. And look at where it got me."

There was a grim silence between them. Gabriel seemed to be staring at the hole in his sock.

Finally, Chase said, "Do you communicate with them?"

Gabriel looked up. "Who?"

Chase gestured to the outside, upstairs. "The Changers. I need to talk to someone in authority. If I can, I'm confident I can get – " He paused to correct. " – us out of here." His mind was starting to move as he focused on the problem. Sister Sheena, definitely, but Brueler could likely get to any number of the miners or lesser lights around the Beavenstock throne.

This time it was Gabriel's turn to snap. Just a bit. "Would that be just you and me or would 'us' include the other three hundred sorry-ass souls down here?"

Of course, the old man was right.

Gabriel offered a sad, apologetic smile. "Look, son, I believe in faith, but I know – I mean *know* like I know the sun rises – that right now it doesn't matter if you're talking three or three hundred Reasoners. If you're down here, there's no demanding anyone talk to anyone anymore, and who the hell is it you want to talk to so badly anyway?"

But Chase was clearly and suddenly focused on something else. "What did you say?"

"I asked who the hell it is you want to – "

"Three or three hundred, you said."

"Three or three hundred. It doesn't matter."

("In the very first round, a list of three hundred," she had said.

"You expect three hundred people to get together as some sort of Super Politburo?")

Those were voices from the past, what seemed like a painfully long-dead past, but one of the voices was his, and the other was the Senator. And the place was a patio overlooking the grounds of Princeton.

"Why did you say three hundred?"

The old man shrugged. "It's as good a number as any."

"Yes, but it's not. It's not any number. That's what the original list was. Three hundred Reasoners to be whittled down to a practical twelve. And how did you know who I am? There's nothing to identify me here." Chase thought. Then the only possible answer presented itself. "You worked with her. Sofia. You were part of the original team. Did you help choose the Reasoners?"

Gabriel smiled, then laughed. "You're young, Chase. I'm old. Old enough to know that there are things we try just because we ought to try them. Almost all of them start with the highest ideals, but most of them don't amount to anything, and all that bluff and bluster and importance comes to nothing. So, as for Reasoners, you may as well tell people you're a member of the National Recovery Act, or the Civilian Conservation Corps, or the Confederacy, for that matter. Same importance. Things come and go."

"So if the Reasoners are finished, did the same thing happen to the others as has happened to me?"

Gabriel hesitated a moment. His expression suggested he wasn't trying to hide something; he simply didn't know. "I can't answer that," he said.

"Well if the others aren't in here as well – then it would sort of suggest that whoever engineered this was only after me."

Gabriel stuck to his guns. "Like I said, I don't know that."

"But it's possible, isn't it? And you know that."

"How you mean?"

"Because I'm different from the others. And it's possible you know why."

"Why you're different?"

"Well, I'm certainly different because I'm the one *they* chose. That's for starters."

Chase saw the change in the man's expression instantly. "You knew about that, didn't you?"

Gabriel looked at the floor quietly. "She said something. Yes."

"You guys gave them strikes, like on a jury. Yes him, no her, yes her, no him. Then they did something no one expected. They sent back a list with a name penciled in. That name was mine. She didn't know why or what sense that made, but there I was. And the part that bothered her – maybe bothered you as well – was that my name was already on *your* list. Already vetted. What sense did that make? None. And the way it worked out, they never put forward another name and they never explained about me."

"If you must know, I said you were a risk," said Gabriel. "For that very reason."

"I would have said so too."

"But Sofia … " Gabriel hesitated just a moment. Remembering. "She said there was something else there. She said you were a natural. She didn't say a natural what, but you were something she felt was badly needed." Gabriel considered his own words. He seemed to go back in time, perhaps to when the Uprising was just a disruption and the Capitol was still run by reasonably thoughtful men and women only fighting for political advantage. Chase waited. Finally, the old man pulled himself out of his reverie. "You said there's something you have to continue doing," Gabriel said. "What's that?"

"It's complicated."

"I'm pretty good at complicated."

Chase gave in. "It's how I think we can get out of this. Not just this building. All of it."

Gabriel looked unsure. "This is a plan you have on your own or a plan you have with others?"

"There are others involved." He hesitated before he said the next name. "One of them is Van DeVere."

For the first time since Chase had got the bean cans to work, Gabriel Soames looked impressed. "Van DeVere? You have actually spoken to him?"

"Yes. But it's not him I need to talk to now. There's another party that's crucial for my plans."

"And who is this other party?"

"The Wolf."

Gabriel stared at him. A long time. And then, slowly, he started to laugh. Not much, but some. Chase may as well have said Julius Caesar, or Casper the Friendly Ghost.

Chase said, "Look, I know that what I'm saying sounds absurd – "

But Gabriel cut him off. "You *know* the Wolf?"

"No."

"But you know who the Wolf *is*?"

"No."

"So you've got something set *up*?"

"I didn't say that either. Why?"

"Because the irony – the incredible irony – is that I just may be able to help you. At least I know someone who can set you in the right direction."

"What do you mean 'someone'?"

Gabriel got up and went to the door. He put his hand on the doorknob. "You ready?"

Chase rose, surprised. "The doors aren't locked?"

"Oh shit no, son. None of the doors are locked here except the truly important ones. It's not about doors down here, it's about not using the hallways. Ever."

To prove it, to Chase's amazement, Gabriel turned the knob and opened the door.

The door opened onto a cream-colored industrial corridor with a dark grey polished floor and a ceiling that appeared to be an endless highway of plumbing and heating pipes and metal conduits for electrical. It was lit by fluorescent tubes, although the one right outside Gabriel's room was flashing, giving off an annoying buzz.

That wasn't the only sound, however. There was a hum underneath the electrical, one coming from way down the hall to the right. An insistent sound, like a strange, cackling murmur. Instinctively, Chase stepped out so he could hear better, but Gabriel yanked him back with a grip of iron. The older man gestured that Chase needed to just stay where he was. The two men stood in the open doorway and listened.

Chase's first thought was that he'd heard this before. On a record album, or maybe some YouTube thing. The Beatles came to mind, but that seemed kind of crazy. Then he realized what it was. Sergeant Pepper. There was gibberish at the end of the Sergeant Pepper album, which he later heard was a backwards tape of the group talking, something tacked on to the end of their masterpiece as a last-minute joke. But it wasn't all that funny, because the backwards talk sounded like threatening, almost demonic chatter.

It wasn't the exact same sound now, but Chase had the same sensation from the disjointed murmurings he heard now coming from the end of the hall; human voices neither talking nor shouting, but whispering amongst themselves in the disjointed tones and discordant tenor of the completely mad. There was an occasional chuckle, mirthless and threatening. Then an answering shriek in a word he recognized. Standing at the door, peering around the corner, he heard a high-pitched voice shriek from some distant room: "Cornflake!"

Peering down the hall from Gabriel's room, Chase could make out what appeared to be dozens of doorways, all to the right, presumably opening into small utility offices such as this one. Likely some of them were even connected in the same way. The murmuring voices betrayed a dark and terrible truth, however, which Chase had never considered. The basement of the Capitol, instead of being occupied by concerned, terrified, but rational and educated people, was perhaps instead populated by beings who long ago had lost control of themselves and transformed by fear and the destruction of their known world into entities barely human. Chase only had to hear their noises to know that he was looking down a corridor of madness and fear and dark anticipation.

Chase glanced back at Gabriel. The old man nodded sadly. "Yes," he said.

From the left, a voice suddenly screamed out. Screamed. The sound slid a knife of pure fear into Chase's spine. He turned his head and looked down the other end of the corridor.

"This place is full of blue madness!" the voice – maybe man? Maybe woman? – shrieked.

Chase made another involuntary step forward, a reflexive action to see where the screaming was coming from. Again,

Gabriel stopped him. "Remember, we don't go there," the older man said.

The shrieking voice went on from the depths of some distant corridor. "The madness is in the water! It's in the crumbs of the toaster! They've poisoned our feet!"

A man's voice, Chase decided. Tinged with a vague accent. Southern? He was so shrill, it was hard to tell.

"Where is the Tin Man? Where is the Lion?" the voice demanded.

Gabriel's grip turned into an iron pincer. He wasn't going to let Chase put one foot into that corridor.

Even though Gabriel was holding him in the doorway, Chase discovered that he could nonetheless see something if he stuck his neck out far enough. The left-side corridor made an abrupt turn not fifty feet from Gabriel's door. At that junction, Chase saw a shadow reflected on the opposite wall; the shadow of bars – like jail cell bars. Bunched behind those bars was the misshapen form of a man, perhaps a very fat man, who looked like he was squatting on his haunches. "It's a cinch Dorothy is the one in charge!" the shadow man shouted.

Then the shadow rattled his cage and offered up the incantation of every prisoner everywhere in time. "I don't belong here!" he shouted. "I know people!"

Chase glanced over at Gabriel, who put a "shh" finger to his lips and offered a nod and, "Wait."

"I know the Woodsman!" the caged man shouted. "I know the Wizard! I know them all. I know Dorothy! And I know the Wolf!"

Chase and Gabriel locked eyes.

Another rattle of the cage. "You hear me? I have talked to the Wolf! Every fucking one of them! Hairy bastards all except above their pointy ears!"

Chase gave Gabriel a questioning look. Gabriel gave him another 'wait' look. Chase waited.

The man in the cage took a good long while formulating his next sentence. Finally it came, although it wasn't offered up in quite the same bellow as the nonsense that had preceded it. "I know Calvin Coolidge," he said. "And mine eyes have seen the glory of the coming of the Lord!"

The expression on Gabriel's face was almost mournful. He slowly drew Chase back into the room and closed the door, quietly. "You understand?"

Chase returned to the center of the room and slowly lowered himself onto the edge of the wobbly chair. He stared at the linoleum floor. Gabriel stood over him. "Two months ago, that man was one of the senior members of the House Energy and Commerce committee. We've been friends for more than thirty years. He was a war hero. Two times!"

Chase didn't know what to say.

Gabriel returned to his cot. He knelt down at its side and searched for something underneath. "I got something here. Maybe we both need." Sure enough he came out with a fabric shopping bag, the kind you buy. He pulled out some balled-up clothes – they appeared to be workout clothes – and then a small purple bag with a drawstring. From this he drew out a squarish bottle with a gold cap. Crown Royal Canadian Rye Whiskey. It looked like it was almost full. Chase was never more happy to see a bottle of alcohol in his life. "Grab that," Gabriel said, gesturing behind Chase.

Chase looked behind and saw a little plastic blue cup, the kind for bathrooms.

Gabriel came over and wiped the cup out with what looked like a clean handkerchief. He filled it halfway up from the bottle and handed it over.

The whiskey blasted Chase awake. In a second, he could feel his head returning to normal size.

"It's amazing what happens to us, isn't it?" Gabriel asked, returning to his cot. "As people." He picked up a brushed-steel traveling coffee mug which sat on the box beside his cot. He gave it a quick cleanout and poured himself a drink. "In – maybe a matter of weeks? – most everyone went from fire and brimstone and 'we shall overcome' to cave dwellers. It happened fast. And some, like Dan there, got to some place a lot farther away than that."

"But … how?"

Gabriel shrugged. "Food. Water. You start fighting over that stuff like food and water and you discover pretty quick that you're not what you think you are. You hope no one else notices what you're turning into. But you can't escape it; one moment you're thinking about the importance of restoring democracy and the Constitution, and the next you're thinking about how to steal your cellmate's water, or wondering if you're strong enough to knock him out for the box of Ritz Bitz he happened to bring to work in his briefcase on 5/22."

Chase tried to take in what Gabriel was telling him. "I tried to picture it," he said. "But it was nothing like this."

"I would imagine that's what it's like when any people are caged. Especially folks who always figured that caging was for the other guy."

Chase didn't know what to say to that.

Gabriel kind of smiled. Sort of. "Thought we were all civilized down here, didn't you? Working together collegially to figure out our escape while the true madmen were up on the Capitol steps?"

Chase nodded slowly. "Something like that."

"Yeah," said Gabriel. "That's the clothes."

"Excuse me?"

Gabriel nodded at his suit jacket and white shirt hanging on the back of the door. "The clothes. Almost from the beginning they said we had to keep our work clothes perfect. The idea is that when they take us up the south stairs and put us in front of the mob, we still have to look like Washington. You understand?"

Chase nodded slowly, as if taking this in for rational consideration, but inside he was screaming to himself, My God, My God.

"They're smart," said Gabriel. "Somewhere they decided the whole thing doesn't work if we look like regular people. That's also why they send barbers around to us every week, and before they take the ladies up, they have someone do their makeup and nails. To look the part. That's what they did to my wife, anyway."

"Excuse me?"

Gabriel took another sip from his traveling mug. "Corinne had a job in the Treasury. She was a junior director at the TTB. That's the Alcohol and Tobacco Tax and Trade Bureau. But they hauled her up early in the first culling and made a big show of it."

Chase felt his throat tighten. "In God's name, why?"

Gabriel grinned. "Well, TTB also collects taxes on firearms and ammunition. You get the problem, don't you?"

Chase didn't.

Gabriel laughed. "Nobody out there believes in taxing firearms and ammunition! That's sin #1."

"So ... what happened?"

Gabriel shrugged. "They made her kneel down and one of those fellows in the Jerseys made a *big* show of that. You know, dropping trou and waving himself as if she was going to put him in her mouth. As if they *hadn't* done that before, which I'm convinced they did. Down here, I mean. Corinne was a very good-looking woman, although I guess I was biased. She was proud. Correct. That's exactly the kind they hate and exactly the kind they have to abuse."

Chase looked at the old man and thought he saw, for a fraction of a second, a shimmy in the hand which was holding the travel mug. Perhaps catching Chase's glance, Gabriel quickly opted for two hands to take his next drink. Eventually, he managed to lower the mug without a shimmy. His voice was steady. "They didn't go that far, of course. They just chopped her head off. The worst part was that they let her head stay there in one of those boxes while some asshole made a speech about the Second Amendment and the right to bear arms without taxation."

"Where were you?" Chase asked. "I mean, did you see this?"

Gabriel shook his head. "I wasn't out there, if that's what you mean. I was in one of the big rooms in those days. Our phones worked then. We saw everything streaming." He glanced balefully at the two cans and string sitting on the floor. "We have gone considerably lower-tech since."

Chase wanted to change the subject. To anything. "The big room?" he asked.

Gabriel smiled a thin smile. He was clearly ready to change the subject as well. He reached over and handed across the Crown Royal so Chase could top himself up. "Well, 5/22 wasn't about a plan, you know. I'm meaning, they didn't have one. They had a plan to attack and take *over*, but they didn't have a plan when it came to housing prisoners and all that. So they herded maybe a hundred or more into the biggest rooms and locked the doors."

"What happened then?"

"Someone told them that all those folks in one room meant everyone was going to die if they kept that up, whether from disease or starvation or just beating the shit out of each other. That's a problem if you're holding a basement full of power brokers. So they decided to spread us out. In some cases twenty to a room, in other cases ten or even five."

"But you have a room all on your own."

"It wasn't always."

Chase was surprised. He waited for him to explain.

Finally, Gabriel said, "A Senator Brubaker – you know who he is? – lived in here with us till just very recently."

"Us?"

Gabriel cocked his head, gesturing to the corridor. "And Dan down there. The one offering us the *Wizard of Oz* reboot. Before he left us in a different way. And two congressional office interns. I don't know what happened to them. They were just hauled out one day. Not chopped, though. I'm sure of that."

"So the Changers don't manage the actual rooms?"

Gabriel shook his head and laughed. "Like I said, they're smart! Eventually they figured out that all they had to do was manage the hallways. In a basement, you manage the hallways, you don't have to worry about rooms, do you?"

Chase was trying to take it all in.

"They got all sorts of badasses to patrol," Gabriel explained. "And you never know when they're coming to check up on things. Terror. That's their thing. And counting."

"Counting?"

"Us. They're obsessed that we're all here and no one's getting out."

Chase was trying to put all this in order in his broken head, but it was starting to feel like too much.

"Who?" he asked finally.

"Who what?"

"Who was the one who told them they couldn't keep everyone penned in one room, that they should spread them out?"

Gabriel smiled, and for the first time Chase noticed the big gap in his teeth. "Guilty as charged."

"It was you, wasn't it?"

"Me."

"And why do you think they went along with that?"

"Have you ever *met* Jeff Beavenstock?"

Chase shook his head. "I've only met her."

Gabriel was instantly fascinated. "Sheena? You've met *Sheena?*"

Chase nodded.

"Now her I'd like to meet," Gabriel said. "But, of course, this whole Washington thing isn't her scene. This is him, through and through. What's she like?"

"Smart. And dangerous." Chase didn't feel ready yet to plumb the depths of his insights into Sister Sheena.

Gabriel was viewing him with a kind of bemusement. "I bet you think she's the smarter one. Compared to Jeff."

"Isn't she?" Chase asked.

"For sure that's what everyone thinks. Maybe from the beginning. Me too. I wonder if that's what everyone's supposed to think."

"What makes you say that?"

"That man is *shrewd*. He has a way. *The* way. I don't mean just the way he presents himself – all of us here have that – but he has that something else."

Chase was aware that Representative Soames was putting Jeff Beavenstock in the same category as himself and duly elected members of Congress; Beavenstock, whose principal tools were anarchy and cutting off people's heads. Beavenstock, as if he were just head of the opposition. Beavenstock, as if he were a political superstar blessed with God-given retail talents.

Gabriel went on. "He can make the complex very simple and he can get right to the heart of the matter. Of course the flipside is that he can't think ahead. It just defeats him. Probably the reason he never got very far in life. Normal life, anyway. And, of course, there's another drawback. Something I've only come across a few times in my life."

"What drawback is that?"

"The fact that the man is utterly dead inside. A living corpse."

Chase had begun to suspect that the commotion Gabriel had heard through his tin cans five days before ("five days ago the place was on fire ... I thought they were going to shake this building to death") was likely the shooting of Beavenstock and the killing of his wannabe assassin. Clearly, however, the old man knew none of the actual details. Chase gave him an update now, carefully laying out the events leading up to and resulting from Beavenstock's shooting in as clean an order as he could manage.

Gabriel took it all in with wonder and an odd look of pleasure. "Wow," he said. "Wow." Then, "I knew something had happened. Big. I asked some of the food guards here, but they wouldn't tell me. Is he dead?"

"He might be," Chase said.

Gabriel sipped his whiskey thoughtfully. "So there's a new culling coming. Has to be."

Chase said, "Except without a leader ... "

"Oh, there's a leader." Gabriel gestured toward his tin cans.

"I don't know who it is, but *someone* is revving them up. Filling them with all sorts of fire. I haven't heard them like that since the beginning." The old man suddenly got caught up in his thoughts. Chase wondered if he was thinking about his wife. It turned out to be something else. "You know, Chase," he said finally, "it's sad. I know all empires fall. But I thought – I really thought – that we had such a good shot."

Chase was surprised. "You think this is it?"

Gabriel nodded emphatically. "Well, it's certainly it for the country I grew up in and the country you grew up in. Maybe that's my problem, and why sometimes I lie here thinking I don't care if they take me next – because I don't really want to live in a different country. Not that it was so wonderful, but I just don't want that much change, Especially at the end. You know what I mean?"

Chase nodded, although he wasn't truly sure he felt it the same way the older man did.

"We just ran out of gas somewhere," Gabriel said. He sounded incredibly weary. "Must have. After all, you gotta be pretty weak to let a bunch of cockroaches take you out like this. Think of it: Folks without any ideas whatsoever came in wearing a bunch of sports jerseys and carrying whatever they'd bought at Dick's or gun shows, and in no time they defeated the D.C. police, the state militia, ran off the Capitol police, and even the transit and prison cops. They killed a whole stack of very important people – including the Supreme Court! – and even got lucky enough that the army didn't crash in on them. Clearly, the patient has been sick a long while. May I?"

Gabriel was holding out the bottle to refill Chase's drink. Chase shook his head. He was already feeling the effects but at least the throb in his skull had been cut in half.

Chase said, as gently as he could, "I'm not sure you can count us out yet, Gabe. There's hope. Someone will come up with a plan better than their plans."

Gabriel pretty much hooted. "Plans?? You think these chuckleheads have a plan?! Boy, you really are new to town, aren't you? Let me tell you something: For all their burning and killing and 'getting back at the power in Washington,' you know what they never once thought about? How to come up with an actual plan that has a chance of working. You hear what I'm saying? They've got nothing."

Chase thought of Sister Sheena's ham-handed new American constitution. Hardly what could be called an actual 'system.' "They've got *Wolf Words*," Chase tried.

Gabriel shook his head. "That thing's just a cobbled-together political tract which relies on the old saw of the guys on top are screwing you, and you oughta get some revenge. How's that going to let anyone know how to run a post office or how to handle the imbalance of donor states? No, they never had a plan, and that's why they agreed to that Compromise, bringing the Reasoners in. What true revolutionary in their right minds would allow something like that? Especially if you're sitting in the catbird's seat. I think these folks were ready to make a deal – any deal – because nobody knew what else to do. Caught the fire truck, that's all."

Chase looked up. It was the same expression the Reverend had used. "Why'd you say that?"

"Well, it's true."

"I mean about the fire truck…"

"Well, they did. But that's not what bothers me the most. You know what bothers me? Really galls me?" Another slug from the travel mug. "How embarrassed I am!"

"Embarrassed? For who?"

Gabriel laughed. "For me! I worked for reforms my entire life. Always trying to help the poor dumb bastard who the fat cats were stepping on. And what happened? Those poor dumb bastards went and killed my wife. Clearly I have misunderstood those motherfuckers my whole life. Otherwise, why am I sitting here?" He laughed again. Another drink. He was getting sauced, and it was clear he enjoyed – no, craved – the company. "You got to understand that I really thought – my whole life – that I was put on the earth to help the poor."

"Maybe you were."

Gabriel shook his head. He reached out to pour Chase another drink. This time Chase took it. "You ever been to Jackson?"

"Mississippi?"

"Mississippi."

Chase shook his head.

"Well, lemme tell you: You ever get a rental from the airport and plan on driving into Jackson, make sure you get extra insurance. The place is nothing but potholes. Tear your car to shreds. Rip the bottom right out. By the time I got to my hotel, I was a nervous wreck, you understand? I didn't ask the desk clerk, I asked the *cleaning lady*, 'Madam, why in the hell do you allow a city government that won't fix those potholes when you deserve better?' And you know what she said? She looked me right in the eye and said, 'Congressman, maybe we don't think we *deserve* better.'" There was a long pause as Gabriel thought about that.

Chase let the old man take the moment. Then he said, "Maybe the Changers think they deserve better."

Gabriel's head shot right back up. "No!" he said. "They do *not* think they deserve better.' They just think others should suffer like them. There's a difference and I see that now. You ever think you can fix things for them or give them enough that they'll see reason, you know what will happen to you?"

"What?"

"They'll kill you, son. Just as sure as they're going to kill me."

2

Chase wasn't sure, but it felt like he slept most of the next day. He only awoke to relieve himself in the black plastic litter can in the corner of the room. He'd apparently already used this before. It was a quarter-filled with pee. When he'd been out for the count earlier? He had no memory of it.

Shivering under his blanket again, he thought about Hog. He was almost sure he was dead. Although they had only known one another a very short time, Chase suspected Hog had been one of the few truly honorable people he'd ever met. The idea that such a man was snuffed out so easily – by who knew what whim – was more than Chase's already crowded and pounding brain could take.

It was evening when he woke up again. Or, at least, he had a sense that it was evening. His headache was almost gone, but he was starving. He was thinking about Hamer and the foil-wrapped nuts in the back of the Escalade. Were they cashews or almonds? Cashews, Chase thought.

Slowly, he pulled himself up. He peered into Gabriel's room, pushing the door open as gently and as unobtrusively as possible.

The old man was writing something on the back of what appeared to be a school spiral-bound report book. What, Chase wondered, would an old man with no hope write?

Then the door creaked. Gabriel looked up. He offered a weak smile. "If you're hungry, you got good timing."

It turned out that three very tired young people delivered the food in the basement of the Capitol. Fellow prisoners ("food guards," Gabriel explained) who Chase imagined had once been Washington interns. They pushed what appeared to have been a mail cart, loaded with boxed food. "Hey Gabe," the young woman said, but there was no heart in it. The two young men just leaned on the cart with their forearms and waited for Gabe to choose his evening meal. And now, of course, Chase's.

Gabriel chose a box of Stove Top stuffing and two macaroni and cheese dinner boxes, the kind which don't require milk or butter. He thanked them and they moved on. Chase, standing in the doorway, looked after them. He wondered if they were going to deliver food to the caged beast just past the turn at the end of the hall, but they turned the corner and were gone. He wouldn't know.

Chase couldn't imagine how Gabriel was going to make a go of his food choices. Both items required water and a stove, far as Chase could tell. He shouldn't have doubted his fellow captive. Underneath Gabriel's cot was a heating plate and a "cookset" that consisted of two glass coffee urns, a couple of bowls, and plastic knives and forks from some long-forgotten Starbucks. Gabriel looked almost shamefaced as he filled the coffee urn from a water jug and began to boil water on the hot plate. "Far, far more than others have," he said.

3

After dinner, Chase learned something else about Gabriel that he couldn't have anticipated: The man did not stop talking. Perhaps it was because he finally had a companion to talk to, or because the particular subject he focused on filled him with such energy and emotional fuel; either way, Gabriel kept up a staggeringly knowledgeable recitation.

His subject was, primarily, the American Constitution. He had a lot of views on it, mostly centered around its horrific flaws and the iniquities it both guaranteed and entrenched. This was interesting enough, but for Chase the truly remarkable thing was just how much Gabriel knew about its history, intention, and the challenges it had faced. Gabriel breezed happily from *Marbury v. Madison* to *Gibbon v. Ogden* to *Dred Scott* to *Miranda*. He spoke as if he had been at every single case himself ("then Justice Tawney, he gets up, and you know what he says?"), and often included his listener as well.

At first, Chase assumed some sort of response was expected. After a while, though, he realized that Gabriel was just happy to be speaking to a new cellmate. Chase decided that this was his therapy, his way of getting through everything that had happened to himself, the country, and the world Gabriel Soames had once known.

It was an amazing performance, and at the end of it, Chase believed the old man was fairly delighted with himself. But then, as they were saying goodnight, Gabriel suddenly embraced him and wept, openly and unashamed. "I don't know what I'm going to do, son. With all this in me and it having meant so much to me all my life – my *life* – when really all it meant was nothing. What am I going to do with that now? Where do I go?"

Chase had absolutely no answer for that.

44. *Taking Stock*

1

As Chase lay on his mat in the room adjoining Gabriel's, his head resting on a pillow which had almost surely once been an arm cushion from an office sofa, he did a little 2 a.m. stock-taking.

Over the past few days he had come to accept the idea, as well as Gabriel's hypothesis, that the Reasoners had almost surely been manipulated into non-existence. By whom exactly, Chase didn't know, but it was surely some group of people or persons who had an agenda of their own. It made sense to assume that one of the Reasoners, or maybe more than one, had played a part in this, just as Sister Sheena had warned, but here Chase was hesitant, not because duplicity was so hard to imagine, but because he'd seen the Reasoners operate.

Their chief value, by and large, lay in why each of them had been selected: the ability to reason. They were thinkers. Planners. Talkers. They were not, in and of themselves, particularly good administrators. Miles Mallickey had been right about that. Without an ability to run anything, Chase doubted that any single or group of Reasoners could orchestrate anything resembling what had happened since the bridge.

And if he needed further unquestionable proof that whoever had betrayed the Reasoners was a superior hand at manipulation, Chase was proof itself. He was here. This said everything. They'd abducted and dropped a Reasoner into one of the basement rooms of the Capitol, and something like that didn't just happen.

The obvious candidate for such activities was Sister Sheena.

However, to make that work, you had to write off the entire parking garage meeting or chalk it up to some strange reverse power play on her part. Chase had trouble doing that. He had stood inches from her. He could picture those piercing eyes looking up at him. With Beavenstock's shooting, Sheena's youth had reasserted itself, had a little conversation with that considerable brain of hers, and come to a very clear decision; namely, that she was going to cut and run the second she could. Was the look he'd seen in her eyes faked? No, Chase decided. It couldn't have been. Real fear.

The next obvious entity antagonistic to the Reasoners specifically and the peace process in general was Miles Mallickey. Miles hadn't been around when the Reasoners program had been dreamt up – so it was something he inherited, pretty much as he appeared to have inherited the thankless job of quasi-maybe Chief of Staff for the entire United States government, or at least what was left of it – and the fact is it flew in the face of Mallickey's core belief in how to manage a crisis, which was military power and brute force above all else. People wanted to take down his beloved political bureaucracy? Kill them. Subtle planning or finesse were not for him. There was also the fact that while it was imaginable Miles maybe – *maybe* – could have one Reasoner shot on a bridge and another murdered and hanged in a closet, he didn't have the means to pluck Chase out of the Reasoner's secure fortress and drop him into the enemy's Capitol basement prison. In the end, Mallickey was just a bureaucrat.

Fortunately, there was one thing Chase was confident of: The person or persons who orchestrated his imprisonment had no intention of him actually dying here. The guillotine was not his fate, any more than he was supposed to die on a bridge or by gunfire in a government building's parking garage.

If they wanted to kill him, they could have already done it any number of ways. No, the intention was either to take him out of the picture for a while or to scare the shit out of him. He suspected both but leaned on the former.

But take him out of the picture why? The only thing he could figure is that his meeting with Van DeVere had triggered a sense of urgency on the part of whoever was behind this. Chase had opened some box, and someone wanted it closed.

Which led him back to the Reasoners. Presuming that Kirsten Pappason and Albert Calinescu were lying dead in the garage beneath the State building, what about the others? Were they, like the Reverend Campbell, all working for the baddies, or were they suffering for having tried to be one of the goodies? Chase suspected most had gone the way of the Reverend; collaborators with the bad guys in order to save their necks, and therefore safe and jolly in an undisclosed location. Morally compromised, certainly, but at least not in the Capitol basement prison. Chase suspected someone like Vin Jansert would have led the charge for collaboration if the choice were ever offered. Not for Vin an empirical exploration of the wretchedness of the Bastille.

As if on cue, his thoughts were interrupted. The Sergeant Pepper sounds had begun their nightly drift down the hall, far off to the right, even though both his and Gabriel's doors were closed. That meant it was either two or a little after two. They were so regular that you didn't need to check your watch.

They weren't as loud during the night as during the day, or as creepy, but Chase could make out them murmuring better at night, and occasionally he picked up actual words. One that kept recurring was "offerings." The other was "sacrifice." Chase wasn't crazy about the sound of either of them.

Sure that his thoughts wouldn't let him fall asleep again, he fell asleep again.

45. *The Jangles*

1

It was in the dark morning of his third day of consciousness – or was it his fourth? – that Chase learned just how the Changers handled discipline belowgrounds.

He wasn't just pulled out of a dead sleep; he was ripped from it as violently as if blasted into the air by a land mine and sucked into the turbines of a 737 jet engine. To some degree, that's all his brain could make of things – that an aircraft of some sort was flying directly into the building, targeting specifically the west front basement where Gabriel and the rest of the miserable unfortunates were caved, and that an air raid siren was being blasted right next to his ear.

He needed to bolt upright. He needed to scream. But he couldn't move an inch, and he couldn't react. Something was holding him down, and no matter how hard he fought, that something wouldn't let go. He feared he would be unable to breathe.

It took him seconds – or longer? – to realize that there really *was* something holding him down, and it wasn't some aeronautical force. It was a seventy-two-year-old man less than six inches his height yet deceptively strong. "Do not go out!" Gabriel was hissing into his ear. "Do not do anything!"

"What the fuck – "

Gabriel clamped Chase's mouth with the palm of his hand. "It's just the morning jangles! That's all it is. Just the morning goddamned jangles!"

The morning *what*??

It took a few more seconds, but Chase was eventually able

to recognize that the sound blasting through his brain was real. Amazingly, it seemed to be getting louder.

Gabriel slowly relaxed his clamp on Chase's mouth, and after a moment or two swung his left leg and his weight off Chase's body. Chase sat up and rubbed his jaw. Gabriel nodded at the closed hallway door and shouted over the noise. "You can look if you want, but remember, you can't step out! Never."

Chase wondered what the catch was, but Gabriel nodded his head. "Go! See!"

Chase got up and approached the closed hallway door, the one with the map and fire instructions on it. The din on the other side was staggering. What would he find if he opened the door? He looked back at Gabriel, who merely nodded again. He said something, but Chase couldn't hear. Gabriel shouted louder. "You got to anyway, for the Pledge!"

Chase opened the door slowly.

If the din had been excruciating before, it was now an ear-splitting scream from the bowels of hell.

Yet once Chase poked his head far enough out, he saw that it wasn't supernatural or biblical in any way. It was, as usual, Changer can-do know-how.

They were coming from the right side of the hallway, and they were traveling in two or three, maybe four, heats of three. They were all Jerseys, and Chase was surprised to see women mixed in with the men. In the first heat, one of the men was pushing a Lawn-Boy 21-inch self-propelled gas-powered lawnmower, which was not just on, it was jacked up as high and as loud as those things can get. In the Jersey's other hand was a Craftsman B215 leaf blower, which was hard to manage physically, but nowhere near the monster the Poulan Pro was – the backpack model, which the woman was carrying. The Jersey directly behind her was whirring away happily with a Greenworks weedwhacker in one hand and a DeWalt 22-inch, 20-volt hedge trimmer, which gave off a surprising 120 decibels. About twenty feet behind this group was the second heat, which was outfitted with similar lawn equipment, all turned on, all turned up high, and all emitting unbearable decibels which blasted off the concrete block walls and polished floors.

Each of these Changers was outfitted with industrial-grade ear protection, wrap-around goggles, and gardening gloves.

They moved at a stately pace, making sure that the unprotected eardrums of every living soul in the basement were rattled and swollen, impaired if not destroyed.

Chase covered his ears and yet almost instinctively stepped out into the hall for a better look. Gabriel grabbed him at the last second and shouted, "No!"

So Chase stood where he was and watched as the Jerseys came closer and closer, and eventually walked right by him as if he didn't exist – except one of them, the guy at the back with the hedge-trimmer, gave him a smarmy and oily grin from behind protective goggles.

Eventually, all three heats passed. In a matter of not even a minute they turned around and came back. Chase retreated into the room, putting his back to the wall and covering his ears. He realized without knowing it that he was screaming. Then he realized that he wasn't the only one.

He took his hands from his ears and held his breath for a second so he could hear. Yes, there was something back there, something behind the godawful motors. It was man made, not machine made; high-pitched and human, souls screaming in torment.

Then, just as quickly, all the engines turned off, and Chase was able to hear the screaming without engine accompaniment.

It was every soul in the basement. Screaming. For relief from the noise, to be let free, to be made into people again.

And then, slowly, the screams began to die down. And just as it began to disappear, an authoritative voice bellowed, rather cheerfully, "Goo-ood morning, lawmakers!"

What the hell was *this*? Chase returned to the doorway and peered around the corner, careful to keep his feet on the correct side of the threshold.

There they were. The Noisemakers. Gathered together in the center of the hallway, maybe fifty feet from where Chase stood. It was the woman from the first heat addressing the opened doors of all the offices. All the other Changers were removing their safety goggles. "It's a beautiful morning, lawmakers, isn't it? Time for your protein fruit smoothie! Time for a jog! Time for a latte! Time to make the world better!" She delivered this with a kind of weird, twisted smile. Some of her fellow Changers chuckled. One of them, however, didn't. He just futzed trying to get his gloves off and looked annoyed. There was something in the way he did this – something in the way all of these Jerseys did everything – that suggested this was a short-straw job in the Changer hierarchy, and they were only trying to make the best of it.

The woman went on. "We're glad you're with us, lawmakers, and we're glad we can all share the fruits of freedom together! And on that subject – "

Suddenly, every voice in the basement rooms screamed in outright terror. These voices belonged to people Chase couldn't see from where he stood, but the power of their shrieks bounced off the walls and ceiling and sent him stumbling backward, right into Gabriel. Gabriel steadied him.

The Jersey woman was neither surprised by the screaming nor perturbed. She merely nodded to the fellow who had been futzing with his gloves and said, "Ethan, you grab me one, will you? Got to be young, though, remember."

The Glove Guy nodded, clearly pissed to be picked for this shit job. He stepped toward the first door open to him. A scream went up from within. He grinned, then quickly reached into the room with a darting grab and – nothing! It was a fake. They screamed. He laughed. Then, with his back to the far wall so no one could see him, he snuck up on the next available open door.

"What the fuck?" Chase whispered to Gabriel.

Gabriel whispered in his ear. He smelled of rye whiskey. "They got to catch them. That's the rules."

"What is this?"

But what Gabriel said is exactly what happened. Glove Guy surprised the prisoners lurking in the doorway of the next room, leaned in and hauled out a young man in running shoes and a filthy T-shirt who instantly began kicking and screaming to be let go.

Gabriel whispered back into Chase's ear. "They got to take the young ones. They take an old one they might screw up and accidentally waste a Congressman or Senator. Beavenstock would go berserk."

The young prisoner, who had carrot-colored hair and freckles across every inch of his body, was trying to reason with them. Such as it was. "No, no," he said. "Don't do this! Don't do this!"

The woman nodded to another Jersey, who put down his leaf blower and helped Glove Guy hold the freckled guy against the wall. Then the woman said in a loud voice, "What's your name, Red?"

Red shook as he tried to answer. "Look, I'm begging you, I'm begging you as a person, as an American, I'm asking you, look, I have family – "

"'Begging you'? What kind of name is that?"

"No, seriously, don't – "

"Tell me your fucking *name*, Red, or this is gonna be a lot worse than you think it's gonna be!"

"Pilar."

"Pilar? Pil-ar?? Are you kidding me, Red?"

"I'm not kidding you at all, I swear, really, please – "

"Pil-ar!" She turned back to the open doorways. "Everyone, Pil-ar has been chosen today to give up something for the sake of freedom! Give up something so we can all live better lives than our parents did, and our grandparents! Give up something because he believes in the American dream, don't you, Pilar? Pilar is gonna make a sacrifice for the rest of us, isn't he?"

Pilar was beyond shaking now. He looked like he was about to lose bladder control. "Please! I'm begging you!"

But the woman didn't care. "Hold him!" she said.

And they did. Glove Guy and Leaf Blower held Pilar against the wall. He kicked and screamed as two other Jerseys stood on either side of them. Each had a leaf blower. On a signal from the woman, each one put the mouth of their leaf blower right up to each of Pilar's ears and, on a nod from the woman, turned them on.

The sound was deafening.

Both from the leaf blowers but also Pilar, who screamed probably the last scream of his own that he would ever hear. When they were done, they released him, and Pilar fell to the ground, whimpering and literally mewling. Glove Guy toed him with vague curiosity.

The woman once again shouted to all the doorways in the corridor. "And now, lawmakers," she said cheerfully, "the Pledge!"

To Chase's astonishment, a listless but completely recognizable recitation of the Pledge of Allegiance started up, an unharmonious and utterly uninspiring incantation from within the various basement rooms.

I pledge allegiance to the flag of the United States, and to the Republic for which it stands ...

Chase turned around, realizing that Gabriel was also reciting it. The old man gave Chase a sharp look, and Chase quickly joined in on 'one nation under God' and continued to the end.

This was a nightmare.

When it ended, Chase and Gabriel were staring at one another. The woman's voice from down the hall shouted, "Good to see you, lawmakers! Have yourselves a terrific day! See you tomorrow! Or not! Someday! But you'll never know when!" Chase heard the Jerseys walking off, wheeling their lawnmowers with them, the rest of their lawn tools clattering in their arms.

Chase just stared into Gabriel's eyes. Gabriel returned the stare.

"They don't come every morning," Gabriel said. "That's the genius of it. You never know when they're coming, which is a lot worse than if they came every morning."

"Why did they ... "

Gabriel shrugged. "*Schrecklichkeit*. You know what that is?"

Chase nodded. "Frightfulness. Germans. World War I."

"Of course, I don't think they *know* that, historically. But I think, like everything else, they figured it out on their own. Because it's inside them. You hear what I'm saying?"

"Why can't they come in the rooms? And why can't we go into the halls?"

Again, Gabriel shrugged. "That was something Beavenstock dreamt up, so he didn't have to build actual jail cells. It's simple: If you get caught in the corridor, you're killed. In exchange they don't go into the rooms. Think about that. It keeps order. If you know you're safe in your room, why would you ever leave if you know what the punishment is?"

"My God," said Chase.

Gabriel shrugged. "It's smart. Just like he realized all he had to do was cage the stair entrances and not the individual rooms. Leave everything else open, for all it mattered."

"Are these people truly Americans?"

"Absolutely."

2

His first witness of the jangles – Gabriel's strangely apt word for the sound torture – destroyed something in Chase. What happened to Pilar took away his sense of time. His sense of urgency. His need. Or, at least, almost.

He thought. And he slept. He slept more, in fact, than he had ever slept in his life.

3

It was so dark when he woke up. Chase needed a moment or two to focus. He startled when he realized that there was someone else in the room. Just sitting there in a chair in the corner, watching him.

Not Gabriel. He could tell that. Someone much smaller. A woman, maybe, or a very small man. For a second, he thought it might be the Reverend, but the build was too slight. Besides, there had always been something comforting about Sarah Campbell's vague slouch in posture, whereas there was nothing comforting about this figure.

He and the person just stared at one another in the dark, two figures without feature, and as Chase began to accept that what he was seeing was real – not a hallucination – he became frightened, because he was convinced that the person opposite was his dead sister, Bea. She had come for him. There was nothing comforting in that.

He decided to roll over and turn into the wall, putting his back to the figure. When he did, he heard the rustling of clothes, as if the person were getting up out of the chair and coming over to him. Then nothing. When he turned back, the figure was gone. Not in the chair. Not in the room.

Chase waited and wondered. He must have done that awhile, because he fell asleep – and when he did, life was terrific again.

46. *The Wizard*

1

Rin said she wanted to meet at a place called the Dead Man's Chest, which was in Soho. Clearly, she hadn't heard the news. "You won't get near it," he told her. "There was a bombing this morning at Tottenham Court station." She said she actually had heard, and it was, in fact, one of the reasons why she wanted to go to that particular pub. She was sure it would be open.

It turned out they were both right. The Chest was indeed open – so one for her – and the entire area was crawling with police and the terrorist squad – so one for him.

Rin being Rin, though, she was able to convince the owner of the pub to let them sit up on the rooftop patio, at the table right at the edge so they could look down on the chaos. There was no one else up there. "Why are we here?" he asked.

"I wanted to see what this was like," she said. He couldn't see her eyes because of her sunglasses.

He laughed. "Only you."

"Only me what?"

"Would want a ringside seat to tragedy and chaos."

They watched the firefighters and the special investigations team as they streamed in and out of the tube station. Emergency vehicles clogged up a length of more than two blocks while foot cops held everyone back for more than a block. The media was everywhere.

"Imagine the people who did this," she said. She meant the terrorists. "Not people. Animals."

"They might say the same of us," he said. "We bombed their country not so long ago."

She shot him a hard look. "You think that's justified? Crude slaughter standing in for justice?"

Realizing this was a serious conversation and where it might go, he tried to lighten things. There was every indication that if he said something objectionable, she would unload on him. "It depends on what your point is. If your point is terror, then it's a very good way. For such a limited agenda."

Her expression darkened. Sometimes there was no grey area with Rin. Black and white. Foolishly, however, he couldn't help himself and went one step further. "There's two sides to every story."

"Two sides to *whose* story?" she asked.

He shrugged.

They sat in silence. She started to pick up her drink but thought better and pushed it away. "We should go home." She was annoyed now.

"We just got here."

"Chase," she said. "I have to tell you something. But you have to promise to listen to me. Do you promise?"

He felt fear then, real fear. There was something about the way she was looking at him. It was her unpredictable look. Anything could come out of her mouth. For some reason – some inexplicable reason – he was terrified that the next thing she was going to say was, "I've been thinking about you and me … "

But she didn't.

She said something much worse.

She said, "Chase, you're in far more danger than you think."

He laughed. "I am? I didn't know I was in any particular danger."

"Well look at it this way," she said. "Even if Hog is alive – and I think he is – I doubt he can get you out of where you are."

Chase looked at her and didn't understand what the hell she was talking about. Then, an awful thought, as awful as if she had started a sentence with, "I've been thinking about you and me … "

Shit. This is a dream.

He felt utterly betrayed. And robbed. He wanted to cry. But we're here, he protested to himself. And we're together, and even if the setting is strange, we *were* there once, we were a finger's length away from one another.

He looked at the stray wisps of hair around her ears blowing in the breeze. It was too windy up here on the second-floor patio, and too cold. Her hair was losing its last vestige of purple. So that made this … September?

"Don't say anything more," he said.

"But I have to."

"No, I don't want to hear it." He pushed his drink away and stood up. "You were right. Let's get out of here."

"Just let me finish."

"No, it was your idea, and now I'm agreeing with you. So let's go back to the flat."

"Listen first."

He looked around. Anxious. Trying to take everything in. Nailing it all down. It was real, dammit. Or was it? He looked at one of the firemen down below and across the street. He looked far too old to be a fireman. Oh shit, Chase thought.

"Listen," she said.

He turned his attention back to her.

She looked right into his eyes. "It doesn't matter how you got in here. The problem is you may not get out well. Do you hear me? Whatever chance presents itself, you have to take it, because things have changed."

"I want to touch you."

"I want to touch you too. But listen to me, Chase. Okay? Look down there. That's what I wanted to show you. Look down there."

He looked down into the street.

"You know what their faces tell you?" she asked.

"What?"

"Chaos is always going to win unless you're brutal."

He woke up then, to a voice shouting at him, but he had to ignore that voice. Instead, he pushed his face back into the scratchy sofa cushion and pulled the thin blanket up over himself. If he could just burrow in tight enough and shut the world out, he could go back to her. He could smell her perfume and touch her skin and see the wisps of her hair moving in the breeze.

But it was hopeless. She was gone, and he was in a miserable little room in the basement of the Capitol building, and the lunatic was shouting again.

Chase opened his eyes and stared at the ceiling. Of course.

It was the man in the cage at the end of the hall. "I know them all!" he shouted, he who had once been on the House Energy and Commerce Committee. "You think Mark Hanna can't reach in here and pull us out like guppies and Sylvester? Think, people, think!"

Mark Hanna? Mark *Hanna*?? Chase had to struggle to find the name. Then it came to him. My God. Hanna was a political hack – the mover and shaker who got President McKinley elected. Hanna was a Senator from Ohio in 1900. What was possibly going through a man's mind – any man – that he reached in and found Mark Hanna and somehow related him to Sylvester the Puddy Tat reaching for guppies in a fish tank?

It almost, but not quite, drew him entirely away from his time with Rin.

Slowly, he started to get up, but a voice stopped him. The connecting door between his room and Gabriel's had drifted open a few inches. From within that darkness, Gabriel's sleepy voice said, "Don't you be going out there."

"I wasn't," said Chase. He tried to peer into Gabriel's room, but the crack between door and doorframe was too thin. The old man's room was pitch dark anyway. "What's set him off?"

"He gets like this sometimes. At night. Not often. But sometimes."

"Mark Hanna introduced me to the Wolf's landlord! And the Wolf shook my hand and talked to me! And the landlord said, 'Dan, you're in so much more danger than you think!'"

The cobwebs in Chase's head blew away almost instantly. What? *What* the hell had he said?

"You okay?" Gabriel asked. Evidently, he could see Chase even if Chase couldn't see him. Gabriel was likely lying the wrong way on his own cot watching out for him.

Rin had said the same thing in the Soho dream. "You're in far more danger than you think."

"*Judy Garland blew the director!*" came the shout from down the hall.

"Nothing," said Chase, and lay back down on the mat, this time on his back. He drew the blanket over himself again. He tried to make out the ceiling. *You're in far more danger.* What were the odds of that?

"You talk when you sleep," said Gabriel.

"I didn't know," said Chase. In fact, he'd never talked in his sleep. If he had recently started, it would be about the worst timing for a habit like that to appear.

"Bad dream?"

"Not especially."

"You were talking about being in the woods. That we were all in the woods. We had to get out because of the forest fires."

But that *wasn't* in the dream Chase had had. Was the old man putting him on?

"No," said Chase. "It was something different."

There was a long silence between them, and Chase realized he needed to tell. It was like the time with Hamer in the car. A feeling he had to tell. Considering where he was, it might be a very good idea. And the old man knew a lot.

He rolled over back onto his stomach. "I want to ask your opinion, Gabriel. About Reasoners."

Gabriel sighed. "I don't know anything about Reasoners, son. I was there at the beginning, but I was nowhere near as involved as Sofia."

"But you understand the idea."

"Such as it was."

"The key criterion was reason. Dispassion. Clear thinking."

"Well, there's no point to Reasoners if they aren't at least reasonable, is there?"

Chase took awhile formulating what he said next. "I have something in my past which is very much *not* reasonable. Something I kept from everyone who interviewed me, and something I tried to keep from the Senator, although I think she knew, anyway."

"Okay."

"A time in my life when I was anything but reasonable. It was a long time ago but it seems to have followed me. The word is wrong but I'll use it anyway. It ... infected me."

There was a silence.

"Infected you how?"

"My reason."

"Which makes you a bad Reasoner?"

"It certainly makes me suspect." He hesitated just a moment. "It's a woman."

"And this woman, she infects you still"

Chase nodded. "Yes. I see her."

"See how?"

"All the time. Here. In dreams. During perfectly normal moments."

There was another long pause.

"You loved her?"

"Yes."

An even longer pause. Chase knew what the old man was going to say. He would say, "But all men at one time in their lives ... " And while true, it would mean he didn't understand.

But Gabriel shocked him. Because instead of that, Gabriel said, "Chase, we *knew* about the woman."

Chase felt himself hold his breath.

"I don't remember all the details, you hear me, but we knew about her. In fact, that was the point."

Chase released his breath. "What was the point?"

"It's one of the reasons why we chose you. It made you human. Your choices."

Chase's eyes had adjusted. He could now make out the ceiling of his room. The acoustic tile. There was a water stain on this side which he hadn't noticed before.

"Judy Garland and those motherfuckers went into the woods all frolicking, but they were full of lies."

Gabriel and Chase were silent, just letting the shout of the mad man echo down the hallway.

We knew about the woman. Senator Sofia had said the same thing, hadn't she? But what did they know?

"And the Spam Man said, 'Fuck you, I'll run for President.'"

"He does shut up, eventually," said Gabriel. "I promise."

"But he's not a Spam Man, is he? He's a secret tuna can man, and Judy Garland says, 'I don't have to run from Kansas anymore, we got fucking wolves in these Maryland woods.'"

Slowly, Chase started to sit up.

"You hear me, Spam Man? You're secretly made of tuna, and we got wolves here in Maryland!'"

Chase wasn't sure he had heard what he thought he'd heard. "What the fuck … " he said.

"The Wolf is in the woods, boys! You hear me, Willy Loman? The Wolf is in the woods!"

The man who had been on the House Committee for Energy and Commerce began to rattle his cage at the end of the hall. *"Tuna!"* he shouted. *"Tuna!"*

Chase was on his feet now.

"I told you!" Gabriel said. "He'll shut up eventually. There's no need to be – "

But Chase was already on his way out the door that opened onto the hall.

Gabriel was up in a flash and pushing through the connecting door, coming after him. "I said you can't go out there!"

This time, Chase ignored him. It was too important. He opened the door and stepped into the corridor. He turned to the left and started in the direction of the booming madman's voice and ran smack into – Gabriel Soames! The old man had doubled around and now threw him against the wall with an astonishing display of strength. "Haven't you been listening? Never in the hallway. At night they *do* patrol! At night they do all *sorts* of shit!"

"The Maryland woods!" Chase protested. "That's what he just said."

Gabriel's face twisted in confusion. "What …?"

The man at the end of the hall filled the void. "*Judy Garland is behind this whole thing! Dumb bitch. And all those people traipsing through the Maryland woods round the woodsman's cottage! If it'd been me, I would have said, Judy, stay the fuck away from my place! Wolves everywhere!*"

It was dark in the hallway, but not so dark that Gabriel and Chase couldn't see one another's eyes. Gabriel looked fearful, but aware. Chase was, for the first time since he had awakened in the dingy little room in the basement of the Capitol, lit from within. He had something now. He had *possibility*.

"No … " Gabriel hissed, but Chase slipped from his grasp and headed down the corridor toward the caged man. Gabriel had no choice but to follow.

47. *The Mad Man*

1

Chase had assumed that the basement rooms between themselves and the caged Congressman were empty, but this turned out not to be true. As he and Gabriel crept down the hallway, it was clear that of the two rooms on the right and the three rooms on the left, at least two of the ones on the left were occupied. The smell, for one. Then, as Chase slowed to peer into the cavernous darkness, he made out what he thought were human beings clustered together just inside the doorways. It was hard to tell, though; he had only the whites of eyes, the shadows of uncombed heads, and bare hands clutching one another, to go by. They clearly did not want to venture anywhere near the light of the corridor or away from the safety of their huddle, but they were also clearly curious about Chase and Gabriel and what the two might be up to. *Cave dwellers*, Chase thought. Neanderthals. Almost, but not quite, human.

Chase didn't realize he had stopped at the second door and was gawking at the shadow figures of power brokers who once were, until Gabriel gave him a shove. Clearly, Gabriel had decided if they were in for a penny, they were in for a pound, but let's pick up the pace! As they moved past, Chase heard one of the people in the rooms whisper an inscrutable phrase: "Spider eggs."

He had believed that the screaming Congressman was being kept in a room at the end of the hall with bars across the door. When he turned the corner, however, he discovered to his horror that this was not the case at all.

Possibly no one could say for certain why or how a Derek

Steel Chain Link Portable Yard Kennel (retail $484) had wound up being stored in the sub-basement of the U.S. Capitol, but it had sat unoccupied and unclaimed in the old tile room for years. It was the kind of cage that kennels kept for Doberman pinschers or zoos used for large mammals, except it wasn't storing any zoo animal now. Instead, it held a human being, specifically a seventy-eight-year-old Mississippian who had gamely represented the people of the Fourth District for the past eighteen years. Man and cage came together when the man utterly lost his marbles at the same time the Changers in charge of the basement stumbled across the cage.

There was irony perhaps in the fact that Daniel Jefferson Williams had always been a large man, carrying 350 pounds on a six-foot-five frame, and therefore to some degree actually resembled a rumpled orangutan.

To support the zoo comparison, the Congressman's cage was not in the room itself. It was pushed up against and was filling the doorframe – likely because that position made the delivery of food easier. This explained why, when the light was on in the room, a shadow was cast on the opposite wall of the corridor, man and bars together, which is all Chase had seen until now. An image considerably more benign than the truth.

The nine weeks of cage incarceration had reduced Rep. Dan Williams from a rather imposing bear of a man to a blob of blubber encased in a large grey onesie, which, like the cage, was also of unknown origin. The massive head of hair which he had proudly Brylcreemed into a daily pompadour most of his career was now a sort of helmet of madness, and the cleanly shaven face had become a jowly mountain range of stubble. The eyes were the hardest to take. Every flash of those eyes told you that Dan Williams was not just crazy but had been *driven* crazy by some contradiction which haunted the inside of his very brain as well as his soul, a contradiction which he was still doing ferocious battle with day after day and, more often – from the sounds of it – night.

The concern over Judy Garland and the rest of her friends –

that which had presumably wakened him from sleep and which he felt the need to express – had him in its full grip even as Chase and Gabriel came around the corner.

"*There are all sorts of them!*" the Congressman bellowed. "*Judy's friends! Lions and tigers and bears oh my but no one said anything about wolves but look all over you'll see their tracks! You can see their –* "

Dan Williams stopped in mid-sentence, looking through the ceiling of his cage as Chase and Gabriel came around the corner. To Chase's surprise, he addressed Gabriel in a perfectly reasonable tone of voice. "Oh, hi, Gabe."

Gabriel hunkered down to a squat and answered in kind. "Dan, this is a new friend of mine. Professor Chase Selby."

"Pleased to meet you, Professor." Dan offered up a sad little attempt at a jovial wave but didn't move beyond that. He really didn't have the room to move. "I'm sorry I can't get up, but I am, as you see, caged." The man had a pleasant southern accent. The pleasantries, however, were suddenly over. "*Professor?!*" he shouted, as if discovering the word for the first time. "Professor *who?* Not Marvel?? From the wagon??!"

"Selby," Chase said calmly. "From Princeton."

"Oh," said Williams, relieved. "Good."

Clearly this man had a very troubled acquaintanceship with *The Wizard of Oz.*

Chase hunkered down to a squatting position. This put him and Representative Williams eye to eye. "Congressman, I wanted to ask you some questions."

Dan Williams seemed to think this made perfect sense. "Why not? I am a knowledgeable man. And well lettered. I also came from a time when they used to have peanut machines, if you can *imagine* such a thing."

"I wonder if you can tell me about Judy Garland."

Once again there was an immediate transformation within Dan Williams. "*That bitch?!*" he demanded. "*She brought the tin man and the scarecrow and the wolf traipsing to the woodman's cottage!!*"

"And when did she do that?" Chase asked.

"What am I, a fucking travel agent? I don't know! All I know is the idiotic woodsman invited her! He let them all in!"

"All four of them?"

"Seven! Eight! Sixty-seven! Who knows?"

"What did they want?"

"I told you! The woodsman's old place! To hide from the witch! Before he built that cancerous monstrosity on the hill! It killed his gin! You can practically hear the damned hippies singing that awful song – the worst one in the whole score! 'We're out of the woods, we're out of the woods, we're out of the woods!' Orgies!"

A hand touched Chase on the shoulder. "Chase," Gabriel said gently. "Please. You're riling him." What he really meant was, "there's nothing here and let's get the hell *back*."

But Chase ignored the hand and kept his focus on Dan. "Congressman, did you ever talk to them?"

Dan looked at him and another wave of sanity seemed to break. At least, he stopped yelling. "When the woodsman's back was turned, yes. When they weren't having their orgies."

"Real orgies?"

"I have every reason to think so. And why not? Everything was a joke with them, the blessed sacrament of sex being the least of their transgressions. Sexual congress, nationhood, ethical and moral understanding..." Then he was gone again. *"If the woods burn their fingers, they brought it on themselves!"*

Chase looked back at Gabriel. To his surprise, instead of offering a sorrowful shake of the head and disapproval, Gabriel was studying his old friend with renewed interest. Something Williams had said. "Dan, is this the place you and *Sheri* bought?"

"Now they're in hiding! Living in fear! And maybe they should be!"

"Dan," Gabriel tried again.

"They're not out of the woods! They're IN the woods!" Dan said, and laughed.

"Dan," Chase also tried.

"They brought us here! Their orgiastic casuistry, wanton mockery of none other than Abraham A. Lincoln!! Does no one care about the rough man from Illinois anymore??"

Chase resisted. "Dan, how do I communicate with them?"

"Communicate? You can't communicate. Only through the survivor."

"Who is the survivor?" Chase asked.

Dan looked at Chase as if he was the one who had lost his mind. The answer, as far as he was concerned, was simplicity itself. "It says on her shirt, dummy!"

Chase had a sensation of the bottom falling out of his body, like free-falling from an airplane or had fallen through the bottom of a ship and was now sinking into the depths of the ocean. He could almost physically feel his brain pulling all the strands together. Things were going to make sense any second now. Unfortunately –

"Oh Christ!" Gabriel hissed one micro-second before an ear-splitting noise cut through every sane thought Chase had ever had and rattled the teeth in his head.

Lawnmowers. Leaf blowers. Weedwhackers and hedge trimmers. Coming toward them.

A very powerful hand pulled Chase from his crouched position. Gabriel screaming in his ear! "I told you!"

Gabriel didn't push Chase so much as shove him. Back down the hallway. Back toward their rooms. The two ran, almost tripping over their own feet. If they were caught, they were dead.

Truth was, it wasn't a terrific distance. And they would have made it if Chase hadn't stumbled as they passed the open doors on the right. It was a brutally unnecessary fraction of a second, but how could he not pause? For when he came around the corner and caught his first glimpse of the Neanderthals, he saw those jagged souls were no longer rubbernecking at the door; no, now they were standing in a circle screaming in agony at the sounds of the lawn engines, their hands raised to the drop-ceiling fluorescent lights like they were engaging in some sort of odd religious worship. It was this that caused the stumble – and the half-second delay at getting up – that did him and Gabriel in.

Because it was just enough time for the first heat of lawnmower Jerseys – three men, one woman – to come around the far corner at the other end of the corridor. They were pushing their lawnmowers and blasting their leaf blowers, prompting screams from within the rooms that swirled up into a full pitched tornado. The second the Jerseys saw Gabriel and Chase out of their room, however – dumbass prisoners actually out of their room! – eyes lit up behind protective goggles, first in shock, then in pure delight. They instantly dropped their lawn tools and made a beeline for Chase and Gabriel, wild dogs having glimpsed fresh prey. These particular wild dogs, of course, had weapons on their belts, and they reached for them as they ran.

Gabriel grabbed Chase by the shoulders and hurled him forward with a shove. Chase was barely able to keep his balance as he slid around the corner toward the open doorway of Gabriel's room. Right on his heels, Gabriel smashed into him with the force of ten men, sending them both hurtling into the room and crashing to the floor.

"What are you doing?" Chase shouted. "They already saw us!"

Gabriel was struggling to close the door with his foot. "The rules say they can't come in here!"

Chase doubted such rules applied now, when they'd clearly been seen outside their room, but it was possible Gabriel knew something he didn't. Maybe it was a grey area?

That seemed to be the case, because when the four Jerseys caught up to them, they skidded to a halt right at the edge of the door frame, their weapons pointed from outstretched hands. They stopped Gabe from shutting the door, but they did not step into the room. "What do you think you're doing, old man!?" one of the men demanded.

"My friend got confused and went wandering!" Gabriel protested. "He's new!"

"Confused?" the woman shouted with derision.

"I was helping him back."

This was greeted with the slow silence of dull thinking. The Jerseys tried to work this out as Gabriel and Chase pulled themselves to their feet. Gabriel helped the Changers along in their thinking. "We're in here now, though," he said. "So that means we're not out there. All's well."

To Chase's surprise, this notion really did carry some weight. Everyone had to chew over this undeniable truth. After a moment, three of the four Jerseys reluctantly lowered their weapons.

Which is when a loud voice from farther down the hall broke through. A husky, belligerent, crude bellow, brought to them alongside the sound of booming footsteps. "What the *fuck* is this?"

The four Jerseys straightened to some sort of attention. This fifth Jersey was heard lumbering down the hall toward them. From the sound, Chase pictured real hard shitkicker work boots. Then, suddenly, there he was, standing behind his comrades in the doorway and peering into the scene in Gabriel's room.

"What the *fuck*?" asked Fifth Jersey. He looked, Chase decided, pretty much like all the others, and yet there was something about him – something Chase couldn't quite put his finger on. In some fundamental way, this man was like no other Changer Chase had encountered.

"We got an agreement," the First Jersey explained to this fifth. "We can't go in."

"*Agreement?*" asked the Fifth Jersey. "Seems to me *agreement* is one of those words that's caused us nothing but trouble."

"About the rooms," the First Jersey explained. "Long as they stay in, we stay out. Those are Jeff's rules."

The Fifth Jersey looked at them, then at Gabriel, then at Chase, then back, then back again. He seemed at a complete loss for words. Then, to everyone's surprise, he broke out into genuine laughter. "You fuckers are having me on!" he hollered. It seemed friendly enough, but there was a slight twist in his tone that warned, "And if you are you'll pay – you'll pay badly." He drew back the laugh just enough to say, "You telling me there are goddamned *rules* here?"

Jersey One looked at Jersey Two, the woman, hoping she would answer. Clearly, she was the smart one in the crew. She hesitated, but she gave it a shot. "Well, not rules exactly, more like an understanding, like I – "

"They *sound* like rules," said Fifth Jersey. "And they sound like fucked-up rules."

"But they're Jeff's rules" the Jersey woman said, and the second it came out of her mouth, you could tell she knew it was the wrong tone and completely the wrong attitude. But she couldn't help herself. Her next words tried to clean things up. "Everything down here are Jeff's rules," she said.

On the face of it, it seemed like a good answer, but there was also something wrong with it in some way, because all the other Jerseys stiffened.

Only the Fifth Jersey took it in stride, as if he had now entered into a friendly political debate. No biggie. "But these are our prisoners, right?" he asked. "That the way you see it? Prisoners?"

Jersey Two knew this was a trap of some sort, but she had to keep going. What was the right answer? She looked at Gabriel, who looked very worried, and Chase, who was trying to work this out. He had a sense something important was happening here but he wasn't sure what. "Well," she said slowly. "Sure. Prisoners."

"Bullshit," Fifth Jersey said.

This took everyone by surprise. Somehow the worst thing was that he didn't shout it, he just said it. All calm.

"They're – *not* – our prisoners?" she asked.

He shook his head. "That's what I'm saying. That's where you're upside down. They're not our prisoners, they're our jailers."

There were confused looks all around, including a flinty-eyed side glance from Gabriel to Chase. The air was charged. This was going in the wrong direction.

"Here, I'll show you," said Fifth Jersey. With that, he took a step into Gabriel's room. Not much more than that, but it was enough to make the other Jerseys almost gasp. And not just the Jerseys. Chase felt Gabriel, standing behind him, tighten up like a drum. But there it was. This guy, this Fifth Jersey, was now standing just inside the doorway.

Fifth Jersey could sense their shock and it pleased him mightily. Then he tried to clarify his meaning. "Our whole goddamned lives, I'm saying. The way they made us live since we were born, and how they're making us live now. You think any of us'd be here if *they* weren't here? You think everyone doesn't want to go home? But them. They're keeping us here. Because we have to deal with them."

Jersey Two had some trouble tracking this idea. "I don't know if you can think of it like that … "

But she didn't get any further because Fifth Jersey slapped her. Hard. Really hard. She staggered with the power of the blow and then, when she righted her head, there was blood across her bottom lip which started to crawl down her chin. She looked dazed and there was something in her eyes like fire. The other Jerseys didn't do a thing, but they were almost as shocked as she was and possibly even more worried.

Surprisingly, it was the Fifth Jersey who reached out to steady her. "That hurt, right? Makes me a fucking bastard?"

She didn't say anything, just wiped her chin and then studied the blood on the back of her hand. There was a lot.

"Yeah, but who did that?" Fifth Jersey asked. "Them or me? You say me. I say, who do you think made me dumb as a fucking dog like this, and violent? I got no finesse. I got no restraint. I'm your basic human garbage, made for digging ditches or shoveling shit. That's why I'm saying don't think even for a second we're in charge. That's bullshit. We're not in charge. They are. And that's why we gotta keep the boot on their neck, every second, or they'll flip it around on us. Listen, you ever been in charge of anything before?"

Jersey Two was scared. She didn't know how to answer. And she still had blood on her lip. "How you mean … in charge?"

"In charge. Running. Like a job. The boss."

"Well, some."

"What's that?"

Jersey Two hesitated, waiting for the next hit. The look in her eye and the way she hunkered her shoulders suggested that she'd probably taken a hit or two already in her life. "Me and my dad ran the kennel."

"Like dogs?"

She nodded.

"You mean it was your business?"

"Yeah."

"That's a lie."

Silence.

Finally, Jersey Two – and you had to give her credit for nerve – said, "No, we owned it."

"You ever get a bank loan?" Fifth Jersey asked.

"Yeah."

"Then you didn't own no business, did you? You own a house?"

"Yeah. My dad's anyway."

"He have a mortgage?"

"Sure."

"So there's a lie too. He didn't own nothing. He just took care of and cut the grass on the bank's house. They could do whatever they wanted to that house anytime. You own a car?"

"Yeah."

"There's another one. You drove the bank's car and had to repair it for them. You send your kids to school?"

"Yeah."

"More lies. The government sent your kids to school. You didn't have no say in it. Not if, not where, now when. You get married?"

Jersey Two was feeling thoroughly beaten. "Yeah … "

"Nope. You made an agreement with the government that you'd pay some guy's debts if he ever ran off or died, and he made the same agreement with the government for you. And you gotta pay to bury the cocksucker as well!"

Everyone thought about this. Fifth Jersey was pleased. "So the way I see it, if every time we think we're in charge of something when really someone else is, we oughta wake up that we're in charge of jack shit. Always." He gestured to Gabriel and Chase. "And these sneaky fuckers? You know what they are? Like raccoons. They get into everything, no matter how well you tie it down. So you think they're the ones on the run, you better think again. We're the ones doing the running because of them. If you think they're the prisoners, you better decide that *we're* the prisoners. Because of them." Having dealt with the Jerseys confusions about how the world worked, Fifth Jersey now looked squarely at Chase and Gabriel.

Chase had only ever seen Jeff Beavenstock on TV. Still, he was pretty sure that he had never seen in Jeff Beavenstock's eyes – no matter how inflamed Jeff got when preaching to his hordes, even when he was encouraging them to use murder as a tool of social change – anything near the casual, unconcerned yet undilutable hatred that was in Fifth Jersey's eyes. It was a stupid face, but the eyes were alight. "So we don't do deals with the folks who are imprisoning us. Because the minute we start doing deals, that's the minute they've won. These boys were out of their rooms. It don't matter if they got back in time. They gotta be punished."

There was a difficult moment. Chase finally filled the silence. He said, "Except you're not going to hurt anyone here."

Fifth Jersey raised an eyebrow. "What the fuck do *you* know about it?"

Chase gestured to Gabriel. "This old guy's well known. The whole point of the Changer movement is publicity, social media, and eyeballs. That's all you've got. So you're not going to waste him down here, where there are no cameras."

Chase had imagined this argument would at least give Fifth Jersey pause. Instead, Chase's point seemed to sail right past him. He was focused, instead, on Gabriel. "Yeah? So what's he so famous for?"

"One of the most respected members of Congress," Chase

said. "Every newspaper knows who he is. Every channel asks him to talk with them. He's known at least four Presidents."

Fifth Jersey considered this. "And you?"

"I don't even belong here."

That made Fifth Jersey laugh. "Me either! Like I just said."

"What I mean is, they're breaking a treaty by keeping me here. That's going to be problematic for somebody."

Fifth Jersey gave him a scowl. Chase decided that "problematic" was a bad word choice. He wasn't sure Fifth Jersey knew what it meant.

"How you figure you're not supposed to be here?"

"Because I'm a Reasoner."

Fifth Jersey's surprise turned to pleasure, and he laughed. "Well, that's a hell of a thing to know! How the fuck *did* you get in here?"

"You tell me."

"I thought there *was* an agreement!"

"There is."

"So what the fuck?"

"Right."

Creepy geniality once again overcame Fifth Jersey. It was the same look on his face right before he hit the woman Changer. "'Cept ... another word for agreement would be 'deal,' right? And I just finished saying that there are no agreements and there are no deals. Like I said about raccoons. You heard that part, right?"

"Yes."

"And I heard you about the thing about him being famous." He nodded at Gabriel. "But I don't know why I'd care about him being famous when he's just a politician and there are hundreds of politicians down here and you're a Reasoner and far as I know there are no other Reasoners down here."

Chase nodded uneasily.

"So," said Fifth Jersey happily, "Reasoner beats a politician in any poker game. So we'll do you. Tomorrow morning. Saturday. Start things off with a *big* bang! Solved!"

With that, Fifth Jersey turned around and started to go. Then he had a second thought and turned back. "You kno-ow," he said slowly, drawing out the "ow." "Maybe we should do it together. You and me. And maybe I'll be the one to actually do the head chopping. They never let me even near that before. I just had to stand there like an asshole by the rope. But if I do it this time, no one will question who the fuck I am, will they? It'll all make sense."

"What will make sense?" Chase asked. He wanted to keep his voice steady, but inside he was grappling with what Fifth Jersey just said. Did this odious man really have such power?

"What they call me."

"What do they call you?"

"Viking."

With that, he went back down the hallway and left everyone looking after him. The way rulers do.

48. *The Rule of Madness*

1

"Reason has left town," the Fox broadcaster said. This was about eleven hours before he left town himself, or was killed. Who knew?

As Chase was quietly losing track of the days during his imprisonment in the west basement of the U.S. Capitol building, the Changers were going through their own metamorphosis. Or purge. Some labeled it a cleanse, or an internal cull. No matter what you called it, everyone could see its effects.

First off, there was no question this guy Viking lit the match, and in the absence of other leadership, his was the direction they were going to follow. But whereas Jeff Beavenstock's ambitions had been a complete overhaul of an elitist and inequitable system, Viking's only thought seemed to be to set one group against the other, fomenting violence to assert power for its own sake.

The name of the game had become "are you a real Changer or aren't you?" Fortunately, because there was no real litmus test or definition for what a Changer was, just about anybody could take part, and just about everyone did. The big issue was proof of allegiance to the cause. You demonstrated this by staying on the Mall no matter what crazy shit occurred. When some folks, particularly the ones with kids, opted to flee – temporarily, they hoped – north across Constitution Avenue until things got back to normal, things began to shift. There was resentment and anger. In the very beginning, of course, folks could do what they wanted, but soon the phrase "Kid Coward" cropped up, which meant traitors who were so gutless that they hid behind the excuse of their families, using their children as a shield. The hardcore believers dealt with suspected Kid Cowards harshly. More than a few dads and even a few families were prevented from fleeing, which meant plenty of children were able to witness some pretty bad things happen to Mom and Dad.

Torture, specifically. It was considered one of the most reliable means of not just dealing with a traitor but getting the traitor to admit they had worked against the Uprising and the Changer movement. Torture in front of one's family is a pretty gruesome thing. Mostly it was men forced to watch their wives being sexually assaulted, but in a number of cases women were forced to watch their husbands being sexually assaulted. A small group tinkered with torturing children to get their parents to confess to traitorous behavior, but they quashed this pretty quickly. The other side of this equation – kids watching parents being tortured – only worked if you believed the *kid* knew something, but even that was unreliable: What kid wouldn't make shit up in order to stop their parent from being tortured?

Another good means of extracting information from folks deemed possible "leakers or speakers" was to dunk them. They did this over by the basin near the MLK Memorial, or even in the Potomac for the heartier of inquisitors. The concept was as old as time: Bind a traitor's hands and legs, attach a weight to their feet, and then "dunk" them into the water by means of a rope and pulley. This would be done repeatedly and at longer and longer intervals until the person either confessed or died, or, on very rare occasions, the dunkers themselves decided the person was telling the truth.

A squad of bikers from Maine came up with a unique concept. Somewhere they landed their hands on a massive crown-and-anchor wheel six feet in circumference. They set it up just past the Korean War Veteran's Memorial. The idea was to strip their victim of all clothing, tie them to the wheel, then spin the wheel. Standing at a distance of no less than ten feet, the interrogators threw lawn darts at the victim, who obviously was unable to prevent the darts from hitting genitals, major organs, eyes, or mouth.

A less resourceful group of younger thugs came up with the

idea of simply hanging people upside down and substituting jackknives for lawn darts. Their preferred victims were women. They particularly liked publicly stripping their clothes off.

As mad as all this was, it paled in comparison to the actions of a group who called themselves the Brotherhood of Truth. This was a group that gave even the knife and dart throwers and dunkers the willies.

For one thing, they were organized. The matching robes proved that. Not bathrobes, though; robes like Franciscan monks, complete with deep hoods and rope belts. For another thing, they were clearly well off, something you really couldn't say about most people on the Mall. They appeared to be, in fact, extremely clean-cut young men from Ivy League universities. With square jaws and perfect haircuts, they looked like rowers, not football players; fencing, not baseball. They were the future rulers of the world, although not one of them appeared to be over twenty-one. Every one of them had a smarmy, self-satisfied sneer. And perfect teeth.

It was with the arrival of the Brotherhood that a long-puzzled-over mystery was solved; namely, who was responsible for the perfectly cut-and-fitted stakes installed on the steps of the Lincoln Memorial? It turned out that the builders themselves – the burly men in their mid-50s who had pulled up the day after Beavenstock's shooting and set to work using their Black & Decker Workmate benches – were not the intended users at all. On the contrary, they were only hired to do the work for those clean-cut college boys with the smarmy grins and hooded robes.

This was made clear on the third night of the first Purity Purge, when these members of the Brotherhood of Truth appeared on the Lincoln steps and presented themselves as the "builders" of the stakes, here to finally reveal their justice in the name of the "once great and future true America."

A young man named Kyle did all the explaining. His nineteen Brothers (Noah, Liam, Benjamin, Elijah, Lucas, etc., etc., etc.) stood behind him. Kyle had short blond spikey hair and a slightly over-large jaw. He smiled a lot, revealing perfectly white teeth, but it was a strange, humorless smile, a jug-like smirk. Kyle said that the Brothers were going to allow everyone on the Mall to join them in their quest for the "distillation of American purity." He then drew a clipboard from beneath his robe (a flash that revealed the robes came from Norstrom's) and read his proclamation.

It was long winded, it was arrogant, but it basically went this way: The Brotherhood had a list of names of absolutely and unquestioned traitors to the Changer cause. However, rather than seek these people out themselves, the Brotherhood were going to pay $5,000 in cash for each traitor anyone in the crowd could bring to them. Then the Brotherhood would mete out appropriate justice as they saw fit.

There was one hitch. All self-appointed bounty hunters had to lay their hands on their quarry within a half hour, or no payout.

People will do a lot of things for $5,000, especially people who have spent the past month or more on a long strip of grass which was now turning into a fetid sewer of mud and shit and disease. As soon as they read out the names, folks scrambled like starved rats, while the twenty Brothers stood and waited. They grinned widely at one another, clearly pleased with the no-effort-required simplicity of their plan.

Soon multiple "Joseph Johnston"s were brought forward,or "Tyron Jeffries"s. The Brotherhood had anticipated this, of course. Their plan was to have the bounty hunters fight it out for who had brought forward the real person named on their list, and to accept the winner's prisoner as legitimate.

For anyone who thought that the Brotherhood were just clever college boys who were simply getting some kicks by dropping a bounty list worth $5,000 a head and thereby unleashing shitloads of chaos, they were sorely mistaken. Yes, the Brotherhood clearly enjoyed watching the shitshow, and certainly they liked the violence let loose when cases of mistaken identity resulted in more than two Tom Smiths being dragged bound and gagged up onto the

Memorial steps, but they had every intention of delivering a good show. And this they did. Big league.

Once the "guilty" were assembled, and once the money was dispensed – usually with someone raising a fistful of hundreds for all to see and the crowd cheering its approval – to the chant of "USA, USA, USA!" – the Brothers made good. They tied the guilty parties to the stakes and burned them alive.

At first no one really believed that was the actual plan, even as the Brothers spread around more hundreds in cash to get helpers to place kindling at the feet of the stakes. It had to be just for show, right? Even when they spritzed the lighter fluid on the kindling at the base of the stakes, most folks assumed it was water. After all, they did look like such nice boys.

But it was real, and they weren't nice boys at all. They had a very clear and specific agenda worked out to the nth detail while getting shitfaced in their dorm rooms, and it wasn't lost on anything that every single name shouted out brought forward a traitor who was Black, Hispanic, or Native American.

In short, the Brotherhood were seriously hardcore. So hardcore, in fact, that some turned away. Revolted or not, however, everyone on the Mall talked about it the next day, and the day after that. In a land of utter madness, the Brotherhood seemed to have crossed a line no one knew was there anymore.

So an even greater crowd showed up the following Wednesday night, especially after the Black & Decker men put in more stakes. After dark, the Brothers appeared again in their robes, raising their fingers in the gangsta salute. They were greeted with cheering and shouting from a crowd even bigger than the previous evening. The Brotherhood clearly intended to repeat their act and repeat it they did. Presumably, as long as they had stakes, they'd repeat it as often as they had names.

For some, this made the act of cutting off heads almost pedestrian. That was almost certainly why, on the Thursday following the third Brotherhood burning, Viking announced that the guillotine would go back into action earlier than anyone had expected. It would be a big three-day weekend, and Viking promised something the Brotherhood *couldn't* deliver.

Celebrity.

2

Gabriel took to reading to Chase rather than pontificating. Chase at first thought this might be an improvement, but when he discovered that Gabriel intended to read *State of Virginia Tax Code* he wasn't so sure. But it was all they had.

So Chase took to sitting in the older man's cell and sipping Crown Royal whiskey and listening to the pleasant voice as it rose up and down, making even Virginia tax law seem portentous and of value. Chase didn't mind as much as he thought he would. It helped him think. For his part, Gabriel drank from his brushed-steel travel mug, although this soon presented its own confusion.

There was something about the bottle which perplexed Chase. The level. It had gone down considerably since their first long talk, even though Chase knew they had shared less than three or four drinks each since then. Presumably, therefore, Gabriel was tippling on his own, although he never seemed drunk and had told Chase that he made a rule of no more than two a night. Yet the bottle was more than a third down, and it was a big bottle.

Chase studied it and tried to understand it as if the very secret of life were involved in the answer. Then he realized Gabriel had stopped reading.

He looked up. "What?" Chase asked.

Gabriel put a finger to his lips. His head was cocked strangely.

They waited, staring into each other's eyes.

Then it came again. It was a distant roar, like a sea wave crashing against the rocks. Then, seconds later, it came again. Only louder.

They didn't need two tin cans and string to hear this.

"What do you think it means?" Chase whispered.

"Bad."

They listened again.

It came again.

Gabriel closed the book and put it aside.

"What?" asked Chase.

"They're back," Gabriel said. "They've started up again."

"What does that mean?"

"Bad. The worst."

Which was dead-on accurate. Because it was the very next morning that they came and got Chase.

49. *The End of Chase*

1

Finally, Chase told himself, he would be able to see what was at the other end of the hall. Who, or perhaps what, was the source of those strange murmurings and weird shrieks which had sent a shivers down his spine, the source of the tornado screams when the lawn tools came roaring in.

Four Jerseys escorted Chase down the hall. Not the Jerseys who had run what Gabriel called the Jangles, and certainly not the four who had wound up in the encounter with Viking – none of whom, by the way, had ever been seen again. No, these were all men – and bigger, beefier, and more intimidating than any basement Jersey.

They seemed perfectly cast for their parts. If you're going to have Execution Guards, they ought to look right. The wrap-around and mirrored sunglasses were spot on, as were the cut-off shirts which displayed massive biceps.

There was no need for Gabriel's tin cans and string this morning. Everyone could hear exactly what was going on outside. The crowd was losing its shit, and its enthusiasm made the walls shudder, even down here in the basement. As if in answer, the disturbed murmurings up and down the hall had increased.

Gabriel had shouted at them when they came to get Chase, but the Jersey guard ignored him. Then, when he tried to physically interfere, one of them swatted him like a fly. Gabriel went crashing into the wall. The Jersey had laughed. That, more than anything, made it real for the older man. He wept and shouted and called them fucking animals. "You can't be us!" he shouted. "You just *can't* be us!"

He had not calmed by the time they cuffed Chase, and he even broke the rule he most assiduously observed. As they took Chase away, Gabriel stepped brazenly out into the hallway and screamed at them. "One day this will all be over!" he shouted at the Jerseys. "One day this will not be you!"

The flying wedge of security was escorting Chase toward the House side of the Capitol and toward the screaming crowd outside. The Changers had long ago discovered that the best way to bring a prisoner out – meaning, where you really got serious bang for your buck – was up the Capitol's central stairs and out through the center door on the terrace floor and then down the steps to the right.

Which is how Chase knew that he was going to finally see whatever was at the end of his hallway.

He wanted to. No, he felt he *had* to know what the murmurings were about, and who or what D.C.'s best and brightest had become. He did not want to believe that the creatures he had seen on his way to Dan Williams's cage – the beings he had labelled Neanderthals – were a true representation of what had happened to everyone down here but he needed to know for sure. How was that possible? This brought him to a surprising revelation – that despite everything, despite the fact that he was almost surely going to his death – curiosity still had such a grip on him.

To his surprise, it turned out there were a number of empty rooms – or at least rooms with closed doors – between Gabriel's room and the first staircase. The other side of the staircase, however, was a different story. At this end every room was occupied and all the doors were open, although there were cheap plastic toddler restraining gates in each doorway, likely meant as a reminder rather than actual restraint. As Chase passed each room, he was given what he wanted: a glimpse of what becomes of the human race once it faces pure undiluted desperation and fear, mixed with months of isolation.

Whatever motor had once driven these people to behave as rational human beings with rational views and a rational perspective on the world which (they assumed) they ran had long since broken down. And these engines had malfunctioned in some strange concert, like toys designed to wind down at pretty much the same time, and – and this was the part that really got to Chase – in a strange uniformity.

The stench was staggering. Evidently, their shit and piss buckets were emptied with nowhere near the regularity of Gabriel's and Chase's. Chase suspected, however, that it was the actual fact of the buckets themselves, coupled with the sheer number of people in each room, which had helped drive them mad; having to urinate and defecate in front of one another was something most of them, almost all with law degrees, previously only associated with prisoners and the dregs of society. That they had become what they had once only abhorred and controlled certainly contributed to breaking their brains.

What also struck Chase was that each room seemed to have its own unique madness with its own insanity brand.

The first room he passed, for instance, seemed to be filled only with Lurkers. These folks clustered just inside their dark, gated doorway. They watched Chase pass with unguarded excitement. They were wild-haired and wild-eyed and one or two of them were literally bare-assed. "Don't let them lie to you!" one of them said. "Don't let them put wooden hangers on you."

In contrast, the next room seemed to be a room of sadness. There was only one person standing in the doorway. She was a woman in her fifties, wearing what may once have been a workout suit, who looking longingly at Chase. "Daryl," she said. "I'm gonna miss you."

Chase nodded as if to say he would miss her as well, but his attention went to the scene behind her. About a dozen folks were down on their knees, each and every one of them stark naked, engaging in some pretty intense prayer. Was this the prime source of the murmurings? The prayers seemed to be Christian, yet the person they were praying to was not exactly Jesus. It was a very portly woman in her seventies, parked in a wheely office chair in the center of the group. Her only garment was an immense flag, wrapped around her and tied with a gold sash. She was intoning encouragement to her worshippers which seemed almost sexual in nature. "Oh yes, give it to me, give me more, let me hear it." So, perhaps not the room of sadness after all. Perhaps the room of worship.

In the next room, only a half-dozen occupants were aware of Chase passing. They huddled just outside the light of the corridor and watched him go, whispering something to themselves that sounded like "Porky Pig meat." Others in the room were huddled together eating dried breakfast cereal from the box. A man was shitting in a bucket.

In the room beyond this, quite a few of the occupants were simply asleep, huddled on top of one another. A dead man was hanging from the ceiling, having noosed a necktie through one of the pipes behind the acoustic tile. "Shit!" one of the Jerseys escorting Chase said, although even at this he didn't slacken his pace. Shit yes, Chase agreed. Suicides would be a problem for the Jerseys: Not only did it deprive them of more meat for the masses, but it weakened their political leverage.

The next room was empty. The room after that was darker than the others, but you could still tell there were people in there. The flash of their eyes, and the vague outlines of unkempt heads of hair let you know. The last room, as Chase turned to head toward the main stairs, was full of more praying folks. They weren't on their knees, though. They were flat on their bellies, arms outstretched.

So this, he thought, was them. The once high and mighty. The speakers at the microphone. The repeaters of phrases like "institutional readiness" and "shift the paradigm" and "project awareness." Every single one of them was college educated, more than half had been elected to something at some point, and almost all of them had spent their lives in pursuit of highly visible achievement – and all had pretty much grasped their brass ring. Even the ones who eschewed phrases like "inquiry resolution" instead of "answer" had once had the kind of supreme self-confidence which, they thought, had equipped them for anything that nasty Fate might want to throw at them. Almost.

Because now here they were, reduced to primitive, mewling, feeble life forms who pissed on one another or worshipped a co-worker in an office chair. They masturbated in doorways or prostrated themselves before nonexistent Gods. How in the world this had happened – how they had been driven to such wild extremes – was anyone's guess, but Chase suspected he knew. Or at least had a clue.

They had Believed. They had Believed in the system with such absolute surety that the collapse of it, its sudden annihilation, had unhinged these winners in ways that losers would never suffer. If you looked into it, you discovered that Jeff Beavenstock had been arrested not once but twice in his life – the first time for stealing his cousin's car, the second time for beating up an undercover cop outside a bar, if *Time* magazine was to be believed. So, Jeff had already seen the inside of a cell and he had already shat in a bucket. Contrast that with Karen Superstar, Chief of Staff to Senator Squarejaw Jones. Compared to Jeff, Karen was from another planet, and therefore her privileged life of complete self-assurance and academic and social perfection would prove her psychological undoing. So now she ran from the light, bare-assed and wild. By contrast, had Jeff Beavenstock been subjected to months of confinement in a basement office cell, he likely would have just taken up whittling, or electrical repair.

Chase and the Jerseys turned a corner, then another corner, then made their way down a corridor Chase was sure they had gone down before. He began to suspect his escorts were lost. He caught one of the Jerseys glancing at the other. Then, on a hand gesture from the biggest, they turned back, turned right instead of left, and went down another corridor.

This didn't appear to be the right choice either. "Fuck," one of them finally said. They had turned left past a row of more holding rooms, full of more Neanderthals, then an immediate right, and now they couldn't find the center stairs. One of them decided to put a firm grip on Chase's bicep in case Chase had the idea of taking flight at this moment of confusion.

They weren't used to anyone *walking* with them, Chase decided. They were used to carrying people out, kicking and screaming. Actually walking with someone had rattled them.

Finally, the promise of exit. They were coming up to a grand flight of stairs. Before they got to that, however, there was another room, or cell, although the much shorter and narrower door suggested it had been some sort of storeroom rather than a traditional meeting room or office. Still, the usual child's barrier was up, promising more miserable creatures within.

They slowed as they got to the stairs, which gave Chase the opportunity to glance into this storeroom cell. An old coal cellar? That seemed about right. Left over from the old days, perhaps, and now used as a stationery closet at one point. But who would the Changers quarter in here and why?

People they wanted to punish harshly, Chase concluded. And, indeed, there were dark shadows inside that miserable little room, vague silhouettes of human beings sitting against the wall or stacked up against one another. Some of them were clearly men, because they had to crouch down beneath the abnormally low ceiling.

The Jersey on Chase's right noticed his interest and grinned. "You wanna see?" he asked. He withdrew his cellphone and quickly slid his finger until he had the flashlight turned on. "You're gonna be interested in this one."

The Jersey shone the flashlight into the tiny little coal room. The people inside immediately covered their faces, protecting their eyes from the light. Slowly, one revealed the expression of a man paralyzed by fear. Chase gasped. He was looking into the eyes of Vin Jansert. And behind him, a red-eyed and slack-jawed Agniew, wearing just underpants. Hydy Horvat sat in the corner far away from them. For reasons Chase couldn't fathom (or maybe could), she was naked from the waist up.

"Quite a sight, aren't they?" asked the Jersey with a sneering chuckle, and then slid his smartphone flashlight to OFF.

"How long have they been here?" Chase managed finally.

"Just before you," said the Jersey. "Looks like someone sure made the wrong deal, don't it?"

2

It wasn't bravery that held Chase in check. It was the sad, pathetic ruination of the Reasoners – magnificent minds all – that kept him from losing himself as the Jerseys led him up the stairs. They, with whom he had once sworn an oath and made a prayer, shoved into the filth and stench of that old coal room, made clear to him the sheer absurdity of the situation in which he found himself, and thereby, the pointlessness of rebelling against it.

Intellectually, of course, he knew he was slated to be the first victim of what they were surely calling the Second Culling (imagine the poor salesmanship if they had called it anything *else*). He knew this meant that he was about to be taken outside to the second level of the west steps of the Capitol and likely forced to listen to God-knows-what bullshit about Chase Selby, Reasoner and traitor from hell, before being forced to kneel with his head in the cradle of the guillotine. He knew there would be a last glimpse of the earth – of light, of air, of people, of the actual physical stonework of the Capitol steps, the blue recycle bucket – and that then there would be absolutely nothing ever again. He knew all this, and yet he believed none of it. Perhaps because he was still thinking about proud and arrogant Vin Jansert covering his face from the light.

So he went with them. Having found the stairs, up they went.

Someone had wanted him here. Someone had gone to a great deal of trouble to get him here. Someone had been directing him without his knowledge. For how long? Since the beginning? Since before the Reasoners had even been dreamt of? Or more recently, since General Williamson (if it *had* been General Williamson) or the Reverend had decided to betray them?

The main floor of the Capitol smelled of summer heat and dust. After the sewer smell of the basement, the breeze blowing through the open doors of the Capitol was so fresh that Chase almost lost his balance.

Now they really tightened their grip on his arms and moved him toward the blinding light of the rear door, practically lifting him instead of letting him walk. This is where the President comes out for inaugurations, Chase thought, then added inanely, they used to do the ceremony at the front door until Reagan said they should move it to the back; he wanted to look west, and if he was nothing else, Reagan was a showman who knew the value of image. The nation's new leader looking out to the reflecting pool and from there to the Lincoln Memorial, was too good to be resisted. What grandeur was promised, what hope symbolized! A country that exists no more, Chase thought, than Rome or Carthage or the Soviet Union.

All Presidents came out these doors ramrod stiff and head erect, ready to face the world. Chase, however, was literally blinded by the light. Now he understood why his escorts wore sunglasses.

Once the Jerseys realized he wasn't going to run, they relaxed their grip on Chase just that little bit; a little stumble and stagger, to say nothing of some shimmy, would do wonders for the crowd. And that's what they got, because when Chase stepped out onto the second-floor terrace of the Capitol building, he did indeed stumble, simply because he was so blinded by the white stone and the sunlight. He couldn't *see* the step. The crowd roared. It deafened him.

They did not take him down the north steps, which would have been the most direct route to the guillotine. Instead, they took him down the south steps, which really gave the crowd a show.

But it wasn't a crowd, of course. It was a sea. A sea of what might have been people, but to Chase appeared to be faces and heads and hats, flags, signs, banners, and guns. Arms waving with clenched fists, they chanted "USA, USA, USA," which was quickly replaced by "SEND THEM BACK," a slogan Chase didn't even know or understand. The crowd screamed at him like a crazed animal braying in rage; they forced themselves right into his face.

There was scaffolding raised high above the crowd. This was for the sound system and the TV crews, set up pretty much the same way they were set up for the inaugural, although in this case there were two towers instead of one.

After his little stumble, Chase was ferociously careful with his footing on the bone-white steps going down. He focused as hard as he could. Yes, it made it look like his head was bowed with emotion, but not falling was more important to him than the appearance of guilt or fear. Guilt had nothing to do with this ritual.

It wasn't until they were at the bottom of the steps that Chase felt it was safe to raise his head. That's when he really saw the guillotine for what it was. Up close, what surprised him was how big it was. It was massive, a god standing over them; the blade was up, of course, and the sunlight hit it perfectly. It seemed to wink at him.

What didn't surprise him was Viking standing right beside it. The only difference since Chase had met him in the basement was that Viking was now wearing a *black* Vikings jersey, almost surely in deference to his self-appointed role as executioner. He also wore black sunglasses. Wrap-around, of course.

As Chase was led toward the guillotine, Viking reached out and someone handed him a wireless microphone. With rock star skill, Viking held the mic high up at the neck and practically screamed into it. "Well all RIGHT!" his voice boomed through the Mall, across the basin and across the Potomac, and, it seemed, right down into the heart of the Confederacy.

The crowd lost its shit.

Viking nodded at his guys to make sure they held Chase where he was, which put Viking and Chase side by side. Viking turned back to the crowd. "I promised you some serious shit and this here is *serious* shit!" There was a roar of approval. "You wanna know who we got first up here? You wanna know what the Viking brought you today?"

A huge "YESSSS!" seemed to roll like The Wave from as far back as the Lincoln Memorial. This crowd was one, no question about that. This crowd was unified. Whatever Viking had meant to do with his purges and Purity Squads – if, in fact, he had ever had any plan at all – it had worked. These people were together. And with his unerring instinct, he was going to bring them even closer in a matter of minutes.

"This ain't no fuckin' Senator you never heard of!" he shouted. "And it sure ain't no motherfuckin' office staffer!"

The crowd booed, showing exactly what they thought of officer staffers and Senators.

Viking stepped closer to the crowd, working it rock star style. "I brought you grade-A top sirloin! Two-inch thick! The best meat you ever put in your dumb, uneducated pie holes!"

They shouted complete approval of such bounty as well as for being uneducated.

Viking went back to Chase and raised his arm above his head, as if Chase had won a prize fight. This close, Chase realized that Viking smelled of vinegar and something else, something foul. Bad hot dogs? "This here's not some Senator!" Viking told the crowd, sounding strangely unsure on the repeat of the word 'Senator.' "He's one of the ones they forced on us, one of the ones we were supposed to listen to, one of the ones who thought *they* were gonna tell *us* what to do!" More boos for this. But they loved booing. "Say hello folks – AND goodbye – to Shay Shelby, a card-carrying Reasoner!"

It was a scream, not a roar. It was orgasmic. They lost their minds, even though they had no idea who Chase was, even if Viking had got his name right.

Chase looked at them. The only thing he could think of was what Gabriel had said to him. "What am I gonna do without that?" Because there was nothing Chase felt for these people. No kinship. No regard. And the fact that he had once thought he shared such things with these people – that he harbored such an absurd belief –

embarrassed him to his deepest core. No geography or the accident of where his parents had sex would ever make these people his biological relatives. They were animals. He was a man. There was no connection.

"Well, what do you think we should do with him??" Viking asked the audience in a solid midway barker voice.

The chant was immediate. "CHOP HIM OFF! CHOP HIM OFF!"

"I can't hear you!" Viking shouted. He moved closer to the crowd and held one hand to his ear as if to show he was hard of hearing. "What was that again? Did you say, 'Have him tell us what to do?'"

The crowd shouted their complete disapproval of this idea.

"CHOP HIM OFF! CHOP HIM OFF!" they repeated.

Viking looked back at Chase. Their eyes locked. Viking smiled, sharing the absurdity of the moment with Chase. "Well, son, what the fuck, eh?" he said. "Sometimes you gotta give the people what they want, right?" He said it almost with commiseration. Then he nodded his head, and the Jerseys who had escorted Chase out of Gabriel's room forced him to kneel at the guillotine.

He was moving underwater. Suddenly their chants of "CHOP HIM OFF! CHOP HIM OFF!" seemed muted. He felt his muscles sludging in slow motion. He looked up and studied the glint of the blade, and it didn't look ten or twelve feet above him. It looked twenty.

Someone walked in front of him and held a blue recycle box up for the crowd to see. They lost their shit again, this time in complete approval. The recycle man spun the box in his hands, and the approval scream became even louder. He did a sort of Harlem Globetrotters thing with it on the end of his finger. They screamed even more.

Chase did what they wanted him to do. Like going to the doctor and submitting to an X-ray. Turn this way. Turn that. Bend here. Bend there. Except in this case, someone nudged his knees from behind and he knew to bend down. Then someone pushed for him to put his head down and he did. He was careful to place his neck squarely on the dirty towel which served as a neck rest. He heard Viking shouting some more bullshit to the crowd, but he couldn't make sense of it. He had other things to do.

Exactly like Warren Potsburger, Chase Selby looked out at the crowd and tried to find something to love. Something he could use for solace as the last thing he saw on earth. He couldn't find anything, but then he saw the trees. They were newly planted saplings at the end of the grass near the Grant Memorial, something someone must have planted in the very earliest spring before the madness began. Chase fixed his gaze on the branches, which were so young they only had a few leaves on them, but they were green, and simple, and perfect. Even more incredible, if he lifted his chin just a little bit, he didn't see the people. He saw just blue sky and a green leaf and that was all there was in the world.

My God, this is going to happen, he thought.

Viking was shouting something else, but Chase didn't hear this either. He was aware of just how close the big man was to him now. Then Viking's arm moved, which meant he was likely reaching for the locking brace, which he would snap into place before reaching for the rope that dropped the blade. But Chase didn't want to be aware of such a gross, vulgar, and obvious action. He just wanted the leaf and the sky. He wanted Viking to do it before he lost the perfection of that image.

Which is when everything changed. And everything went silent.

Not all at once. Viking had just said, "Well, are you READY?!!" and the crowd had roared that it was more than ready, it had been ready for a hell of a long time, yeah, let's get back to the killing, man. But then, suddenly, the folks up front weren't shouting like they had been, and the folks around them were now stepping back and suddenly *they* weren't shouting like they'd been doing, and soon it rippled outward – rippled out like some odd inverted sonic wave, like a skipping pebble across a pond. Soon the folks behind them were asking "what is it? what is it?" and then everyone was craning to see on the giant view screens. What was going on?

What was going on was that the crowd on the grass in front of the Capitol steps, the folks with the best vantage point on the killing action, were separating, parting like the Red Sea, and allowing a very small figure to come through them. A figure they all knew, yet none had ever seen in person. She had always left the Capitol to Jeff Beavenstock, and therefore had yet to honor its steps with her cat-like grace and cool intensity.

Sister Sheena literally parted them, and in doing so she sucked the cameras on to her every movement. The crowd grew silent. She wore the dark combat pants and the black T-shirt that said SURVIVE and her hair was tied back the way they all knew, and the sun literally bounced off her sunglasses. And directly behind her, his hand on her shoulder in a protective guiding gesture, was Hog, in his Harley vest and jean jacket. Wearing his bandana. Hog. Whose every gesture said, "Don't even think about it."

With or without Hog, she was a magnetic figure, and suddenly Viking looked absurd. Like a slob. Dumpy. A loser. And when she rose up to the top of the steps and the crowd gasped with recognition, in that one *second*, Viking was no longer even Viking. Suddenly he was just Lowell Grange again – and who, when you thought about it, was Lowell fucking Grange?

At the top of the steps she just looked at them all. That's all she did. Just looked. And slowly, but not too slowly, everyone shut the fuck up. Until you heard nothing but the wind blowing through the little saplings planted last spring.

She reached out a hand. It was a long, slim hand, with perfectly manicured nails. It took Viking a second, but eventually he realized what she wanted. Clumsily, he handed over the microphone. She slowly brought it to her mouth. But not too close.

Finally she spoke, and what she said stopped them all. Stopped everything.

"This," she said, "is not what we're going to do today."

50. *Egress*

1

The silence hung there a good long time. This was where she shone. This was what she was a master of. Sister Sheena knew how to hold a crowd. So she just stood there, perfectly balanced, as if waiting for someone to challenge her. But of course no one would challenge her. Most of the crowd was just trying to deal with the fact that she was there at all. Sheena. On the Mall. Talking to them.

She spoke again. "You are going to listen to me. And I am going to say it again. *Not today.*"

At first, it had taken Chase some time to draw his attention from his leaf and his little patch of sky and instead take in that which was literally altering his very existence. Sister Sheena first, then Hog. He tried to make sense of it, but the pieces of the puzzle wouldn't fit. Then her voice broke the confusion. With that first sentence, he knew he wouldn't be dying here today. Then, slowly, he raised his head and sat back on his haunches. Viking had not yet put the locking brace in place, so there was nothing to stop him and no one tried, not even the man himself, who was standing less than twenty inches away.

Sister Sheena let the crowd think about what she had said. She gave them a good long while. Then, just as they were starting to shift from one foot to the other, she put the microphone to her mouth again. "We have *much* scarier shit to do. Much worse."

The crowd perked up at this news, clearly intrigued. Whatever this was, it sounded good.

Microphone up again. "Because now we know." She turned and

looked directly at Viking, her sunglasses like the ruthless eyes of some giant insect. "Don't we?"

Viking, who had never laid eyes on Sister Sheena in his life – who, in fact, had never laid eyes on a woman anywhere near as striking as Sheena – fumbled for an answer. He had nothing. But he gave it a shot, and out croaked a sort of half-assed, "Sure." Viking's henchmen, standing just a few feet away, gave him an odd glance. Viking felt that glance like a small knife wound.

Sister Sheena turned back to the crowd and moved to one side of the steps. A graceful, confident movement. Where was the girl he had met in the parking garage, Chase wondered? She had been transformed. Back to the revolutionary. For now, anyway.

"Have we uncovered the enemies from within our own ranks?" she asked.

The crowd wasn't sure what to do with this question, but a very tall man with a backward Viking helmet decided he liked the question. He shouted out "Fuckin' bet!!" and cupped his hands together in vigorous applause. Others took up the call. "Yeah!" They applauded themselves and their viciousness at rooting out enemies.

But Sister Sheena didn't seem impressed. "You can do better than that!" she berated them.

So they let it rip then. A huge self-congratulatory roar.

The sound was like cover. It gave Chase time to look past Sheena to Hog, who was standing on the top step of the stairs but one. Hog, whom Chase had last seen on the cement floor of the parking garage, bleeding out his life, or so Chase had thought. They locked eyes now, only for a second, but long enough. Chase knew to stay where he was.

"You know who did that, don't you?" Sister Sheena asked. "Who uncovered our enemies? Who exposed the traitors?"

There was a bit of confusion on this, until she pointed one long, sword-like finger. "He did!" she said, keeping the finger there, and the crowd erupted again, this time thumping and whistling as well as shouting and applauding.

Viking didn't know what to do. This was attention he had never received before in his life. Attention someone *else* was awarding him.

Sister Sheena now moved to the other side of the steps, but she kept that finger pointed at Viking. A perfectly manicured laser beam. "*He* did!" she said. "*He* said there are traitors in our midst, *he* said there are those who are not true to our cause, he said there are those who are trying to tear us apart! And who listened to him?" Sheena stopped and pivoted so her body was flat to the crowd. "Fucking *no* one!"

The crowd booed this, not in disagreement, but because they were caught up in the story. They knew what Sheena was saying was spot on. No one had listened. That was the goddamned truth.

Slowly, Chase rose to his feet. Amazingly, no one seemed to notice or care. No one except Viking, anyway. The two of them locked eyes for just a second, and then Viking looked away, back at Sheena.

"Fucking no one except our fucking enemies!" Sheena shouted, and the crowd roared complete agreement with that, whatever it meant.

She lowered the microphone. She waited them out. Then, when they realized she wasn't going to go on until they shut up, they shut up.

This time, she was so quiet you had to lean forward just to hear her. "And what have we learned? We've learned there are enemies. Bigger enemies than we ever imagined. I'm not talking about those assholes up on Pennsylvania Avenue and I'm not talking about the fucking jokers we got in here." She gestured to the Capitol building. Then to Chase, for the first time. "And I'm not talking about this guy, either." Her eyes were very careful not to lock with Chase. She turned back to the crowd before that could happen. She asked the mob, "Do you really think for one second that any of those comedians could fool us? You think any of those clowns are smart enough to get inside us and fool us and almost defeat us from within? Well?"

The answer was a huge and resounding "No!"

"That's right," she said. "They couldn't manage the virus, they couldn't manage the government shutdown, they couldn't manage the Recession. They couldn't manage jack shit. So clearly our real enemies are not from here, are they?"

There was a strange hesitation from the crowd. She prodded them.

"Are they??" she asked.

"Nooo," came a half-hearted murmur. The crowd was clearly confused. What was Sheena saying?

"They're foreigners! And they want to destroy us!" she said. "They've always wanted to destroy us, since 1776!"

There were a few shouts of outrage at this, but she still didn't have them.

"What I'm telling you," she said, "is that our fight has only just begun. We have new battles ahead. Unless – of course – " She practically hissed on the *unlesssss*. "Unless you're saying we're done. That you can't fight anymore. That you can't fight anyone, anytime, anyplace." She pointed again at Viking. This time it was a direct question. "You!" she shouted. "Do you think we can't fight anyone, anytime, anyplace?"

Viking was on the spot. The simple truth is, he had no idea what she was talking about, but he had a pretty good idea that he had to say something to look strong. All eyes were on him. Viking looked at his closeup on all those goddamned jumbo monitors spread across the Mall. Fuckin' TV. The *world* was watching. He wanted to snatch back the mantle of authority she'd just taken a chip out of.

"We can take on anyone," he finally croaked.

That they liked. They cheered. They shouted. They knew defiance.

Sister Sheena turned back to the crowd. "You listen to him. And you ask yourself, when the tanks finally roll in, when the tanks finally roll in to fight *with* us, when the tanks come in and show our enemies just how powerful we are now, who do you want leading you?" Again, she pointed at Viking.

There were shouts of "Viking! Viking!" and Sister Sheena seemed pretty pleased with that. She put the mic back to her mouth. "Because that's what I'm talking about here. Not other Americans fighting us, but other countries. That's what time it is. That's where we are. That means it's soon time for bombs, not blades. It's time for us to bring in the heavy artillery in our name. It's time to show real, unimaginable, unquestionable, wrath of God power!"

The crowd lost its shit then. They were all for wrath of God power, and she let them shout and yell their defiance all they wanted.

Viking, for his part, seemed pleased that Sheena was saying he was the right man to lead this new battle. A battle against nations. And why not? Hadn't he shown what a commander he was?

Until one voice up front said the word Chase had most feared. Perhaps even Sister Sheena feared.

"BULLSHIT!" someone shouted.

This elicited a small chorus of boos, but when the voice again shouted "Bullshit" the boos turned to laughter. Everyone leading a cause knows that laughter is just about the worst thing you can hear if you're trying to keep the troops on side.

The laughter began to ripple through the crowd.

Sister Sheena glanced back for just a second, and Chase saw it; for one lightning strike of a milli-moment there she was – the high school girl – and she was scared shitless.

Chase took an instinctive step toward her, but held himself back when Hog gave him a sharp, darting glance. This was followed by a strangely tentative step up that last Capitol stair. There was something strangely unsteady about that step, and it concerned Chase.

But she came back, Sister Sheena did. She stood with a hand on her waist and the microphone up. She said, "Someone's calling bullshit! I want to *know* who's calling bullshit! You call bullshit on me, you better get your fucking ass up here!"

They cheered that. They loved that.

The voice from somewhere just below the steps – a man's voice

— shouted out, "Who says there are other *countries* trying to destroy us! Who?"

Soon the chant was taken up. "Who!" "Who!"

Hog took another step closer.

Sister Sheena decided to go center stage. That put her no more than ten feet from Chase and Viking, staring defiantly back at the crowd. She held up one "STOP" hand and waited for the crowd to finish their catcalling. Finally, they did.

She had an answer. She had an answer that they couldn't ignore, or laugh at, or jeer. She said it simply, and it shut them down instantly.

"The Wolf," she said.

There was complete silence.

"The Wolf says it," she repeated. "The Wolf told *me*."

Chase could feel Viking looking at him. He dared to look back. What he saw was a man who was no longer sure that he wanted to be where he was. A man who could imagine the simple joy of being able to lift himself out of who he was at that moment.

Sister Sheena reached in her back pocket and removed a folded piece of paper. She held it up for the whole crowd to see. "How about I read this?"

Slowly she began to unfold the paper, and the crowd waited for her to do it. She took her time. Finally, once it was open, she began to read. "'Stop shaking the tyrant's bloody robe in my face, or I'll believe you want to put all of us in chains.'" She looked up into a sea of confused faces. She read on. "'There is a time for hand-to-hand battle, and there is a time to let cannons do what they're built to do. When the enemy is not your neighbor, it is time to use cannons.'"

Okay, this made sense. This they understood. There were a few shouts of agreement. Sister Sheena read on. "'There is a time when you have won the battle in the field, and that's when you move on. There is a time when your local enemy is too small for your attention, and that's when you turn your eyes to the greater combat, and you unleash fury as never seen before.'"

There were very loud murmurs of approval for this part as well.

Sister Sheena suddenly held the piece of paper up to the wind. In her outstretched hand, it looked exactly like what it was; an act of defiance. "The Wolf has written to me to deliver a message to you! We have won this battle! We have defeated our small enemies, and we have defeated the enemies from within, and now it's time to unleash the fury on our bigger enemies! It's time to destroy those motherfuckers who want to destroy us! What I want to know is, are we with the Wolf, or do we betray the Wolf?"

When you put it like that, there was no question. The crowd roared its approval, so strong, so powerful, that both Chase and Viking took a step back.

Still holding the paper above her head, Sister Sheena shouted into the microphone, "Do you want me to take your answer to the Wolf??"

The answer was a resounding "YES!"

"And what is that answer?" she shouted.

As one they shouted back. "WAR!"

"Fucking right," she murmured, and they loved that. She started them chanting "WAR!" as she strode from one side of the steps to the other, holding the piece of paper above her head. "WAR!"

Then she switched it up on them, but she did it so quickly, no one seemed to notice. Soon everyone was back to chanting "USA! USA! USA!"

That's when she nodded at the Jerseys to let the rope down. They weren't sure about that, but when Hog stepped forward and began to pull it down himself, they went along with his natural authority, and soon the diehard front row Changers were streaming onto the Capitol steps, just as they had on the day of the attempted assassination of Jeff, shouting "USA! USA!"

Everything became incredibly confused very quickly. Chase was pulled into the crowd. He resisted, until he realized it was Hog doing the pulling. He yanked both of them, Chase and Sister Sheena, down the steps and through a whole crew of guys Chase hadn't noticed before, but all of whom looked a great deal like Hog. It was a human corridor of Harley-Davidson vests and jean jackets, all armed men. At the end of this Pretorian guard was a large black Jeep Wrangler with its back door open. Chase and Sister Sheena were hurled into this with an unceremonious shove.

"Fuck!" Sister Sheena said. The rear door of the Jeep was hammered shut. The car pulled away, a path cleared for them.

51. *In the Buick Regal*

1

Chase had expected Neil would be the one behind the wheel, but of course that was impossible. The last time he had seen Neil, he had been giving Chase cover fire in a gun battle that promised to end only one way. Neil was almost surely dead.

However, the driver of the Jeep did look familiar. He was big – not as big as Hog, but big – and wore a leather jacket and ski cap which also looked familiar.

Hog, in the passenger seat, registered Chase's confusion. He nodded at the driver. "Levi."

"Levi," said Chase, trying to remember where and when.

There was a grunt from Levi, who was focused on navigating the Jeep through the crowd – shades of Chase's first day in the city, when a Hells Angels escort attempted to get him as close to the Capitol steps as possible, wading through the sheer madness and exuberance and high spirits of the Changer revolution. Now, however, they were heading *away* from the Capitol.

"You have no idea how pleased I am to see all of you," Chase said. That was putting it mildly. His heart was thumping at four or five times its regular beat. He was in physical shock and he knew it.

He looked at Hog. Hog made a very small gesture in Sister Sheena's direction. She was sitting in the seat behind Hog.

Then Chase realized who Levi was, and why he had seemed familiar. Levi had been with Sister Sheena in the Watergate parking garage the night of the clandestine meeting. Hog with Chase, Levi with Sheena. And here they all were, together again, winding their way slowly – achingly slowly – through the mob of rabid Changers.

"How are you alive?" Chase asked Hog.

"One in the leg and one in the hip," he said. "You don't die from that."

In the leg. That explained why Hog had simply dropped in front of him in the parking lot shootout. Chase had assumed it had been a mortal back wound. Leg was something else. And another in the hip. Which also explained why Hog had such a strange gait escorting Sister Sheena through the Capitol crowd, and why he appeared to be having difficulty stepping up onto the second level of the stairs. It hadn't been judicious hesitation. He was still injured.

"Where are we going?" Chase asked.

"Away from theses jokers, I hope," said Sheena. She was peering out her window through the bug-sized sunglasses. Clearly, the crowds unnerved her when they were this close.

"It will clear up ahead," Hog assured her. And it might. They were now heading up 1st street. Peering ahead across D Street, it looked like the crowd was going to be much thinner the farther north from the Capitol they went.

"What's the plan?" asked Chase.

"North," said Hog.

"North where?"

Levi glanced at Chase in the rearview mirror. "We just have to get out of the city."

"Are we on the run?"

"Probably," said Levi.

They were now past D Street. Chase realized that there were no vehicles or motorcycles in front, beside or, when he looked back, behind them.

When Sister Sheena spoke, Chase wasn't sure who she was talking to. "That crowd was with me. Did you see that?"

He looked over at her. Her gaze was locked on that passenger window. She seemed so brittle, like she would snap in two from tension. It was impossible to reconcile this with the figure of swagger and bravado who had literally strutted across the Capitol steps.

"Yes they were." He wanted to thank her, but that didn't seem what she wanted right now.

"But not totally with me," she said.

"How do you know that?" Chase asked.

She shrugged. "You always know when they're with you and when they're not – if you've got them, or if they're wandering. And if anything sticks."

"And?"

She turned and looked at him, although he only saw himself reflected in her glasses. "I didn't leave them with enough." She was angry, like a comedian or musician who knows they had a bad night and refuses to be talked out of it. "I thought it was a mistake to go up there."

"If you thought it was a mistake, then why did you do it?"

She gave a nod to Hog. "Ask your man."

Chase looked at Hog. For his part, Hog kept his eyes on the road.

"A very persuasive fellow," she said.

They were turning now, going around the train station. The streets, Chase realized, no longer resembled even the thinnest reflection of normal Washington. This was now a war zone. Filthy, covered with litter, graffiti, store windows shattered, and pretty much deserted. Clearly, things had seriously degenerated while Chase was imprisoned underground.

"And how did he persuade you?" Chase asked.

Sister Sheena returned her attention to her window. "Apparently you made a deal with Van DeVere and the whole goddamned army. I don't want to be on the wrong side of that shit. I have to get out, just like I told you."

So she hadn't changed her mind since the Watergate garage. She was still looking to find a way out of the fix she found herself in; still believed there *was* a way out, and that the fix was pretty much everyone else's fault. She had merely been along for the ride.

Then Chase caught himself, and recalled her performance on the Capitol steps. The leaf and the sky were the last things he had expected to see in this lifetime. He owed her.

"What you did was remarkable," he told her. "The real thing. The reason doesn't matter."

"The real thing what?" she asked.

"Heroism."

Slowly, she raised her sunglasses. It wasn't that she didn't believe him, it was more likely that no one had ever told her she was heroic before.

"So you owe me one, Beaver." she said.

"Beaver?"

"As in *Leave It To.*"

There was something about the way she said it; she was making sure he knew he owed her. Put that fear together with the rest of her, especially the look – the sunglasses, the SURVIVE shirt, the perfect hair, the nails – and it all made him think of Garth Brooks.

Chase didn't know anything about country music, but everyone in America knew who Garth Brooks was. He was the sometimes-heavyset country singer in the black cowboy hat who reflected the true heart of America. Except he wasn't that. Or he wasn't just. In 1999, Garth released an album as Chris Gaines, a goth musician "persona" Brooks adopted; a wraith-thin ghost with soul patch and eyeshadow. Neither the music nor Chris's appearance was anything like Garth. When Chris Gaines didn't gain traction, Garth went back to being Garth and everyone decided to forget the weird goth aberration, except Chase had thought it was a game changer: it meant that *Garth Brooks* was an act as much as Chris Gaines was.

This is what Chase had known since the garage meeting and was confirmed today. Sister Sheena, sitting beside him in the Jeep, was simply an act. An invention. Nothing more. And the person behind that act – who probably didn't know how or why she could turn it on or off any more than Garth knew how he could do what he did – was, at the moment, scared stiff.

"You hear what I'm saying?" she asked. "I protected you so now you protect me. That's the way I see it."

But Chase, before he agreed to anything, had a more pressing question he needed answered. The only question.

"How did you get in contact with the Wolf?" he asked. "And how long have you been in contact?"

She looked back at him, and for the first time there was something more than sulky self-concern in her manner. She looked genuinely shocked. "Why?"

"Because it's possible that's the only shot we've got now," he said. "I need to speak to the Wolf, whoever or whatever they are." Then, remembering what motivated her most, he added, "*And* the key to protecting you and giving you what you want."

"You want to know about my relationship with the Wolf?"

"Everything you can tell me."

She reached in her pocket and slowly removed a crumpled, half-folded piece of paper. It was the Wolf letter she had waved at the crowd. She handed it to Chase.

Chase looked at it. The handwriting looked like it belonged to a middle school girl, with large loops around the lowercase "l's" and "b's." Bic pen. The paper was lined.

On it he read:

Wolf shit —

Tyrant's robe blood — chains —

Yah yah — hand-to-hand

Cannons?

Use cannons on neighbors — or guns — bigger — artillery

Chase looked at the paper awhile, then back at Sister Sheena. Her eyes were locked on his. "You get it, right?"

But he didn't. For a while, he just stared.

"I never talked to a Wolf in my whole fucking life," Sheena said. "Who *knows* what that shit is all about. Hippies in the woods I heard. Jeff sure never knew. We just said we did."

Chase took that in, then looked down and stared again at the sheet of paper – clearly, Sheena's notes to herself on a bogus Wolf quote from a bogus Wolf letter. He thought of Representative Dan in his cage at the end of Gabriel's hall. Dan talking about the men in the woods.

A plan began to formulate in Chase's head. Even though he couldn't quite make out its full shape, or even its rough outline, something was starting to build.

He folded the paper and put it in his pocket, then addressed Hog up front. "What about the others?"

Hog, who was holding onto the bracing strap above the passenger door, kept his focus on the very deserted street ahead of them. They were going northeast now, entering the industrial side of the city. Storage units out here. Carpet factory warehouses. You made fast time on these wide streets when there were so few cars on the road. "Calinescu died," Hog said. "In the parking garage. So did Pappason. She died instantly."

Chase took that in. "And do you know about the others?"

"We never found them in the State building."

"We?"

"Neil and me."

"Neil?? You mean Neil did make it out?"

Hog nodded.

Chase tried to understand this. He remembered standing in the lobby of the State building, holding Tyler's dead body and hearing the elevator from the parking garage start up. "So that was you?" he asked. "Coming up in the elevator from the parking garage?"

Hog nodded. "We left the garage and went looking for you. We sure couldn't take the stairs. We were pretty banged up."

The pieces were starting to come together. "What did you find?" Chase asked.

"Security all dead, including those young kids in the jackets. But no Reasoners, dead or alive."

Chase wanted to tell Hog that he knew exactly where the Reasoners were, or most of them, anyway, but he was still assembling facts.

"Do you think they were Changers?" Chase asked. "The bad guys?"

Hog almost laughed. "Those guys in the parking garage? No fucking way. They were military. Trained somewhere and trained together. Maybe Van DeVere double-crossed you, sent a hit squad ahead while you were having lunch."

Chase thought about that. "No," he said. "I don't think so."

Hog nodded. "The only clue I ever got was when one of them went down. His helmet came off."

"And?"

"Mohawk cut. The old-fashioned kind."

"Does that mean something?" Chase asked.

Hog shrugged. "You tell me."

Chase looked out his window. He tried to think. They were passing a McDonald's. It was closed, pretty much permanently; a car had smashed through the front window and been left there, stuck forever. Someone had spray painted across the back window "Quarter Banker with Jews."

Chase said slowly, "Someone who could pull that off and take everyone by surprise *and* turn the Reverend – to say nothing of getting me placed in the Capitol dungeon – is somebody. But who?"

Hog said nothing.

Chase looked at Sheena. She returned the stare with something like – anger? Fear?

Chase looked back at Hog. "What about Brueler?"

"Clipped in the shoulder."

"You mean he made it out *too*?" Chase asked in amazement.

Hog nodded.

"Where is he?"

"You're about to find out."

2

They pulled into the parking lot of a vast industrial yard labeled Store Smart, which advertised itself as "America's Safest Self Storage Cubes." It looked to be pretty false advertising, however, as the electronic front gate with the razor wire – the one which was meant to slide across the driveway entrance – was lying in the gravel parking lot with only one hinge keeping it attached to the perimeter fence. Access to Store Smart now seemed to be more a case of "come and go as you please" rather than "America's Safest."

Surprisingly, none of the brightly painted storage garage doors were bashed in yet, although someone had gone a little crazy with the spray paint. FUCK DRURY, said one, referring to the last known President; also, EAT THE RICH; also, and more concerningly, I JUST ATE 2 COPS.

Levi carefully edged the Jeep through the demolished gates and slowly steered around the big storage sheds. Around back was where the Store Smart enterprise met up with the Washington Union rail tracks.

A Buick Regal was sitting by the tracks, waiting patiently for them. It had smoked windows. You couldn't see who was inside.

Chase had a strange sense of foreboding about that car, as if whatever was inside were some kind of poison or would reveal something to him he truly didn't want to learn.

Almost as if reading his thoughts, Hog said, "You probably want to do this one alone."

But Chase hesitated, and Hog misread the hesitation.

"The area's safe." As if for confirmation, he glanced at Levi and Levi nodded. Reassuring, perhaps, yet Chase couldn't help noticing that Levi also reached into his denim jacket and checked the Glock neatly holstered there.

Chase opened the back door of the Jeep Wrangler and climbed out. His feet made too loud a noise on the gravel. He shut the back door of the Jeep and went around the front and walked directly, if slowly, toward the passenger door of the Buick Regal. His footsteps really were just too damned loud.

The Regal door opened with the nice, satisfying whisper of a brand-new car. Chase got in.

And tried to hide his shock.

The man behind the wheel may have once been Tom Brueler, but he sure wasn't Tom Brueler anymore. This was someone else. Confident Brueler – union negotiator, head of the table, the watchful eyes and the scowl under the heavy brows, the expensive suits and the rich watch – replaced by a much smaller man. His neck appeared to have shrunk two sizes and there were wattles where there hadn't been wattles before. He still wore the expensive suit, but his body swam in it. Even the watch seemed too big on the wrist. He looked like a cancer patient, although Chase knew that wasn't it at all.

Tom Brueler's courage and belief were gone. Someone or something had ripped them out of his body.

Still, he turned from where he sat at the wheel (he'd been sitting there keeping his hands at ten and two, even though the car was parked) and offered a crepey smile with teeth that seemed Osmond-sized, even if now dull old-man yellow. "You have no idea how glad I am to see you," he said.

Chase was so rattled by his friend's appearance that he had to struggle to grab hold of a clear thought. Focus. But he couldn't. One question wiped out all other thoughts: How the hell had Tom become so debilitated so quickly?

For a micro-second a very simple answer nibbled, but then it went away, and all he was left with was an image of Gabriel's Crown Royal bottle and the copious amounts of booze Gabriel seemed to drink in such a short period of time, even though Chase never saw him drunk.

Then the image was pulled away, because Brueler was speaking.

"Go back," Chase said.

"I said I don't know how much you know"

Chase gestured to the Jeep sitting twelve feet away to their right. "I've been getting a crash course from them. And what just happened to me back at the Capitol was a pretty good indicator."

"Well, yes," said Brueler slowly. My God, was he just going to keep his hands on the steering wheel like that? The car was in park! "The wheels are really off now. Not just here, but across the country. Everywhere. You were right, Chase. A revolution hates a leadership vacuum. And when there is a leadership vacuum – "

"That lunatic who calls himself Viking," Chase said, interrupting him. "Where did he come from?"

Brueler offered up his hands in frustration. "Who *knows*??" Then the hands went back on the wheel, but not before Chase discovered why he used the wheel: Untethered, Brueler's hands shook. "He just appeared, and his message was pretty terrific for all the folks disappointed with the lack of violence. 'There are traitors amongst the Changers, and we have to find them and kill them.' So back to more killing. It almost made us miss Beavenstock. They went for it, of course. Because they're hungry."

"Went for it how exactly?"

What followed was Brueler's brief, palsied recitation of what most everyone inside Washington now knew; a tale of lynchings, forced drownings, dunking parties, burning people at the stake, and fatal lawn darts. And that was just on the Mall. It was a pattern of mad violence which was being repeated in all sorts of inventive ways across the country. Brueler tried to offer up a smile at the end, as he asked, "So, who are we, Chase? Who are we, really?"

It was no different than the look Sheena had given him in the Jeep. The look that said *Fix This*. The same look Gabriel had given him as the old man searched through what he imagined was his own wasted life. Tom, like Sheena, like Gabriel, maybe even like the Reverend in the closet; *fix it*.

But that thing about Brueler's physical state was still bothering Chase. He had to understand it. "Tom, how could all this have happened in a couple of weeks?"

Chase was staring at Tom Brueler's emaciated hands as he said it. He couldn't take his eyes off them. They, of course, were the answer. Chase's brain knew that, just as he knew the secret to the Crown Royal bottle. "How long have I been gone?"

Brueler looked at him in surprise. In a small voice he said, "Well, it's been more than a month since we saw General Van DeVere, Chase."

Chase heard the words but didn't react. He wasn't sure how he wanted to react. A month! It was impossible, yet it explained so much, including a D.C. that resembled no D.C. he'd ever seen.

But he couldn't get caught in the specifics. He had to focus on what really mattered. "So … " He struggled for the next sentence. "Is the General still there?"

Brueler's gaze met Chase. "He got in touch with me once. He said he was waiting to hear from you."

Chase had imagined that all of his plans had been erased. But with this information there was something. A possibility. A chance, even? "Tom, how did you survive?"

Brueler seemed relieved to be on safer ground. "By a miracle!" he said with a horse-faced smile. He gestured to the Jeep with an unsure hand. "And your man Hog. I got hit, but in the shoulder. I crawled under the car and moved myself as dead center as I could. There was a lot of gunfire, I tell you. Finally it was just feet circling the cars. That was when I was most scared, because I knew they were checking, and I knew they'd find me. But the face that peered under was your man. He and his friend hauled me out. They took me up in the elevator with them and dumped me in the lobby while they searched the rest of the building. They were looking for you and the others. Did you see – Tyler?"

Chase nodded.

"It's not hard to figure out what happened. Someone betrayed us. All of us. Someone very close to the Reasoners."

Chase shook his head. "Not someone close to the Reasoners. It *was* a Reasoner."

Now it was Brueler's turn to be surprised into silence.

"It was the Reverend," Chase said. "She made me think she was the last survivor, but that was just to get my guard down. She set me up so they could get me out of there and dump me in the Capitol."

Brueler shook his head. "No."

"I sat with her, Tom. In a closet. I know."

"No, I mean, yes, she set you up. But because that was the only choice they gave her. They said she had to sacrifice you or all the other Reasoners would be killed. So, she made the only … " He paused to find the word. "*Reasonable* choice she could."

Chase was stunned. "How do you know all that?"

"Because she killed herself, Chase. And left me a note, asking to be forgiven."

The shock wasn't that Sarah Campbell had killed herself. The shock was that he hadn't considered this scenario before. He hadn't believed in a woman he had found faith in.

"Forgiven by …?" Chase asked.

"You!" Brueler let that sink in, then cleared his throat. He didn't sound so good. "As it turned out, they were lying to her the whole time. The other Reasoners were taken, and no one has heard from them since. I assume they're also dead."

"Actually, they're not."

Brueler looked up with a start.

"They're under the Capitol," said Chase.

Brueler was shocked. "Did you talk to them?"

Chase shook his head. "Somehow I wound up with better accommodations. Private, and on the other side of the building."

Brueler considered this, then gestured to the Jeep. "Maybe that was your friend's doing. She certainly went to extra lengths to get you off the hook – literally – this morning."

Chase almost laughed. "It was someone more powerful than Sheena. Tom, we need to continue with the plan I had. It's the only way out of this."

"What are you talking about?"

"What we talked about with Van DeVere. We have to keep pushing on that. But it still only has a 50-50 chance of success, especially now that these people have a taste for a different kind of blood. But we could change all that. Sell it. I'm pretty sure I know where to start. But we need help."

"Such as?"

"Do you have a private congressional contact information?"

"Nothing like that was part of our structure."

"So who would?"

Brueler hesitated only a fraction of a second. "Mallickey."

"*He's* still alive?"

Brueler offered a weak smile. "Guys like Mallickey are always still alive. And he'd certainly have access to information about anyone in Congress or the Federal government."

"Then he gets us what we need."

"Which is?"

Chase gestured toward the Jeep and Sister Sheena. "She sends a message."

"To who?"

"A man named Woodman. Or Woodsman. Which is why we need the information from the directory."

"You've lost me."

"And it has to be Sheena because I'm pretty sure she's Judy Garland."

"Chase, you're starting to worry me."

"An old man told me. A real patriot. The trick is just getting through the code that's rattling around in his brain."

"His name is Woodman?"

"No," said Chase with a smile. "Woodman or Woodsman is the long-time neighbor of Representative Dan Jefferson Williams. Williams and his wife Sheri have a secret country place out in the wilds of Maryland somewhere. Woodman and his wife are or were neighbors. They used to live in an old farmhouse out there, but it sounds like they built themselves a more exotic place in recent years.

On the other side of the property. So the farmhouse and all the land around it was rented, and for the past few years rented to some very strange people."

Chase didn't go further into the *Wizard of Oz* details, or the fact that Representative Williams had mixed the Wolf up with the Cowardly Lion and/or Scarecrow, depending on where he thought he was in the story. It was probably better if Brueler thought things were actually coming from a source based on the planet Earth.

"And Mallickey's going to tell you where the Congressman's place is, which leads you to Woodman, who is delivering the message to who?" Brueler asked. "The Wolf? To do what? Talk to Sheena?"

"Yes," said Chase. "But the message from Sister Sheena is just an introduction."

"Meaning?"

"Meaning the person the Wolf is really going to talk to is me."

"What are you talking about?"

"I have to be the one to meet the Wolf. Because I think we already know each other."

52. *The Big House and the Old House*

1.

Linden Woodman wondered if perhaps he was losing his mind. Or already had.

He had finally finished boarding up the rear windows of the Big House – a ridiculous name which Ginny had put on it, a joke at first but it had stuck – so now he was able to focus on the west side. He was two days behind schedule, but that didn't matter as it was just his own schedule, so he could let it slide a bit.

No, he thought. That was wrong. Be honest. The reason he had come up with the schedule in the first place was because he didn't think he could let *anything* slide.

Linden stood on the crest of the Big Hill where the Big House sat. He looked down into the valley, where all the greenery was just starting to be peppered with ochres and yellows. He liked to imagine things looked the way they had back when the area had first been settled, in 1770. He liked to imagine the village then. A different kind of revolutionary times. Times had been bad then. Uncertain. But Linden couldn't believe they were as bad as now.

He went around and considered the west side of the house. As with the rear, he wondered why in the hell he and Virginia had designed the place with so many damned windows. And why so many fucking round ones? But he knew. This had been their great achievement, right? Life's accomplishment at sixty-five. Everything had to be perfect and no expense spared. The unbearable thing to contemplate was that at the very moment they finished the place – that night of the wine and those steaks that took forever to cook in the firepit and the unbelievably fantastic sex in the master bedroom overlooking the valley – Ginny had less than ten months to live. Her clock had been counting down even then.

Now Linden was stuck with a house he pretty much hated, loaded with too many windows that were idiotically round, and two Sjoberg worktables currently doing overtime in the massive front driveway. The worktables and the Makita table saw and DeWalt circular saw were set up alongside the massive delivery of three-quarter-inch plywood from the Lowe's in Steffenville. Linden supposed he could have hired Ignatius MacDonald to do the window boarding – after all, Ignatius had been their handyman for years – but Linden was a man who believed that sometimes you had to cut your own wood, just as you had to shoot your own dog.

And maybe Linden was embarrassed. He didn't want Ignatius to see that he, big manly Linden, once a roaring bear in the government security service, was scared.

But Linden surely was. Scared shitless, in fact.

He hadn't been. Not at first. Not even when all the crazy shit went down in the hick towns. Back then, he'd just been disgusted. Who were these clowns who didn't know how to tamp down street brawls? Was this the best the new generation of Security Ops could do? And where was the National Guard? Then, when law enforcement and reserves began to abandon their posts, he wondered if he'd lost his mind. Abandon their *what*? Again, who, and what the fuck? And what about the Insurrection Act? Of course, no act to stifle violent uprisings means anything if there's no one around and willing to fight fire with fire, so …

Then the assault on Washington. The complete collapse of law enforcement, almost like they were in on it. That idiotic ruling from the Supreme Court. The military absence. Then the beheadings. He had been numb, as had most of the country, simply because it had seemed so absolutely impossible.

If there had been any real fear back then, it had been for Dan Williams, with whom Linden had shared this side of the hill for more than twenty years. Every day Linden had watched CNN, sure that any second he'd see Dan dragged out and made to kneel at the Great Guillotine. But it hadn't happened. In time, Linden supposed that the Reasoner Compromise had saved his neighbor, or at least bought him a reprieve. As long as there was the option of some sort of peace accord – or whatever the hell those Reasoners were supposed to do – Linden told himself that Dan was safe.

Except now. Now, Linden didn't think anyone was safe.

The shit had clearly hit the fan when the Reasoners had fucked up with whatever their moronic escapade to drag the military into things had been, and when the idiots' leader had been shot. Since then, what? Something was going on. Shit bad enough that CNN, Fox, and MSNBC had started to adopt a pretty strange tone. Starting from the moment of the Beavenstock shooting, each day had got scarier than the last. Now the talking heads on the channels were talking about "uprisings within the uprising" and "outbursts of violence on the Mall," even if they didn't give any specifics. They said things like "allowing for crisis self-management" and "shifting the focus." You didn't have to be Harlan Coben to know they were covering for something. Once Linden figured out how to navigate Twitter, he got an even clearer focus. He had a pretty good idea the nets were covering up their own complicity in some pretty unbelievable shit.

So most nights now, Linden sat up in the attic office space, the one with the round window and the truly stunning view of the valley (a window he almost never looked out anymore), and trolled Twitter or that thing they called Parler, or Gab. Holy shit. Here you got a way better sense of what was going on. And what was going on – at least on the Mall – sounded like America right off the chain.

There were creepy and spooky suggestions of lynchings and ritualized physical abuse. Some nutbars called these "interrogations," but Linden could read between the lines: The lunatics had turned on one another and were tearing each other's throats out. Or, more accurately, burning each other at the stake, if *that* crazy story could be believed. And if that was what was going on at the Mall, what was going on in the rest of America?

Iris said it was all true, but of course Iris believed everything. If Ginny had been the sister with her eyes on the here and now, Iris was the one to believe Oswald worked for Russian aliens from Roswell. Iris believed the entire Uprising had been the work of the Russians. Linden wasn't entirely sure where she was getting all that shit, but he had unearthed a few underground sites which harvested this kind of stuff, so he imagined Iris was going there, or worse.

The problem wasn't that she told him all of her crazy theories. The problem was that she was starting to convince him. What, after all, was too much these days?

As he set about marking the next cuts for the 72x96 windows, jockeying the plywood around so that it was braced properly across the two work benches, making neat assertive pencil lines with the aid of his four-foot level, he wondered exactly what he thought he was keeping out. Did he really think the crazies were going to find their way out to the rolling hills northeast of Maryland and specifically rip his house apart? And if they did, did he think that some plywood was going to protect Ginny's dream world from people who burned their enemies at the stake?

Linden didn't think any of that, but he knew he had to do something, because something was better than nothing, and if he was doing it now rather than three months earlier, perhaps that was just because the threat now felt closer, and if a threat feels closer, a man boards up his house. Linden couldn't rationalize things much more than that.

His phone vibrated in his right front pocket. For a second he imagined it was the numbing of his sciatica acting up, but no, it really was the phone again, and he knew exactly who it would be.

He ignored it, and instead marked a perfect square and the point with an "X" from his pencil. Big, so he couldn't miss it hiding behind the blade guard of the circular saw.

By the time he had the plank clamped down properly, the phone buzzed again. This time he looked.

Yep. Iris.

He paused just a moment. Always the same thought. She was his dead wife's sister. She was all alone. She was probably going (gone?) crazy in that egg-box condo overlooking the Treasury building. He was one of her few real contacts with the outside world. So …

Fuck it. The phone went back in his pocket.

He was three-quarters of the way through the long cut when the phone buzzed again. He veered off by an eighth of an inch. Fuck! He stopped the cut, carefully withdrew the saw, let the guard fall, and placed it on the board. He took off his work gloves and goggles. He checked his phone.

This time it was just a text message. "CALL ME." He called. The minute she picked up, he let his sister-in-law have it. "Sometimes I'm doing things!"

She gave as good as she got. "Don't tear *my* tits off! I didn't shit in the living room and turn it into an outhouse!"

Who knows where she got her expressions? "If it's about the article in *Kos* or *Jacobin* or *Democracy Now*," he said, "I've already seen it." A total lie.

"Someone got footage of those burnings. I told you they were real! Do you want me to send them?"

Linden slowly lowered himself onto the top of his step stool, and this time his sciatica *did* cut into his leg. "No," he said. "I don't want to see."

"*They're burning people alive down there*! At night I can see the flames from my place!"

"From the beginning they've had campfires," said Linden, suddenly incredibly wearied. "You yourself told me that. It's probably just that." Oh, but he knew otherwise, didn't he? So who was he trying to convince?

"That's a tautology," Iris said. Now she was chewing something. A Clif bar, he imagined. It was all she ate. "'You yourself.'"

"I'm cutting lumber, Iris," Linden said.

"And this isn't a chat."

"What is it?"

"I've been contacted by someone who wants you to help."

"Help with what? And who goes through you to get to me?"

"A man named Brueler."

That stopped Linden cold. If he hadn't been sitting already, he'd sure sit down now. Instead, he just focused on the electrical cord of the DeWalt and wondered if there was a bit of a fray there at the end. He'd have to look at that. "O-kay," he said.

"You know him?"

"I've heard of him." This was another lie, but Linden didn't share any of his past professional history with Iris, and he imagined she was pretty much the same. For thirty-five years Iris had worked as a counsel for the Federal Labor Relations Board, and conspiracy theorist that she was about everything else, you couldn't get boo out of her about the Board. Modern-day hysteria, sure. Anything "real" from her work, never. Once a public servant, always a public servant.

"He says someone asked him to have you deliver a message to your neighbors." Chomp, chomp on the Clif bar.

Now Linden felt his balls grow cold. Did he hear that right? He hoped he hadn't. His neighbors. The Great Contradiction of Linden Woodman's life. But they weren't just neighbors, were they? No, not by a long shot.

"Are we talking neighbors like Congressman Williams or are we talking –"

"The freaks in the Old House," said Iris.

Fuck. Why had he even *told* her about them?? It had been a moment of weakness and he'd known it at the time. Well, now the chickens had apparently come home to roost. Linden imagined that this was what it was like to open the door and find the cops standing there, saying they wanted to talk to you about your teenage son. Not that Linden had ever had a son, teenaged or otherwise, but he could imagine.

"Why doesn't Mr. Brueler call me himself?" Linden asked.

"Because this is Washington, Linden."

"What's the message?"

"I don't know. I'm not sure Brueler knows. Sounds very shaky."

"So how does this work?"

The smoothly efficient Labor Relations Board counsel within Iris kicked into gear. "If you're game, you're going to get a call in about five minutes from the person who *does* know the message. The source, as it were." Another crunch and a chew from Iris. Peanut butter crunch Clif bar, Linden guessed. "And then, as I understand it, the folks who need to be connected are then connected. That's what this Brueler wants. Me to connect you. And he said something else."

"What's that?"

"That this isn't a thing you can refuse."

Linden took that in. A long time. The only thing he knew was that he didn't want this. Whatever it was. But old habits die hard. What had his life in Ops been, if not a matter of doing things you didn't want to do, and admiring your own strength for doing them anyway? But he had to be careful. "Iris, is this a load of bullshit?"

"Yes, Linden, this is a load of bullshit. I'm calling you with a load of bullshit."

"Fuck."

He hung up. He stared at his phone. Then he went around to the back of the house. He looked down into the valley.

2

They were only a mile and quarter down the hill road, but most of the time he managed to convince himself that they were a state or two away. Just like he managed to convince himself that the Big House was the only property he owned on the hill. Yeah, but he still managed to cash their check every month, didn't he? Even if he washed his hands a bit after.

The unbelievable fact was, they had seemed kind of comical when they first approached him about renting the Old House and its six acres. "The Old House" he and Ginny had called their getaway place – well at least until they pulled savings enough together to build the monstrosity with the round windows. There were just three of them then, two guys and a girl, and they had seemed like a throwback to another time. Hippies. Students at George Washington who were working on their masters. Or two of them were. Wasn't one supposed to be writing his PhD thesis? Linden couldn't remember which was which. They needed peace and quiet for their work and wanted to be out of the fray. Political philosophy students, although one of them, the big one, had done a tour of Afghanistan. Then, one day when he had been delivering some extra wood he'd had lying around, Linden discovered the other one doing some target shooting out back. With a .9mm Beretta, no less. Turns out he had also done service, although this one in Somalia. Turns out they'd all done some sort of service. So who *were* the people he'd rented his old house to?

Yeah, and why hadn't he kicked them out? That was a question he asked himself a lot of nights lately. It had only been a one-year lease, and even if the renewal was automatic once you took that thirteenth check, Linden could have dreamt up plenty of reasons to get rid of them. Too many people, for one. He'd rented to three of them, but soon there were all sorts coming and going – young men in particular – and who the hell were they?

Then Ginny got sick and died. Linden knew he wasn't exactly in the best head space then, and wondered if his concerns that he'd accidentally rented the old farmhouse to a neo-Manson family weren't a tad irrational. Besides, he liked the money, didn't he? He didn't need it, but he liked it, and they paid more than double what anyone else would pay. Anyone in their right mind, anyway. Which was sort of the problem.

Last autumn he had begun to have truly serious doubts. The land around the old farmhouse was pretty vast, but from the porch of the Big House you could see a lot of things. Particularly headlights at night. Particularly if you were content to sit there drinking yourself comatose night after night, which was pretty much Linden's chief recreational activity after Ginny died.

From the top of the hill it was easy to see. Trucks came and went at odd hours. Men walked the dirt roads leading in and out of the property all night, as if guarding the place. There were high-powered flashlights. Every now and then he heard shots at hours when no one should be target shooting. Other times he heard shots and shouts from the clearing, sounds which reminded him not of conflict, but of something more ominous: basic training.

Then he decided to finally find out what was going on. It was his property, after all, and his goddamned right. Still, he used the excuse of coming down to check if the main hydro-electric wire had fallen during the storm the night before. When he pulled into the farmhouse yard, however, things were a lot different than the day he'd come across the tall one doing target practice.

On that day, there had been just the old Toyota pickup and the Subaru shitbox. Now there were six pickups. All new. All green. Parked in a row. And beside them, a row of three electric golf carts, the kind old geezers use in Florida or California.

Linden wound up talking to the short one with the frizzy hair and scrappy beard. The kid might have been nineteen, might have been thirty. Either way, he assured Linden that the power was just fine, the line actually had gone down in the storm, but "some of us" were "good with high-voltage electrical power" and so they put the line back up themselves and secured it. WTF?? The kid also assured Linden that they were very happy with the financial arrangement. What he didn't say, but what was abundantly clear, was that he wanted Linden to get the fuck off the property. Linden obliged, but not before seeing something he knew he wasn't meant to see. Just as he was getting back in his truck, Linden glimpsed someone coming out onto the porch of the farmhouse. A man he'd never seen before. Bare chested, he had a coffee mug in hand. Over his shoulder was a Heckler & Kock HK416. Sitting down to enjoy the morning air and drink his first java of the day, he sure looked comfortable with that weapon.

You should have kicked them out then and there, Linden had told himself many times since. You don't know what they're up to, but it sure isn't studying for any master's degrees in political science. So why didn't you? You, who know exactly what this kind of shit might be. That was part of your job for more than thirty-five years, or did you forget that? So …

Because Ginny died, that's why. Who the hell was paying attention during all that?

True. But Linden had been paying attention enough to tell Dan Williams, hadn't he? The two of them had got themselves good and maudlin drunk that one night, sitting on the then-newly finished deck overlooking the valley, and talking about just how fucked the world was. Somehow they got around to Linden's tenants. Linden had talked too much and invented fanciful theories. It had turned funny, eventually, but in the morning Linden suspected that Dan hadn't been as amused as Linden imagined he'd been.

Because of the freaks in the Old House. That's what Iris had said. What the hell could that mean?

As if in answer, his phone rang. He looked at the number. He knew it wouldn't be Iris, and it wasn't. PRIVATE CALLER. The last thing he wanted to do was answer PRIVATE CALLER.

After four rings he answered it, focusing his attention on the tips of the pine trees across the driveway. "Hello?"

To his complete surprise, it was a woman's voice. "Linden?"

He knew who it was right away. Over the past six months, he had spent too much time staring at cable news, and then all the crap he viewed over social media …

"Do you recognize my voice?"

Her voice was as distinctive as the T-Shirt. SURVIVE. "Yes."

"I need you to deliver a message for me. Are you gonna do that?"

Linden was silent.

"Do you need me to tell you *why* you're gonna do that?"

Linden said, "Sure," and was stunned to hear a quaver in his voice.

"Because you could redeem yourself, Linden. For being such a goddamned fool."

Linden listened.

53. *Traitors*

1

They had been slicing through the woods for more than forty-five minutes now, with no turns on the two-lane roadway, the speed unwavering. Neil was behind the wheel. Hog was riding shotgun, literally. Brueler was beside Chase in the back seat. They stared out their respective windows at the impenetrable lines of pine trees.

In the equally silent car behind them. Sister Sheena was being driven by Levi – the man who kept her safe, or hoped to. He had his work cut out for him. Already, things were popping up on social media about Sister Sheena having "shammed" everyone on the Capitol steps. A few brave souls even posited that Sister Sheena had been the one behind the insurrection against the insurrection: the leader of the traitors. So she had been right; it wasn't a matter of *if* they would turn on her, they already were. So whatever was going to happen tonight, she had a stake.

Chase was trying to keep his head clear, but it was hard. He kept thinking about his sister. At first he didn't know why. Then he began to see the connection.

It was the crackle in the air. The sense of a skittish, uncertain lightning bolt that skips across the landscape, looking for a place to land. You feel it but you don't know what it means.

Sitting in the back seat of the armored car as it cut the dark forest in two, Chase felt the crackle but something else as well. A sense of unreality. How else to explain that the pine trees which lined each side of the road seemed to be leaning in closer the farther the cars went? They seemed to be almost leering at him, daring him to keep going as they sped farther into the mouth of the beast. The jagged pine trees were like the teeth of an enormous dog.

The cars kept on, the speed unwavering.

Finally, Chase spoke. "This is it."

Brueler assumed the comment was directed at him. "What do you mean?"

"There are no more options. This has to end now. We have to find resolution here."

"Have to?"

"That's what I'm saying." With that, Chase resumed his study out the window. The pine trees were starting to look black. "Otherwise things keep escalating. No cap. No end."

"I'm an optimist," Brueler said. "I believe there are always more options." Except he didn't sound like he believed it. This new, emaciated Brueler didn't sound like he believed in much of anything anymore.

"No," said Chase. He felt absolutely sure. "We've come to the end of the road."

Unbelievably, at that very moment, they *did* come to the end of the road.

At least, they slowed and turned.

Hog was carefully reading instructions he'd written down in a small pocket-sized notebook, his phone's GPS having lost its signal a good half-hour ago. There were murmurings up in the front seat as Neil expressed doubt, but Hog said something like, "We're here," and so they turned into a passageway between conifer pines and firs.

Apparently there had been instructions to douse their headlights, because Neil quickly flicked the switch on the signal stalk indicator. The car behind them, driven by Levi, killed its lights as well. Everyone dropped their speed.

Soon they were in dark woods, the cars moving slower than a man could walk. Neil was very nervous. Hog cocked the cannon on his lap, which was partly hidden beneath a 76 roadmap. "Easy," Hog said. Whether the instruction was for Neil or everyone else in the car or even himself, it was hard to tell.

Up ahead, men suddenly stepped out from the trees. They wore Stars and Stripes bandanas over their faces and each carried a semi-automatic rifle in their arms – but casually, the way men used to weapons do. They also moved their bodies like military, even though they were just wearing jeans and T-shirts. One of the T-shirts had the words "The Blood 13" splattered across the chest. The Blood 13 what? A team? A band? Then Chase realized: the colonies. The original colonies.

This fortress guard was obviously meant to intimidate, but Chase felt a different emotion: relief. He looked over at Brueler to see if he felt it too, but the man just looked terrified, trying to assess from the right, left, and behind them, just how many armed strangers were moving in on the car. But he caught Chase's glance. "What?" he asked.

"The hair," Chase said.

The apparent leader of the welcome team, the largest and most muscular, approached the driver's window. He did not wear a bandana or try to disguise himself in any way. Instead, he seemed very comfortable with who he was. He had a Mohawk haircut and wrap-around sunglasses circled around the back of his neck.

Neil lowered the driver's window.

Mohawk pointed to a barely visible clearing to the left of the dirt road. "In there."

Neil nodded and shifted the car into Drive.

They parked in the clearing but sat in the car, awaiting further instruction. Sister Sheena's car pulled in beside them. Neil and Levi exchanged concerned looks across the two vehicles. Chase could just make out Sister Sheena sitting in the back seat opposite him. She was staring straight ahead.

Finally, two electric utility vehicles pulled up behind them, the kind Parks and Rec custodians used. A bandana-masked man was in the driver's seat. Another armed bandana man sat in the back, at the right.

Mohawk and his pals gestured everyone out of Chase's car. Chase's team obeyed instructions and made their way to the first utility vehicle. As they climbed in, Chase caught Brueler's glance. He was pale as a ghost. His eyes said it all: 'I don't think we're doing the right thing.'

Sister Sheena and Levi got in the second vehicle, with Sheena lifting her sunglasses up onto her head as she climbed in.

The instant Levi's ass hit the bench seat, both vehicles took off, making their way through impenetrable wooded pathways so narrow that branches and leaves scraped at their arms and shoulders. Occasionally they had to duck their heads to avoid low-hanging branches. It seemed never-ending, and Chase suspected they were being re-routed for the sake of confusion, or they were being tested in some way. The only objects of interest were the tents. You could see them hidden back behind the pines. Military-style, A-framed things in khaki green or cammo. Three in a group of four, then another small cluster, then another. How many people were out here? Doing what? Training? So many of them, Chase noted, had Mohawk cuts.

Just when Chase was ready to say, "Okay, that's enough," they broke through the foliage into a large clearing. There were two buildings here. One was an old farmhouse. The other was a shed, possibly a small smokehouse. The farmhouse was lit by warm, yellow incandescent bulbs. The smokehouse was dark.

There were a number of people standing around in the clearing, as well as two more of the Parks and Rec vehicles. They were parked alongside a row of Toyota Land Cruiser pickups, maybe six in all, identical green, parked side by side.

Most of the people in the driveway wore bandanas. One, very conspicuously, did not. Instead, he wore an immaculate pearl-grey double-breasted suit. He separated himself from the group and strode toward Chase and Brueler before their utility vehicle even had a chance to slow.

"Now this is very good! Terrific! You're all here!" Except it came out 'heey-ah.' The first thing Chase thought of was Foghorn Leghorn. But of course it wasn't Foghorn Leghorn.

He no more belonged out here in the Maryland woods than he belonged in the jungle or in the middle of the Sudan, and yet, somehow, he made himself seem comfortable everywhere. The suit was immaculate, and the cuffs and collar of the white shirt literally glowed out here in the night. "Chase, I'm so glad you got out," Ambassador Macomb said. But it was the boots that identified him. Those distinctive five thousand dollar snakeskin cowboy boots.

Chase climbed out of the Parks and Rec vehicle and stared at the man in front of him.

He wondered why in the world he hadn't seen it before. Now, standing opposite the Ambassador, it seemed perfectly obvious. The rational man who only ever behaved for rational advantage. He was, in many ways, perhaps the ultimate Reasoner, if reason and not passion were the litmus test. In this, he succeeded where the rest of them failed. Chase realized the older man was dressed exactly as he had been the first time they met, the first day the Reasoners convened, including the boots.

So it had not been General Williamson who had betrayed them. It had been Macomb. Did that mean Macomb killed Williamson himself? Unlikely. The Macombs of this world did nothing for themselves.

Macomb reached out a hand to shake Chase's. Chase didn't pull back. He was still trying to take it in.

"I think, no I *know*, we are going to have a profitable discussion," the Ambassador said. There was none of the cool, almost chill pragmatism of the man Chase had worked alongside as a Reasoner. No, this was pure rah-rah. This was pure political theatre.

Chase watched as the Ambassador went around him to shake Brueler's hand. Brueler looked just as stunned as Chase. Watching Macomb, Chase wondered if maybe Brueler was right. Perhaps this was a mistake. After all, if the treacherous man was truly pleased with how things were going, what did that say?

"I think we can go right in," Macomb said. "Soon as they do the once-over."

"The once-over" turned out to be a pretty thorough body frisk before they could even mount the first step of the falling-down farmhouse. Two large men in jean jackets, neither wearing a bandana but both with Mohawk haircuts, stood at the stairs ready to do the frisking. Sister Sheena, it seemed, would not be awarded the courtesy of a female body frisker. Chase was surprised at how roughly they handled her. She accepted her fate with cool stoicism but slapped – no, slammed – one hand that went too far.

Hog had left the cannon – and all of his weapons – in the car. Still, they frisked and fussed about him and Neil and Levi the most. They pretty much waved Macomb through, however, mostly because he seemed to take afront at the idea that he would be searched at all. "Let's all remember who's who now," he said, with a touch less charm than usual. He sounded like a man who knew he might walk out of that farmhouse a king, and those who mistreated him would be remembered. The guards didn't touch him.

Chase couldn't help but wonder, though: If Macomb really was wearing the exact outfit that he had worn that first day he met the Reasoners, then that meant he was armed. There would be two handguns strapped to each thick shin just above the soft leather of the cowboy boots. Was this why he waved off the frisk as an affront and why he was so pleased they let him in without further examination?

Of course, by the time Chase discovered the answer to that question, it was too late.

54. *Of Wolves and Wild Dogs*

1

The house didn't look like anyone's idea of a political headquarters. Nor did it look like the home of leaders of a radical revolutionary movement. It looked, if anything, like Mom and Dad's summer place, circa 1978, with peeling wallpaper and mismatched cottage furniture. There was a bookcase in the corner stuffed full of John Jakes, Colleen McCullough, and Robert Ludlum paperbacks, with board games stacked above that. Was this someone's actual house or a carefully designed set, stage dressed to send a message?

Beaded curtains off the main room gave a peek into a tiny railroad-style kitchen. The vent above the chipped white enamel electric stove was grease-stained and the stove itself spotted with what looked to be blotches of spaghetti sauce. There were actual dishes in the sink. It's real, Chase, thought. These people, whoever they are, are actually living here.

Cheap floor lamps lit the living room. There were rag rugs on the floor, frayed and coming apart in the middle. Someone had repositioned two armchairs, a small and comforting-looking loveseat, and a straight-back kitchen chair so they were all looking toward the dining area.

Clearly it was here that a meeting – or audience? – was to take place. The long family dining table had been placed lengthwise, with five chairs spaced across the window side, a kind of mock Supreme Court setup. The table was lit by a single hanging lamp with a 1960s fringe around the edge. Chase took careful note of the five chairs.

Was this the answer to the great mystery confirmed? The Wolf really was a group? A panel?

Ambassador Macomb followed Chase's gaze and seemed to read his thoughts. With his usual grace, the older man slithered into one of the armchairs and said, "Chase, what always struck me as remarkable too is the sheer number of misconceptions about what the Wolf is. I admit I was susceptible to all the same absurd speculations. So, you can imagine my surprise to discover just how wrong I was."

"Wrong in what way?" Chase asked.

The Ambassador shrugged. "Robespierre is not always mad. In this case, Robespierre may understand us better than we understand ourselves. As a people. That, and we should keep our minds open."

Listening to this – Macomb's talk just to fill space – all Chase could think was, "Oh yeah, he could do it." Kill General Williamson personally. Anything to put Chase and the others off the scent and cover his own ass.

Instead of betraying this thought, however, Chase nodded as if in agreement and looked toward Brueler, who was just staring at the Ambassador, still wide-eyed with disbelief at the man's treachery. Chase looked over at Sister Sheena. She seemed to be sizing up the room, perhaps looking for an exit. Levi and Hog stood behind her.

Ambassador Macomb went on. "In truth, I have learned a great deal more in this house than I have imagined possible, and certainly more than I have given. I guess you always can teach an old dog new tricks."

This was political speak, nothing more. Macomb had hitched his wagon to what he thought was the surest winner, and now he was trying to sell everyone else on the sheer wisdom and rationality of what he had done. But how long had he been in bed with them, Chase wondered. Perhaps from the beginning?

Macomb went on. "The interesting thing, though, is that *you* were right, Chase. You hear me? You were right."

Chase glanced back at him. "Right about what?"

"That we must go to the source. And that's what the Wolf is.

The source. *Wolf Words* are *Das Kapital*. *Wolf Words* are the *Declaration of Independence*. The *Magna Carta*."

"Or *Mein Kampf*," a voice said.

Chase spun around and saw, to his amazement, that it was Brueler who had said this. Everyone else stiffened, but Brueler didn't seem to care. So, the real Brueler was still in there somewhere. Chase offered him an appreciative smile.

"I wouldn't think so," said the Ambassador after an awkward, even concerned, glance around the room.

Almost as if in answer, there were the sounds of closing doors from behind the beaded curtains. There were people moving around in the back passageway of the house, where the bedrooms likely were.

Obviously, something was about to happen, because the four sentry Mohawks in the living room seemed to stiffen. Ambassador Macomb rose from his chair, as if he expected the President himself to enter, yet clearly he also felt the need to explain something to Chase. Something awkward, and maybe even embarrassing. "Chase, you're a very clever young man, but I'm not sure you truly accept the value of misperception when building a public movement. Even deception. And, of course, mystery."

"I thought public movements were based on conviction and belief," said Chase.

Macomb offered an indulgent smile. "All I'm saying is, when you combine mystery with a strong doctrine you have a very powerful tool."

"What mystery are we talking about?"

"The mystery of the Wolf," said Macomb. "Enormously powerful. When revealed, it becomes something else again."

Chase didn't understand what that meant, but it seemed Macomb was telling him that he was about to be disappointed. That the Wolf, when revealed, could not withstand public scrutiny or would not satisfy the people as something to worship. Which, of course, might scuttle all of Chase's plans – although, how could Macomb possibly know his plans?

Almost as if in answer, and before Chase could respond, men came through the beaded curtains. Chase tried to mask his shock, but he knew it showed. Oh yes, the Ambassador had warned him, but not forcefully enough.

There were four of them, but two were so alike as to be almost twins, with shabby dark hair and scraggly beards, and whippet-thin bodies. If you were to draw the image of the ISIS wannabe revolutionary, these guys would fit the bill, except they seemed more like teenage boys playing the part of a revolutionary in a school play than the actual article. The only difference between the two was that one wore glasses and the other didn't.

Behind the Scraggy Twins came a large, handsome young man with military haircut and bearing. He carried a notepad under his arm. In cammo pants and khaki T-shirt that almost, but not quite, covered what promised to be a mural of tats, he might be a new recruit taking night classes. But there was something dark and disturbed behind those blue eyes. He took in the sentries with a nod.

Behind this Soldier Boy came the Slob. A colorful Hawaiian shirt, elastic jeans, a smartphone in hand. He was also bearded, but it was shaved so close to his three chins that it might simply be stubble rather than a plan. The hair was curly. At least he looked smart. Smarter than the other three by a country mile.

The four of them moved behind the dining room table and took their places, two on either side of the center chair, which remained empty. Clearly someone else was expected.

Chase looked back at Ambassador Macomb as if to say, "Is *this* the Wolf?"

Macomb seemed almost apologetic. "There's no question that this great cause has benefited from a mutuality of interests among a great many warriors. It's enormously dynamic, proving everyone pulls their oars in the direction of a single cause."

Pulls their oars? What the fuck was he talking about?

Chase glanced again at Brueler, who looked just as baffled as Chase. Then at Sister Sheena, who gave Chase a small, almost imperceptible shake of the head. 'This is bullshit,' it said. 'We should get out of here.' Chase suspected she was right. But curiosity had him in its grip again.

He gestured to the four guys settling themselves at the table. "These guys are not the Wolf," he said to Macomb.

The Ambassador smiled. "The truth of what the Wolf might be is at once quite different from, less than, and greater than, whatever one has probably thought. And you, more than anyone else, Chase, will appreciate this now."

"Why me more than anyone else?"

Macomb seemed to be struggling for an answer.

He's going to tell us that the Wolf is just some hybrid body of malcontent incels, Chase thought. Not even bomb throwers. That the doubters and cynics were right; just a crew of guys who managed to pull it together and create the manifesto for a social movement or a second semester political science project without thinking through the consequences. Too much Marx and Corona beer.

If that were true, then Chase's plans would fall through his fingers like sand. He was already starting to recalculate, yet he was also mindful of what he had said to Brueler on the way there: that this was it, their one shot. And that was also true. Therefore, what was there to recalculate?

"I'm not sure it matters who the Wolf really is," said the Ambassador. "What I am trying to express is, the association between the Wolf and the Changers has always been one of inspiration and action. The Wolf has been the inspiration, but the action has been theirs." He looked at Sister Sheena, almost accusatorily. "Hers. And Beavenstock. And now others."

He's backing away, Chase thought. From what? Chase decided to be as direct as possible. "You need to cut the crap, Macomb. I have plans, there are things we need to do, and I didn't come here for cat-and-mouse politics."

"A cat," said the languid voice behind them. "Not a mouse."

The room turned.

She came through the beaded curtains like she was weaving her way through parting water. She was lean and graceful and careful in her movements. In theory, she was presenting herself to them, but the power was all hers. She had her beauty and the element of surprise, but of course she had much more. She had the essence of pure dynamic energy.

Chase felt his breath leave his lungs and his body stop its normal functions. He didn't breathe and he would never know if he blinked at that moment.

It was Rin.

Of course it was.

Rin, wearing a loose caftan of black and orange silk and a shimmery gold neck piece that on anyone else would look gaudy and absurd and ridiculous, but on her conjured up images of an Egyptian queen. She wore simple thin sandals, also gold. Her hair was pulled straight back and held by a tortoise shell clip. Again, so simple. She was more beautiful than he had ever seen her – or any woman.

She looked only at him. No one else. Obviously, she had known it would be him, just as he had never imagined it would be her.

Rin. So beautiful. The whimsy and the wicked humor still in her eye. His Rin, as he had imagined her and remembered her for a thousand and one nights.

But *not* the woman he had seen in the crowd. Not the woman with the sunhat. That woman had been the younger Rin. Because she had been a memory, and memory doesn't add years, memory keeps trapped in amber the things you need to keep trapped in amber.

So it turned out the woman in the crowd had been a hallucination after all. This Rin, however, was most definitely the real thing.

The room was silent as she and Chase sized one another up. They must feel it, Chase thought. They must all know. The way she was looking at me, almost grinning as if to say, 'See? I got you, didn't I? I got you, Chase.'

But there was something else in her expression. It took awhile for him to understand it. Wonderment. Not at who he was or the strange circumstances that had brought them together again, but simply that he was here and that she was here too. That they were in the same room together again. Finally.

He imagined he could smell her perfume. The rich oil in her hair. Her very skin.

He had not realized until this moment that *his* Rin had been a girl. He knew it now because the person in front of him was very much, and so definitely, a woman.

"Manhattan," was all she said.

Brueler asked it first. "Do you two know one another?"

"No," said Chase.

"Yes," said Rin.

It was the first time he could recall where she had told the truth and he had lied.

The Ambassador gestured Rin to the table. "Why don't we all sit down?" He nodded the others toward the more comfortable-looking living room furniture.

What a ridiculous character he is, Chase thought. Not a great statesman after all, nor a wise mandarin. Not even a southern gentleman. Just a shady political hack looking to back the best horse he could find who might also support him. Nothing more. How could Chase have been so naïve in his assessment of this man?

Then he looked at Sister Sheena again. She was simply staring at Rin, awestruck. And why not? Rin was the real thing. In the shadow of Rin, Sister Sheena suddenly seemed so obvious. And young. A pop star from the year before whose cachet had suddenly vanished.

In fact, no one sat down until Rin took her place behind the dining table, flanked by the four flunkies. As she did, Chase admired just how carefully all this had been stage managed. Even how the 1960s fringe lamp was placed. The light hit the gold piece on Rin's neck just so. She seemed to shine like a goddess, even if the lamp fixture itself was hanging low enough that Rin's eyes were in shadow. But that was surely part of the stagecraft too. You couldn't see what she was thinking.

Rin adjusted her seating position and revealed slim, bare legs and the gold sandals. She gestured that they all sit down.

As they did, as Chase sank into the nearest armchair, he thought, I so want her. Again. We could find a way to work all this out and then we could be together. We could love one another again. I could wake up to her. I could make her laugh. I could taste the salt from the sweat on her bare shoulder.

But there was no romance in her voice when she spoke. She merely brought her hands together and said, "Explain it to me." This was something he had never seen in Rin, even if it had been hinted at in all her various and outrageous plans: Rin the leader. This was a role she had grown into at some point since their parting.

That's when Chase put it all together, like a carousel of old family slides.

Sofia Puccelli leaned into him, almost threatened to kiss him when she said, "They chose you."

They chose you.

Putting him on the Reasoners panel after Puccelli had to stride up to the guillotine for that unnecessary execution (at whose order?).

The protection of him, the near misses, the almost but not quites. Someone with enormous power. Someone who could make true believers do almost anything.

But why?

Rin looked as if she understood his mental calculations. Again, it felt like just the two of them in the room.

"The Key bridge," he said. "Tay Hamer. That was because you never expected me to get that far, wasn't it? So you had to do something. Who set that up?" He gestured to the four guys flanking her. "Surely not these guys."

Rin sighed and smiled at the same time. "Surely you're not going to litigate …"

"Yes. Because I want to know."

For just a moment, she seemed to debate with herself if it was worth getting into. Then she gestured to her sentries standing around the room. "These are my very closest friends. They have friends. They have even more friends. You can imagine the rest. People are very dedicated to the cause. Not the Changers cause – that's one thing – but something else that's much, much bigger."

Chase struggled with his next question. "Are those – the much, much bigger people – the same people who carried out the attempted assassination of Beavenstock?"

That seemed to annoy her. She was instantly defensive. Old Rin. "Don't be distracted by comic book characters, Chase! I've never actually met Jeff Beavenstock. Obviously I was pleased when he appeared – why not? He represented nothing but chaos – but unfortunately once he gained power he didn't know what to do with it. He began to find ways to settle. That couldn't be."

"So your belief is chaos?"

"Chaos is the great and most powerful gasoline." The way she said it, they might as well have been sitting at the Dead Man's Chest pub in Soho, debating over pints of beer. "There are no great changes in the course of history without the key ingredient of chaos."

"Chaos leading to what?"

She shrugged.

In that shrug, Chase began to understand what had happened. Where she had gone with those talents she had been given. That mind and that anger. He slowly got up from his chair. He felt the sentries tense around him, but he also felt Levi and Hog tighten as well. He stepped forward and leaned on the dining room table, leaning into her. Rin's four accomplices shrank back. She didn't. Not an inch.

"You never believed in anything like the Reasoners, did you?" he asked.

"What makes you say that?" she asked. She was smiling, but with a real smugness.

"Because if you're truly dedicated to chaos, then you wouldn't be in favor of any agreement between the Changers and the government. It would have flown in the face of what you wanted to prove, which was how impossible it was to keep the country going as it had been, whereas we thought we were trying to restore order."

"You're ridiculous," she said, as she had often said when teasing or dismissing him. "And right, of course. After all, why would I want you to be part of a team that I thought was doomed to failure?" They were playing a game he remembered. 'What if.' They had played it so many times. 'What if Hitler had won?' 'What if Booth had missed his shot?' 'What if the Watergate burglars had got away?'

He hesitated. "I don't know. Any more than I can imagine why you would have put me on the Reasoners if you didn't believe in the Reasoners."

"To be clear, I didn't put you on the Reasoners," she said. "I had someone put you on the Reasoners."

"But you were willing to go along with it until … when?" Chase asked. Then he answered his own question. "The bridge." He felt he was on to something. "Did the bridge happen simply because you learned about our interest in reaching out to General Van DeVere? From – " He looked over at Macomb, who was removing a thread from the razor-sharp crease of his pant leg, a pant leg which had risen just enough to reveal the top of the cowboy boots and just a hint of Velcro strap. Yes, he was wearing the same outfit. Almost surely why he wouldn't be frisked. "Him," Chase said, gesturing to the Ambassador. "He horned his way into our little group and he told you what we wanted to do. So, General Williamson was set up to deliver a phony Van DeVere to us and a phony meeting was set up and then the attack on the bridge took place. To turn the Changers against the Reasoners and break the agreement and create even *more* chaos." What he was saying sounded reasonable to Chase's ears, but there was something wrong with it. He just couldn't place what it was, but it didn't quite jell. He went on, though, almost as if trying to convince himself. "And that's where the plan to have Beavenstock shot kicked in. Chaos on top of chaos. Pit the two sides against one another again. And then … " He stopped. "Somewhere you got the idea you had to bring the Reasoners in. Capture them. It … " He stopped. He straightened up. He didn't have it. He knew he didn't.

Rin knew too. She leaned forward and spoke like a schoolteacher to a troubled student who almost, but not quite, understands the algebraic principle. "Part of leading, Chase, is making sure that your followers understand which options can't and won't succeed."

Chase stared at her feet beneath the table. He focused. Then, when the answer came, it was obvious.

"Or it didn't start at the bridge," he said. "The *Reasoners* were a setup from the beginning."

She didn't say anything.

This idea began to catch fire for him. "That would mean *everything* was a setup. The idea of reaching out to General Van DeVere was a setup. The Ambassador pushed that. The bridge was a setup based on threats of nuclear weapons falling into the wrong hands, which you manufactured. And the Reasoners were always meant to be captured. Everything we were doing had been planned maybe months before. We were always following your script."

She didn't say anything, but he could tell from her expression that what he had just said was largely true.

"But something went wrong, didn't it?" Chase asked. "And I think I know what it was." He pointed to Hog, who seemed much more interested in all of the other participants in the room than in following what Chase was saying. "Him," Chase said. Only then did Hog glance up at Chase. For only a second. Chase stepped next to Hog. "No one anticipated a protector from amongst the Changers. And because of the protector, I was able to secure a real meeting with the real Van DeVere. That wasn't supposed to happen, either, nor was I supposed to cook up any sort of a plan you couldn't control." Chase looked back at Rin. "That's when you realized you really had to clamp down on things. Kill me or scare me, but either way you had to take me out of the picture. So, through your minions you arranged to have me captured and put in the basement of the Capitol." He studied her. "But did you really plan to kill me?"

She had been looking away when he said that, but now she shot a look at him. Rin anger. Everyone was a toad. "*That* was the maniac's idea." She practically bit the words out.

Chase smiled. She had revealed herself. "Another thing you hadn't anticipated. The psychopath with the sideburns. The people's choice. Not yours. Am I right? Where did he come from? Out of nowhere." He looked back at Sister Sheena, who had an angry, almost combative look. Then back at Rin. Her look wasn't all that different. "He calls himself Viking. Who could count on such a lunatic catching fire? Certainly not you."

"You don't always know," said Rin, "what will crawl out when you move a rock."

"Well, if your religion is chaos, that's what you get. Chaos breeds chaos. Suddenly the crowd wants a Viking, and next thing you know rich teenage boys are paying to burn people alive at the stake and grown men use human beings as dart boards. That's what pure chaos buys you."

She looked at him. He was making her angry.

Chase couldn't help himself. He liked that she was angry. He pushed further. As they had always done with one another. "You look at it that way, that guy Viking is nothing more than the natural outgrowth of cheap writing and second-rate revolutionary dogma – "

She bristled at that. He saw it, and in that instant he knew that what he had suspected since Rin had walked in – before she'd even sat down beside the Sad Sacks – was true: Rin was the *sole* author of *Wolf Words*.

Which explained everything.

" – which leads to the incitement to violence of simple minds and YouTube revolutionaries and – " He glanced over at Sister Sheena. He gestured to her without apology. " – pop star thinkers and reality-TV philosophers."

Rin didn't like this line of talk. "What is your plan, Chase? Why did you come here? Of what are you trying to convince me?"

"The Wolf needs to endorse a plan," he said simply.

"What plan?"

"To make it clear to the Changers that they've won."

"That they've *what?*"

"Won. And if she says those words – " He gestured to Sister Sheena. " – and the Wolf says that what Sister Sheena says is true, then I guarantee you the United States Armed Forces will enter Washington D.C. – in fact, most of the cities across America – but they'll be on the Changers side. And because of that strength, the Changers will form a leadership. They'll have won. And the madness will stop."

Rin looked at him a long time and then she swallowed something. He knew what it was because he knew her so well. It was a laugh. She was going to laugh, but she managed to hold it in. "The madness will stop under whose leadership? I hope you're not thinking me."

"Of course not. I didn't even know you were part of this until ten minutes ago."

"Then who?"

Chase shrugged. "Well, I was thinking Vin Jansert."

There was a moment of shock – real, stunned shock – and then she burst out into laughter. She looked at her Sad Sacks. The Sad Sacks smiled back at her, even if they didn't get the joke. "*That* asshole??"

Chase shrugged. "Bigger assholes have been President of the United States. Don't count Vin out so quickly. He has a huge following, he's despised by the left as much as the right, no one really knows his politics, he's terrific at bullshit and he's good on TV. He probably has seventy-five-percent name recognition across the country. All that's a lot of something."

"He's a clown."

"A clown yes, but maybe he can be convinced to be less clownish. After all, right now he's living in a coal cellar beneath the U.S. Capitol. Also your doing, I imagine." He looked back at her. "Pretty cold, Rin. Pretty merciless."

She shrugged. "Your friends were all window dressing." She nodded graciously at Ambassador Macomb. "With certain exceptions."

"Window dressing for what?"

"For you, Manhattan. Window dressing for your true destiny."

"We were talking about potential leaders."

"I never left the subject."

Chase stared at her. Was she serious? Was that what this was about all along? Could she really be that mad? He tried to stay on track.

"Okay, if not Vin, then one from the other side. Obviously, you were thinking about Jeff Beavenstock as the leader at some point, but then you had him shot. So that leaves us … " He gestured to Sister Sheena.

Rin looked at Sheena. "You don't buy *her* bullshit, do you?"

"She's still fit for the part."

Rin shook her head. "Her star is waning."

"She saved my life."

"She got lucky with that."

It was as if they were talking about the odds on an upcoming prizefight and Sister Sheena wasn't even in the room. But as Sheena's attention ping-ponged from Rin to Chase and back to Rin again, it was clear she wasn't offended. Instead, she looked afraid. Very afraid.

"You don't understand," said Rin. "Leadership takes more than words and slogans. You have to be merciless and dedicated to principle."

"Which principles are those?"

"You tell me, Chase. Tell me how your great plan works. With a new leader and the Changers convinced they've won the day, what happens?"

"Peace," said Chase. "A sort of peace, anyway. Good enough for the next generation maybe."

"Peace."

There was a moment as she considered that word. Then Rin stood up. Everyone came to attention. Even Chase. "And what does that get you? I can make clear to you that no one wants peace. Our natural state is war. We've shown that time and time again."

All eyes were on her as she came around the table. In that microsecond, Chase shot a glance at Hog. Hog returned his gaze. His expression said he was ready.

"Man's nature may be combative," Chase said, "but I believe his natural objective is peace."

"Well it's not *my* objective," said Rin. She was now standing maybe four feet from him. He *could* smell her perfume. She was so close to Macomb that the Ambassador, seated, was almost looking straight up at her. "My objective is – "

"Yes, we've already established that your objective is chaos," Chase said. "Which is what you've got on the Mall now and in Viking and in the thousand other Vikings behind him. But take a look at that guy, Rin. Take a look at what he promises, and then tell me we don't all need to move on to something else. True chaos takes away even your control."

Chase knew this would anger her. Rin treasured control. It's why she had left him so abruptly. Why she had kept confusing him about who she was and where she came from.

But she surprised him this time. "I was going to clarify that my objective is to move on to something else. Because we have reached the end of the era of our Third Great Experiment."

He stared at those lovely eyes and wondered, What the fuck is she talking about? What he managed to say, however, was, "You're going to have to fill me in on that one."

She smiled, genuinely pleased, and moved away from him, walking a small circle, back and forth, in front of the dining room table. And with that she began to expound. She began to expound as perhaps no one has expounded since Lenin. Or worse. "Our first Great Experiment was when we made the transition to growing crops and attempting to establish an agrarian culture, which we were not attuned to. It was a goal we as a species never achieved or succeeded at, to this day."

Was she serious? Chase asked, "Is that what we're talking about? What we were doing ten thousand years ago?"

"That's where this starts, Chase." And she began again.

Chase had the sense he had heard this before. Then an image came to mind. Rin, in the Earl's Court flat in London, trying out pitches on him of the radical documentary films she wanted to sell to the BBC. He had dismissed her off-the-cuff ramblings as half-baked notions meant to provoke leftish executive producers to take a flyer on her. But she had fought back. She said, usually with a glint of humor in her eye and a slight mischievous grin, that the idiots would buy "anything that smacks of radical revisionism." She remained sure of this, even though none of her ideas ever wound up rewarded with a commission. Chase had always felt it was because she had never truly believed in what she had dreamt up and spouted.

Here, however, in this strange throwback farmhouse in the Maryland wilderness, he was witness to the final metamorphosis: There was no humor in her, no grin, no glint in the eye. Nor was she putting up a mock argument just to create an opportunity for herself. No. She had the look of a true believer, someone who had seen her work put into action time and again over the past year and given substance. She had seen zealots draw around her and give her meaning; seen violence caused by her worst instincts and given purpose. Through these graduations, she had become, finally, someone who had drunk her own Kool-Aid.

She was going on: "The Second Great Experiment was the Age of Revolution and the attempt at democracies, which obviously failed … "

There was no way, Chase realized with an absolute finality. There had probably never been a way. He knew her too well. There was only one way, in her hands, that this was going to end.

"Democracy was a fantasy," she continued. "Beautiful, but a mass delusion, and eventually will be seen as a blip on the world's socio-political and economic evolution, like the tulip market mania, or the Soviet Union. Laughable fetishes that in time proved unnecessary."

There were awkward glances around the room. Not from the Sad Sacks. No, they were staring at her with complete adoration. And not from the sentries, because they were also part of the band. But certainly from the people who had come with Chase. Hog and he locked eyes again. Chase looked from Hog to Sister Sheena. Then to the Ambassador. The Ambassador was looking away, perhaps in embarrassment, perhaps for an exit. Staring at the Ambassador, Chase knew what had to be done. To save any of this. To save them all.

"So what *is* the Third Experiment?" Chase asked Rin.

Rin stopped where she was and looked at him. "I just said it. Chaos. Madness. Call it what you want. The Age of Purification. I don't care. But from it, you get the Darwinian Rise of the Superman."

She went on to explain the Darwinian Rise of the Superman.

Chase focused on her mouth and her eyes. Her mouth moved like a child's toy, capable of a thousand variations and contortions; graceful, subtle, nuanced, yet it all seemed mechanical and unreal, as if some super force had programmed her, or she was one of those holographic Presidents who talk at Disneyland. Her eyes, however, were the opposite. They seemed lit by an irrational and unpredictable yet immense force, like summer lightning in a country field and the crackle in the air. And wherever the landing was, it was for sure havoc would be wrought.

She is actually not right, he had thought long ago, and the power and danger in that idea had made him leap up and escape onto the tiny iron balcony of their flat, gasping for air. *She is actually not right.*

This Rin went on. *This* Rin could not be stopped, certainly not by an action as puny as Chase stepping out onto a balcony. No, her worst tendencies had taken deep root and were now embedded. She had become the worst side of herself. "In *this* age we're going to need to restructure to create a new paradigm, a system that propels us forward as a species, and not perpetuating old, antiquated, and unnecessary systems. Ask yourself only true questions: Why do we need the South? Why do we need an industrial North that produces nothing? We must burn our acreage to regenerate the soil."

Rin, but not Rin. A Disneyland robotic Rin. A version of Rin. And yet, also, Rin.

Chase didn't need to think it out or parse out the possibilities or the pros and cons. This was what being a Reasoner was, in the end, he realized. It turned out it had nothing to do with reason at all. It was the simple understanding of what secured life and what promised death, and embracing the solution that would guarantee survival, no matter how unreasonable.

If she was in fact the Wolf, then the Wolf had no intention of allowing anyone to move forward with any plans beyond pure violence and chaos. It was not just a matter of the Wolf not interfering; this Wolf intended to stop them on the only road to anything resembling an ordered world.

Chaos. Her religion. She had been honest about that. Perhaps to get back at the toads. Or anger at BBC rejecting her. And fury. And the rise of some special, unnamed supermen.

Her mouth kept moving. Her eyes flashed.

He saw his duty with total clarity. In life, there is often only one answer to a question. How to avoid getting a speeding ticket? Slow down. How to stop the flood in the kitchen? Turn off the tap. How to stop this madness all around them? There was only one action.

While she was talking – spouting – Chase gestured Ambassador Macomb to come toward him.

Macomb, realizing that in some fundamental way things were not going as he had wished, stood up and took a step toward Chase.

Chase put a comradely arm on his shoulder and leaned in to whisper to him. Macomb tilted his head forward to hear. Chase gripped his neck, long enough to startle and incapacitate the older man, and long enough to reach down to his shins and the top of those ridiculous cowboy boots, where he found the two guns strapped to the garter holsters. Macomb's hand reached down to stop him, but Chase bent the man's arm back to prevent him and heard a crack of brittle septuagenarian bone.

Hog was already moving, so that by the time Chase had removed the first gun from its Velcro strap, Hog had the second. Far more experienced than Chase with firearms, Hog didn't struggle to undo the strap, he just tore it off. He also bent the Ambassador's kneecap so the older man went down on his back, knocking over a small end table and lamp.

It wasn't that everyone else moved in slow motion. It seemed, in fact, that they didn't move at all.

None of them. Not Brueler, the sentries, and most of all Rin, who finally paused in her recitation, her mouth half-parted, her eyes finally landing on something of enough interest to distract her from her monologue of hate and retribution and complete chaos.

It was Chase. Chase as he turned and shot Macomb in the face, killing him instantly. He had intended to shoot him in the chest because it seemed less gruesome, but the purely rational part of his brain said he didn't know how to shoot someone in the chest with assurance he'd hit the heart, so it had to be the face.

As the life literally dipped and yawned out of the Ambassador, everyone else was silent but *very* focused.

Which is when Hog pressed the Ambassador's second gun up against the back of Rin's head. Hog wasn't looking at Rin, or the sentries, or Levi. He was only looking at Chase. They were locked in an intense, terrified stare. For her part, Rin's eyes were also locked on Chase, and for the first time she looked truly worried, as worried as she had once, long ago, when the train started to pull out of the station and appeared ready to take her and her trapped bag with it – that she might smack into the iron post and destroy herself. He had saved her, as perhaps she was not supposed to be saved.

Finally, Hog spoke. "What do you want me to do?"

Chase looked at Rin. Beautiful Rin.

Then she said something. One word.

"What?" he asked.

"You," she said.

"Me what?"

"It was always meant to be you, Chase. Always."

"Meant how?"

And then she smiled. It was such a beautiful smile. A Venus.

An angel victorious. She had been proven right all along about something. "You'll find out."

Hog tightened his grip on her but never took his eyes from Chase. "Tell me what to do," he said.

Chase would never know if the single word he uttered was why Hog pulled the trigger. Or if it was due to Reason. Or not. But Hog pulled the trigger.

Epilogue

"The Great Unfairness"

55. *The Statue*

1

The Chairman of the House Committee on Security and Safety, the Honorable Changer Gabriel Soames, had taken to walking to work every day, and why not? The man had survived endless months trapped inside the basement of the Capitol building, and as any ornithologist will tell you, once the cage is opened, the bird doesn't want to go back in again. Ever.

Moreover, Gabriel was a bachelor (well, a widower, technically), and there was nothing to keep him at home once he was up and shaved and showered, which was happening earlier and earlier these days. So, he began leaving his townhouse before six sometimes. He often extended the walk, taking in the empty streets of Washington before the city even began to rouse. He couldn't say that he enjoyed everything he saw out there, but at least it was starting to look very much like the Washington he had known for the first half of his adult existence, when life had been enjoyable. His walk was easier once he became a familiar sight to the Street Guardians. After a while, they even let him pass without having to present his papers, always offering a polite nod.

At first, it had been Gabriel alone. But after a few months, and once the blossoms came out, joggers started to appear, just like in the old days. Gabriel was glad to see them, and even came to recognize one or two. They would exchange a friendly nod of the head as they passed one another, the old man striding along and the young Olympic gods striding past in New Balance shorts.

No earbuds, though. No one jogged with earbuds anymore.

Gabriel usually cut down 17th Street and walked along Constitution toward the Capitol building because you couldn't, of course, walk on the Mall. Not yet. The whole area had been fenced off for the replanting and the new monuments, which meant that from the Lincoln Memorial all the way to the Capitol everything was once again a mess, except that now it was a mess of construction and landscaping equipment, irrigation pipes and service portables. Gabriel wasn't sure he would want to walk on it anyway, or if he ever would even once it was open.

If you walked east along Constitution Avenue, however, and kept your gaze centered slightly to the left, you could convince yourself that everything was as it had once been long before. They had done a terrific job of dealing with the buildings. The Archives in particular looked utterly untouched, and someone had thought to add white fencing instead of black around all the federal buildings, which, combined with the flowerbeds and hedges, added an almost homey feel. All of this was from the mind of someone who imagined Washington as it had been, say, circa 1938, back when FDR was in office and the world was a hell of a lot quieter. Someone with a thirst to travel back in history. And despite the unreal Disney aspect of it all, Gabriel approved.

In the old days, if he had come through from the Mall, Gabriel would have entered work from the west steps of the Capitol building – the back – but since the Great Victory he had discovered that he simply couldn't do that anymore. It wasn't the guillotine. That monstrosity had been wrenched out almost a year ago now, but that didn't mean he still didn't see it, in his dreams yes, but also sometimes in the clear light of day.

Instead, Gabriel made his way to work these days by trudging up Northwest Drive on the north side of the Capitol and making his way around to the "front" of the building. Gabriel always did his best to keep his gaze turned away from where the great blade had once stood, and usually picked up his pace.

This morning, however, he saw something out of the corner of his eye. He couldn't avoid it. The sparks, for one thing. And the men in masks. My God. Whatever it was, it was immense, and towered over the steps even higher than the killing monstrosity.

Terror leapt into his chest. They're assembling another one!

But then his rational brain took over. Reason.

He stopped at the foot of the steps and looked up.

Yes, it would rise much higher than the Great Guillotine. Was that on purpose? It had to be. Gabriel had seen the very earliest plans – every single member of the Changer Caucus had seen the original plans and been consulted – but he'd chosen to absent himself from offering an opinion on this particular aspect of reshaping Washington. But really, had they ever made it clear that they were planning on making the thing so damned big?

There were two crews of workers overseeing the whole operation. One was clearly an engineering crew and the other was a welding gang. The welders were the folks with the masks and the source of the sparks. They were the assemblers of the massive statue, and they would be the ones to secure it in place for all time and all history.

The argument over the monument had been long and hard. The Changers, who held a one-seat majority over the Democrats in the Senate, would get what they wanted, of course, but when their deputy leader, Miles Mallickey, was removed (for tax fraud, of all things), the majority was reduced and the decision got thrown into the Leader's office.

The Leader, of course, cast the deciding vote. He probably always assumed he would. Everyone knew that this was a pet project of his. *Very* important, they were told. In fact, one wag at the *Washington Post* suggested that the desire to maintain control in this particular case was almost certainly the source of the Mick's tax problems. Sister Sheena, as always, made the announcement in the Leader's stead. Also, as always, she made it all sound like the only possible solution. The same way they announced the Med-All plan.

Still. Why was it so damned *big*?

Gabriel stood at the next-to-top step – ironically, although he didn't know it, the same step on which Hog had stood as Sister Sheena addressed a sea of Changers hungry to see Chase Selby's head chopped off – and wondered at the whole thing.

He saw a man roughly his own age sitting on one of the benches at the far side of the steps. He was immense. Truly immense. He seemed to be leaning forward under the sheer weight of his own bulk, strands of hair from a truly massive head of grey blowing in the wind. He was smoking a cigarette. You really didn't see people smoking cigarettes anymore, even though it was no longer illegal, but for some reason, it gave Gabriel comfort.

The hulk seemed immensely interested in the erection of the statue.

Gabriel didn't address him until he got that much closer. "Dan?"

Congressman Dan Williams looked up, surprised. Then offered a small, almost sad smile as he took in his old friend. "Gabe," he said. He edged his bulk over to the right side of the bench, giving Gabriel just enough room to sit down. Gabriel did. Barely. The two old friends looked at the statue being assembled forty feet away from them. "In the old days," Gabriel said, "I never knew you to rise even ten minutes before call. Or, really, ever, if you could avoid it."

"Today I am overseeing," Dan drawled, nodding at the statue.

Gabriel was surprised. "This is you?"

Dan nodded.

"I thought you were Heritage and Nationhood."

"I am. This finally fell under us."

"The statue?? Under Nationhood?"

"What is it," asked Dan, "if not part of building a nation? Besides, we have all sorts of unusual fiefdoms. Last week he gave us the internet. The whole thing. Not just Free-Fi. *The* internet. And all the free schools fell into your lap. If I didn't know better, I'd say he was targeting me specifically."

Gabriel studied the statue awhile. It really was a hell of a thing to see. Two of the engineers and one of the welders moved a human hand the size of a car door into position. The other workers were assembling what appeared to be enormous brass arms.

"I still don't get it," Gabriel said after a moment or two.

Dan gestured to a blanket-shrouded rectangle leaning against the north steps. "It will make even less sense once you see the damned plaque. That's it there. They were changing the name right up until last night. Until the Leader sent the directive, anyway."

"He wanted to approve the *name*?" Gabriel asked.

"Nothing left to chance on this one," said Dan.

"And what is the name?"

"You ready?"

"Go."

"*The Great Unfairness.*"

Gabriel held back his laughter. Almost. "You're kidding me!"

Dan gave him a glance out of the corner of a glinty eye and then he too laughed, so hard that he coughed and coughed until a smile finally cleared it. "Gabe, you think I'd shit you? *The Great Unfairness.*"

"What does it mean?"

Dan shrugged. "Who knows with him? Unfair to who? And who was the victim of the unfairness? And has it all been set right?" Dan thought about that a moment, and looked out across the Mall, with its mess of caterpillars and tractors and snow fencing. His expression darkened. "*Has* it all been set right, Gabe?"

Gabriel could see Dan was going into himself a bit, so he spoke just to nudge his friend out of that particular – and dangerous – darkness. They had been there before, the two of them. "They say he wants to change the name of the party now."

Thankfully, that worked. A grin broke out on Dan's face. He loved political gossip above all else. "I'm hearing that too! On the committee, someone said they expect to see the caucus room sign changed any day now. He'd do it without asking, I bet!"

The two friends chuckled at the sheer audacity of this. Then came the hard part for Gabriel. It's why he had avoided Dan in the halls and deked out early at the renewed swearing-in after Congress was reconvened. But he couldn't avoid it now. So, he just said it.

"How *are* you, Dan?"

Dan shrugged. "Mentally? Who knows? I still wake up thinking they're coming for me and that I'm in the kennel cage again. But I can't walk away now and I can't resign. I mean, I have, I've tried it three times, but it keeps coming back. He asks me to stay. What am I supposed to do?"

Gabriel didn't know what to say.

Dan said, "It's like he can't and won't release the old guard. He wants to reward us, or maybe we're a connection to the past he doesn't want to let go. Do you know he's even got that old con artist Agniew running the Department of Energy? He never lets anyone go."

"Window dressing," said Gabriel.

Dan looked confused.

"Van DeVere runs just about everything that needs real hands-on running," Gabriel said. "We're all window dressing."

Dan shook his head. "I don't think so. I think he really means to put it back. In some way."

"Absolute power, Dan. Remember?"

"I remember."

It felt unpatriotic to talk this way. They both had – the whole *country* had – an image of General Van DeVere and his troops rolling into Washington on October 1, Great Victory Day. It had been the liberation of Paris, the release of Kuwait, the fall of the Berlin Wall, all rolled into one, with Van DeVere center stage on top of the troop truck in aviator sunglasses and private's hat. Except the folks cheering had been the Changers, not Parisians, and it wasn't a restoration of government, but the creation of something new. It's just that at that time, no one had understood that. All they knew is the Changers had won.

The two men stared at the statue. The arms were being fixed into place. "I don't get it," Gabriel said.

"They're putting the stimulus bill on the floor today," Dan said. "You hear the deal they made last night? Three hundred billion for the oil sector and not an ounce of accountability. All to keep Oklahoma and Texas in the fold. And you know what? I think they'll stay."

"What does the Leader say about that?" Gabriel asked.

Dan lit another cigarette. "You know exactly what he said. He said if it passes with sixty-one percent, he'll sign it no questions asked. He doesn't step in the way of that kind of thing. Mark my words, Gabe."

Gabe thought about that. "We'll see."

After a few moments, Gabriel got up and went in, but he still entered from the other side and didn't cross where the guillotine had once stood. You don't like to break new habits.

2

By 7:30, the Capitol building was filling up as it always had. Smart young people in businesswear strode toward far-flung offices while frumpy older folks strolled with a trail of plucky ass kissers behind them. Fifty-year-old men in skinny suits ran ahead of everyone else to show how active and fit they were.

At first, Gabriel thought there had to be something wrong with the men's room up at the south end. Then he realized it wasn't the men's room at all, but the caucus room beside it. People of all stripes were gathered together around the doorway, watching with a sort of stunned amazement.

Gabriel approached slowly, but once he saw what was happening, he almost laughed. Except, of course, it wasn't all that funny. He thought to himself, My God, it actually *is* happening. It really is.

Two men in paint-splattered overalls – an extremely familiar sight around the Capitol – were carefully replacing the wooden sign outside the Changers caucus room. They had replaced the word *Changers*, and now, in simple, bold lettering it read, *Federalist Party Caucus Room*.

3

It took them all day. Throughout the course of business hours and the hours when tourists were most prevalent, folks came by and did a little gawking, and just about every tourist took a picture of themselves standing in front of the monument that, most likely, would last hundreds of years if Washington precedent were any gauge, but the workers didn't put the finishing touches and the plaque on until well after the Capitol had closed down for the night and the tourists were gone. It was after dark, and they finished by electric work lamp.

As a result of this timing, very few people were there to see her in all her glory on her first night overseeing the Capitol Mall and the reflecting pool.

Gabriel had been right. She was a foot taller than the Great Guillotine, which was on purpose. She looked out across the Mall from the steps of the Capitol to the Lincoln Memorial and there was no question that had she been real she could have seen the whole way, just as she was seen; a radiant beauty in classical robes, hair combed back, exquisitely adorned by the necklace and earrings of a classical goddess, an empress, a majestic bronze monument to the Great Uprising. At her feet were emblems of the valiant battle fought and won – half-size versions of men in wolf hats and women in T-shirts and ball caps, children, and even a disabled girl.

That statue was of Rin. Rin nineteen feet tall, towering over all she surveyed, bronze Rin, identified as the author of *Wolf Words*, she who had launched and won the renewed battle for liberty.

Of her assassin, Ambassador James Macomb, nothing was said. Nor was anything said about the manner of Macomb's death at the hands of Sister Sheena, who fought to defend the founder in one of the last great battles of the movement. The plaque made it clear that Rin represented all forgotten and disenfranchised Americans and symbolized "The Great Unfairness."

The dedication of the statue was signed by Van DeVere, identified as Chairman of the Joint Chiefs of Staff and Commander of all United States Armed Forces. Of course, the plaque *should* have been signed by the author of the sentiment and the designer of the monument itself, but he never took credit for anything.

It was just like he didn't use the title 'President.' Technically, that's what he was, but everyone knew not to use the word around him. Some said it was because, for him, it smacked of the Old Days and he always wanted to stress how much things had changed.

However, most Americans said there was another reason. A simpler reason.

They said it was just because Chase didn't like it.

About the Author

Wilson Coneybeare has written movies, television, theatre, and radio plays. Most recently he wrote the feature film *American Hangman*, which premiered on Netflix. A proud Canadian-American, he estimates he has driven his family across the continent twenty-seven times. *A Feast of Wolves* is his first novel.